The Foundling

Linda Hayner

Bob Jones University Press, Greenville, South Carolina 29614

Library of Congress Cataloging-in-Publication Data

Hayner, Linda K.
    The foundling / Linda Hayner.
        p.   cm.
    Summary: Abandoned on the porch of a London church in 1644 at
the age of four, Willy eventually becomes an apprentice while never
quite giving up hope of finding his mother.
    ISBN 0-89084-941-2
    [1. Abandoned children—Fiction.   2. Apprentices—Fiction.
3. Mothers and sons—Fiction.   4. London (England)—Fiction.]
I. Title.
PZ7.H3149115Fo   1997
[Fic]—dc21   97-10574
                                                                              CIP
                                                                              AC

The Foundling

Project Editor: Steven N. Skaggs

Designed by Roger Bruckner

Illustrations by Vincent Barnhart

Cover: Giraudon/Art Resource, N.Y. Lorrain, Claude. *Harbor with
Setting Sun.* Louvre, Paris, France.

© 1997 Bob Jones University Press
Greenville, South Carolina 29614

ISBN 0-89084-941-2

15   14   13   12   11   10   9   8   7   6   5   4   3   2   1

to D. L. W.

Contents

Part 3: The Apprentice

Acknowledgments

I wish to thank the staff of the Guildhall Library in London, England, for their kind assistance. I am indebted also to my British friends whose lives provided many ideas for the characters in this novel. Dawn Watkins, mentor and friend, deserves special mention. Her teaching, encouragement, and suggestions were invaluable throughout the writing of this book.

—L. H.

part 1
The Nurse Child

Chapter 1

January 1644

Jack Crumpton hurried along the dark, wet street. An old red-and-black scarf protected his neck and lower face; his cap was pulled down over his ears. His coattails whipped in the wind, and his hands were deep in his pockets.

"Ha! What foul weather. And me, checking locks and testing chains. I'll do no more tonight. Only a fool would—"

His foot slipped on the cobbles. He staggered, arms flailing, towards a deep gutter.

"By all the saints!"

He teetered on the gutter's edge. With one more windmill of his arms, he regained his balance. He jerked his coat back in place and hugged it to himself.

"A close one there, Jack. Fall into the gutter tonight and it'll be the dogs that find you. No, even the dogs are in their holes tonight. Only the likes of you out doing his duty." He sniffed loudly. " 'We've a constable's job for you, Jack,' they said. 'Just a quick turn about the ward each evening, Jack,' they said. 'It'll put a bit of coin in your pocket, Jack,' they said."

He splashed through a puddle hidden in the shadows.

"By all that's—"

He drew in his breath as the cold water filled his shoes.

"Wet from the knees down. Probably be my death. No Old Jack, then, to clear the streets of cutpurses and footpads. They'll be sorry, that's what; yes, they'll be sorry."

The damp air worked through his coat. He stepped into the protection of the porch of the parish church and rearranged his scarf. He pulled his cap down farther, then blew on his cold fingers.

Over his reddened knuckles he saw the hem of a cloak disappear into an alley. The clatter of wooden clogs echoed against the walls, then died away. He wondered for a moment what would bring someone out in this weather, and after curfew too. Well, he thought, whoever had run down the alley was safe from him; he wasn't chasing anyone tonight.

"Eh? What's that?"

He listened, barely breathing. Without moving, the Constable peered up and down the street and into the alley.

"Who goes there?" He cleared his throat and tried again. "Who goes there?"

The wind sighed around the buildings. Shutters and signboards swung on creaking hinges. He could hear the river as it raced through the pillars that supported London Bridge.

"You're hearing things, Jack. Best be getting on."

From a corner of the porch came a tap and two light thumps. The Constable froze in his steps; the back of his neck prickled. He heard the dry scuffing of cloth being dragged over stone.

"Hello?" He could barely hear his hoarse whisper.

Cold sweat trickled down his back. He'd never checked the dark corners of the porch when he'd stepped into it.

The Constable shivered and his teeth chattered. Run, run for your life, he thought, and he gathered himself for a dash down the street.

"My name is Willy."

Jack Crumpton whirled around. He saw nothing. He searched the deepest shadows. Still nothing. He wiped his nose on his sleeve and took half a step to the right.

Why weren't the lanterns lit so he could see, he thought. A body could die right here at the church door because some fool was in a hurry to get home.

"Wind's playing tricks on your ears, Jack," he muttered and sidestepped to the peg where the lantern hung. His fingers fumbled with the flint.

But there was no vagrant, only a bundle of clothing tied up in a blue shawl. The Constable swung his lantern over the ends of the porch where someone might crouch. No one. He turned his attention to the bundle. No doubt some charitable householder had deposited it there after the church doors had been locked. Crumpton set the lantern down and rubbed his hands together. He certainly deserved to be first to sort through the clothes after the trials of this watch. He could use a pair of stockings, soft and thick, to keep his feet warm. And gloves. He'd been hoping to find a pair with most of the fingers still attached. He pulled the bundle towards him. The knot in the shawl proved difficult with his fingers so cold.

"Never mind, I need—"

Two small shoes stepped close to the bundle. "My name is Willy."

"What's this?" Constable Crumpton jerked straight. "Didn't look behind the pillars, did you, Jack?" He lifted the lantern and held it so he could see better. "Left at the church door, are you?"

"That's mine." The boy gathered the bundle in his arms.

The Constable pushed himself to his feet and hung the lantern on its peg. He knotted his scarf tighter, pulled at his cap, and pushed his hands deep in his coat pockets. "You don't say so, now."

"My mummy gave it to me."

"Your mum? Is she here?"

Willy shook his head. "She said to stay right here."

Crumpton leaned closer. Willy hugged his bundle tighter and backed away.

"Well, it's fortunate I stepped in for a moment. This is bad weather for waiting on the porch. You might take a bad cough, weaken your lungs. Maybe you already have. Best be finding someone to take you in."

"My mum, she said to wait here."

"And how long might she be gone?"

Willy shrugged.

The Constable pointed to Willy's bundle. "This yours?"

Willy nodded. "All my clothes."

"Your mummy left you and all your clothes?"

"Yes." Willy drew himself up. "And she said the Constable would collect me very soon."

"Really!" The Constable pulled his hand from his pocket and jabbed his chest with his thumb. "I'm that very person. It seems you're to come with me." This was the third child he had found abandoned in the parish since Christmas. The infant girl had not lived long enough to be christened. He did not know about the boy.

"Are you really the Constable?" Willy studied the old man.

"Indeed I am. Now let's be off and find us a warm place for the night, eh? I'm near frozen, and you've not stopped shivering. We'll be following your mum's instructions."

At Willy's slow nod, the Constable scooped up child and bundle. "Let's see what Master Perry will do with you. I always take the little ones to him. I don't know that he will take you in, mind, but he's never yet turned one away. He'll know what to do with you. He's a churchwarden."

Sheltering the boy, the Constable stepped into the street and ducked into the wind-driven mist. He walked as fast as the slippery footing allowed and within three minutes approached a large house. He shifted Willy to one arm so he could raise the iron door knocker.

Down the street, deep in a doorway, a lone observer heard the sharp crack a moment after the knocker fell. She saw a servant open the ornate doors, allowing warm light to flow into the street. The Constable stepped closer, speaking rapidly and gesturing toward the child he held. The door closed but was soon opened by the master of the house. He nodded at the Constable and motioned the servant to take the boy. He dropped some coins into the Constable's outstretched hand and turned back into the house. The door swung closed and was locked for the night.

When the door closed, the silent figure turned away. The hem of her tattered cloak fluttered briefly in the wind as she left her hiding place. Her wooden clogs thudded dully as she turned towards her room at Mistress Garret's house. There was no hurry, for she could afford no fire tonight.

Meanwhile, Constable Crumpton surveyed his three pennies. "Master Perry is a fine and generous man."

He hurried towards his room and fire, fingering the pennies. There are at least a dozen ways to spend this, he thought. Maybe some gloves with fingers?

He shook his head. "No, they'd be a waste of good coin . . . A juicy sausage and white bread. Now, there's a treat." He licked his lips in anticipation. Crumpton envisioned himself seated comfortably in his favorite public house, near a large fire, with a tankard in his hand. He smiled. "Ah, you're a fortunate fellow, Jack."

Chapter 2

"Yes, madame." Master Perry nodded to his wife. "The Constable brought another foundling last night. Left on the church porch. Not a baby, this one, but a little chap about four years, I should say. Says his name's Willy . . . for William, I suppose. A nasty night to abandon a child." He sipped his tea. "Most refreshing, this tea . . . We'll have the old women out looking for the mother soon enough."

"And until she's found?" asked Mistress Perry.

"Probably won't be. Not even Crumpton saw anything. Though considering his ability to overlook everything but a warm corner, I'm not surprised." He set down his cup and reached for another slice of bread.

Mistress Perry frowned. "Here's the butter. When will the vestry meet?"

"On Wednesday, as usual. In the meantime, I must contact some of our parish nurses. Surely one of them will take the boy. If I can settle the details before Wednesday, it will merely be a matter of the vestry agreeing to what I've arranged. Until then—" He raised an eyebrow.

"Why do you insist on taking in every abandoned child?" Mistress Perry blinked back tears.

"It will be for a short time, a few days only, Amelia." Master Perry reached across the table and took his wife's hand. "We have this conversation each time Crumpton brings a foundling to our door."

"Why can't he take them to the Overseer? Doesn't he know how hard it is for us . . . for me?"

"But we have so much; it's our duty—"

"Our duty." She slipped her hand from her husband's grasp. "Who will care for him I cannot say. The maids will be busy cleaning."

THE FOUNDLING

Master Perry swallowed the last bite of his breakfast. "Cleaning, is it? I'm off, then. No man should be standing near mops and brooms being swung about like flails."

A small smile rewarded him.

"Best leave as soon as can be, or I'll have a mop in your hands. Getting those little girls to work will be almost impossible."

Master Perry rose. Amelia had set the foundling out of her thoughts. Cleaning after the Christmas festivities would keep her mind occupied. Prodding the maids to work would take all her ingenuity.

He smiled when he recalled entering the pantry abruptly during the holidays and catching Gillian and Marie propped in a corner devouring a mince pie. They probably had been sick for two days. He chuckled, finished buttoning his coat, and stepped into the street.

Willy awoke, yawned, and stretched. He propped himself on his elbow.

"Mummy?"

He was alone, in a big, white room, lying on a cot with a soft pillow and white sheets. He pulled at his blanket. No, there were no holes in it. This wasn't his blanket or his cot or the room where he and his mother lived. He caught his lower lip with his teeth. He remembered the cold, dark porch and the funny old man who had carried him to a warm house. He looked around.

Next to his cot stood a much bigger bed. Nobody was sleeping there. Willy leaned way over to look under it. He knew from the stories Mummy had told him that monsters often hid in such dark places. There were none there now, of course, because they always disappeared during the day. But they left those balls of dust behind. That's how you knew they'd been there. He checked under his cot. There was a chamber pot but no dust balls. He'd still have to be careful not to let his hands or feet dangle from under his blanket at night. Monsters could move in anytime.

Next to the big bed was a table. There was a small mirror above it and a stool in front of it. His mother had a stool just like it, but hers had a leg that was too short. Willy could make it rock back and forth when he sat on it.

Across the room stood a tall wooden cabinet. It had two doors that were decorated with drawings of birds, leaves, and flowers. It looked like a garden. A half-empty coal scuttle sat between the cabinet and the fireplace. The trunk next to his cot was plain wood.

He got goose bumps when he threw back his blanket. He was wearing a long white garment that pulled up over his knees when he slid out of bed. Beside his cot was a rug; the colors whirled around on it like the colors of the spinning top he'd seen in a shop window. He stretched one foot to the rug and poked at the small, hard lumps of braiding with his toe.

Willy shivered, gathered up his nightshirt, and ran to the fireplace. The fire warmed his front, but the cold hearthstone made him hop from one foot to the other. He pulled the rug to the hearth, sat down, and tucked the flannel nightshirt around his toes.

Where was he? Where was Mummy? Willy put his thumb into his mouth and stared at the fire. Something stirred in the back of his mind. He took a second look at the room. His thumb popped out of his mouth and his eyes grew round. Mummy had told him stories . . . was he where the king and queen lived? That would explain why he had a bed of his own and was wearing something long and white. Kings and queens were very rich and had their own beds and thick warm clothes. They lived in rooms with white walls, slept in beds with thick straw mattresses, had beautiful rugs on wooden floors, and had finely decorated cabinets. This was just like Mummy's stories.

"So you're out of bed."

Willy whirled around. Standing before him was a girl, perhaps twelve years old, in a plain brown dress and stiff white apron. Her hair was tucked under a cap, and her sleeves were rolled to the elbow. She wasn't pretty enough to be a princess.

"Come with me," she said. At the door she waited for him. "Come on then; you're to have a bath."

A bath? thought Willy. His breath caught in his throat. Surely kings and queens did not have to stand under the pump in the street and have cold water splashed over them. His mother had held so tightly when she jerked him out of the mud puddle and marched him to the pump. In spite of his kicks and squirms, she'd scrubbed him clean. He'd gotten water in his eyes and mouth and had coughed until his sides hurt.

Willy studied the girl's face. Definitely not a princess, he decided. How much of a protest would she allow?

Then she smiled and held out her hand. "My name is Marie."

Willy submitted. He stood up, pulled up his hem, and took her hand. He tiptoed and hopped beside her down the icy hallway floor.

Marie opened a door. Light and heat poured out. Across the room a fire wrapped around a great pot, one like the butcher had, a pot big enough to hold a little boy. An old woman bent over the pot. Just like the witches in tales . . .

Willy stiffened and pulled back. Then he was off the floor, tucked under Marie's arm so tightly that he could hardly breathe. She went towards the fire. Its heat poured over him, and the water bubbled. This was not the king's house, he knew. This was the house of the evil monsters. His mother had warned him this would happen if he misbehaved too often. He was going to be dinner for the monsters! Willy struggled for breath for his last scream.

Cook looked up. "Now he's a fine one, ain't he? Takes one look at my kitchen and sets himself to raise the ceiling."

Marie clapped her hand over Willy's mouth. "Now shush. You've nothing to carry on about." She turned back to Cook. "Mistress insists he have a bath. He came from heaven knows where. She won't have him in the house unless he's made presentable."

"The tub's in the corner." Cook returned to her stirring.

Marie whisked away Willy's nightshirt and left him shivering and too stunned to run while she filled the tub with water. Then she grabbed him and swung him into the water. His second outcry ended in a squeak. The water was only warm, hardly hot enough to cook him. Marie folded his nightshirt.

Willy glanced at Cook. All he could see was her back as she bent over her pots. So this was how spells were cast over people.

"Sit down." Marie pushed Willy down into the water and went to work. She might have been washing the floors for the scrubbing she gave him. The washing flannel came at him again and again. She washed his hair, and soap ran into his eyes.

"If you would sit still," Marie scolded, "this would be over sooner."

"Don't forget the ears," reminded Cook. "And mind the water on my floor."

Marie attacked Willy's ears. When his head, inside and out, was clean to her satisfaction, she put her hand over his mouth, pinched his nose shut, and pushed him under. He came up sputtering and stinging from his first full bath. Willy rubbed his eyes. They were watering and his nose was running. He coughed and fixed an injured expression on Marie. She dragged him out of the tub, then rubbed him briskly with a towel. Willy had never seen skin this color before. He was pink all over.

Then Marie dragged a shirt over his head. It caught one of his ears and pulled it. Willy shook his head hard and saw a warning in Marie's eyes. She pushed each arm into its proper sleeve and fastened the neck, then turned the sleeves back at his wrists.

Willy frowned. This wasn't his shirt. The shirts his mother made for him always fit just right. He looked up to tell her.

"Lift your foot . . . Right. Now the other foot." Marie pulled his breeches on and pulled the straps over his shoulders. They were too long, so she tied them in a knot in back to shorten them. "Now turn around so I can fasten the buttons."

Marie sat Willy down and pulled stockings on his feet. They were dark gray with no mending in the heels or the toes. Then she put new shoes on him. This isn't right, he thought. Where are my own clothes? Mummy made them just for me. Willy's lower lip trembled. The heavy cloth of his new clothes scratched him. The new shoes were stiff and squeezed his feet.

Willy kicked off his shoes and tried to pull off his socks. He fumbled with the buttons on his breeches and started to wriggle out of his shirt.

"Why, you little brat!" Marie roughly tucked his shirt back in, pulled his stockings up, and replaced his shoes. "That will be enough of that." She bit out each word.

Marie stood back and pushed a curl under her cap. She wiped her face and then her hands on her apron.

THE FOUNDLING

Cook peered at Willy. "Needs his hair cut." She nodded to Marie. "Mind this floor, girl." Cook shuffled to the table. "His breakfast is ready. He'd best be here on time tomorrow. I'll not make a second breakfast again."

Another maid entered with a small basketful of rags. "Some nanny you are," she said to Marie. "If you don't quiet him soon, Mistress will be here laying us all by the ears." She kneeled before the fire. One by one the rags went into the flames.

"Nasty things, so worn we can't even use them for cleaning. Look at this shirt!" She held it up with thumb and forefinger. "No child should have to wear such as this." She tossed the shirt into the fire.

"Mine! My shirt!"

"You'll have more shirts and better. And cleaner." She added more clothes to the fire.

"Mine!" Willy ran to the basket and grabbed at his belongings. Marie dragged Willy back. "Oh, do give him a shirt, Gillian. We can wash it. Or give him those breeches." Marie pointed. "I don't want to hear much more of his wailing."

"No, they're to be burned, all of them."

Willy screamed. He kicked at Marie's legs, but she was too quick and her skirts hid his target.

"Give him whatever's cleanest," she said. "I won't be scolded because of a screaming brat." Marie caught up the blue shawl and shoved it in Willy's face. "Now be still," she hissed.

Willy grabbed his mother's shawl and wadded it up against his chest.

Mistress Perry swept into the kitchen. The maids jumped up and curtseyed, standing with their eyes lowered and their hands clasped before them. Cook merely looked up for a moment.

"What is going on here? The whole house is disturbed." Mistress Perry's foot tapped impatiently. She addressed the younger girl. "Gillian?"

"Yes, mum?" Gillian curtseyed again.

"Why is that child carrying on so?"

"I suppose because I'm burning his old clothes. He wants them, mum."

"Keep him quiet. Finish here and come immediately to the front parlor."

Willy snuffled loudly and wiped his eyes on his shirtsleeve.

"Mum?" Marie curtseyed.

"Yes?"

"The boy hasn't eaten yet, and Cook says I must clean up the water from his bath."

"Feed him and clean as Cook instructs. Then come along. I don't suppose he can be left here?" Cook shook her head without looking up. "Very well, bring him along, but you must see to him."

The girls curtseyed.

"Mum? What's his name? What do we call him?" Marie asked.

Mistress Perry shook her head. "I'm sure I don't know." She left the kitchen, closing the door softly behind her.

"His name's Willy. I heard the master say so this morning," said Cook, and she lapsed back into silence.

The girls returned to their tasks.

Gillian handed Willy's old breeches to Marie. "There's something in the pocket. See what it is."

"You look; you're doing the burning."

"Oh, no. I'm not sticking my fingers into a little boy's pockets. Besides, you have brothers. You're used to it."

Marie took the breeches and poked at the pocket. A wad of paper rolled out across the floor. She snatched it up, glancing quickly at both Gillian and Willy.

"What is it?" asked Gillian.

"A twist of paper."

"Let me see." Gillian held out her hand.

"It's just paper. I'll keep it to help light the fire in my room." And Marie dropped it into her apron pocket.

Willy sat at the big table. Cook set breakfast before him. This was certainly no spell from her huge black pot. He ate white bread and butter and fruit preserves. There was cold milk too. Willy licked his milk mustache and looked up to see Cook watching. He ducked his head and tried to frown at her from under his eyebrows. But she gave him a wide, toothless smile when she leaned forward to give him another slice of bread and a piece of dried apple. So he smiled back just a little.

Marie motioned to Willy. He jumped down from his chair. Marie said, "What do you say to Cook?"

Willy said nothing. He looked from Marie to Cook and back to Marie.

"Say 'thank you,' Willy."

Willy hid his face in his sleeve. A hard nudge brought a whispered "thank you." He held on to Marie's apron with one hand and his shawl with the other as Marie led him out of the kitchen.

Cook swept the bread crumbs from the table into her hand. A likely lad, she thought, and smiled again.

Chapter 3

The maids hurried, arguing over who would wash the windows and who would polish the woodwork. The pails they carried thumped against their legs, and water splashed their aprons. They pushed open two heavy doors and entered the parlor. Willy followed.

It was the largest room he had ever seen. It was big enough for a king. A fireplace took up nearly one whole wall. Another wall was full of windows. There were chairs and tables everywhere. The red carpet that covered much of the floor felt soft under his feet. He couldn't hear his own footsteps. He squatted and poked his finger into the nap. The stiff, deep wool scratched his hand. It wasn't as soft as it looked.

Mistress Perry left the room carrying a basketful of wax-covered candlesticks. Gillian began polishing a heavily carved chair, and Marie started washing the windows.

Willy went to the fireplace. It looked like a huge cave, big enough for a whole family of monsters to live in. But it was daytime and they wouldn't be there. He stepped in. Gray ash puffed around his ankles. When he looked up, he could see a small, round patch of sky.

"Come out of there this instant." Gillian stood on the hearth, her hands on her hips.

Startled, Willy grabbed one of the andirons to keep his balance.

"Look at you. Up to your ankles in ash. Now your hands are filthy as well." She pointed to the hearth. "Come here!"

Willy backed farther into the fireplace. Gillian leaned in to snatch him. "Back away from me, will you?" She balanced on the edge of the hearthstone and tried to reach him.

"Gillian, get back. You'll fall in yourself if you're not careful." Marie came over to the hearth. "Go on; get back to your polishing. Here, Willy." She stretched out her hand. "Come stand on the hearthstone so I can brush you off before Mistress returns."

THE FOUNDLING

Willy took Marie's damp hand and stepped out. She gathered her rag and wiped his hands. Then she picked up a broom and brushed his legs. "Turn around." She brushed his back clean and wiped off his shoes.

"Now go sit down, and don't move unless you're told to, or . . . I'll take your shawl away." She gave him a swat to hurry him to a large chair by the windows.

Willy sat clutching his shawl. Smells of polishes for pewter, brass, and wood swirled around him. The swishing of brooms, the clatter of pails, and the brushing of the thick upholstery were loud. Dust floated in the sunbeams that shone through the windows. He wondered why the bits of dust didn't fall and why they spun and danced when someone walked past his chair.

When the sunbeams disappeared, Willy watched traffic in the street. It wiggled past, distorted by the uneven window glass. Men and women became tall and thin, then short and fat; horses and wagons stretched and squeezed as they went by.

When the work was done, Mistress Perry moved around the room. Occasionally she pointed to something and one of the maids rushed to polish a spot or brush away a bit of dust. Finally, all their work seemed to please her.

She stood near the middle of the room where watery beams of the winter sun shone once more, giving the parlor a semblance of light and warmth. Willy saw her lips part in a half smile. He could not know that for a moment she almost expected three children to burst through the doors tumbling over each other, shouting, eager for her attention. But when she turned, she saw only two tired maids and a waif, none of whom touched her heart. The light in her eyes died like the disappearing sunbeam. She pressed her lips together and motioned the maids to leave. Willy followed Marie back to the kitchen.

That afternoon Willy lay on his cot. He had never taken a nap before. He and his mother had always gone to Cheapside in the afternoons to beg. Occasionally someone gave them a small coin. More often a constable told them to move along. Willy turned over and punched his pillow. He had never slept alone before either. He had always curled up with Mummy. She'd made him feel warm and safe. He tucked Mummy's shawl under his cheek.

When they had gone out together, she scooted him out of the way of draft horses and oxen pulling wagons. She never let him dawdle in front of the public houses, although he tried to look in. Mummy grabbed him by the elbow and directed him around rubbish in the streets. One day he found a red ribbon that he knew would be beautiful after it was tidied up. Mummy wasn't so sure. She had, however, been able to sell the shoe buckle he pulled from a pile of rotten vegetables. The knitted cap hadn't been as good a find even though it had only two holes. He had found it under a dead rat, and Mummy said it was very nasty and she would never get the smell out. He threw it back into the gutter. One day he'd found a halfpenny. He'd kicked aside some rags and there it lay. We had some cheese with our bread that day, Willy thought. And it was my halfpenny that bought it. He smiled.

"I'll squeeze you 'til you squeak," his mother would say. And he would wait until her hug was so tight he could hardly breathe, then squeak for her. He would hide under her apron while she whirled around looking for him. They both laughed when she found him and told him how clever he was to find such a hiding place.

I haven't seen Mummy at all today, Willy thought. He wanted to tell her how he had obeyed and waited for the Constable. He wanted to tell her of his adventures and of the nice witch in the kitchen. But most of all he wanted to hug her and have her hug him until he squeaked. He tried a squeak lying there on his cot, but it wasn't a very good one. He closed his eyes and saw his mother down the street. She walked away and didn't hear when he called to her. He started to run, but she turned a corner and disappeared. He was left alone among strangers.

A noise awakened Willy. Through his half-opened eyes he saw Marie take her hand from the door latch.

"I thought I'd never have a moment to myself," she muttered. "That nosy Gillian!" She glanced at Willy who lay completely still.

Marie drew a twisted paper from her apron pocket. "It's too heavy. There has to be something . . . " She sat on her bed and untwisted the paper. Something gold slipped through her fingers and off her lap. She snatched it from the floor. "How beautiful!" she whispered.

Marie turned a golden brooch over and over in her hands. The burnished metal reflected the fading light. On its cover, engraved swirls formed the initials *WH*. How had such a piece of jewelry found its way into a little boy's pocket? Marie pressed a small catch and the brooch opened, revealing a lock of hair and a miniature portrait. She glanced at Willy. There was no mistaking the resemblance. Willy's mother? It had to be.

Marie bit her lower lip. What shall I do, she thought. Give the brooch to Master Perry? He'll give it to the vestry. They'll sell it and use the money for Willy. Not that they'll need the money—they'll take care of him whether they have it or not. They'll surely never allow him to keep it.

Her hand closed over the brooch. It's so beautiful. It would be a shame to sell it. Why couldn't I keep it? Who would miss it? No one knew Willy had it. No one knows I have it. So, it isn't as though I'd be stealing from anyone. Who would it hurt?

"Marie, are you going to the shops for Cook?" Gillian called down the hall. "You should go now before it rains."

Willy peeked in time to see Marie run to the wardrobe and pull its door open. She tucked something into a fold of clothing and whirled around as Gillian entered the room.

"Shhh, you'll waken Willy. I'm coming." She took a deep breath and closed the wardrobe. Her hands shook when she picked up her cloak.

Willy waited until the maids' steps died away before he threw back the blanket, kicked off the sheet, and ran to the wardrobe. He could hardly wait to discover Marie's secret. He opened the wardrobe door and patted the folded clothes. Nothing. He emptied the shelves one at a time. It's in here, he thought, I saw her put something in here. He pulled her shifts out, one at a time. A golden object tumbled to the floor and rolled under Marie's bed.

Monsters or no, he dived under the bed. He crawled out covered with dust, his fist closed tightly around Marie's secret.

Willy opened his hand. He was holding Mummy's brooch. Marie shouldn't have this. It didn't belong to her. He had to return it to Mummy.

Willy opened the door and looked up and down the hall. Where was the door to the outside? He ran to the left, upstairs, through rooms, downstairs, into and out of passages. Sometimes he could see outside, but he could not find the way out.

The swish of skirts stopped him. He looked up into the stern face of Mistress Perry.

"Gillian! Come here immediately!"

Gillian came running. Mistress Perry and Willy faced each other, neither moving. Mistress Perry made a vague gesture. "Take care of . . . him." She walked away, barely stepping aside as she passed.

Gillian reached out and gripped Willy's shoulder. "Come with me."

Willy wrenched away. "No! I want my Mummy!"

With a swoop she grabbed Willy's stiff body, clapped her hand over his mouth, and hurried him back to the servants' quarters.

"What have you done, you little wretch?" Gillian surveyed Marie's room. "Marie will have your head, and so she should, you ungrateful brat." She sat Willy on his cot and stooped to pick up the clothes. "You should be ashamed! I'd not have cared for you as Marie has, let me tell you." She shook out a shift.

"I want Mummy!" Willy started to get off his cot.

"Get back up there." Gillian sat Willy down with a thump and shook a finger in his face. "Listen to me. Your mother doesn't want you. She left you last night and she's not coming back. You'd best make up your mind to that. You'll never see her again."

Willy struck at Gillian. She caught his hand. "Don't you dare! She left you on the church porch for someone else to take care of. She doesn't want you anymore."

"Mummy!" Willy sobbed into his shawl, hiding the golden brooch against his chest.

"You can cry all you want; she's gone."

Willy sobbed louder. "I don't want to stay here."

THE FOUNDLING

"Don't worry. You'll probably be gone tomorrow or the next day . . . as soon as a nurse is found. You can't be gone too soon for me; Mistress doesn't want you here, either. You stay on your cot until dinner, or you'll be punished."

Gillian slammed the door when she left.

Willy snuffled once and then again to clear his nose. His mother's shawl was wet from his tears. Gillian's stupid, he thought. Mummy does love me. She does, she does, she does! And I have this!

He opened the brooch and looked at the tiny painting inside. His mother looked back at him with just the faintest smile. She was beautiful, but Willy liked her best when she laughed out loud. He touched the lock of hair.

Mummy had told him how her husband, Willy's father, had given it to her a few weeks after their wedding day. They had been very happy when Willy was born, so they named him William after his father. But everyone knew it would be confusing, because when Mummy called for William, she would get two answers. So baby William was called "Willy." Willy liked that story, even though he did not remember his father. Daddy had gone to war and died fighting a bad king.

Soon after, four soldiers had come to live in Willy's house. They were rude and made Mummy cook for them. She didn't like that at all, so she packed her trunk and took Willy to London. She sold her belongings one by one to buy food. Except the brooch. She would never sell that. Willy closed the brooch and listened for the click of the catch.

Now he wanted to give the brooch back to Mummy, hear her laugh, and feel her tight hug. He would be so good that she would never leave him on the church porch again. Willy looked out the window. It was dark. He'd have to wait until tomorrow. He pushed the brooch under his straw mattress. It made a small lump, so he slid the brooch up where his pillow would hide it.

Master Perry was pleased with his day. He could not send supplies to Fairfax's parliamentary army quickly enough. An agent of the King's army had also come to him, but secretly, asking to buy supplies. Master Perry could have made handsome profits from both sides. But, besides being an ethical man, he was a strict Parliamentarian, and he had refused.

His manservant took his cloak and hat. Rodgers was a fine sort, Perry reflected, punctilious to a fault in his duties. He was also well-read and could converse intelligently on many topics. Or, if Perry desired a more demanding exchange, he could debate matters of politics and religion. His ability in financial matters had earned him a position as a clerk at Master Perry's warehouse. And he was a good friend.

Perry sat down and stretched his legs to the fire. He looked with chagrin at the mud caked on his boots. If he had tracked mud through the house, Amelia would be more than a little upset. He was as bad as the children had been.

Rodgers interrupted. "Mistress has been detained, James, but she instructed me to bring the tray along. She asks you not to wait for her." Then catching sight of the muddy boots, "Oh dear, shall I remove them for cleaning? Yes, yes, that's better. I'll fetch your slippers."

"Thank you," said Perry and took a slice of cold meat pie.

Mistress Perry entered moments later. She sat beside her husband and arranged her skirts. "Just a small slice for me, if you please."

They sat quietly before the fire chatting of the cold weather and the promise of more rain. They spoke of his relatives and hers. The cleaning of the front parlor was rehearsed along with the besetting sins of Marie, Gillian, and other members of the staff.

"And Willy, how is he?"

"The boy? He spent the day with Marie and Gillian. You'll have to ask them. They're all in the kitchen just now."

"He's just about the age of our Daniel."

"Never say so. You do your family a disservice to mention a gutter child in the same breath with one of your own children." She stared into the fire. "He will be gone tomorrow?"

"Or the day after, perhaps. Unless we have some word of his mother. Unlikely, of course . . . " Master Perry's voice trailed off into silence.

Chapter 4

Wednesday afternoon the officers of the parish of St. Pancras, Soper Lane, met in the vestry house. They agreed to purchase one pickaxe, one large ladder, and an iron crowbar for repairs to the church. They chose a committee to view houses and assess their values for parish rates. Then they itemized payments of relief to the parish poor.

"Well, if she insists on not attending divine service, Goodwife Franklin should not receive her bread and cheese. Many others would gladly have it," said Richard Jackson, Overseer for the Poor.

"Is she able to attend?"

"Of course. Goody Darby saw her at the shops Saturday last."

"Perhaps another warning?"

"She's received two already."

"One more, then." Speaker Rand looked around the vestry. "Richard, please warn her once more and inquire more closely into why she does not attend Sunday services."

The Overseer nodded while the parish clerk scribbled notes in the book of minutes.

The Speaker continued. "Is Master Garvey still in Newgate for debt?"

"He is."

"How much debt does he owe?"

"According to Mistress Garvey, five pounds, twelve shillings, eight pence. She is unable to pay. Either we help Garvey with his debt, or he'll remain in prison. Then we'll have his wife and child laid to the charge of the parish as well."

The clerk's pen scratched in the silence.

"The war has ruined him; I believe he would find a way to repay the parish. But he must be free to work."

"Aye, let's help him. A solid man, he is. Get him out of Newgate before he dies of jail fever and we have no choice but to support his family." Old Arthur Dewe pulled his cloak closer and hugged himself beneath its folds. He always sat next to the fire.

"Any further discussion? No?" Speaker Rand addressed a stout man whose short legs did not allow his feet quite to reach the floor when he sat down. "Henry, do we have sufficient funds in the poor box for Garvey's debt?"

Henry's eyes flew open. He shifted, seeking a more comfortable position, and stuck out his lower lip as if in thought. He cleared his throat.

"Yes, yes, of course."

"We can cover Jim Garvey's debt?"

Henry put the fingers of his left hand to his forehead and let out his breath in relief. There was enough to cover the debt. "By all means," he said, "with a bit left over, if I'm not mistaken."

"Please see to this immediately. Add sixpence for Garvey's immediate expenses if you have it." The Speaker hesitated. "Is this satisfactory? . . . Very well. Now about the boy left on the church porch Monday last."

The old man by the fire made a noise of disapproval. "Another foundling? How many already this winter, and January not half over?" If he had announced a rise in rates, the response could not have been more immediate.

"Any idea who his parents might be?"

"We should swear out warrants for arrest."

"I shudder when I hear of these urchins being left here, there, and about for someone else to care for. Why, I remember just two years ago—"

"Yes, yes, it's inexcusable. Problem is these hard times pinch everyone."

"Let these beggars go back to their own parishes. That's where their help should come from."

"Why everyone comes to London is beyond me. Let them go home, I say, and—"

"It's the war, you know. Men taken into the army, women unable to provide for the children. Houses and fields destroyed. No wonder they come to London."

"We're short of funds too. Can't be denied. If many more shops and houses are closed up, we'll have no one left to pay rates."

The clerk waited for business to resume.

"Just last week George Parker told me that their vestry swore out warrants for the arrest of two young scamps. They'd been begging and loitering about the parish for several days. Up to no good, I'll wager. They went straight to Newgate. Won't be causing trouble for some time, I daresay."

"Gentlemen, we could continue this indefinitely, but my wife expects me home this evening. Very frankly, I'd like to oblige her." The Speaker motioned for silence. "Constable Crumpton discovered the boy about nine o'clock last Monday night. The boy has since been kept by James Perry. Thank you, James." The Speaker nodded in Perry's direction.

"Have you kept an accounting of expenses? Ah, good." He took the list of figures offered to him. "He required all new clothing? Are you being generous again, James? He really needed everything from caps to stockings? Total is ummm . . . "—he ran his finger down the list—"twenty-five shillings, seven pence, one farthing." He turned to Churchwarden Whiteing. "Please see this account settled, Tim." Again to Perry, "Has the boy been properly christened?"

"He says his name is Willy—for William, no doubt. But, no, I do not know that he has been christened. Since we have no knowledge of the mother, I suggest we christen him William Pancras." Perry looked around.

"Can't we be a bit more imaginative?" Arthur Dewe asked. "We always name our foundlings after our parish. Why not name him after the street where he was found—?"

Speaker Rand stared the old man into silence.

Perry continued. "I have inquired about a permanent nurse for him. Neither of the nurses in Ware has a place. They would like the money well enough, but each has five or six children already. So I asked Margaret Bessie whether she would take in a second child. Here are her fees."

Perry passed a second list of figures to the speaker.

"James, this seems a bit high."

"Willy is not an infant. He'll take more in diet alone than a newborn."

"Yes, quite. And, I'm sure we will receive regular requests for new clothes and shoes for him." Speaker Rand handed the list of figures to one of the Overseers of the Poor.

The Overseer studied the paper. "It is a bit more than we usually pay, but Goodwife Bessie is one of our best nurses. She seems to take a genuine interest in her charges, feeds them well, keeps them clean and their clothes well mended. I've heard she also insists on their presence at divine service and at catechism. You know she reads and can write. But, to answer your question, the fees for Willy will be more than another nurse would charge. She's worth every farthing, though . . . In fact, the overall expense may be less because her children are seldom sick. Yes, Goodwife Bessie will do nicely. Willy is a fortunate little fellow that she will take him."

James Perry sat back and relaxed, pleased that his suggestions met with the vestry's approval. He leaned forward again.

"Now about his christening."

"Ah yes, the christening." Speaker Rand addressed the minister. "Reverend Scoppe, will you be available at all tomorrow?"

"Tomorrow will be fine. Better make it at, say, eleven o'clock. We have relatives in the house, and I'm sure to need a respite about then."

"Just so. I'll notify the pensioners to attend and stand with the child. They'll be a bit disappointed that they won't get to choose his name. They argued for two hours over the name of our last foundling." The Speaker shook his head. "Who will bring . . . Willy, is it? . . . along to the church?"

Perry motioned with his hand.

"You, James? Very good."

The meeting ended and the clerk laid his pen aside, waiting for each man to sign the minutes. Goodman Dewe shuffled away from the fire and out of the chamber with his cronies. Henry slid out of his chair, muttering at his stiff knees and sore back. He limped to the door. Other men lingered, more than one commenting on James Perry's interest in the latest foundling.

Perry turned his steps towards home, a quiet dinner, and perhaps some reading. He was pleased with his arrangements for Willy . . . about the age of Daniel—

Nearly a year had passed since he had held his son, comforted him, prayed his fever would break. He brushed his hand across his eyes, remembering the three trips to the cemetery last winter. He and Amelia buried Daniel first, then each of the girls. Even now he was relieved that he was wealthy enough to own a vault to protect his little ones. He didn't want to think that any of his children, even in death, might be cold.

Soon after, Amelia's health had failed. Blaming it on London's cold, damp air, they had traveled to the mild countryside of Cornwall and busied themselves with the daily trivia of living. They found an old stone cottage surrounded by an overgrown garden. Cleaning, sweeping, and mending its fabric occupied their days. By early summer the garden with its trailing roses was the envy of the neighbors. The Perrys even attended some local gatherings where new acquaintances never asked after the children. But each evening, when there was little to occupy mind or hand, the shadow of the preceding winter crept back, dulling the golden green of the sunset.

Physically, Amelia had grown stronger. Yet her demeanor altered subtly. The shadow never left her. Though she moved and spoke and looked the same, it was with no light of soul. It was she who had proposed their return to London and, through autumn and into December, had immersed herself in the duties of housewife and hostess. Never had she been so busy. Yet, Perry wondered, for all of her holiday preparations, had she ever truly enjoyed herself? The house, the festivities, the attention to every detail became ends in themselves, engineered to fill each waking moment. The end of the holidays and the arrival of Willy emphasized that their lives were as empty as their house. And Willy would go to Margaret Bessie's after the christening.

Perry was surprised at his sense of loss at the thought of Willy's going.

Chapter 5

The next morning, Willy straightened his sheet and blanket. He compared his bed with Marie's. Hers had no wrinkles at all. He pulled his blanket hard to make it as smooth as Marie's, put the pillow over the lump made by the brooch, and went to breakfast.

In the kitchen, he exchanged winks with Cook. She wasn't a witch at all. He ate bread with lots of butter, sprinkled with herbs. It was delicious. Then he had a bowl of oatmeal with milk and honey. He saw the tub sitting in the corner. His bath hadn't been so very bad. Over there was the cabinet that held the dishes. The one next to it was full of tablecloths and serviettes. He'd seen them when Cook opened the door. There were candlesticks, pots and pans, and serving platters on shelves above the fireplace. Willy looked carefully at the fireplace with its huge kettle that swung over the fire. He'd stay away from there for a while, just to be safe.

Marie brought in a tray full of breakfast dishes. She put them down and left. Willy licked his fingers, thanked Cook, and slipped from the table to follow Marie. He was sure she knew how to get outside. All he had to do was be there when she opened the right door. He waited while she cleaned up the dining room. Then he followed her when she carried linens to the laundry. He never left her for a minute while she swept and dusted two other rooms. Finally she put her broom and rags away, but though she opened many doors, none led to the street.

For the afternoon, Willy decided he would follow Gillian. Perhaps she would show him the way to the street.

Gillian scowled at him, but he ignored her and followed her through the house. She stopped in almost every room to collect dirty clothing and linens for washing. Willy even picked up some clothes she dropped. When they reached the laundry, he sat down on a stool by the door. The steamy air smelled of mildew and soap. The damp floor was slippery, and water beaded on the cold stone walls. Gillian tugged at the tangled linens, ignoring sharp tearing sounds. Her face became redder and redder from her exertions. Her ruffled cap drooped over her right eye. Willy saw her lips move, saying words he could barely hear.

"I shouldn't have to do this . . . or mind that brat. Marie's the house servant; I'm Mistress's personal maid. My hands will be a sorry sight when she calls me to help her dress for dinner. I must ask Cook for some lard to take the redness away." Gillian pushed her cap up with the back of her hand. "That old hag probably won't give it to me. She's as sour as a quince."

Gillian lowered a sheet into the boiling water. Willy watched her without moving. A rolling bubble splashed over the lip of the cauldron onto her foot. She screamed in pain, grabbed her foot, and hopped around the piles of laundry. Her skirts flapped around her legs; her ruffled cap slipped lower and lower over her eye. She stumbled over a pile of dirty clothes, lost her balance, and fell against the mildewed wall. Her shrieks of pain alternated with wails of disgust.

Willy couldn't help himself. He laughed out loud.

"Get out! Get out of here!" Gillian aimed a scrub brush at Willy, but his place was suddenly empty and Cook stood at the door. Gillian froze, then lowered her hand and replaced the brush on its shelf. She let go her scalded foot, pushed herself from the wall, and stepped off the pile of clothes. She folded her red hands over her wet apron.

"Cook, may I have a bit of lard? The kettle boiled over on my foot. I'm sure a bit of lard will soothe the burn nicely."

Cook chuckled. "See me after you've finished the washing, dearie. I'm sure there's some lard we can use on your foot. In the meantime, straighten your apron and cap." Cook stepped back into the hall where Willy watched in safety. "Come along, sprout. I need an opinion on a spicy cake."

Willy licked the last crumbs from his plate. Then he showed Cook how Gillian had grabbed her foot and hopped all over the laundry room. Marie bustled into the kitchen, set her baskets on the table, and raised her eyebrows at Willy's behavior.

"Gillian hurt her foot," Willy explained. Then he fell against the wall, finishing his performance for Cook.

Cook laughed. "That girl never was any good at household chores. Fancies herself a lady. She'll be complaining of her burns and bruises for a fortnight. Ah, well . . . Now, Marie, how were the markets?"

"Sugar is dearer than we thought, but the vegetables look good, considering the season."

Marie had gone to the market? Cook rolled the onions around and examined the carrots. How had he missed Marie's going to market?

"Yes, quite nice, quite. No soft spots. Put the sugar in the chest. Mind you don't spill any." She paused. "Any eggs?"

Who cares about eggs? thought Willy. I want to see my Mummy.

"The other basket," said Marie. "Fresh this morning, they are. If you still want a goose, the butcher just 'round the corner has three large ones hanging in his window. I'm surprised he has any to sell with Christmas just past." She shook the last of the sugar into the chest, closed the lid, and snapped the lock shut.

"That's the lot." Marie brushed her hands off. "Where are you going, young man? Why aren't you in bed? It's long past time for your nap." She swept him out of the kitchen.

Willy climbed onto his cot and kicked off his shoes. He lay back and pulled his blanket up to his chin. Marie would soon leave, and he could continue his search for the door to the street. He waited until she had hung her damp cloak before the fire and left the room. When he could no longer hear her steps, he slipped out of bed. He was straightening his stockings so he could put on his shoes when she came back, carrying an armful of clothes. Her sewing basket was perched on top.

"Get back in bed this instant." She stood there with the clothing balanced on one hip. Her free arm pointed to Willy, then to his bed.

Willy crawled back onto his cot and once more pulled his blanket up.

"It's a good thing I returned." Marie sat down on her stool. "Understand this, little man: Mistress does not want you wandering about the house untended. I'll be staying here until you are asleep." She shook out a garment to find where it wanted mending. "Make up your mind to it, you'll not be running about today." Marie threaded her needle. "Do you understand me?" She looked at Willy. "Do you? Answer me!"

Willy scowled at Marie so she wouldn't be able to see any tears in his eyes. He sucked in his lower lip. "Yes," he said and rolled towards the wall so he could not see her. He rested his head on his mother's shawl and his hand on the small lump under his pillow.

A log settling in the fireplace woke Willy. He rolled over. Marie had left. He lay back with a yawn. Alone! He sat straight up. He heard no footsteps in the hall, so he swung his feet over the side of his cot and set to straightening his stockings again. One nearly slipped off and dangled from his toes. His new shoes were stiff and hurt his feet, but he got them on. He jumped from the cot, pulled his shirt straight, and tucked it into his breeches.

His shoes squeaked when he walked, and the heels sounded like hammers on the floor. His breathing filled the room. How had he suddenly become so noisy? Willy stilled his breathing and tiptoed into the hall. He passed door after door, but now he knew where some of them led. He passed Gillian's room and stuck out his tongue at it. Then he turned around, screwed up his face, stuck out his tongue, and made donkey ears at Marie's door. Satisfied, he continued past the servants' passage to the upstairs.

He opened one of the doors at the end of the hall. Its latch clattered in the silence. He cringed and looked over his shoulder. No one. He pushed the door open. The hinges screeched. Willy scurried through and pushed the door shut. The boom sounded like thunder. Surely someone had heard that. No one came. He stood still until his heart stopped pounding and he could breathe again.

He had entered a small room with a stone floor and many windows. In the middle of the room stood a table set with tiny dishes. A large covered basket leaned against the wall by the fireplace. In a corner, a rocking horse waited patiently for its rider.

Willy inspected the table and dishes first. The table was just the right height for him. Though the plates, cups, and saucers were covered with dust, someone had set them out with care. Two dolls, seated in a nearby chair, waited for the party to begin. Their fine gowns had faded and the laces yellowed, but Willy thought both of them very pretty. The rocking horse was as grand as the horses ridden by the rich men of London. Willy stroked the mane and forelock, the pink muzzle, and the white blaze. The horse's saddle and bridle sparkled with red and blue jewels. He knew just how to sit on a horse from watching the men. He combed the horse's mane through his fingers and looked at the dolls at the table. Would anyone mind? The dolls smiled back and no one else disapproved, even though Willy stood there for some time, waiting.

The horse was taller than he expected and rocked while he tried to climb on. Willy grabbed a handful of mane and the saddle and pulled and kicked until he was high enough to swing his foot over the saddle.

In his mind's eye he rode down Cheapside and all the people moved aside for him. The horse rocked faster. He waved and nodded to acquaintances, proud to be seen on such a steed. His friends called out inviting him to dinner, to play games, to—

Those were real voices right outside the door! Willy scrambled off the rocking horse and crouched motionless on his knees.

"Did you hear that? Certainly, there's no one in the garden room?"

"I rather imagine not," came the reply. "Madame allows no one in there."

The voices faded with the footsteps.

Willy did not move for a long time. Then a movement in the garden outside caught his attention. He went to the window and pushed his nose against the cold glass. The garden was small and uninviting with its yellow grass and unkempt bushes. In the corner, a swing moved to and fro in the winter wind. Willy ran to the garden door. He pushed and pulled; he tugged at the latch, but the door would not open. It was getting dark. He'd have to hurry! He shook the door again, then he looked about for another way into the garden.

Shadows filled the room. He couldn't see the horse in the corner. He could barely see the table in the center of the room. The door by which he'd entered had disappeared in the shadows too.

For the first time, Willy felt the penetrating cold and shivered. He didn't want to play anymore. He wanted to get back to the warm light of the rest of the house. It was dark, time for monsters to come out. He cowered on the floor, too frightened to move.

"I told you, there's no one in here—" The playroom door swung open. Two figures stood in silhouette.

"I heard something, I tell you."

"Like as not it was the wind rattling the doors. Come along, we've much to do before Master returns." And the door swung shut.

Willy started to shout "I'm here! I'm here," but the door closed too quickly. He was instantly up, moving as fast as he could towards the door. No monsters caught him. He saw a sliver of light along the edge of the door, found the latch, and, with a sob of relief, pulled the door open and ran into the hallway.

For the next few minutes he wandered aimlessly through the house. He'd forgotten about getting to the street. He wasn't even sure how to get back to his room. He stopped in a small room that would have been dark but for the fireplace and a lamp burning on a table. Some coats hung on wall pegs. A carved door took up nearly one wall. Willy warmed his front and then his back at the fire. He was feeling hungry. Far away, he heard noises and talking, but he had no idea how to get to them.

A key rattling in the lock broke into his thoughts. Someone was coming! He would be found and sent to bed forever. Willy ran into a dark hall, but muted voices echoed all around him. Footsteps paused. Panic-stricken, he ran back to the fire. He whirled this way and that. The great door opened. Willy ran to the table in the entrance hall and crouched beneath it.

He peeked out as two men entered, each wrapped in a long, heavy cloak. The intruders closed the door behind them. One of them removed his gloves and reached for the fastening of his cloak. He saw Willy and paused, then let the other take the cloak from his shoulders.

"Thank you, Rodgers," he said, handing him his gloves.

"Will you be needing any help, sir?" Rodgers looked significantly at Willy.

"I think not. The little chap seems more afraid of us than we are of him . . . Young man!"

Willy crawled out and stood up. Not knowing what to do, he started turning back and forth, his hands stuck in his breeches' pockets.

Master Perry looked Willy over, speaking to himself. "Not at all like Daniel, but still . . . "

Rodgers shifted the cloaks.

"Willy is it?" Master Perry handed his hat to Rodgers. "I'm Master Perry, James Perry. This is my house."

Willy took his hands from his pockets, clasped them behind him, and settled back on his heels, still swinging back and forth.

Master Perry leaned down. He smiled and held out his hand. Willy studied the eyes before him. His decision made, he shook hands.

"I'm very pleased to meet you, Willy . . . Do your shoes hurt your toes?"

Willy nodded.

"Sit down. Let me help you." Master Perry knelt down, removed the offending shoes, readjusted Willy's stockings and put his shoes back on.

Willy watched him work, occasionally stealing a glance at Master Perry's face.

Master Perry patted Willy's foot and stood up. "There, that should do it. See if they're not better."

Willy rose, wiggled his toes, and took a step. The shoes did feel better, and they didn't squeak as much either. "Thank you, sir," Willy said.

"Aha! Some breeding here." Master Perry smiled. "Come along, young man. Let's leave this drafty room." He swung Willy up on his arm.

Into the entrance hall came the light step and rustling skirts of Mistress Perry. Her greeting died on her lips. "Sir," she gasped, "what are you doing? Gillian, this instant! Get him out of here!" She whirled away and stared into the fire.

Gillian flew to her Mistress's aid, bobbed a curtsey, and took Willy from Master Perry. Mistress Perry's cries followed them down the length of the hall.

"You see? Just as I told you? You saw him, a child raised in the gutters; he can't even dress himself properly. And he has no breeding, none at all. He sneaks about. Sneaks, I say. He's not to be trusted. And you bring him, along with every other child born in the street, into our house, and treat him like one of your own! Get him out—tonight—now!"

Master Perry led his wife into their sitting room.

"Amelia, you must recognize that we have a little boy in the house. You can ignore or despise him, but he's still here and will be for one more day."

"I don't want him here. I never wanted him here, James. Why did you take him in?"

"What would you have me do with him? Leave him on the porch? Have the Constable take him home? We've taken in other foundlings. It is our duty to help wherever we can when there are so many homeless and unfortunates in the City." He paused. "Is it because he's about the same age as Daniel would be? Willy's a bit like him, you know." He stared into the fire. "Amelia, I loved Daniel more than I thought possible." His chin sank to his chest.

"And you expect a castoff to take his place?"

"No, Amelia—"

"I won't have it, never. I'll be glad when he's gone!"

Anger was always her first response to any remembrance of their children. Perry agonized for his wife, struggling for composure. Soon, he knew, she would act as if nothing were amiss. She completed her metamorphosis and smiled at him.

"I'm sure dinner must be ready. Will you come now?"

"Rodgers will announce dinner. Sit down, please?" He sat down and held out his hand.

Amelia looked, but Rodgers did not appear. She frowned and laced her fingers together.

"Yes . . . yes . . ." She sat on the edge of her chair.

So fragile, Perry thought. The veneer of composure so thin. When will she come to terms with our loss?

"Amelia, I—" James searched for a way to lighten the mood. "Both Gillian and Marie will be happy to be free of their extra responsibilities. From what Rodgers tells me, they've been led a pretty dance." There, now he'd done it, spoken of household affairs that centered on Willy. He pressed his lips together and waited.

A small smile, however, rewarded his effort.

"Gillian isn't very good with children, is she? Marie, now, has little brothers—" She blinked back unbidden tears. "Poor Gillian, she isn't very good at much. Her advice regarding my new waists simply is not to be borne. I should look a fool if I wore them as she suggests." She looked at her husband.

Yes, he thought, that's better. He loved her for trying.

When Rodgers appeared to announce supper, he found his Master and Mistress seated before the fire. They were very still, so he withdrew unnoticed. Tonight, supper would be served a bit later.

Chapter 6

When Gillian carried Willy away from the entrance hall, she slowed her pace so she could overhear the exchange between Master and Mistress Perry. Then she rounded on Willy.

"You're a fine one, you are. See what happens when you're about?" Her arm squeezed Willy, and he began to squirm. She tightened her grip more. "Try to get away from me, will you?" She cuffed his ear. "Going to cry now, are you? Well, we'll soon be rid of you, and none too soon, if you ask me." Gillian barged through the kitchen door and plopped Willy on a stool. She gave him a look that told him he'd better be still. Gillian then settled onto a bench.

"I haven't seen Mistress so upset since last winter. I was helping Mistress with her wardrobe this afternoon." She checked her audience. "She had received some waists from the seamstress, and you know how she values my opinion—"

Marie sniffed loudly and turned her head away.

"You may sniff, Marie, but you could use some advice yourself, particularly on the way you—"

Gillian's voice faded under Marie's level gaze.

"Yes, well." Gillian studied her fingers. Still red. There had not been enough lard left from tending her scalded foot to do much good. She hid her hands under her apron. "But to continue. When Mistress went to greet Master, I followed discreetly should she need any assistance."

"Eavesdropping," mouthed Marie.

Gillian went on undeterred. "I heard the most dreadful scream and without a second thought, I rushed to her side. There she was, her hands clutched over her heart. Nearly swooned away, she was, from seeing this piece of baggage," she nodded at Willy, "fawning all over Master. How he condescended to allow a child of such low degree to even touch him, I can't imagine. I soothed Mistress as best I could. When she became calmer, I suggested Master take his wife to the sitting room while I carried Willy back here."

THE FOUNDLING

Willy edged off his stool and stood by Cook. She continued to knead dough for tomorrow's bread, nudging Willy aside from time to time. Marie rolled her eyes and returned to her mending.

Exasperated, Gillian changed tactics.

"And I'm heartily weary of Willy. He's been nothing but trouble since he arrived. To be wandering about the house where he's no business makes one wonder. What was he doing, looking for things to steal?"

Cook gave her dough a sharp slap.

"Is that why he was going through your wardrobe yesterday, Marie?" Gillian sat primly, her hands folded under her apron.

Marie's needle halted in midair. The brooch!

"I thought things looked a bit out of place," she said slowly.

Gillian, pleased to be the center of attention once again, pressed on. "Yes, well, I tidied up for you. Then I caught him yesterday afternoon wandering through the house—prying into rooms and closets like a petty thief or cutpurse. You'd best check your things, Marie."

Willy disappeared behind Cook's skirts.

Gillian continued her narrative. "And this very afternoon he made a pest of himself in the laundry room. He's a very naughty little boy."

Cook delivered a stunning punch to her dough.

"He'd be better off in Newgate with his own kind. I, for one, do not appreciate having to constantly look after him."

"Oh, do be still." Marie piled the mending in a basket. "I've been the one who's had to look after him along with all my other duties."

"You have not done a very good job of it, letting him wander all over the house doing who knows what, and upsetting the Mistress as well," Gillian said.

Marie jumped up. "As if you cared about the Mistress. You bow and scrape to her to get out of the real work, always whining and whimpering. If she knew how useless you really are—"

Gillian rose. Her voice shook with poorly controlled anger. "You're jealous because Mistress likes me best! You know she does,

so don't you dare condescend to me, you . . . you kitchen wench!"
She whirled to leave.

"Oh, no you don't!" Marie caught her sleeve and spun her
around. Her hand flew to Gillian's cheek in a sharp slap, and Gillian
crumbled to the bench, her apron over her face.

"You horrible creature," she wailed. "Now Mistress will have
proof of what I've told her time and again. You'll be turned out ere
another day passes!"

Cook whirled from her kneading, dribbling a trail of flour on
the floor. "This is my kitchen and you'll mind yourselves! Both of
you think you're worth so much. Ha! You whose families apprenticed you for only two pounds each. If you are unsure of your places
in this household, be sure that I know—Gillian!"

"Yes, Cook?" Gillian snuffled and dabbed at her eyes, now as
red as her hands.

"There's flour on the floor. Sweep it up immediately!" Cook
nodded when Gillian hesitated. "Yes, you."

Gillian felt the rough broomstick on her chapped and tender
hands. Tears stung her eyes all over again. She dragged the broom
across the floor, scattering the flour in all directions.

"Marie!" Cook's voice snapped out again.

"Yes, Cook?"

"Lay the table for dinner."

"Yes, Cook." Marie bobbed her head and went to the dining
room. When she returned, Gillian was still struggling with the
broom.

It was late evening before Marie could return to her room; Willy
was already in bed and asleep. Too late! she thought. Tomorrow,
while he's at his christening, I'll see if the brooch is still in the
wardrobe. If not, I'll turn this room inside out if I have to. She
dropped her clothes in a heap, blew out her candle, and climbed
into bed.

All night long Marie dreamed that she was being dragged off to
Newgate Prison as a common thief. Willy stood and watched. The
brooch glimmered where it was pinned on his shoulder. When she
reached the prison, the wolf-faced keeper demanded money for her

diet, but she had only a farthing. So he thrust her into a small, dark cell crowded with other starving thieves: men, women, and children, and fastened the door with heavy chains that rattled and clanged—

Marie awoke and sprang from bed. Air, she needed air! She jerked open the door and found Gillian bending to retrieve a small bucket and shovel.

"So sorry." Gillian's voice purred. "I was just on my way to clean the sitting room fireplace."

Marie slammed the door. Friday morning! How could it be, and she had slept through the rising hour. Slept! She was exhausted! Even Willy was no longer in bed. She pulled her hairbrush through her hair, hurrying to get to breakfast.

Marie ran into the kitchen where Rodgers was watching Willy spoon preserves on his third piece of bread and butter. "The boy must be hollow," he said to her. "He eats as much as a grown man and he's still thin. Of course, he may just be making up for lost meals."

Marie made a face. She took her plate and sat as far away as she could. Even so, she kept her eyes on Willy.

When Willy at last pushed his plate away, Cook came around the table.

"Just a moment, sprout."

She took Willy's chin in her hand and pulled his face toward her. Then she gathered up a corner of her apron, spat on it, and went to work. In spite of Willy's wiggling, Cook wiped his cheeks, his chin, and the corners of his mouth, and swiped at his nose for good measure.

"You're a piece, you are. How do you manage it? There's enough food on your face for a second breakfast." She scrutinized her work, turning Willy's face from side to side. "There you are," she said and pinched his cheek.

Willy pulled back. He rubbed his cheek and then his lips to wipe away the scratchiness of Cook's apron.

At that moment, Willy gave a cannon blast of a belch. Cook froze, still holding the corner of her apron. Her eyes opened wide, and she put her hand over her mouth. Her shoulders began to shake.

The corners of her eyes crinkled shut and little tears appeared. She sat down at the table stifling her gasps in her apron and wiping her eyes.

Willy, dismayed, reached up and put his hand on Cook's shoulder. But he couldn't think of anything to say to remove his offense. He looked helplessly at Rodgers who was bent over coughing into his handkerchief and dabbing at his eyes.

Marie stopped eating and looked from Cook to Rodgers. Both of them laughing at the little barbarian! Their breeding isn't any better than that little fiend's, she thought.

Finally Rodgers cleared his throat. He patted his face dry, then folded his handkerchief and returned it to his pocket.

"Have you quite finished breakfast, Willy?" he asked.

Cook's shoulders shook again. "Oh, aye, he's finished, and what a finish!"

"I'm sorry," Willy said in a small voice.

Cook patted his hand, her face still in her apron. "Thank you, sprout. Now run along with Rodgers."

Rodgers put his hands on his knees and pushed himself up. When he at last held out his hand, Willy took it. They had reached the door when Cook raised her head.

"Who'd have believed he had it in him?" she cried, and collapsed on the table.

"Well, what might you expect from rubbish—" Marie began.

"Oh, do shut up," Cook said between gasps, "and get to your work."

In Master Perry's private chamber, Rodgers lifted Willy into a chair.

"Will that be all, James?"

"Yes, Rodgers. Thank you. I'll ring when we're ready to leave."

Rodgers bowed himself from the chamber. Willy faced his host.

"Do you remember me, Willy? I introduced myself yesterday when I came home."

Willy nodded. "You helped me with my shoes."

"Yes, I did. Now I would like to get to know you better." Master Perry smiled at the boy. "Do you know how old you are, Willy?"

Willy held up four fingers, carefully folding his thumb across his palm. He looked at his hand and bit his lower lip in concentration.

"Willy, do you know your mother's name?"

Willy studied the face in front of him. Of course he knew his mother's name. Was this man making fun of him? Willy nodded.

"Well?" Master Perry paused. "What is her name?"

"Mummy," replied Willy immediately.

Perry smiled. "Does she have any other name?"

Willy thought, then shook his head.

"Do you remember where you lived with your mother?"

Willy nodded.

"Please tell me."

Willy began his description. Master Perry shook his head. Willy's home was like that of hundreds, perhaps thousands, of poor who came to London. Eventually most found themselves living in one-room hovels, garrets, or cellars, with little or no furniture and little food, clothing, or warmth. Some died in the streets. Just last week a poor man had been found dead in Houndsditch. No one knew who he was. And only yesterday a vestryman from St. Bride's parish had told him of alleys stuffed—yes, stuffed was the very word—with poor, and no means to care for them.

Willy had stopped talking. Master Perry looked up.

"Thank you, Willy." He thought for a moment. "Is Willy your only name?"

"No. My other name is William, like my father."

Perry sat back in his chair. So much for that. Willy had been his last resource since investigations in and around the parish had been fruitless. Neither Willy's mother nor his home would probably ever be found. The Constable and elderly parishioners who went about questioning women who roamed through the parish had been unsuccessful as well. The parish would definitely have to take responsibility for Willy.

Master Perry rang for Rodgers.

"Please collect our coats. I'll take Willy this morning. You go on to the warehouse." He turned to Willy. "Come along then, young man."

Rodgers met them in the entrance where Willy had hidden under the table. He helped Willy button his coat.

"Will you stop jumping about? Now give me your hand." Rodgers slipped a mitten on. "Now the other one. Right. There you are; now, don't lose them." He patted Willy's shoulder and opened the door.

"Shall we expect you at the warehouse later?" he asked Perry.

"I think not. Carry on; lock up as soon as the last wagons leave. Come, Willy. We're off to your christening."

The door opened onto the street. Willy clapped his hands. "Let's find Mummy!" he said and bounded down the steps.

Marie let the lace curtain fall back into place. At last he was gone, and she was free to check on the brooch. She picked up a basket full of candles. If she met Gillian, it would appear as though she were at work. And, in fact, I will be, she thought. So many candles need replacing. I'll just start in my room.

The brooch was not where she had put it. But then, Gillian had said that Willy had pulled everything to the floor. She fumbled through her shifts to make sure she hadn't overlooked it. Then she went through each shelf, leaving twisted and tangled clothing in her wake.

"No, no, no, it can't be gone. Where is it? Oh, please—" She chanted over and over.

Finally, she turned the articles in the bottom of the wardrobe onto the floor.

The brooch wasn't there.

Willy must have found and taken it. "The little thief!" Marie bit her words short.

She searched the room mentally while she refolded and replaced her clothes. Suddenly she laughed. The answer was so simple. Where else would he possibly put it but with his mother's shawl? She closed the wardrobe and went to Willy's bed. She flipped the pillow on the floor and shook out the shawl. No golden brooch tumbled out.

THE FOUNDLING

Marie chewed her lip in frustration. She had so little time; she had to finish replacing the candles. Cook would scold her if she were late to help with dinner preparations.

Where could he have hidden the brooch? She picked up the pillow and was about to replace it when she spied a small lump under Willy's blanket. Afraid of disappointment, but pushed on by her greed, Marie slowly lifted Willy's blanket and straw mattress. The brooch gleamed at her from its resting place.

"Oh, yes!" She snatched it up, letting the pillow fall back. She cupped it in her hand and felt it grow warm. It was as though the heat came from the gold itself.

Find a hiding place! But where? She dismissed the chest by Willy's bed. Too obvious and too easily opened. A dress pocket? No, he'd pulled her clothes out once. He might do it again. Behind the mirror, under the mattress, high on the mantle? No, no, and no! The fireplace? She pulled at a couple of bricks, but neither was loose.

One of the hearthstones shifted under her foot. She pulled her apron and skirts aside, fell to her knees, and clawed at the edge of the stone. The dry mortar crumbled and she lifted the stone free. With the poker she gouged a hole large enough for the brooch. Perfect!

Marie wrapped her treasure in a handkerchief and laid it in the hole. She replaced the stone and swept the dust and mortar into the fireplace.

"There, let him find that!"

She wiped her hands on her apron. She put new candles in the candlesticks and straightened Willy's bed. She even folded the shawl and put it under his pillow. At the door she surveyed her handiwork. Perfect! No one would ever know.

Chapter 7

Willy squealed in delight at the beggars, the carters driving their animals, the hawkers calling out their merchandise, men and women hurrying by, apprentices on errands for their masters, servants out shopping, the damp air fresh and cold on his nose and cheeks. He took a deep breath. "Outside!"

"This way, Willy—Willy!"

Willy twirled around.

"Come along. We'll be late for your christening." Master Perry gestured and set off down the street. "Are you warm?" He looked down at the woolen cap bobbing alongside him. He pulled his own scarf up under his chin. It wouldn't do to become ill; it was that time of year. He shook his head free of memories in time to see Willy's cap bobbing toward a heap of refuse.

Irritation swept over Perry. Why hadn't the scavengers removed this mess last night? He'd have to speak to the ward officers about this—

"Willy! Do get out of that rubbish!" He reached Willy just as he poked a new blue mitten beneath some filthy green rags. "Oh, no—put that down." Master Perry shook a muddy green ribbon from Willy's mitten.

Willy stooped to pick it up again. "We could sell it. I'll wash it. Mummy will need it."

Master Perry pulled him along.

"Mummy must have the ribbon. She needs my help, but I'm not there. She—she gets more when I'm with her. She said so—"

"Do be still and come along. You don't need to pick up rubbish anymore."

Willy hung back. "Mummy needs it because . . . because . . . she . . . they—I mean, we could buy cheese . . . ."

Master Perry stopped. He reached for Willy's hands but thought better of it when he saw the wet, dirty mitten.

"Willy." Master Perry's voice was low. "Listen to me. Do you know where your mummy is now? No? I don't know either. You see, we couldn't give the ribbon to her."

"Yes, yes, we can so." Willy's lower lip quivered. "I'll find her."

Master Perry pulled out a handkerchief and held it to Willy's nose.

"Blow."

Willy blew.

Master Perry straightened up with a groan. Why couldn't children be taller? Willy hiccupped, and Perry bent again to his level.

"Willy, let's get your mummy a new green ribbon, or any color you wish. Just in case we find her. Won't that be better than giving her one you found in the rubbish?"

Willy gave a tentative nod. Of course, no ribbon could match the one now under the wheel of the carter's wagon.

"Right, off we go. We really must step along now."

They stepped into a shop full of ribbons, hats, and flowers. Willy touched a flower and sniffed it. "It's not real." Master Perry looked around.

"Are you being served, sir?" asked a clerk.

"Um . . . no. Ribbons, yes, ribbons." He cleared his throat and sidestepped an apprentice laden with hatboxes. "Ribbons, if you please, green ones. Willy, you do want a green ribbon?"

Willy nodded.

"Yes, well then," he paused, not quite certain how to proceed. "How much do you suppose I'll need?"

The clerk rescued him. "Enough for a nice hat, sir?"

"And how much might that be?"

"Two or three ells at least, sir."

"So much? We don't really need but this much, I think." He held his hands about three feet apart. "Will this be enough, Willy?"

At Willy's assent, the clerk cut the ribbon, wrapped it in paper, and handed the small packet to Master Perry, who gave it to Willy. "Here's your ribbon. Now we must be off."

When the shop door closed behind him, Perry exhaled. Had he been holding his breath since he entered the shop? He grinned to himself. Women's shops . . .

Willy had the ribbon out of its packet. He gasped at the wealth in his hand. "Mummy will have cheese with her bread!"

Master Perry herded his charge through the streets. For the first time he looked carefully at the beggars, wondering what a length of new ribbon would mean to each. Bread and cheese instead of bread alone? A newer scarf or warmer outer coat? Some coal for a fire barely able to hold the damp chill of winter at bay? How did they live on so little? These people must be cold and hungry all of the time. He could give each of them tuppence—Perry's mind stopped. He'd spent more than tuppence on Willy's ribbon.

Suddenly Perry understood much about Willy and his mother and why she would abandon her son to the parish. Their lives had been reduced to the value of a bit of ribbon in a rubbish heap. Willy's mother had done what she could to ensure that her son would be cared for. Perry glanced at the length of new shiny ribbon in Willy's tight grasp. One end hung loose and flapped about as Willy swung his arms vigorously and trotted to keep up. For reasons Perry didn't quite understand, he was now embarrassed by that thin green banner and wished he'd bought at least an ell.

A woman with three children clinging to her skirts approached them. Perry looked for her badge identifying her as a licensed beggar. She had none. He was about to step around them when he saw Willy's ribbon from the corner of his eye. Master Perry looked into the mother's face. Exhaustion and hopelessness were all he saw. Her children shivered in their thin coats. The badge lost its importance. He gave her a penny for each of them.

"Four pence!" The woman gasped. "Bless you, sir, bless you!"

Master Perry touched his hat to her. Certainly she deserved that minor courtesy. Four pence, that was all they had. What would happen tomorrow? He shook his head and stepped into the churchyard.

"Here we are, Willy. Soon you'll have a proper name—walk around the puddle, please. That's what a christening is partly for, you know."

Willy dabbled a toe at the edge of the muddy water. "My name is Willy."

"And my name is James." He edged Willy around the puddle. "But I have a second name as well. Soon you'll have a second name. It will be Pancras, Willy Pancras. How does that sound?"

Willy said nothing.

They entered the church just as it began to rain again. The pensioners who attended each christening, as much for the refreshments as to serve as witnesses, edged forward. Willy held Master Perry's hand tighter.

"Chin up, Willy. I'll be with you. These people are here to witness your christening. Now, where is Rector Scoppe?"

In a side aisle, Constable Crumpton spoke to Widow Boggins. "I found him, I did. On the porch. I can show you the very spot. Quite the little chap, that one. Spoke right up, he did, told me his name. 'My name's Willy,' he told me, clear as day. Never cried a whit."

Crumpton eyed the sweetest morsel in the parish. When Widow Boggins's husband had died just after Lady Day last, Jack Crumpton felt it his duty to look in on her. To help as needed. Those first visits had been uncertain; one never knew about widows. But Mistress Boggins was undoubtedly the most gracious woman in the parish. And those tiny hands—

"You found him, did you? And how was he?"

"Eh?" The Constable looked closely at the woman who dared interrupt his conversation. Youngish, tattered clothes, a beggar. He was immediately all business.

"You're not of this parish." It was a statement more than a question. "You can't beg here. Move along." He pushed her towards the door. "Move along, I say."

"I stepped in only to get out of the rain," she said. "And I always enjoy seeing a little one christened. Another life, new hope . . ." She looked toward the ceremony in progress.

"Not a baby, this one, but a little boy. Promising lad, if I do say so myself. We'll have a bit of a celebration, drink and bread, for those standing with him." The Constable smacked his lips. "Ah yes . . . Not for you, of course, since you're not of this parish." His eyes narrowed. "What is your parish?"

The woman shifted her position; her reddened hands pulled at the thin cloak over her shoulders.

"Well?"

"I'm living near the wall in St. Bride's parish."

"You have no badge from St. Bride's?" Crumpton stuck out his lower lip and clasped his hands behind his back in judgment. He should take her in hand and usher her to the parish boundary. He glanced out the door. Rain continued to fall.

Widow Boggins plucked at his sleeve. Crumpton tried to concentrate on his duties. It was hard while she stood there.

"The boy's a fine one, Jack. I'm pleased you found him." She nodded to the stranger. "Listen to him laugh. Pleasant to hear that in the Lord's house."

Crumpton glanced at the widow. That dimple in her plump cheek, the twinkle in her eye. Almost made a body forget—what had he been doing, anyway?

"Mistress, please," he growled in his most authoritative voice. Ah yes, the woman, the one with the tatty cloak, must move along.

The rain pelted down harder still.

Crumpton reconsidered. Come to think of it, very few beggars actually have badges, he thought. Nice when they do, though. At least then I know they have a license to beg. Could let her stay until the rain lets up. Show the widow I know how to do my job and be a bit kind as well.

He opened his mouth to pass along his final decision, but Mistress Boggins had already filled the pause.

"Jack Crumpton is a fine man," he heard her say to the woman. "I'm sure he's been a help to me. And he does us all a fine service at watch. I'm certain you'll be able to stay until the weather's cleared." The widow turned to the Constable.

"Mistress Boggins!" The Constable drew himself up to his full height. It was one thing for him to decide to be kind, quite another for someone else to decide for him. "If you please! I'm an officer of the ward and I must attend to duties here."

"Of course, Jack. Go, do what you must. I'll chat with—what is your name, dearie?—while you're busy."

"You misunderstand." He felt his control of the moment slipping away.

THE FOUNDLING

"Not a bit. Get along with you." Widow Boggins shooed the confused Constable away. He was only somewhat mollified over his undignified dismissal when he overheard her continue.

"Why, just a fortnight ago he found a baby left in Samuel Clutterbuck's doorway. But for the Constable's quick work in getting that child to Master Perry, I'm sure it wouldn't have survived. What a cough he had! The baby, not the Constable, though he does take on when he's been out in the rain. Then, this week he found another child. That's him being christened now."

The stranger turned toward the gathering. The short ceremony was nearly over; individuals were already moving to the refreshments. "I must leave now," she said.

"You're cold! Well, of course, you are with only that cloak. Come along, dearie." Widow Boggins had the beggar by the elbow. "I have somewhat to say about the clothing the parish collects. Most of it is for the army, but I keep my eye on the poor women of this parish for the vestry. Let's see—" She opened the door to the vestry and pulled the stranger along. "How nice! A fire! Some of the vestrymen must be meeting today. Go warm yourself, dearie."

She opened two chests. "Clothes for the ladies . . . yes . . . yes . . . and these too." She draped the clothing over the back of a chair.

"My name is Ma—Sarah, and you are entirely too kind."

"Shush. Try this waist . . . Sarah. No, no, put it on right over the one you're wearing. With both you'll be much warmer. It's a bit large, but it has all its buttons." Widow Boggins stepped back for a look. "That will do. Now, put this underskirt on. And take this shawl and wrap it right 'round . . . Here are some stockings. They're rather short, won't quite cover your knees, but I see only one small hole."

Sarah hesitated.

"Come, come. Sit down and pull them on."

Sarah did as she was bidden and slipped her feet back into her clogs.

"Mind, you mend that hole before it grows larger."

"Yes." Sarah stood before the widow. "I thank y—"

"Nonsense, it's only right that the needy should receive from those who have enough and to spare. I happen to know that all of the parish women have all the clothes they need right now. Except for Beulah. I don't know how that woman's mind works, but she's gone and pawned her clothes again so she could—never mind. She really puts my back up with her antics. We'll get her clothes back again, never worry. There, you see, a story about Beulah brightens 'most any day. Dry that tear. I've done no more than what is proper."

Widow Boggins shepherded Sarah back into the sanctuary. "Now where is that man when I really need him? There he is. You stay right here, dearie."

Sarah leaned against a pillar.

"Woman! Here's the Overseer with something for you." Constable Crumpton bustled toward the beggar with the widow and the Overseer for the Poor in tow. The Overseer dropped a penny into Sarah's hand.

Sarah bobbed her thanks. When she looked up, she saw the Constable holding out a small parcel.

"Leftover bread. Can't let it go to waste, now, can we?" He smiled triumphantly at the widow.

"Oh, thank you. You are too generous."

Master Perry brushed by with Willy, whose laugh once again carried through the church. Sarah followed them to the porch and watched the boy trying to match strides with the man. He looked well cared for and very warm with his scarf tucked well in. She brushed a hand across her eyes, then stepped off the corner into the noonday traffic. Her new shawl fluttered behind her and caught momentarily on the rough stone wall.

Chapter 8

The front door closed behind Master Perry and Willy. The man removed his gloves, then his hat. Willy removed his mittens, then his cap; he laid them on the table next to Master Perry's. Master Perry unbuttoned his coat and removed his scarf. Willy did the same. Master Perry took off his coat and hung it with his scarf on a hook. Then he stood aside and tapped a hook for Willy. Willy stepped forward and hung his coat and scarf as Master Perry nodded his approval.

"Off with you, now, little man. I'll see you after you eat."

Willy strode through the house. He knew his way now. He knew where those stairs led and who lived in the rooms he passed. He stopped in his room only long enough to tuck his ribbon under his pillow, next to Mummy's shawl. Then he went on to the kitchen. Willy liked the kitchen; he liked Cook, and she liked him. Willy liked his lunch. Marie and Gillian entered, and he almost liked them.

After lunch, Marie took Willy back to Master Perry's private chamber. The chairs stood as they had that morning. Warm firelight flickered off the dark wood paneling. Willy climbed into his chair. Pictures of people hung on the walls. Willy hadn't seen them before, and he wondered if Master Perry knew them all. Through the window he could see the gloom of early afternoon, but the outdoors gray didn't dare come into this room.

Master Perry entered and sat down behind his desk. He shuffled the papers and looked at Willy. Then he rearranged his pens and brushed invisible grains of sand onto the floor. He wiped a bit of wax from one of the candle holders. It absorbed a great deal of his attention.

"Willy." Master Perry paused, then rushed on. "This afternoon you will be going to live with Goodwife Bessie."

Willy looked hard at Master Perry, who picked the wax from another candle holder. They both stared at the small, white lump in Master Perry's palm.

"She's a very nice woman who has no children of her own, so she takes care of boys and girls who don't have mothers and fathers—you'll like her—" Master Perry's voice was very low. "You'll like her, Willy. She has another boy staying with her. He will be someone for you to play with . . . " His voice faded.

Willy watched Master Perry's face, trying to understand.

"You can't stay here." Master Perry tried a smile. He glanced at the boy, then studied the heart of the fire on the hearth.

Can't stay here? Willy shook his head back and forth. Master Perry didn't want him?

Willy peered hard at the face before him. It was hard to see through his tears. His throat closed and he breathed in great gasps. He jumped down and stood gripping the arm of the chair. Master Perry didn't want him. But—Master Perry had been his friend this morning. He'd bought Mummy's ribbon.

Master Perry rose and came around the desk. "Willy, you simply can't stay here. It just isn't done. Foundling children are sent to nurses in the country—it's better for them, for you. Here, let me dry your eyes."

Willy backed away and dragged his shirtsleeve across his eyes and the heel of his hand back across his nose. Master Perry grimaced, so Willy snuffled as hard as he could. He rubbed his wet hand on his breeches and looked up defiantly.

Master Perry pushed his handkerchief back into his pocket and sighed.

"Willy, will you let me explain why you cannot stay here?"

Willy eluded the outstretched hand.

"Stand still a moment. Willy!"

Willy disappeared down the hall and around a corner. Master Perry stared after the boy. Of course, Willy must go to a nurse. There was nothing else to be done. Theodore Hinkle had taken in a foundling permanently. But then Hinkle's family was of country stock and he a manual laborer. A good cordwainer, though. And the boy seemed to be doing well in his new family and learning a trade.

For a moment Master Perry studied the chair where Willy had been sitting. No, he thought, it would be highly inappropriate even to consider taking Willy in. No one knew who or what his parentage was. Amelia would never accept him.

What am I thinking? Willy will be better off among people of his own station. He'll be cared for, taught his letters and a trade proper to his position. Yes, he'll be better off.

He returned to his chair and sat down heavily. Why am I so fond of this little chap? he wondered. I've never taken a foundling to a christening before. Always left that to one of the Overseers. And buying ribbon? Even Amelia can't get me into those shops . . . Perhaps because he reminds me of Daniel. Perry shook his head and rang for Rodgers.

"Is all well at the warehouse?"

"Quite. All the carters left before midday. There are crews storing shipments newly arrived, that is all. Hudgins is overseeing their work."

"Good." Perry looked at the floor. "I must ask you to take Willy to Goodwife Bessie's this afternoon. I don't believe that I—he's upset right now, you understand. I believe the little chap thought he would be staying here. Well, what else could he think? He's hardly old enough to know the way of the world, is he? And so much has changed for him these past days." He looked at his friend. "I'm sorry to send you out again on such a day—"

"Of course, I quite understand. I'm certain we'll do well. I'll see that all the preparations are made." Rodgers hesitated. "The churchwardens must be kept apprised of the boy's progress. Perhaps the occasional visit—?"

"Thank you, Rodgers." Perry held his palms to the fire. Already the house felt emptier.

Willy ran toward the kitchen. Cook liked him; Cook would let him stay. But he ran into Marie, and she wouldn't let him pass. She took him by the arm so hard that her fingers hurt him. She pushed him into her room.

"Now you settle down. One more kick and I'll turn you over my knee." Marie shoved Willy toward his cot and swatted him hard.

Willy stumbled and fell on the rag rug. Master Perry didn't want him. Marie hated him, and she wouldn't let him get to Cook. He felt the warmth from the fireplace and turned towards it. The fire dissolved into sparkles through his tears.

THE FOUNDLING

Marie opened a large satchel and started packing Willy's clothes. "Just a couple more hours of you." She glanced toward the hearthstones. She packed three shirts and two pair of breeches, a waistcoat, and a pair of shoes.

Willy climbed onto the cot. He pulled his shawl from under his pillow and wrapped himself in it. The green ribbon came out too. He pushed it away.

"Come on, then," Marie said. "Get up. I must pack your linens and blanket." Willy ducked under his blanket.

Marie slapped another pair of stockings into the satchel and went to the cot. Willy felt her bony fingers trying to take his blanket away. He rolled into a tight ball, and Marie dumped him and the blanket on the floor. "Give over, you little wretch."

Willy howled as Marie ripped the linens from the cot. His pillow flew to the floor. She yanked again at the blanket. "Shut up, and give me that blanket!"

Willy tumbled out and landed on his back, still howling.

"Pick up your pillow and bring it here. Now!" Marie's voice rose. She dropped the blanket and grabbed Willy's shoulders. She brought him to his feet with a hard shake. "Obey me!"

Willy managed a scream.

Marie's jaw stiffened. Her lips turned white and barely seemed to move. "You're the Devil's own, you are, and I don't have to put up with this." She slapped Willy, then snatched the blanket and stuffed it, unfolded, into the satchel. She added Willy's pillow, threw in the green ribbon despite his protests, and snapped the satchel shut. "Mistress says you will go to Goodwife Bessie's. And good riddance, I say."

Marie took the satchel and left the room. The door slammed shut on her skirts. She yanked the material free with a ripping sound. Shreds of material trailed from her hems. She did not care. In a little while the knot in her stomach would go away. The brooch would be hers.

She dropped the satchel under the vestibule table on her way to the kitchen. Outside the kitchen door she stopped, straightened her clothes, and smoothed her expression.

"Mistress will be so happy when he's gone," she said to herself. "And so will I." She lifted her chin and entered the kitchen.

Chapter 9

Rodgers bundled Willy into his coat and scarf. The little boy stood woodenly. Rodgers had already coaxed him to the kitchen where he washed his face, wiped his nose, and combed his hair. Might as well have saved the effort, he thought. Nose needs another wipe, and his hair still sticks up in the back. How do mothers manage? He held his handkerchief out to Willy.

"Wipe your nose."

Willy stared at the wall.

Rodgers moved the handkerchief toward Willy's face and, in a moment of inspiration, grabbed Willy's head with his other hand. So that's how it's done. Must remember that: steady the head. He smiled at his success. But that hair . . . another problem altogether. Yes, well. Rodgers pushed Willy's cap firmly down over his ears.

"Ready, are we? Come along, then. We've a good walk before us." Rodgers put Willy's shawl in the satchel and propelled the boy to the door.

Outside, Willy shivered and sneezed. He wiped his nose on his mitten.

The two walked in silence.

"Willy, look at all the people running about. They're trying to get their work done before it rains again."

There was no response.

The first drops fell. Rodgers turned a corner. Willy did not follow but went straight on. Rodgers glanced back as Willy walked right into a woman's billowing skirts.

"Mummy?" Willy looked up, startled.

The stranger pushed him aside and walked by. "Brats! Can't a body walk peaceably about her business without tripping over begging brats?" She stalked away.

Raindrops fell faster. Willy's eyes ran with tears, and his nose began dripping again. He stopped short in the cold rain.

THE FOUNDLING

One of his bright blue mittens slipped off and fell to the wet cobbles. Rodgers came back and picked up the mitten and then Willy. He held the boy tight against his shoulder.

They entered a public house a moment before the afternoon drizzle became a downpour.

"Abominable weather, what?" the host greeted his guests. "Aha, place by the fire?" He led them to a table which he whisked free of crumbs with one flick of his towel. He smiled, "And now gentlemen, what'll it be? Something hot, I'll wager."

At Rodgers's nod, he trotted off and soon returned with two steaming cups. "I can hardly keep up with custom this afternoon. The weather brought more shivering folk in today than came in all last week. Good you stepped in when you did. Raining. Drink up and have another." He took Rodgers's coins. "Thankee," he said, and hurried back to business.

Rodgers hung their coats and scarves near the fire. He ran his fingers through his hair and looked around. Ah, yes, the mittens. He laid them on a bench by his gloves to dry. He held his handkerchief out to Willy, who took it and blew his nose.

They sat side by side. Willy slid up against Rodgers, who put his arm on the back of the bench. They sat surrounded by the warmth of the fire and sipped their hot drinks. The raindrops rolled from their coats and sizzled on the hearth.

"Willy, I'm going to tell you a story . . . Um, do you like stories?"

Willy nodded.

"There was another little boy, much like you, who lived in the country. He had a younger brother and a sister. His father was a good farmer. His mother kept chickens and cooked and made cider and sometimes worked in the fields with her husband.

"The little boy gathered the eggs. Those chickens were forever getting out of their pen and laying their eggs everywhere. It was very difficult to find them all, let me tell you.

"Twice a week in the winter the vicar gave lessons in reading and arithmetic. All the children attended his classes because the mother and father thought knowing how to read was very important, even for their little girl.

"When the little boy was about your age, five I should say, his father and brother died of influenza. It was very sad."

Willy waited for him to continue.

Rodgers cleared his throat. "The mother could not pay the rent for the farm, so she took her little girl and boy to London. They walked for a long time and slept under hedgerows at night.

"There was no place for them to stay when they reached London, and they soon ran out of money. They became beggars. The boy's sister died the next winter. His mother could not pay the fees for her burial. If it hadn't been for the kindness of an Overseer—" He shook his head.

"Then the mother became very ill and could not go out to beg. They were very hungry. She took her little boy to a church and told him to stay there until someone came to help him."

"Like me!"

"Yes." Rodgers's hand brushed the head at his side, not minding that it needed combing. "He never saw her again."

Willy looked up. "Who found the little boy?"

"Actually, one of the ladies of the parish found him and took care of him. Like you went to live at Master Perry's house for a few days."

"Then what happened? Did the little boy have to leave like me?"

"Just like you, Willy. But the story has a happy ending. The little boy lived with a nurse and, when he grew older, he was apprenticed to learn a trade. Then he could work and never be hungry again."

Willy sat quietly, holding his warm cup with both hands.

"Well?" Rodgers brushed Willy's head with his hand. "How was that story? Did you like it?"

"Yes, but . . . " Willy wrinkled his brow and looked up.

"But, what? It was about a little boy much like you."

"What about the princess?"

"The what?"

"You left out the part about the princess and the dragon and the knight on a great horse. Mummy's stories always—"

Rodgers's laughter filled the room. "The little boy grew up, but he hasn't found a princess yet. We must be on our way; the rain has stopped."

Rodgers and Willy left the warm fire and stepped into the street.

"Thank goodness the wind has quit blowing. Still, it's cold enough." Rodgers pulled his collar up, then reached for Willy's hand. "Where are your mittens? Willy, I want you to put them on. A man of breeding does not walk around with his hands in his pockets."

They walked through the busy streets. Willy looked everywhere for a familiar face or street or building. Once a butcher shop caught his eye, but it wasn't the one he knew.

"Are we still in London?" he asked.

"Yes, we are. It's a big city, isn't it?"

They reached Cripplegate. The heavy wooden gates were swung wide and traffic crowded through. The gatekeeper peered down from his room in the stone tower. When Rodgers and Willy went through the gate, the noise of the traffic echoed off the stone walls like thunder. Willy walked closer to Rodgers.

"Now we are outside the City, Willy. Mind the carts." Rodgers glanced around. "Here, clean your shoes on this rock. Yes, get that mud off, and I'll carry you on my shoulders."

Willy weaved slightly on his new perch. "I see everything, even the vegetables and coal inside the carts."

"I see I should have checked your shoes better." Rodgers tried to brush the mud from his coat. "Well, there's no help for it now." He bent to pick up the satchel, and Willy lurched forward. He grabbed Rodgers's hair.

"Your needn't hold on quite so tightly. You'll give me two bald patches."

Rodgers swung along, pointing out the houses and gardens outside the wall. They passed some small orchards and some common land where cows and geese grazed on the yellow winter grass. Two boys guarded them and chased away the dogs.

Willy looked back at the huge London wall.

"Stop your wiggling, or you'll have to get down."

"Mummy doesn't know where I am. I want to go home."

"I'm sorry, Willy. I don't know where she is."

"She's back there." Willy twisted and pointed, pulling Rodgers's hair.

"Ouch! You will like Mistress Bessie." Rodgers turned down a narrow lane and stepped into the garden of a small cottage. "You must get down. Let go my hair."

No one answered the door, even though Rodgers knocked several times. Finally the door opened.

"Good day to you," the woman said. "Come right through and do mind your head."

Rodgers ducked through the door. "Good day, Mistress Bessie."

"Where's the lad? Caught in your coattails, is he?"

Rodgers pulled Willy to the front.

"Mind the cat; mind the cat." Mistress Bessie booted a fat, orange cat aside. "A good mouser but always underfoot. A trial she is, but a fine mouser. Please sit down . . . just there."

Rodgers hid a smile and sat down. He pulled Willy onto his lap. Mistress Bessie spread her skirts daintily and perched on the edge of her chair.

"This the boy? Looks likely enough. Not sick is he? No weakness of the lungs? Stomach complaints? Fevers? I cannot—will not—keep a child who is constantly unwell. Though in this weather it's a miracle we don't all take to our beds. It wasn't so long ago I said to the baker . . . the baker? Yes, the one just this side of Houndsditch—"

Rodgers glanced around the room. The floor had been swept clean, and the woodwork polished with beeswax. A broom was propped against the table. Mistress Bessie shared her chair with a bucket and cleaning cloths.

She lived better than most nurses. Some said her husband had left her an income from a small farm in Middlesex. She didn't need to take in children to live as so many nurses did. She took them in for company, and to be sure, so she said, that they received a proper breeding.

"That's settled, then."

Rodgers started. "I beg your pardon?"

"Weren't paying attention, were you? Thought I'd catch you. I said it's settled; I'll keep him."

THE FOUNDLING

"Thank you." Rodgers set Willy down beside his chair. "I must excuse myself and return to the City before dark." He buttoned his coat.

Willy glanced at Mistress Bessie. He took a step toward Rodgers.

"No, Willy. You must stay here. I'll visit whenever I can. Good day, Mistress." He lifted the door latch and stepped into the late afternoon. The cat followed and rubbed against his legs, leaving a trail of orange hairs behind.

"Good day to you. Don't concern yourself about the boy." Mistress Bessie began to close the door.

"Willy," Rodgers said.

"Yes, of course. Children his age adjust so quickly. He'll be at home in just a day or two."

"He's lost everything, you know. He's very lonely."

Rodgers touched his hat brim to her and walked away.

Chapter 10

Mistress Bessie closed the door and kicked the rug against it to keep out drafts. Willy still stood by the chair where Rodgers had been sitting. "There's a good boy—no tantrums." She picked the cat up and waved away the orange hairs that floated upward.

"Willy? Please mind the cat. Her name is Button." She pushed Button and her cloud of orange hair at Willy.

Unthinking, he took the cat.

"No, no. Here, put this hand under her back feet and let her rest against your shoulder. Now you can stroke her with your other hand."

Willy jerked his head back at the loud rattle next to his ear.

"Button's purring. That means she likes you and she's expecting you to stroke her or scratch her head."

"I don't want to." Willy tried to hand Button back. "I want to go home." Button wouldn't budge.

"This is your home now, and Button needs someone to take care of her."

"I don't want to."

"Button needs a friend. You see, she has no one to play with. Hold her for a little while, then I'll come and take her from you."

Button settled against his shoulder, her head just below his ear. He touched the orange fur lightly and let his fingers sink into it. Button purred louder. He let his hand slide down the cat's back. Button wiggled and settled closer.

Mistress Bessie guided him to a small stool by the fire. "That's right," she murmured. "Mind the cat."

Willy leaned against the outside of the fireplace. The warmth of the bricks and the buzz in his ear soothed him and his eyes grew heavy. He remembered Master Perry seated behind his desk picking wax off the candlesticks. He thought of Gillian who hopped around the laundry room when the kettle boiled over on her foot. He was glad to be away from her, and Marie as well. She had tried to steal his picture of Mummy.

Cook's face came into focus. She was pushing more bread and jam across the table. He never minded that she didn't have any teeth. She could actually touch her chin with her nose. She had shown him one day when no one else was around. Willy saw Rodgers sitting by the fire in the public house talking to him as though he were a grownup. But even Rodgers had left him.

Mummy loves me, he thought, but I can't find her and she doesn't know where I am. His eyes filled with tears. Maybe he would have to leave here as soon as this lady didn't like him anymore.

Willy lifted his arm to dry his eyes. Button's hair stuck to his wet face. He shuddered and spat cat hair off his lips. Disturbed by the commotion, Button left Willy's shoulder and curled up in his lap.

Willy shivered again and tried to brush away the hairs stuck to his face. He could feel some of Button's hairs in his throat. He couldn't even cough them loose. Stupid cat. He would have said it out loud, but he was afraid to open his mouth and let more hairs in. He wiggled his legs to make her get down. Button curled into a tighter ball and purred louder.

Willy pushed her head away. "Get down, Button." He coughed and sneezed at the same time and shook all over. He could not get rid of those orange hairs. Button roused and stretched. She licked his hand. Her tongue felt like tiny scrapers. Willy jerked away and studied the place where she had licked him. It looked all right. He poked her nose with his finger and Button obliged with another sandpaper lick. Willy held his finger up. "That tickles. Do it again." He poked her and Button licked him once more.

"You kissed me. Do you like me?"

Button stretched and purred. Willy bent over and whispered, "You can stay on my lap as long as you like." He rested his hands on the cat, pushed his fingers deep into her fur, and leaned against the warm wall. His eyes closed.

When Mistress Bessie entered the room a few minutes later, Button jumped down. She was hungry.

Mistress smiled at the little boy covered with orange hair. She laid him on a heavy blanket in front of the fire, then took his satchel and unpacked it. She set aside his shawl and green ribbon. The treasures of children no longer surprised her. After spreading his sheets and blanket on his cot, she carried Willy in, dressed him in his nightshirt, and tucked him in.

Perhaps, as her friends said, she was a bit old to take in children. No, definitely not. The children gave her a reason to rise each morning. She wasn't going to let herself become a self-centered, dried-up bit of apple, good for nothing but huddling around a fire complaining about creaking joints.

She left the door to Willy's room ajar. Not that my shoulders don't bother me some in this cold weather. And my knees pop and snap if I walk too far. She settled herself by the fire and picked up her knitting. This'll keep my fingers nimble, anyway.

The fire warmed her feet. Her wooden needles clicked. Yes, now that she knew Willy's size, she could make him a proper jumper. Knitted clothes always kept one warmer. Time was, she thought, I did this for my own family. Gone now. George to the New World. What was the name of that island? He's growing sugar, he said. Funny, one didn't think of sugar growing. Salt didn't grow; pepper did, though. Supposed to be a lot of money in sugar if all went well. Maybe, someday, I'll just have me a bit of that sugar.

She smiled. George says he has no need of jumpers, or even vests, on his island; it's that warm all the time. She shook her head. Hard to believe.

Her needles clicked on, and yarn rose from the ball that twisted and spun in the basket by her chair.

There's Margaret's family. I never understood why her husband moved them to Southampton. London is a fine city for merchants. What's in Southampton? Smugglers! My son-in-law wouldn't dare—would he? What'll happen to Margaret and the children if he's caught? He never did think beyond the moment. Well, perhaps he's not smuggling. Wouldn't put it past him, though. Shifty eyes and all.

Her needles thrust furiously in and out. She leaned over her work to pick up a dropped stitch, then held it up for inspection.

THE FOUNDLING

Children's jumpers took little time because they were small. She must be careful not to get the arms too long on this one.

The front door opened.

"Peter? Is that you? Kick the rug in front of the door. How did your lessons go? How's the Vicar? Put your book safely away."

Peter dropped his coat and book on the floor and went to the fireplace.

"Peter, books are very dear!"

Peter put his book on a shelf. "The Vicar sends his greetings. He'll visit soon. My lessons are so hard to learn. All the older boys say that they do not need Latin. Why must I learn it? Jonathan says his father will allow him to stop his Latin."

"You must have Latin if you want to be a lawyer."

"I want to be a soldier."

"Nonsense, both your parents expressed their wishes quite clearly on a number of occasions. Your father left a sizeable bequest to see you through Cambridge. Their wishes will be honored."

Peter never won this argument.

"I'm hungry."

"Growing boys usually are. And don't change the subject. You've just hit a rough patch. You'll get through it."

"You're knitting a new sweater. Is there another little boy here? That's my old sweater. Why did you tear it up?"

"That sweater was too small for you." She laid her knitting aside. "I'll fix you a bite, then you can study before you go to bed."

"Did you put the baby in the bed by the fire? I'll bet you gave him the best blankets and my pillow."

"Peter! Mind your tongue. He's just a little boy. We needn't go through this again. You are my first responsibility always. These waifs who come to me have no home. Most can't remember their mothers and fathers. They have nothing. But you . . . " She paused. "Come here."

Mistress Bessie felt Peter's arms go around her waist. She hugged him, then smoothed his hair. "Don't worry, Peter. I loved your mother. She was like my own daughter. That makes you my grandson in a very special way."

Peter's stomach rumbled and he giggled. "I'm hungry. And did you give him the best bed?"

"No, I did not. Your bed is your bed. Master Perry sent all his linens with him, so your blanket and pillow are also untouched. Now that's enough of this foolishness. Let's eat. A boy can't study on an empty stomach."

Willy awoke. He couldn't remember where he was. He hugged his shawl. The room was in dark shadows cast by the glow of the embers in the fireplace. Vague outlines of furniture disappeared as he drifted back to sleep.

He felt a heavy thump on the foot of his cot. His eyes flew open. A big, dark shape stood by his feet, blocking the fire's glow. He must have let his hand or foot hang over the edge of the cot. Everyone knew that monsters stayed under the cot unless they knew there was something good to eat up above. Willy's heart beat so hard it hurt. He tried to get his hands free to defend himself, but he was rolled up in his blanket. Hairy feet now stepped on his stomach. The monster inched its way up to Willy's chest. He struggled, but the monster held him down so it could reach out and touch his chin with its cold nose. It's going to eat me! Willy tried to roll and toss the monster off, but his blanket held him fast.

Content with the spot she'd picked, Button lay down and purred.

"Button!" Willy's voice shook. "Move, Button." Willy gasped for air. "I can't breathe!" Button slipped off his chest and settled by his side.

"I thought you were a monster." But he was glad that Button liked him and had curled up by his side. Together they fell asleep.

Chapter 11

Peter stared down at Willy. Another baby, he thought. I wish they'd not come at all. They break my toys . . . jumble up the room. They whine and cry; Mistress always takes their side. He's small enough, though. I can take care of him. Peter reached down and fingered a corner of Willy's shawl. Ha! A mummy's boy. He nudged Willy's cot with his toe.

"Time to get up. Mistress won't keep your breakfast any longer. C'mon. Get up."

Willy yawned, fought free of the covers, and rubbed his eyes. He rubbed his nose while he stretched.

"Is Willy up?" Mistress Bessie called from the kitchen.

"He's awake." Peter bumped the cot again. "You'd best hurry or I'll drop Button on you."

Willy opened his eyes. "Where's Button?" he asked.

"She's outside killing birds and squirrels and mice. Then she eats them and blood gushes out—" Peter warmed to his topic.

"Peter!"

"Yes, mum, coming." He turned to Willy. "Get up, now, or you'll be in trouble."

"Is Willy up yet?" Mistress asked again.

"I guess so. Hal's waiting for me." Peter's voice faded as he went toward the door.

"Don't forget your scarf."

Peter sighed. If it weren't so cold out, he'd leave his scarf on the hook. Instead, he wrapped it around his neck twice and tucked the ends into his coat.

"And your cap."

Peter clenched his jaw and pulled on the cap.

"And your—"

"Mittens!" Peter exploded. "I know, I know. Do you think I'm a baby? I'm leaving now."

"Be back by noon."

"Yes, mum." He slammed the door behind him and ran into the freedom of Saturday morning.

Willy peeked through the door to the kitchen.

"You sit here and eat your breakfast." Mistress Bessie pointed him to a chair.

Mistress Bessie's bread and jam were almost as good as Cook's, even though her kitchen was much smaller and didn't have half the pans and kettles that Cook's kitchen had. Willy glanced at the corners of the room. He could see no tub for baths. And no one came in carrying linens or dishes.

"Are we alone?" Willy asked. "Do you have any servants?"

Mistress Bessie hung a towel before the fire. "Dear me, no. Never needed any. You mean like Master Perry has?"

Willy nodded. "Rodgers and Marie and Gillian. But I only like Rodgers."

"My house is small. I can do everything myself, though I do get busy sometimes. That's black currant preserves. Do you like it?"

Willy nodded again.

Mistress Bessie's cloth wiped the table around Willy's plate. "You must learn not to spill when you eat." She scrubbed a crusty spot. "Maybe even Peter will learn someday."

"Peter?"

"Yes, the other boy who lives with me. He's outside with his friend Hal. He woke you this morning. Now, if you're quite finished, let's get you ready for the day."

She sized up her new charge. "You're old enough to take care of yourself and to learn simple tasks. Best start now." She led the way to the bedroom.

"This is where you will keep your clothes." She opened a wardrobe. "Here are your shirts. On this shelf—"

"These are my clothes?" He saw shirts and breeches and stockings and shoes and coats and everything. He stepped forward and touched some of them. "Mine?"

Mistress smiled. "Yes, Master Perry sent some clothes along the same day the vestry agreed to send you to me. You're extremely fortunate, you know. Master Perry has taken a special interest in you." She turned back to the lesson. "And I expect you to keep your clothes tidy and not put dirty clothing back into the wardrobe." She closed the wardrobe door and turned a small piece of wood to keep it shut.

"Each day you will tidy your cot. I'll show you this morning, but after this you will do it yourself. Come 'round and help me." She pulled the sheet straight.

Willy pulled the blanket so hard that it nearly fell to the floor. He looked up.

"Hmmm. This may take a bit longer than I thought." Mistress pointed. "Make it hang the same on each side. That's right. Help me pull it over." Together they pulled the blanket even. "Now tuck it all in under your mattress like this." She tucked in sheet and blanket together. "You try it."

Willy picked up the edges of the bed covers on his side and shoved them under the mattress. He patted the lumps flat.

"This will take practice, but you must make your bed every morning. Let's finish." She smoothed Willy's attempt. "That's the way. You'll learn soon enough. See how Peter's done his."

Willy scrutinized Peter's smooth bed. "Peter's big."

"He was little when he started. He learned quickly and so will you. Now, get dressed. Put your nightshirt in the wardrobe. Fold it up first, mind. I'll be in the kitchen."

Willy shivered and pulled his nightshirt off. He dropped it on the floor so he could stand on it, then scooted it across the floor to the wardrobe. After he dressed, he folded his nightshirt and laid it carefully on a shelf. In a corner lay the green ribbon. He pushed it under some stockings and slammed the door of the wardrobe. He spun the knob that held it closed.

Button came in and arched her back against his legs. Willy picked her up around the middle, then set her down.

"Button, you're very fat."

He wandered into the sitting room. Through the window's wavy glass he could see Peter and Hal trying to jump over the garden fence. Willy thought that neither was a very good jumper even though they removed one rail from the fence, then another. He sat down to watch.

THE FOUNDLING

Peter ran at the fence, pumped his arms hard, kicked one foot out, and sprang into the air. He didn't fly gracefully over the fence at all. His foot slipped in a muddy patch, and he landed in a heap with one foot caught on the fence.

Hal came over and set his friend upright. They talked for a few moments, gesturing at the muddy spot. They studied the mud. They tried scraping the spot smooth with the sides of their shoes. Hal put some leaves on it. The leaves slid éven worse than the bare mud, and he fell on his back with one leg sticking straight up.

Willy smiled around his thumb. He pulled his stool closer to the window.

Hal scuffed the leaves away. He looked uncertainly around the garden, then went straight to the garden walk and loosened one of the paving stones in the path. He shouted something to Peter, who ran over for another stone. They put them in the muddy place so they would not slip.

Willy heard a door slam. Mistress Bessie, with measured tread, rounded the corner of the cottage, her broom like a stave, ready for battle. She waggled the broom handle at the two boys. Willy could see her lips move, but he couldn't hear enough words to make sense of them. Hal and Peter ducked the broom and put the stones back in the garden path. Mistress stood over them until they were finished, then she tested their work by walking up and down on the path. The boys, muddy and wet, stood first on one foot then on the other, not daring to look up. Then she saw her fence. Mistress's broom came up in a smooth arc.

Willy had seen men flogged in the streets of London, but never had he seen a beating administered by a furious woman with a broom. He leaned forward until he could feel the cold air next to the windowpane. Peter and Hal fell to the ground. They rolled around trying to get out of the way, but only rolled into each other. Mistress Bessie's black shawl flapped around her shoulders with each stroke. Willy pressed his forehead against the cold glass. He caught his breath when Hal escaped and ran from the garden, clearing all four fence rails with ease. Willy clapped.

Peter still rolled on the ground, his arms and legs flying in all directions. Willy's breath clouded the window. He swiped the fog away in time to see Peter scramble to his feet.

Mistress Bessie reached out and grabbed his ear. Willy could tell because Peter's head was tipped way over on one shoulder, and he was walking as though only one of his legs was really long enough to touch the ground. Mistress dragged Peter to the fence. He picked up the rails and carried them to the house. Mistress gestured once more toward the fence, waved her arm above Peter's head, and entered the house.

Peter stood still until the door latch settled in place, then he ran to the garden gate. He stopped and looked back at the fence section he and Hal had turned into a low hurdle and paced off what seemed an adequate approach. He started his run at the fence with a hop and a skip. Willy clenched his fists and pressed against the window, urging Peter over.

"So the rascal's at it again, is he?"

Willy turned to see Mistress Bessie behind him. She rapped sharply on the window.

By the time Willy whirled back to watch Peter, he lay draped across the fence like a muddy doll. One arm moved, then a leg. Peter pushed himself up and limped off after Hal.

"He'll do himself a mischief, he will." Mistress Bessie went to the fireplace and warmed her hands. Then she turned and warmed her backside, shaking all the cold air out of her skirts. "I've broken two perfectly good brooms on that boy since Boxing Day!"

Chapter 12

Cook straightened from her oven and looked around the kitchen. He brightened us up no end, she thought. Now the table's clean . . . no rings from glasses sitting in spilled milk . . . no bread crumbs or jam spots. No sticky fingers pulling at my apron. No child pestering me with questions. She set her lips in a hard line that stretched nearly from ear to ear. No little boy to listen to my stories. Ate what was set before him too. Never a complaint. Always said a pretty thankee. Had good manners—knew he wasn't supposed to belch out loud. Cook chuckled. Yes, that rumble would have done a thunderclap proud. Rodgers had nearly fallen off his bench . . . Even though he just left today, now it's empty here, empty and dull.

She wiped the already spotless tabletop again. Why I could—indeed—I could bake him a treat. Rodgers can take it when he visits. Jam tarts, sticky buns, sweet biscuits, what does the sprout like best?

Master Perry sat back from dinner. "Well, my dear, the house is quiet once more."

"It is, rather, isn't it? Really, James, we should give a party. All of our friends are in London for the winter. The house is clean. Time to get rid of the winter doldrums."

"I meant that I miss—"

"—seeing guests about the house? I do too. All the noise, the bustle, happy smiles. Why, do you know that Beatrice Ingram's father agreed to her marrying that fine young man from Middlesex at the Somerses' party, just last week? I wonder how many parties they attended just so they could spend time together? Beatrice's father was not about—"

Master Perry looked around the room. No little boy, but then, Willy had never been in the dining room. Why, then, did he expect to see him? No mischief . . . no screeching maids or crowing laughter. With an effort he turned his attention back to his wife.

THE FOUNDLING

"If you wish to have a party that lasts through the night, you have my blessing and my open purse. Pray only keep us from bankruptcy." He leaned over and pecked his wife on the cheek. "I'll be in my chambers scraping the coins together. Please send Rodgers along with a coffee. I'm becoming rather attached to my evening cup."

In the kitchen, Rodgers looked over Cook's preparations. "Is the tray ready?"

She nodded. "I'm not sure about those beans, but I think I've got it right tonight. Ground them a little coarser. Be sure to tell me what Master Perry thinks. Last time he said the coffee was so strong it curled his tongue. I'm sending extra hot water and milk along just in case."

"Frosted buns and raspberry tarts?"

Cook looked squarely at Rodgers. "I reckon the Master'll need a good natter tonight. Cheer him up. You too." She paused. "You going to visit him?"

"Just now, as soon as the tray is ready."

"Don't be silly. Will you visit the boy—Willy?"

"Yes, the vestry needs—"

"Nah, don't try to fool me. The vestry doesn't need anything and you know it. Margaret Bessie has never needed checking. She's a fine nurse. You're going for yourself and the Master." Cook harrumphed and withdrew her arthritic finger from the end of Rodgers's nose.

He shifted. "Our duty to the boy—"

"Willy!"

"Yes . . . Willy . . . is over at any rate—"

"Ha! He's got to you. I knew it." Rodgers opened his mouth to speak, but Cook went on. "Don't deny it. I see it in your face." She wiped her hands on her apron. "You don't suppose you could carry a bit of a treat to him for me when you visit? Something small, not a whole cake."

"Why, you old prune! Got to me, did he? Ate his way right to your heart, I don't guess." Rodgers laughed.

"The poor mite needed fattening."

"You loved cooking for him. You loved having him around."

Cook sniffed. "Always stepping on him, actually."

Rodgers raised one eyebrow.

"Well, will you take something along for him?"

"I'll do my best. What with all the extra clothing Master Perry is sending along—"

"Hire a porter to carry the clothes!" Cook's arms flailed the air. "Will you carry a cake to him?" Rodgers's smile broadened. "That's it! I'll not say another word. Go along before the coffee gets cold. Why anyone would drink something that looks like used mop water . . ."

"Is that you, Rodgers? Do come in. Let me help you with that tray."

"Shall I pour, James? Cook has altered her procedure once again. She hopes to duplicate what you call the 'rich flavor' produced by the new coffeehouse in Bow Lane." Rodgers sipped delicately. "A bit more milk, I think . . . Yes, that's it. She may have done it."

Perry inhaled the aroma from his cup. "The smell alone is refreshing." He sipped as well. "Very nice. Should we import more? It seems to be rising in popularity."

"Our store at the warehouse is nearly gone. It will not last through March. Perhaps we should purchase some from other companies now, in small quantities, of course, before scarcity drives the price up."

"Let's look into that. No reason not to make a profit when and where we can. Mistress Perry is planning a party, no date yet, but"—he smiled—"we'll put the coffee bean profit to that." He raised his cup to Rodgers and both men drank.

In the silence, the raindrops dripped down the chimney, hissing when they hit the fire. Shadows from the candles moved on the walls. Both men removed their shoes and propped their feet on small stools.

"Amelia hates when I do this, you know. She says my feet smell."

"Really? One of the drawbacks of marriage, I suppose."

THE FOUNDLING

Rodgers slouched down farther in his chair, pushing his toes closer to the fire. His deep sigh of comfort became an audible "Ahhhh."

Master Perry struggled up from his chair. "What say I put this tray between us . . . so. We can reach what we like. More coffee? Cook outdid herself. And these tarts—" He bit into one and finished his thought, sending pastry crumbs flying, "—are exceptional."

Rodgers flicked some of the crumbs from his vest.

"Sorry. My manners are deplorable this evening, but it is good to forget the world and put my feet up. So, you returned before the showers began?" Master Perry's voice held a tone of studied indifference.

"Oh yes, no excuse to nip into a pub."

"And how did the afternoon go?"

"Very well, I thought."

"I see you met the cat."

"What? Oh, yes, Button." Rodgers looked at his trousers. "I can't get the hairs off. I believe I'm condemned to wearing orange ruffs around my ankles for days or even weeks. Fattest moggy I've ever seen."

"And Mistress Bessie?"

"She'd been tidying up when we arrived. Seemed well and comfortable."

"So . . . no immediate needs for either of the boys?"

"Not that I could tell." Rodgers licked his thumb and finger clean. A quiet voice came from Perry's chair. "Tell me."

Rodgers described their trek across London and their chat in the pub. Master Perry smiled. "You'll somehow have to work dragons and knights and damsels in distress into your next telling."

"Caught me off guard, I must say."

"So that's how you came to London?"

"Pretty close. There were so many others in the same situation. I sometimes wonder just how many the influenza carried off." Rodgers gazed into his coffee cup.

"A sad story that has been repeated too many times to count. Perhaps that's how Willy's mother came to London."

"Of course, there's the war now, and families losing everything to the armies."

"Not to Cromwell's men, I hear. He's been known to execute men who plunder the countryside. Still, war's a nasty business." Master Perry loosened his collar farther so his chin could rest comfortably on his chest. After a moment, he said, "Please, go on."

Rogers described Willy's fascination with the busy city streets and his complete lack of knowledge of the world beyond the City wall. "I put him on my shoulders to keep him safe. Now Marie is working on the stains his shoes made on my coat."

"Didn't you check his shoes?"

"Yes, but it seems little boys' shoes hide mud more effectively than I knew. But Marie says not to worry . . . I should put her to work on these trousers." He clicked his tongue and shook his head. "To continue—"

He told of their arrival at Mistress Bessie's, his brief conversation with her, and his departure. When he finished, neither man spoke. The silence deepened.

Finally, Master Perry stirred. "She's very good, you know, really the best."

Rodgers nodded, and the silence stretched out once again, punctuated by the crackling fire. A small log collapsed into red coals and he roused.

"It's so quiet. Even Marie and Gillian are arguing less. There's less chatter in the kitchen. I miss turning a corner and finding him there: no stockings, clothing askew—"

"—shoes unfastened—"

"—hair flying in all directions. The house seems quite empty." Rodgers spoke softly. He tilted his coffee cup. It too was empty.

"A child fills the void . . ." Master Perry's voice trailed off.

Marie rushed down the hall. Gone! He's gone! No more prying eyes or dirty little hands pulling my clothes out of the wardrobe. My room, my privacy, my brooch! She kicked the laundry room door open and, with a flourish, dropped the basket of clothes.

"Don't run off," Gillian called. "Stay and talk. I've been here forever."

THE FOUNDLING

Marie hardly heard and didn't care. She ran to her room and closed the door firmly behind her.

Now! She hurried to the hearth and fell to her knees. She snatched the loose stone from its place. Her hand trembled when she picked up the brooch wrapped in her handkerchief. Slowly she unwound the soft cloth.

The brooch once again lay in her palm. Her breath caught in her throat. She tilted her hand to allow the firelight to glow deep into the gold. "It's mine! I'll keep it forever."

She went to the mirror and pinned the brooch to her collar. It didn't look quite right there, or even on her shoulder. Ah yes, that's right. Right in the center at the neckline. Must hold my chin up so everyone can see it, she thought.

Marie turned to the left and right watching the light flash from the brooch. She posed again and again in front of her mirror.

"Where can I wear this right away?" she asked her mirror image. "Susan's party next week? Wouldn't that be too perfect! They'll be so jealous. And my hair—" She pulled her hair back and up. "No, let's see—" She pulled it to one side and tried to curl a brown lock around her finger. Yes, much better. And, my best dress . . . the dark gray wool with the white collar. "Perfect! Everyone will be jealous, none of them owns—they're too poor—"

She froze. A poor apprentice! The words thundered. Too poor to own such a piece of jewelry. Her hand flew to her throat. She felt sick. Tears stung her eyes.

No, no, no! she thought. There must be a way!

But Marie knew there was no way to explain the golden pin. She might even be accused of stealing it.

"My mother . . . she gave it to me. No, as poor as we are, who'd believe—I found it! That's it. So why didn't I turn it over to Master Perry or the Constable?" She snorted at the thought of the Constable.

And there was the problem of the portrait inside it. She unpinned the brooch and opened it. The lock of hair fell to the floor. She threw it into the fireplace. Next she tried to loosen the miniature with her fingernail, then with a hairpin. It was no use; it wouldn't move. She closed her hand around the brooch and sat heavily on her bed. She'd never be able to wear it in her whole life.

Chapter 13

February 1644

A fortnight later, Rodgers visited Willy.

"Why, you should have hired a porter!" Mistress Bessie threw the door open.

"Please take the little basket. Cook tied it up well, but I've had to carry it dangling from my finger. I've no feeling left, up to the elbow."

Mistress Bessie set the basket in the crook of her arm and stepped back, allowing Rodgers to enter.

"And what's all this?"

"Master Perry sent a new cap and mittens for Willy. And shoes. Little boys go through them so quickly. I purchased some stockings and a small toy or two." He set his parcels on the table.

"This is all very well, I'm sure, but you'll quite spoil the boy, raise his expectations. New clothes and toys." She clicked her tongue. "Get to thinking better of himself than he ought."

"We're depending on you to help keep him from that."

"It will be more than a spot of bother, but I'll do my best." She lifted the basket in her hand. "And what's in here?"

"I really don't know. Cook insisted on sending something along. Willy spent a lot of time with her, and she tried to fatten him a bit."

"He ate everything in sight, did he not?"

"I believe so."

"He certainly does at my table. As much as Peter and more—especially bread and jam." She picked up two bundles of clothing. "I'm just thankful the vestry gives a bit more to keep a growing boy. I've often wondered how nurses with five or seven children manage. Well, they don't manage, and that's the long and short of it. Never have quite enough to eat. And their clothing!" She paused for breath. "But enough of that. My children get the best I can give, even if it comes from my own pocket. Is this parcel clothing?" She added it to her load.

"We—that is, the vestry—wouldn't think of allowing you to pay for Willy's food and clothing." He leaned forward and placed some coins on the table. "A bit extra."

"From the vestry?" Mistress Bessie looked shocked. "They never sent me extra before without my personal request."

"From Master Perry. He's very pleased you took Willy."

"You make yourself comfortable. I'll just put these parcels away." She returned a couple of minutes later and picked up the conversation. "Perhaps it's not my place to ask, but what's Master Perry's interest in this child?"

"No direct interest, of course. Hadn't seen him before Constable Crumpton brought him to the door. But the date was almost a year to the day after the burial of his own son. He lost his daughters as well to the influenza. It's still a sad household. So there were those memories and Willy was, or rather is, just about Daniel's age."

"None of my business, of course." Mistress Bessie shook herself. "Fancy a cup of tea? I've just begun drinking it. It does take the winter chill off an afternoon." She picked up Cook's basket and went to the kitchen.

Rodgers settled back and watched heavy clouds, pushed by cold, gusty winds, race past the window.

The front door opened and slammed shut.

"Kick the rug against the door!" Mistress Bessie's call was followed by muffled thumps of someone kicking the rug against the door. Then Willy ran into the room.

Rodgers stared. The boy had grown in just two weeks. Certainly he wasn't as thin as he had been.

"I say, young man!"

Willy careened on through the room. His coat was unbuttoned, his scarf still wound around his neck. His nose was running, and he was using his mittens to dry his eyes.

"Willy!"

Willy might have run into a brick wall. Without a word he spun and dove into Rodgers's lap.

"What a greeting! Let me see you. Willy, do let go." He put his arms around Willy, lightly at first, then tighter. He patted his back a couple of times. Finally Rodgers sat Willy on his knees and pulled off his scarf.

"This is a very nice scarf, Willy. Is it warm?"

Willy nodded.

"And your mittens. What's this bit of string?" Rodgers followed the string up one sleeve and down to the other mitten. "Clever, that. We should have thought of it. Mistress Bessie is quite a seamstress." He dropped the scarf, coat, and mittens on the floor beside his chair and turned Willy to face him. "Now what's all this about?"

"Peter and Hal." Willy's tears began again, and he rubbed his sleeve across his face. "Peter and Hal won't let me play with them."

"Oh? Well, perhaps it's a game for bigger boys. They'll let you play when you grow a bit more."

Willy shook his head.

"Perhaps they thought you didn't know how to play."

"I did so."

"Well, what game were they playing?"

Willy's lower lip trembled. "They were throwing a ball and chasing it. I could do that." He nodded and pressed his case. "I could do it very well. But Peter said I couldn't, and he wouldn't even let me try."

"Hmmm."

"They are both naughty, aren't they?"

"Hmmm." Rodgers looked around the room for some clue to the proper response. "I . . . uh . . . well, perhaps they'll play with you later."

"I don't think so; they're not nice to me. I tried to show them I could throw with some stones from the garden. They went a long ways. I'm very good, you know."

"You threw stones?"

Willy nodded. "Very far, like this." He drew his hand back over his shoulder and swung it around. "Right over the bushes and the fence and into the lane."

"That sounds very good to me."

"Yes, and some went so far I couldn't see them."

"Really! That's quite an accomplishment. If you keep practicing, perhaps one day Peter and Hal will see how good you really are. Willy, you didn't throw the stones at anything?"

"Oh yes. I'm very good, you see. I hit the fence and . . . "

"Yes?"

"Hal."

"You hit Hal? Was he hurt? Were you trying to hit Hal?"

Willy studied Rodgers's left shoulder.

"That's shameful, throwing stones at people. What about Peter? Did you throw stones at him too?"

Willy let out a great sigh. "No, he ran away. Then Hal ran away too, and I was all alone." He spread his hands wide and looked straight at Rodgers. "They weren't nice to me at all."

"Let me tend the fire." Rodgers hid his smile as he stood Willy on the floor and prodded a new log into the grate. He studied the arrangement and knocked the ash from the poker. "There."

He stood up and looked down at the boy's face. "Now, Willy—" No, this won't do, he thought, and bent down. "Now, Willy, throwing stones at people, even at Peter and Hal, shows very poor breeding. You must find some other way of dealing with your problems. I—"

"What's breeding?"

"Eh? Oh, that's the way you were taught to behave—your manners—and I don't want to hear of you doing this again. Do you understand?" Rodgers caught Willy's chin and tipped his face up. "Do you?"

"But—"

"No excuses."

"Are you angry?"

"No, but you must promise not to throw stones."

Willy nodded.

"And tell Peter and Hal that you're sorry."

"But they—"

"No excuses. Men of breeding always say they're sorry when they're wrong . . . Will you do it?"

Willy looked into the crackling fire. Finally Rodgers heard a faint "Yes."

"Good. Now, I really must straighten up. Aha, I hear the rattle of dishes. Perhaps tea is ready."

"Tea?"

"Mistress Bessie and I are going to have a cup of tea. It's very good on such a cold day."

"Can I have some?"

"Yes, you may." Mistress Bessie maneuvered a tray into the sitting room and placed it on the table. "I've brought you a cup, and I thought you'd like to have some of the cakes Cook sent along."

"Cakes? For me? Cook sent me cakes?" He looked at Rodgers.

"Just for you. She wouldn't let me leave until I had them. You won't mind if Mistress Bessie and I share with you?"

"What kind are they?" Willy ran to the table and stood on tiptoe to see what was on the plate. "Are there any black currant?"

"Shoo; go sit down." Mistress waved him away.

"Do you know Cook hasn't any teeth and she can touch her chin with her nose? She showed me one day."

Mistress Bessie handed a steaming cup to Rodgers. "Would you like some honey?" She passed the small pot to him. "You know my son is living in the sugar islands. He's promised to send me a packet of sugar someday."

Rodgers dribbled some honey into his cup. "Thank you." No sticky drops anywhere. He relaxed.

"Willy, sit down so I can give you your tea. It's already sweetened. Here, I'll put it on the stool, and you can sit on the hearthstone. Be careful, the cup is hot."

Mistress passed around the cakes, letting Willy take two.

Willy tried to eat and drink exactly as Rodgers did. Eating one of the cakes in only two bites was difficult. He had to push the second half into his mouth with the palm of his hand. His cup slipped and some of his tea splashed on the stool. Mistress didn't notice, so Willy wiped the stool dry with his shirtsleeve.

He listened to Rodgers and Mistress Bessie talking about people he didn't know. There was a war somewhere. The King was losing, which Willy thought rather sad. Kings were great knights who rode wonderful chargers. They saved beautiful princesses and then married them and lived happily ever after. He took another cake and wasn't noticed.

"More tea?"

Startled, Willy returned from fighting the Black Knight. He nodded.

Mistress sweetened his tea, then served Rodgers. They talked of buying and selling sugar. Willy thought of Peter and was glad he wasn't there to eat any of his cakes.

"I'll just wash up." Mistress Bessie broke the spell and disappeared through the door.

"And what shall I tell Cook about her cakes?" Rodgers asked Willy.

Willy smacked his lips and smiled.

"She thought you might like them. She'll be pleased. Now tell me, do you like Mistress Bessie?" At Willy's nod, Rodgers continued. "You don't always fight with Peter, do you?"

Willy leaned very close to Rodgers's ear. "Peter can't jump. I saw him try, and he fell every time. Mistress beat him with her broom for breaking her fence. Hal jumped better when he ran away."

"And where were you when this was going on?"

"By that window. Mistress Bessie beat them both. She was very angry." Willy nodded and smiled.

"I wish I'd seen that."

"Her shawl flapped all around, and she made them put the stones back in the path."

"What were they doing with them?"

"I don't know."

"I noticed part of the fence was down. Mistress prizes her fence because it protects her roses."

"Mistress doesn't have any roses."

"Not now, but she will have. She's trimmed them back for the winter. Mind you don't get into them. Where's Button today?"

"She's outside. At night sometimes she sleeps with me. But not on me; she's very heavy. She catches mice, you know."

"She does? A good cat is valuable. She can keep a house or barn free of mice and other little animals."

"Button eats them."

"I imagine she does. I've brought you something. Bring me that small parcel." Rodgers untied the string. "Here's a top, some chestnuts, and—close your eyes—here."

Willy gasped. In his hands was a fine wooden horse with a real mane and tail, and on the horse's back was a knight dressed in armor and carrying a shield and lance. "For me?"

"Yes, all for you. Do you like them?"

Willy nodded vigorously.

"Let's put the horse on the table while I show you how to make the top spin." Rodgers slid out of the chair and onto his knees. He pushed the rug back, then wound a string around the top and set it spinning in a whirl of color. It danced across the floor, wobbled, and fell. Willy crawled after it.

"Do it again."

Rodgers wound the string again. "This top has almost the same colors as your jumper. Why are the sleeves so long?"

"So I can grow into it, Mistress said."

Rodgers tossed the top onto the floor. "Pretty, all those colors. Want to try?"

Willy didn't have much success.

"It will take a bit of practice. You'll soon have it." Rodgers threw the top out once more. "Now the chestnuts. You can play any game you want to make up with them, but we always drew a ring on the ground and tried to knock each other's out. Here, let's try."

Rodgers pushed the stool to one side. "Now we don't have a proper circle so let's use the marks on these boards as boundaries. If you hit my chestnut beyond that mark, it's yours." Both he and Willy dropped some of the smooth, brown nuts in the area. "And I'll try to hit yours past that spot. Here are the ones we'll throw."

Down on their knees, circling, aiming, shooting, around they went, groaning when they made a bad throw, laughing at the good ones. Rodgers showed Willy how to cradle one of the nuts in the crook of his first finger and flip it out with his thumb. They flipped two into the fireplace and three more behind pieces of furniture.

Mistress Bessie appeared in the door, wiping her hands on her apron. "It'll soon be dark. These short winter days don't leave much time to be out and about, do they? You're welcome to stay, of course."

Rodgers sat back on his heels. "I'm not sure I can get up. I haven't done this since I was a lad." He grasped a chair and pulled himself up. "I'd best be on my way. Let's put the room to rights, Willy."

"Oh dear." Mistress Bessie sighed. "You're quite covered with Button's hair."

Rodgers looked down at his clothes. "I don't understand," he said. "Button wasn't in all afternoon."

"No, but she is in and out all the time." Mistress brushed at the hairs with no effect. "You look like an early spring caterpillar, rather." She covered her smile with her hand. "Not meaning to offend, but you really are a sight."

"Perhaps I should wait for darkness to go abroad. I doubt even the cutpurses and footpads will have anything to do with me." He slipped on his coat. "Never mind. We have a maid who does wonders with cat hair. I'm sure she won't mind obliging me again."

Mistress Bessie thought to herself, I'll bet she will mind—a lot. "Well, good day to you. Willy, are you going to say goodbye?"

Willy appeared, carrying his new treasures. Most of the chestnuts were stuffed in his breeches pockets, giving him a slight waddle.

"Can I come too?"

"No, your home is here, now. I'll come again as soon as I can."

"Will Cook send cakes with you again?"

"I'll ask her."

"And thank you," prompted Mistress.

"Thank you very much."

Rodgers set off down the road. What an afternoon. He breathed deeply of the cold, damp air. I haven't had so much fun since . . . when? He shook his head and smiled. If Master Perry enjoyed Daniel as much, he thought, I can begin to understand a little of his sense of loss. He stepped through Cripplegate into London and picked his way through the cobbled streets. Constable Crumpton joined him at the edge of the parish.

"A good night to ye," he said. "What brings you out so late? Business for Master Perry, I'll wager."

"It just happens that I've been to visit the child you found about four weeks ago. Willy, you remember."

"And a likely lad if I do say so. Tell me, sir, how is the poppet?"

"He's well. Very well, in fact. We are pleased with his progress." Rodgers paused before the Perrys' door. "Good night to you, Jack. Have a care."

Pleased? he thought. Why, yes I am, and so will James be too. Willy is quite a lad.

And he would tell James all about the visit, but how could he include the moment he felt Willy's arms clinging to him, or the laughter when the conkers flew into the fireplace? Rodgers was not sure he could put that into words.

Chapter 14

Willy practiced the next morning with his top. He wound the string around the spindle and tossed the top to the floor time after time as Rodgers had shown him. Sometimes it fell at his feet and lay there rocking back and forth. Other times it flew across the bedroom, and he had to fetch it from under Peter's bed or from behind the wardrobe. It seemed that he spent hours untying knots in the string. Finally, the top whirled perfectly to the floor and spun and skipped across the boards. Willy crowed.

Willy saw a flash of orange, and a swat by Button sent the top flying. Once again Willy crawled behind the wardrobe.

"You silly cat. I made it go just like Rodgers did . . . and you ruined it."

Button backed away, watching the top.

"Go on; go away." Willy waved his hand, and the top spun from his fingers. Red, green, yellow, and blue twirled across the floor once again. He snatched the toy up before Button could get to it.

"Did you see that, Button? Did you?" He put his nose right up to the cat's. "I can do it again too. Just watch me. Watch this!" He twirled the spindle in his fingers and dropped the top. It fell over after only two turns. "I wasn't ready that time. Here, now. Watch!"

Button's attention never wavered.

"There! Look, Button, there it goes! I'll bet Rodgers can't do that without the string." Willy turned to the cat. "Yes, he will be surprised. Watch when he visits again. Are you listening?"

Button backed under Peter's bed. She settled and arranged her back paws under her. Her swishing tail soon lay still and straight. Only the tip twitched. She drew her front paws well back under her shoulders. Her chin nearly rested on the floor. An occasional ripple of excitement went down her back. When the top flew out of Willy's fingers, she sprang, batting it until it flew around the room.

THE FOUNDLING

Willy threw the top again and again for her, clapping and laughing when she made an especially good pounce. He didn't hear the door open.

"What have you been doing all morning?" Before Willy could answer, Mistress Bessie went on. "Look at Button. She's panting! What's that between her paws? Has she caught a mouse?" She lifted the cat. "Your top!"

"I spin it, and she chases it."

"You've been playing a game with her? Did you have fun?"

Willy nodded. "So did Button."

"It's time for her to go out now, and you have to eat. We must go to the market."

On market day all the shops and stalls opened, and people from the country and village came to buy and sell and to see their friends. In the street, hawkers sold pieces of ribbon and inexpensive lace. Farmers stood by the chickens and geese they wanted to sell. Mistress wasn't interested in the animals or the shops that sold harness and farm tools. She dragged Willy right past all those interesting places and into the fishmonger's stall. Willy wondered how the man with the huge red mustache and heavy canvas apron could stand the smell of the fish. There were always lots of cats around too.

"What'll it be today? Jellied eels? Mussels? Bream, trout? I have a nice carp here, a dainty morsel not commonly had."

Willy looked at all the fish arranged on the table. They stared right back at him.

Mistress pressed the carp with her finger and then bent over and sniffed it.

"Fresh-caught this morning, I assure you." The fishmonger turned the fish over for her. "Nice firm flesh—you can't do better."

"Looks fresh enough, but I don't know . . . " Her voice trailed off and she glanced around the stall. "It's a bit more than I want to pay."

The fishmonger cleared his throat. "It's a fine carp. Perhaps I could sell it for—" He stopped to think. "Six shillings and not a farthing less."

"I'll give you four shillings, sixpence, and not a penny more," Mistress shot back.

Willy never understood why she argued about the price of fish. In the end, however, she bought the carp, and both she and the fishmonger seemed happy with the final price of five shillings, two and one-half pence. With a flourish the fishmonger wrapped the carp in paper and handed it to Mistress. She put it into her basket.

In the vegetable stalls, Mistress handed Willy her basket. She wanted to thump, poke, prod, and squeeze the vegetables. The vendors all protested and tried to get her to stop, but they all wanted her to buy their beans, onions, or carrots. Willy thought she didn't need to buy any vegetables at all. Neither he nor Peter liked them.

They stopped for cheese and eggs at another shop. After selecting a large piece of soft, yellow cheese, Mistress turned her attention to the eggs.

"Are these fresh? You seem to have a lot today. Some of these aren't left over from two or three days ago, are they?"

"Mistress, I beg your pardon?" said the offended shopkeeper. "All of the eggs are fresh since yesterday. Just hold them up to this candle. See for yourself."

"Well, it's my experience that hens do not lay well during the damp and cold of winter." She held a number of eggs up to a candle. "I'll have these six."

She put the eggs on top of the vegetables and cushioned them with straw. "Come, Willy."

Only one shop remained unless Mistress was going to stop and buy a packet of pins, a pair of stockings, or a piece of material. But she went right into Willy's favorite shop, the bakery.

He breathed in as much of the wonderful bakery smell as he could. He could almost taste the bread and cakes. The baker winked at him and chuckled. Willy liked the baker's laugh because his stomach bounced up and down underneath his apron.

Mistress usually bought some one- or two-penny loaves of brown bread.

"And a treat for the lad?" The baker handed the loaves to her. "I've hot cross buns, muffins, cakes, and scones."

THE FOUNDLING

"Willy, you may choose something for yourself and something for Peter. But do not take the scones. I can make them just as easily at home, and I believe they're quite the best. Better than these."

He chose two hot cross buns. As they left the store, he heard the baker say to another customer, "Mistress will have her little joke at my expense. The scones—these with currants, these with cheese—are excellent."

Willy trotted along, carrying the bread and buns in a cloth bag. The shops and stalls were already closing. The farmers collected their animals and headed them towards home. Someday, when I'm big, he thought, I'll come to market. I'll stop at all the shops I want to see, and I won't take home fish or vegetables.

Peter was home when they returned. Willy found him in the bedroom watching the top twirl across the floor. The string dangled from his hand.

"That's mine." Willy picked it up.

"Leave it alone. I'm not hurting it." Peter moved to stop him. "Besides, where did you get a top?"

"It's mine! Rodgers gave it to me." Willy stood clutching the top.

Peter reached out to take it. "You don't know how to make it work. I'll show you."

"I do so." Willy backed away.

"Then why did it take me so long to untie all the knots in the string? Give it to me."

"No, it's mine."

"I can take it from you, you know."

"It's mine!" Willy hunched over his toy to protect it.

"Let me have it. It should be mine anyway; I can make it work. You can't." Peter grabbed Willy's hands and began prying them open. "You're just a nurse child. You aren't supposed to get toys. Nobody cares about you."

"No, no, no!" Willy bent lower over the top.

Peter bent over him and continued to pull Willy's fingers apart. "C'mon, give over." He cuffed Willy.

"What is going on here?" Mistress Bessie's voice snapped both boys to attention.

"I just wanted to show him how to make his top go, but he won't let me touch it. He's a selfish, naughty little boy."

"Peter, be still. The top is Willy's." She paused. "But, I'm sure he won't mind sharing with you since you don't have one. Isn't that right, Willy?"

Willy's lower lip trembled. "It's mine. Rodgers gave it to me, just to me."

"Let me have it," said Mistress.

"It's mine!" Willy backed away.

"If you can't share, you shall not play with it either. Give it to me."

Mistress never wavered, and he put the top in her outstretched hand.

After she left, Peter said, "There, see what you made her do? Why couldn't you let me play with it? You really are quite awful, you know."

Willy tried to push past Peter and out the door. Peter blocked his way. "You stand still and listen to your betters."

He pushed Willy back and drew himself up. "You folks come from the gutters; you have no family; you run from your proper places in the country expecting the City folk to take care of you. Why, all of you should be shut out of the City walls or clapped into Newgate as sturdy rogues." He thought for a moment. "You're a charge on the poor relief that simply can't be borne. A blight on the fabric of . . . on the fabric . . . People who will never become productive citizens. And . . . who steal and rob and cheat and . . . and . . . always get in the way." Peter stopped. He glared at Willy. "You're just awful, the lot of you! Hal's father says so!"

Willy had little idea what Peter had said, but he could answer the last charge. "I am not. I am not awful!"

"Yes, you are just awful. And don't forget that this is my room. I was here first and I don't care how many toys you get, Mistress loves me. She takes care of you because they pay her, but she doesn't love you."

Willy stared at the door for several moments after Peter slammed it behind him. Peter's footsteps sounded towards the kitchen. He wanted to chase Peter and tell him that he was just awful too. He wanted to run to Mistress as Peter was now doing.

But he stood alone in the middle of the bedroom he shared with Peter. He had a huge lump in his throat. His chest ached, and he could hardly breathe. Mummy's shawl was under his pillow. He ran and pulled it out and wrapped it around his shoulders as tightly as he could.

The room darkened as twilight faded into night. At last, Willy wandered to the sitting room. The candles had not been lighted, so he continued to the kitchen. Even that room was quiet and shadowy in the late afternoon. Light from Mistress's bedroom and the sound of voices drew him. Through the partly open door he saw Mistress and Peter sitting on the edge of her bed.

"So you see, there's no reason for you to be jealous of Willy," Mistress was saying.

"He has toys, nice ones, and he shouldn't have. His clothes are as nice as mine, and he's just a foundling. He doesn't even have a proper name."

"Willy's mother did abandon him. Perhaps she wasn't able to care for him any longer. As for his clothing and toys, I have nothing to say about them. A wealthy and influential man has taken an interest in him. Perhaps he's doing a bit much and giving the boy a wrong idea about what his life will be like. Whatever, Willy's here and will stay until he's apprenticed—"

"Or he dies."

"Well, I certainly hope not! I'm sure I take better care of my children than that!"

Peter broke the silence that followed.

"Why did they have to die?"

"Your parents?" Mistress reached out and gave Peter a hug. His head rested against her shoulder. In the hall Willy pulled his shawl tighter around his shoulders and wrapped his arms around himself.

"Why did they leave me here? Why didn't they take me with them? Did they . . . abandon . . . me?"

"Not at all. They wanted to visit in the City. It was such a hot summer. I told Grace again and again that the City was not a healthful place to be, especially for a baby. So she left you with me." She smoothed his hair. "Peter, you were not abandoned. And we had such a time. I took you to market and you were so clever, the baker gave you a tiny bun with too much sugar on it. You were sticky for a day after. Then the message came—the plague—your parents were in a visited house and had to be locked in with those who were sick." Mistress spoke slowly.

"Why did they go if they knew the plague was there? Why didn't they stay here with us?"

"Your mother had been so long in the country. She wanted to visit her friends. And we hadn't heard about the plague. I'm sure they would have stayed here if they'd known."

Willy stood silently. He'd seen sick people in the streets. Some had died right there. He shivered.

"The Vicar says God decides when people will die. I don't think God is fair."

"Peter! You mustn't speak so. We are all God's creation, and He can do with us as He wishes. Don't blame God. We must thank Him for leaving us together. Now, let's have a hug and a smile." She glanced at the window. "Look how dark it's become. You must be hungry."

"What about Willy?"

"What about him? You must learn to get along with him. Remember, your station in life requires condescension to all beneath you. While you are his better, you also have responsibilities to the meaner sort. Now, while I prepare a meal, your books would like your company."

Peter pulled a long face.

Mistress smiled. "You look just like your mother. Now, give us a hug and get on to your lessons."

"I just wish . . . I mean, I can't remember . . . I want to see both of them again."

Willy felt sorry for Peter. Maybe he would never see his mummy again. Never play a game with her. Never hear her stories. Willy shook his head slowly.

Mummy . . . he thought. The stories . . . the games . . . He wanted to be with her again, to go back to London to find her. She'd left him for a long time. It was time for him to go home. And give her the ribbon. Willy's head bobbed up and down.

Willy spun on his toes and ran to his bedroom. He wanted to look at his brooch.

He pulled his pillow down the bed. He had put it in there to hide it from Marie! Willy dropped the shawl so he could push both hands into his pillow. Nothing. The mattress had no lump. He threw the pillow on the floor, then the blanket and the sheets. He rolled the mattress down the bed and started at the sacking that lay on the ropes.

Nothing!

Willy surveyed the darkening room. Where?

"The wardrobe!"

He kicked his way through the bed covers and spun the catch on the wardrobe door. It swung open by itself. The room was too dark to see well. The wardrobe looked like the entrance of a cave.

Too dark! Willy closed his eyes tight. He could barely breathe around the knot in his throat. He knew there were dust balls under his bed. That meant the monsters came often; maybe they were there now, waiting. A crackling, hissing, crumbling noise made him jump and hit his head on the wardrobe door so hard that it hurt. He forgot his fear long enough to open his eyes. In the fireplace a tiny tongue of flame shot up from the log that had settled in the grate. Around it the coals glowed a dull red.

It wasn't much light, but it was enough for Willy to find his candlestick. He rushed to the fireplace and lit his and Peter's candles and another one he found on the mantle. He let his breath out. Those monsters had been very close. His hand trembled. Three candles would have to be enough; there weren't any more in the room.

He stood once more before the wardrobe. Starting with the lowest shelves, he reached way back and patted around his clothes. Nothing. Shirts, stockings, and breeches joined the bed covers on the floor. He found his chestnuts and the horse and knight Rodgers had given him. His green ribbon slid to the floor. There was nothing more. His brooch wasn't there. He checked his cot again and then the wardrobe. He even dared to look under his bed, then Peter's. It wasn't there, either.

He'd lost it, Mummy's picture. Willy slid to his knees and laid his head on the bottom shelf of the wardrobe. Tears rolled from the corners of his eyes. When he straightened up to wipe his nose on his sleeve, a corner of his mother's shawl caught his eye. He fell on it and pulled it and his toys from Rodgers close.

Mistress Bessie entered some time later to call Willy to supper. She found him wrapped in his shawl, lying on a pile of clothing. He was clutching some chestnuts and his knight and horse. The green ribbon lay by his head. She pressed her lips together and reached out to shake him awake. She stopped when she saw his tearstained cheeks and heard his shaky sigh. His hands closed convulsively around his treasures while he dreamed.

What had gotten into him? And burning three candles at once. She blew out two of them and stirred up the fire. She shook out a shirt to refold it, then decided Willy should tidy his clothes. She laid the shirt in the wardrobe. The boy needed a stern talking to, but for the moment she lowered the latch and went back to the kitchen.

Chapter 15

Winter-Spring 1644-45

To those living in the cottage outside London's wall, it seemed that winter meant to stay forever. The sun rose at midmorning and disappeared by half-past four. Even then it never shone for long, and when it managed to brighten the day, it did nothing to warm the icy, wet winds that blew in from the North Sea. Clouds raced across the sky, casting gray shadows over the land below. Sometimes the clouds were lighter and the sun seemed about to break through. Other times they hung so low and dark that Willy felt he could reach up and touch their flat undersides. And always they brought rain.

On better days the rain fell quietly in a light drizzle, shrouding Mistress's garden in a perpetual fog. People and animals passing by appeared as ghostly figures, and then they faded back into the fog, voices and thumping cart wheels muffled by the blanket of damp. On the very worst days, wind-driven raindrops sounded like small pebbles hitting the windowpanes. Water dripped constantly from the roof, making puddles all around the cottage.

When the skeletons of bushes and trees thrashed in the storms, Mistress smiled at her wisdom in having had the branches lopped off the tree that stood next to her cottage. It looked bare and forlorn now, but those branches would grow again, healthy and strong and much less likely to snap off and come through the roof. Her gaze fell to her flower and herb gardens. Even her rosebushes held no promise of spring. The rain continued to pound the remains of last year's plants to a sodden brown pulp.

Peter still went to school every day, and Willy and Mistress visited the market. She bundled him up in coat, scarf, cap, mittens, and heavy stockings. In the end, however, the damp always soaked through all the layers of clothing. When the wind pulled at his scarf and coattails, Willy thought he'd never be warm again and ran for the fire of the sitting room. All winter the cottage smelled of wet wool clothes hung to dry.

THE FOUNDLING

Willy often sat by the window, watching squirrels search for last autumn's buried acorns. They didn't cheer him up very much even when they chased each other through the garden and around the trees. He remembered Mummy's smile and her brown eyes, but without the brooch picture she seemed very far away. Now he carried her shawl with him all the time, except when he was outdoors.

Evenings became the best part of the day. Mistress came in and pulled heavy draperies over the door and all the windows. Try as she might, she never could keep all the drafts out. They sneaked in and made the drapes move gently, as though the cottage itself lived and breathed. Then she lit the candles, selected a book, and settled into her chair by the fire. After arranging her heavy skirt and shawl, she called Willy to her lap. She read him stories about Vikings and their longboats.

"Longboats?"

"Ummm . . . like the ferryboats on the Thames but much longer, with a square sail and places on each side of the boat for men to row."

"When there was no wind?"

"Precisely. And the boats had heads of fierce creatures carved on their front ends."

"Why?"

"To scare people so they would run away and the Vikings could rob their houses. And it worked. When villagers saw those strange boats, they ran away. Then the Vikings came into the villages and took whatever they wanted, sometimes even people."

"Even little boys?"

"Sometimes."

Willy sat up on Mistress's knee. "Well, they wouldn't take me. I can fight." He brandished an imaginary sword.

"Do sit still."

Willy settled back.

"There was a king." And Mistress picked up the story from her book of how Alfred of Wessex was strong enough to stop the Vikings.

These were good stories with great battles and brave deeds, but Willy's interest waned when he found there were no knights riding chargers. The Vikings didn't have enough room in their longboats to bring horses. And Alfred's men fought without heavy armor or horses. The stories about King Arthur were a lot better. King Arthur and Sir Lancelot defeated the enemies of Camelot in battles and tournaments. The Knights of the Round Table even saved fair maidens from dragons and lived happily ever after.

Willy tried to remember every detail so he could pretend with his own knight and horse. Already he'd won some fine battles and saved the kingdom at least twice. The monsters under his bed didn't bother him quite as much, either, unless it was very late at night and the fire burned low in the fireplace.

Mistress also loved to read about the New World. Willy found it difficult to imagine any place where there were no cities, just endless forests where dragons and unicorns roamed. A creature that looked like a huge bear, but had no head, lived there too. Its eyes, nose, and mouth were on its chest, and it had a roar that scared all the animals for miles around. The people who lived there had red skin and dressed in animal skins and feathers.

"How do they keep warm?"

"They buy nice woolen blankets from English merchants."

"Really?"

"Yes, really."

"Feathers?"

"I have it on the best authority."

"Oh."

Once Mistress read of people who had huge feet. When the sun shone too hot, they lay down on their backs and held their feet over themselves to provide shade.

Willy looked at Mistress in disbelief.

"I'm just reading the story. It says they live in Patagonia."

"Pat—a—"

"Patagonia. That's part of the New World."

Winter could not last forever, and by the end of March the days were noticeably longer. The storms became less fierce, and the sun melted the ice around the puddles. The first green grasses appeared on the commons. Colts and calves wobbled behind their mothers. Ducklings and goslings waddled after their mums to the pond. Button disappeared for several weeks. When she returned, she carried a mewing kitten in her mouth. Soon there were five kittens crawling on Willy's blanket. Mistress said the kittens might stay by his bed until they were old enough to go outdoors.

Green leaves appeared on the trees. On Mistress's tree the leaves hung in round bunches at the ends of the trimmed branches. Each branch looked like an outstretched arm with a bouquet of leaves grasped in its fist. Woolly caterpillars inched into the garden. Willy let them crawl over his hands and up his arms. He put some in his pocket to play with later. Mistress made very sure he emptied his pockets himself after that.

If Mistress didn't like caterpillars very much, she positively declared war on snails. In her herb garden and small rockery she found twenty-three one spring evening. Already they had eaten some of her flowers, leaving only bare, chewed, and very short stalks where there had been blossoms. It didn't seem possible that the snails could do so much damage in one night. Willy examined one closely and couldn't find its mouth at all. Mistress took all the snails she found to the commons pond. She said with a grim smile, "The frogs will eat them."

Then the cottage was fixed up. The workmen brought their tools, and Willy helped them all. A glazier reset some loose windowpanes. The plasterer, a taciturn man, smoothed a wall so it could be painted. Willy wondered how the wet plaster stuck. He gave it an experimental poke and made some small indentations in the finished wall. The plasterer smoothed the wall again and warned Willy away with a stern look. The carpenter took his turn and mended the fence.

The fence had been a great source of embarrassment to Peter all winter because the rails he and Hal had removed lay where everyone could see them and ask why they had been taken down. Mistress made Peter tell the story of the fence jumping several times. He had secretly tried to repair the fence, but the rails wouldn't stay up.

Finally, the painter came to paint the outside of the cottage and the fence. The painter was the most fun. He didn't mind that Willy touched the fresh paint to test it. With a flick of his big brush, the fingerprints disappeared. When Mistress would have made Willy go away, the painter tut-tutted, saying he had four boys of his own and fingerprints all over his house.

"How very droll," Mistress said. "Nevertheless, I want no fingermarks on my wall."

The painter let Willy help paint the fence. Mistress rushed out of the cottage with a canvas apron for Willy and lighter cloth covers for her precious roses. She'd learned from previous springtimes that painters not only painted what they were supposed to, but they also painted everything else around them with splatters.

Small birds returned to build nests in the thatched roof of the cottage. Each morning their songs awakened those within. The birds flew down to the garden, rested for a moment on the rosebushes, then darted back into the air. Soon hatchlings climbed to the roof and tried their wings.

Rodgers continued to visit rather more frequently than was absolutely necessary. Urged on by Master Perry and Cook, he trekked across London every two or three weeks. During these walks he tried to figure out what it was about Willy that had drawn so many to him. A number of foundlings had been taken into the Perry home, but none of the others had affected its residents so strongly. Perhaps, thought Rodgers, James still misses Daniel. And Cook? He smiled. She had certainly become one of Willy's admirers. She said it was because the sprout ate whatever she fixed and never whined over foods he did not like. According to Cook, there wasn't anything Willy wouldn't eat.

And why did he enjoy seeing Willy, he asked himself. Was it the sight of a little boy jumping up and down in excitement? Or maybe the impetuous hug around the legs? Perhaps it seemed Willy was a happier version of another boy long since a man. Perhaps he just wanted one foundling to have a happy life.

Rodgers recalled his own confusion and loneliness when he had been passed from household to household with never a chance to form any lasting ties. He had not had a Master Perry or Cook to take an interest in him. No, after his christening, he had been sent to a series of nurses. The last one at Ware had taken in more children than she could care for. There had never been enough to eat.

THE FOUNDLING

Rodgers remembered hungry days and cold nights. Only when the parish sent representatives to check on them had the children been tidied up and fed well. If the vestryman gave each child a penny, as occasionally he did, the nurse took each one as soon as the visitor disappeared around the first bend in the road.

Yet Rodgers did not think of those days as bad. All the children were treated the same, and though many died soon after arriving, that was simply the way life—or death—was. He'd been fed and clothed and given a place to stay.

When he reached the age of eleven, the vestry apprenticed him to a shoemaker for twelve years. Too young to begin learning the trade, he had quickly learned that his master really wanted a servant to sweep his shop and keep the fire going. The shoemaker's wife made him beat carpets and fetch water. He had slept on a pile of rags by the stove.

His good fortune began when the parish vicar persuaded his master to send him to school for a couple of hours each week. Rodgers supposed the vicar did want to teach him to read and cipher, but the lessons were also a way for him to add a bit extra to his inadequate stipend. It didn't matter, because Rodgers learned his letters, read every book he found or could borrow, and soon was better educated than his master.

Eventually, Rodgers learned how to purchase leather for his master. His ability to strike shrewd bargains caught the eye of a young merchant, but Rodgers's master would not release his valuable apprentice from his indenture. Finally, James Perry offered to purchase the remainder of his apprenticeship for an annuity of five pounds until Rodgers was twenty-three and his apprenticeship legally ended.

And he had flourished. Perry introduced him to the broader world of the merchant and to a much greater world, that of friendship. Rodgers had never had a close friend—no, more correctly—he'd never allowed himself any friendships until he met James. Perhaps it was that closeness he wanted to give Willy, to keep him from the loneliness of his own life. Whatever the reasons for his growing affections for the boy, Rodgers was afraid. What if

Willy outgrew him? Maybe those hugs around his legs that nearly threw him to the floor would stop. Rodgers winced.

He turned into Mistress Bessie's garden. Yes, there was Willy watching from the window. Before he could rap on the door, it flew open and Willy dragged him inside. After delivering Cook's treat and exchanging pleasantries with Mistress, Willy and Rodgers decided on a walk.

"Then you must wear a jumper," said Mistress.

"It's warm out."

"Don't argue. Put one on or you cannot go out walking."

"I'll see to it." Rodgers herded Willy to the bedroom. Willy selected a blue jumper that Mistress had knitted for him.

"What's this?" Rodgers picked up a green ribbon that fell from the wardrobe.

Willy pulled the jumper over his head and looked up. "That's just an old ribbon," he said.

"It doesn't look very old to me. Is it Mistress Bessie's?"

"No, it's mine. But, I don't like it." Willy pushed first one arm then another through the sleeves of his jumper.

"Don't you like the color?" Rodgers pulled the ribbon through his fingers.

"I just don't like it."

"Oh. I think it's very pretty. Did Mistress give it to you?"

"That man bought it for me. The man who helped me with my shoes. In the big house." Willy's arms described a large square. "He sent me away."

"Master Perry?"

Willy shrugged. "He bought it in a store full of flowers that weren't real."

"Oh, yes." Rodgers ushered Willy out the door. "It was Master Perry." Rodgers still held the ribbon.

Willy reached up and took it. "It's mine."

"I thought you didn't like it."

"I'm going to give it to Mummy someday."

"You really should take better care not to soil it, then." Rodgers pointed to the dangling ribbon. "You won't want to give anyone a ribbon you've dragged in the dirt."

Willy hung the ribbon around his neck and twirled the ends with his fingers. He followed Rodgers into the lane.

"Would you like me to put it in my pocket?"

Willy pulled the ribbon from his neck and wound it around his hand so he could put it in his own pocket.

They walked into the village. The leaves of the trees rustled above them, and the flowers nodded as they walked by. They passed a dog lying on his side, asleep in the warm sun. Farther on, a tortoiseshell cat sat on a window ledge cleaning her face. She stopped and watched Willy and Rodgers walk by.

"Pretty moggy," said Rodgers.

"Button is prettier, and she cleans her face all the time. She sleeps on my bed."

"She must like you a lot."

Willy nodded emphatically. "She does. She plays with me, and sometimes I give her treats. Did you know she likes to lick the butter off bread? Mistress lets me give her little pieces from my breakfast, and Button licks the butter right off."

"She doesn't eat the bread?"

"No, I have to pick that up."

A few moments later Rodgers stopped in front of a small shop. "Would you like a sweet?"

"Really?"

"Let's go in and see what we might like."

It took several minutes for Willy to choose two pieces of gingerbread with candied orange peel baked right in. He and Rodgers left the shop and found a dry spot under an oak tree. They ate in silence, careful not to let any crumbs fall.

"My, that was good." Rodgers leaned against the tree and licked his fingers clean. Then he reached out and pulled Willy closer.

Willy rubbed his sticky fingers on his breeches. "Do you like me?" he asked.

"Why, yes, very much. Why do you ask?"

"You bought me gingerbread the same way I give Button bread and butter. I love Button."

"Really?"

"And Cook sends me cakes."

"Cook likes you too."

Willy took the ribbon from his pocket and pulled it out straight. "Does Master Perry like me?"

Rodgers looked down in surprise. When he saw the ribbon, he said, "Yes, he does. I'm sure that's why he bought you the ribbon."

"Oh." Willy put the ribbon across his knees. "I want to give it to Mummy because I still love her." He tried to press some of the creases flat with his fingers.

"Would you like me to show you a way to keep it clean and nice?"

Willy handed the ribbon to Rodgers, who wrapped one end around his finger to start a roll. When he finished, he pulled a short piece of wool from the seam of his coat and tied it around the roll. "Now you can stick this in your pocket and keep it nice."

Willy stood up and put the ribbon back in his pocket. He patted it in place. "It's safe now," he said.

"And don't forget," Rodgers went on, "how much Master Perry likes you. He likes you so much that he sent you to Mistress Bessie because she could take care of you better than anyone. He sends you clothes as well."

"You bring me toys."

"Yes."

"And you come to see me and play games."

"Yes. And a fine time we have too."

Willy stood in front of Rodgers; his gaze never wavered. "Do you love me?"

Rodgers hesitated for the shortest second, then he opened his arms.

Willy fell against his chest, put his arms around the man's neck, and rested his head on his shoulder.

Rodgers hugged Willy tight, and tighter still.

They were both surprised when Willy squeaked.

Chapter 16

April 1645

Gillian patted the neat pile of folded clothing on Mistress Perry's dressing table. A job well done she thought, but, oh I am tired. She yawned and stretched, swinging her arms out and back. "Ahhh." She pressed her fingers into the small of her back.

"Gillian?"

"Yes, mum?" She turned and dropped a quick curtsey.

"Are you quite finished? Yes, I see you are." Mistress Perry rested her fingers on the folded clothes. "What do you think, my dear? Can I be ready by seven o'clock?"

"Ready, mum?"

"Yes. Master Perry and I are meeting friends at the theater and dining with them afterward." Mistress smiled at Gillian's expression. "Well?" she prompted. "Can we do it?"

"Oh, mum, yes, mum. Of course we can. Oh my, what a surprise; you're going into society again. Pardon my saying so, mum, but you've stayed away much too long, though I understand and all—" She flew from wardrobe to chest to jewel box before coming to rest in the middle of the room. "I'll come and help you with your hair—" She ran out of the room and right back in. "A bath, mum? Yes? I'll see to it." And she ran out again.

"Well, I just don't believe it. Going to the theater?" Cook pulled two leather buckets from a corner closet. "See that the fire is properly laid under the large cauldron." She thought for a moment. "It's good, very good. Mistress should be getting out again. I wonder what brought this about." Cook stirred a stew to keep it from scorching, tapped the wooden spoon on the lip of the pot, and set it aside.

Gillian ran back into the kitchen. "Cook, where's the lavender? I want to sprinkle some in the bath."

She followed Cook to a small locked cabinet. "Isn't it just wonderful? Mistress leaving the house after all this time? Just let me have the packet. I'll bring back what we don't use." Gillian held out her hand.

"This packet must last until the lavender blooms again. You may have this much." Cook poured some of the dried blossoms into a small cup. "The bath will smell sweet enough."

"But this is special! Everything must be perfect. Let me have some more, please." Gillian checked the contents of the cup. "A bit more?" She smiled her brightest. "Please? For Mistress?"

Cook shook a few more blossoms into the cup. "That will have to do. Now off with you."

"Thank you, Cook." Gillian ran down the hall, up the stairs, and into Mistress's room. She pulled the bathtub from its closet and pushed it close to the hearth. She poured the lavender in and ran downstairs to check the heating water.

The fire crackled and wrapped itself around the bottom of the cauldron. Gillian dabbled her fingers in the water. Only warm. Time enough to dash to the linen closets for washing flannels and towels.

Soap! It too smelled of lavender. If I'd only known earlier, thought Gillian, I'd have wrapped her towels around the soap so they'd smell good too. She dropped the soap into her apron pocket and ran to the laundry room. Little bubbles were forming on the inside of the cauldron. Not quite hot enough. She couldn't get any more wood under the cauldron, so she took the flannels, towels, and soap upstairs and put them on a small table beside the bath. What else? What else does a lady need? A ribbon to tie up her hair. Gillian laid a blue ribbon in pretty coils next to the soap.

"Gillian? Is the water warm yet?"

"I'm going to check this moment, mum." Gillian curtseyed towards the door of Mistress's dressing room and ran to fetch the water. Six trips and twelve buckets of water later, she called to Mistress Perry, "I'll fetch some cold water should you find your bath too hot."

Gillian caught her reflection in a mirror. What a fright! She pushed her hair back under her cap and dipped a corner of her apron in the bath to wipe her face and hands clean. She'd get a fresh apron before she brought the cold water up. After all, a lady's maid should look, well, like a lady's maid. Her cheeks were flushed and her hands red, but the bath smelled sweet and everything was laid out so prettily. She left for the last two buckets of water.

Marie met her outside the laundry room.

"Bath time, eh?"

"Oh, yes. Master and Mistress are going to the theater. I'm so excited, I hardly know which way to go first. It's been so long since Mistress needed me to help her dress for an evening out. Excuse me, she may need this cold water for her bath."

Marie took in the clean apron and Gillian's excitement. "Don't forget to clean the laundry room."

"I'll be down as soon as Mistress is ready."

"Oh, and Rodgers won't be here to help you empty the bath. You'll have to do all the tidying up yourself."

Gillian's spirit would not be dampened. "That's all right," she called over her shoulder. "I really don't mind at all."

Marie stepped into the laundry room. Gillian's dirty apron lay on the floor. There was water splashed everywhere. The fireplace needed cleaning out and more wood brought in to replace what had been used. Marie smiled and thought Gillian wouldn't be quite so congenial after she'd cleaned this up. Could she keep Rodgers busy so he wouldn't be able to help empty the bath?

"It was quite a surprise when she wanted to go out. I mean, Rodgers, I'd asked her before, but she was not interested."

"Your shirt, James."

Master Perry pushed his arm into a sleeve, shaking out its folds. "I confess, I'm a bit nervous and eager at the same time. I hope it won't be too much for her."

"I've called for your carriage. There will be hot bricks at your feet and lap rugs. You'll be as comfortable as we can make you. Your cravat—"

"More trouble than they're worth, don't you think? I don't suppose I could just forget it?"

"Not really."

"I thought not. Certainly women have no article of clothing as uncomfortable. There, that should do it."

"Waistcoat . . . and coat." Rodgers patted the shoulders into place. "I hope tonight goes well. By the way, what play will you be attending?"

"I never asked, but George—you remember him, he deals in India cotton—does find the best entertainment, so I'm sure we'll have a good evening."

"I heard that his country house was overrun by some of the King's army."

"It was. George says he'd have lost a great deal if it hadn't been for his steward. The man grabbed a musket and held the soldiers at bay. Not soldiers, really. Looters. His tenants stood shoulder to shoulder as well. Some of his fields were trampled and cottages set afire, but his house was saved and no lives were lost. Of course, everyone hurrahed for the King . . . "

"But they're not Royalists—"

"Not a bit. When one faces part of the King's army, however . . . There, how do I look?" James Perry lowered his brush.

"Really, quite dashing. All the ladies will want your attention."

"Perhaps, but it is Amelia I wish to please." Perry drew a deep breath. "Let's go meet my wife."

Movement at the head of the stairs caught Rodgers's eye as he and Master Perry went to the sitting room. Gillian mouthed the words "Are you ready?" With a wave and a grin, Rodgers nodded and went on.

Gillian flew back to Mistress Perry. "He's waiting in the sitting room . . . Oh, mum, you do look ever so lovely. I wouldn't have thought the green would flatter you so."

"Thank you, Gillian. And, I must say, you've done very well this evening. Please fetch the small red casket from the table. Yes, that one. Mr. Perry gave me these as a wedding gift." She opened the box.

"How beautiful! The stones are the exact color of your dress." Gillian fastened the clasp of the necklace and stepped back to admire. "You look like a queen."

Amelia Perry smiled at her reflection. "Perhaps you exaggerate a bit. But this is a special evening and I want to look my best."

"Your cloak, mum."

"You needn't wait up, Gillian."

"Thank you, mum, but please ring if you need me."

"Let's go down and meet Master Perry."

Long after the Perrys had left, Gillian wiped the last drop of water from the bathtub and straightened to relieve her back. She glanced around Mistress's chamber again. All had been cleaned and tidied.

"Gillian? Ready to move the tub back? If you'll open the closet, I believe I can get it in." Rodgers tipped and rocked the tub across the floor. "How ever," he asked, "did you drag it out and all the way to the fireplace?"

"I don't know, really. I guess I was so excited about Mistress going out, that I never thought about it." Gillian closed the closet.

My hands look awful, she thought. And my shoulders and knees are as sore as my hands are red. And there's still the laundry room to tidy. She sagged against the closet.

"We did good work tonight."

Gillian tried to focus on Rodgers. "What? Oh, yes, we did." She smiled, recalling the Perrys' meeting in the small parlor. "It was rather like sending two young people off on their first formal outing, wasn't it? I am so nervous for them."

"Mistress Perry looked beautiful."

"And the Master, dashing." Gillian blushed. "I'd like Joseph to look at me like that someday."

Rodgers nearly laughed at the prospect of any young swain smiling at the tired, damp girl before him. He caught himself. She'd worked much too hard to be laughed at. Instead he smiled gravely. "I'm sure he, or someone else, will, Gillian."

"Not in my present state." She looked in the mirror. "I look shattered. I'll never be rested again. Look at these hands!" She waggled her fingers at him. "Still, it was worth every effort, wasn't it?"

"You've done well this evening." Rodgers bowed in recognition of her efforts. "Now if you have nothing else for me to do?"

Gillian stood rooted to the floor as Rodgers's footsteps faded on the stairs. He bowed to me! Her jaw dropped. To me! He thinks I did well! She ran to the door. "Thank you! Thank you for helping me!"

Gillian went down to the laundry room. Water covered the floor and bits of wood lay scattered about. How awful it looked. I hate this room, she thought. And I'm so tired. Still, there was Mistress Perry's praise and the kind words from Rodgers. Gillian smiled. It had been worth all the extra effort. But I am going to be more tidy next time, she promised herself as she sank to her knees. She wrung her rag out. I can do something right. I can be a lady's maid—

"Don't miss that bit over there." It was Marie.

"Of course not." Gillian dropped her rag on a small spot and hoped Marie wouldn't stay long.

"Look at me when I speak to you."

Surprised, Gillian sat back on her heels and looked up.

"You think you're someone special after all of Mistress's compliments. Mind yourself. Don't think you'll be getting out of the real work around here."

Gillian looked around her. The laundry room was the worst of all places to work as far as she was concerned. She opened her mouth to say so, but Marie cut her off.

"I guess you couldn't get Rodgers to help you with the laundry room. I'm surprised he helped you at all."

"He offered to help. I never asked him."

"He's much too important around here to help the drudges." Marie leaned against the doorway. She looked as though she'd hardly turned a finger all day. "Remember your place." She whirled away.

She's jealous of me! Gillian shook her head. How could that be? She crawled to the last wet spot on the floor. And getting meaner by the day. We used to have some fun together. Now I can't do anything to please her. What happened?

Gillian emptied the ashes from under the cauldron into a barrel kept by the back door. Cook would use them to make soap. From where she stood, Gillian could see Marie's silhouette in her bedroom window. She was bent over, looking at something in her hand. Gillian propped the ash shovel against the barrel and dusted off her hands. When she looked at Marie's window again, the light was out. I'm not going to bother about her tonight, she thought. I'm going to bed!

part 2

The Scullery Boy

Chapter 1

August 1652–September 1653

Eight years! He had lived with her more than half his life. The low mound of dirt at his feet was all that remained of his life with Mistress Bessie. Will clenched his teeth and swallowed hard. I can't cry, he thought. I'm twelve and a half, nearly a grown man.

"Will, it's time to collect your belongings."

"I want to stay." He shrugged Rodgers's hand off his shoulder.

"Will—"

"No, I want to stay." He pushed his fists deeper into his pockets and turned away.

"We must get you settled." Rodgers put his hands in his pockets. "The Vicar says you may stay with his family."

A clod of dirt rolled from the low mound. The sun-dried clay fell to powder under Will's prodding toe. He remembered trotting off with Peter to the Vicar's school, eager to learn to read for himself all the stories he had heard from Mistress. For a moment he saw the scholars arranged on benches reciting their lessons. He had been the smallest. The Vicar had lifted him to his place and begun. Will had run home that day to recite his first lesson. Mistress had been as pleased as he had. A smile tugged at the corners of Will's mouth; a tear splashed on the dust at his feet.

The flowers on the grave wilted in the warm sun. Perhaps he should get a cup of water for them; they would stay fresh longer. He and Rodgers had cut the roses from Mistress's own garden, then wrapped the bouquet in paper and tied it with his own green ribbon. The blossoms smelled as though all the warmth of summer had been gathered into them.

Will bent over and touched what had been the most beautiful of the blossoms. Its deep red petals were edged with brown. His fingers rested on the green ribbon. After a moment, he untied the bow and pulled the ribbon free. He wound it into a spool, smoothing the wrinkles as he went, and put it into the small pouch Mistress had made for him when he was a little boy.

Just two days ago Mistress had packed Peter's chest for his first term at Cambridge University. She had written the trustees of Peter's estate and demanded more money for better clothes. Her boy would not go dressed in coarse cloth when fine, soft wool was available. His shirts were to be made of cambric, not rough kersey. No canvas for his coat, but a heavy wool with a matching scarf. She checked each ell of material for flaws, hovered over the tailor to judge each cut and stitch, and harassed the cobbler to assure comfortable shoes and boots for Peter. Twice she returned garments because of work she considered poorly done. Then she chose sheets, blankets, and bolsters for his bed.

When all was packed, she purchased fine black wool for Peter's academic robes. Here Peter balked. He decided to take the material and have the robes made in Cambridge. He was tired of standing to be measured, standing to be fitted, and standing to be jabbed by tailors who were trying to please the sharp tongue and pointing finger of Mistress Bessie.

Yesterday Peter had left with all the clothes any son of a middle-class landowner might need. Resting at his side was a hamper of food for his journey; a letter of credit was in his pocket. Mistress had hugged him and kissed both his cheeks. Will gave him a manly handshake before the carriage rattled away.

During the walk home, Will had noticed that Mistress was tired and that she was not walking at her usual brisk pace. He asked if she missed Peter already. Yes, she did; he was like her own son. But it was time for him to prepare to take his rightful place in the world, she said. To do that, he needed to study law so he could govern his own holdings wisely. "Peter's estate may not be very grand, but he has great opportunity to do well. And he can't do that still bound by my apron strings." She had blinked rapidly and sniffed delicately into her handkerchief, then put her hand on Will's shoulder to help her walk.

When they reached the cottage she said, "Tomorrow we'll work in the garden, but now I must clean up. Packing always leaves such a mess." And she went for her apron and broom.

Part 2: The Scullery Boy

Will had gone to the garden to find Ginger and Mustache. Both cats had inherited the fine mousing abilities of their mother and had taken up her crusade against local squirrels and field mice. Ginger had the same color as Button but was very thin no matter how much she ate. Mustache looked a great deal like the gray tomcat down the road. But instead of being all gray he had a white patch on either side of his nose. He was also a fighter. Both of his ears looked like flags tattered and frayed after a bad storm.

Will sat and leaned against the fence so he could give the cats a good scratch behind their ears, down their necks, and under their chins. He was leaning against the section of fence Peter and Hal had torn down. What would the men at Cambridge think if they knew about Peter's escapade?

Ginger went looking for an afternoon snack, and Mustache nudged Will's hand for more scratching. "Now it will be my job to mow the grass and lop the branches on the bushes near the road," Will said to the cat. "Already they grow faster than I can cut them back. And there are repairs that should be done in the cottage before the autumn rains. Mistress should begin buying wood and coal for the cold weather too. Prices are lower now than they will be in October and November." Will nodded to himself. Yes, he must mention these things to Mistress.

Mistress came around the cottage, carrying her twine and pruning shears and dragging a rake and hoe.

"I've done as much as I care to in the cottage. We can walk through the place without stumbling over packing boxes and trunks. Who'd have thought there would be some left over? I decided I wanted to be outside in the garden. It's such a beautiful afternoon."

Will stood slowly, stretching his muscles. He carried the twine and rake while Mistress pruned her roses.

"Look at this one." She cupped the bloom in her hands. Will looked and nodded. It was beautiful.

"Better tie this to the stake. All those buds are just ready to pop open." She moved on, puffing from exertion. "One more, over there." She pointed to her trailing roses. "Next year they just might drape all the way over the front door. Won't that be pretty?"

"They smell good too." Will had handed her a length of twine. "I'll rake up the branches."

"Take the twine and bundle them. They'll be good kindling when they're dry." Mistress had stretched to tie the last branch in place.

Later that afternoon, Will had read to Mistress. He read well and seldom had to spell a word so she could tell him what it was. She sat with the late summer sun lighting the knitting in her hands. Eventually, she rested her work in her lap and put her head back. Will hesitated.

"Go on, go on. I can't imagine why I'm so tired, but let's have the end of the story."

He had read on, looking up occasionally. Each time Mistress nodded for him to continue. Twenty minutes later, Will set aside Robert Ingram's description of the New World. Ingram made Virginia sound like a fairy tale. Everyone knew there were many other more accurate accounts of Virginia. Captain John Smith's tracts told how difficult it was to live there because of disease, rebellion of the settlers, and attacks from the Indians. Still, he and Mistress thought it would be nice if there really were gold nuggets lying around to be picked up and people wearing necklaces of perfect pearls.

"Mistress."

She frequently fell asleep now when he read to her, so Will put the book aside and tiptoed past. She still hadn't stirred when he went outside. He and his friend Jack wandered to the village and returned, watching farmers coming from their fields in the late evening sunshine.

Then Jack's mother had called him in. Will called goodbye over his shoulder and ran into his own parlor, slamming the door behind him. Mistress was still in her chair, head back, eyes closed. She never stirred.

"Mistress?" He shook her gently. She didn't waken. Her hands were cool.

"Mistress?" Will stepped back. She wasn't breathing. He ran to Jack's house.

Jack's father had set off at once. He notified Master Perry, who had arranged Mistress's funeral.

And now it's over, thought Will. Just one day . . . it happened so quickly. I wasn't even with her.

Will stood by her grave, not quite able to believe. If he went home to the cottage, he was sure he'd find Mistress sweeping the kitchen or tending her roses, just as he and she had tended them yesterday.

"I have to go home," he said.

"You must stay with the Vicar for now," said Rodgers. "The vestry will decide very soon what's to happen, where you'll go next. Another nurse—"

"I don't want another nurse."

"For the moment you'll stay with the Vicar."

"Can I stay with you instead?" His question hung in the air. He felt a hand rest lightly on his shoulder and pull him a bit closer.

Rodgers spoke so quietly that Will could hardly hear. "No. I'm sorry, Will. That's not possible."

Chapter 2

Will followed the Vicar. They passed Hal's house. Hal didn't live there anymore; he'd been apprenticed to a cobbler just a few weeks before Peter left for the university. The walls of the cottage needed whitening, and much of the roof wanted rethatching. The open shutters let breezes move easily in and out of the unglazed windows. The cottage looked the same as it always had, and that offended Will. It should somehow look different, be in mourning with him.

He pressed his lips together and stared at the dusty road. Even the carriage ruts and mudholes looked familiar. He wanted to kick every stone from its quiet rest in the sun and break down the edges of the cart tracks so they wouldn't remind him of yesterday, saying goodbye to Peter, working in the garden with Mistress, reading to her, finding her so still in her favorite chair.

Then they passed Mistress's cottage. Will almost expected to see her in the garden, or see smoke from the kitchen fire where she was preparing supper. Instead he saw closed shutters and a lock on the door. Still it looked perfect, sitting under the trees. The whitewash on the walls was bright against the dark wooden beams. The garden walk was swept and the roses well tended. But when Will would have turned into the lane to the cottage, the Vicar kept walking.

Will felt lost—confused and lost. How could Mistress have left him? Didn't she care? As soon as he asked the question, Will knew Mistress cared. He may not have been her favorite, like Peter, but he was the one who had sat on her lap when she read. He and Mistress liked the same kinds of stories. Peter never sat still long enough to hear them. She had taught him how to take care of the roses. Peter was never interested in them. At least he didn't like to spend a lot of time tending them.

THE FOUNDLING

The roses. Will recalled the bouquet on the grave. He shook thoughts of the funeral service from his head. He wanted to think of the days Mistress, Peter, and he had lived and worked together.

When Peter had grown big enough, he'd had to paint the fence and whitewash the cottage. Peter was no happier about that than Will was pleased with his new job as window washer. They discovered there was no rushing through the work because Mistress hovered over them, directing and correcting. In the meantime, she cleaned the inside, top to bottom. Every spring the three of them spent two or three days refurbishing the cottage. When they were finished, they'd go into the lane and stand looking at their handiwork, one of the prettiest cottages north of the London wall.

Button had always brought a litter of kittens home in the spring. It took them days to think of good names for all of them. Ginger and Mustache would probably go to Jack's house to live. His brothers and sisters would keep them scratched and petted. They'd buried old Button last winter under the wallflowers. She was a good cat, Will thought. A fine mouser.

He wanted to keep these pictures clear in his mind forever, so he thought about them a lot, going over every detail.

The Vicar called back to him without ever turning his head, "Step along, Will. I must be back in time for evensong."

Will hurried a few steps. Where were they? They had passed the parish church where he and Peter had gone for their lessons. "I thought you lived back by the parish church. Where are we going?" Will asked.

Vicar Richards drew himself up. "I've received another parish, and a fine one it is, I might add. The parish house is much larger, and I now live as befits my station as an educated man."

"Who is the Vicar for the old church?"

"Why, I am, of course." The Vicar sounded surprised. "Many men hold more than one pulpit. It's one of the few ways we can get a living income. My family might soon have starved on the income from the old church. No one paid his tithes. If it hadn't been for the fees my parishioners had to pay me, and fees from my scholars, my family would have lived in rags and begged in the streets."

Part 2: The Scullery Boy

Will thought that the Vicar's family had always looked rather well off. His daughter had ribbons for her hair, and his sons wore shoes with buckles. "Well, who will preach in the old church?" Certainly no one would want the living if it were so poorly endowed.

"I will, of course, whenever I can get away from my new duties. That won't be every week. I'm afraid my new parish will require a great deal of my time. The folks there pay their tithes, and some of them are quite wealthy. But I shall serve as needed, or hire a curate to lead services in the old church."

They walked on. The setting sun cast a golden light over the fields and houses. Finally, the Vicar stopped. "Here we are. Lovely house, isn't it?" He admired his good fortune for a moment. "I am willing for you to stay here as I told the vestry. Mr. Perry seemed agreeable to the arrangement as well. But you no longer come to me solely as a student. While you are here, you must earn your way because I'm receiving little enough to feed and clothe you.

"Therefore, you will make yourself useful in the kitchen and quickly undertake any task given you by any member of the household. You will eat with the servants, and you are not to be in the front rooms of the vicarage unless you are sent on an errand or called for. Is this understood?" Vicar Richards raised his eyebrows.

"Yes."

"See that you don't forget. And remember that you are not to use the front entrance. That is only for my family and guests." He thought for a moment. "Oh, and Will, you are not to play with my children or be seen with them."

"Yes, sir."

"Obey the rules; keep your station. I shall try to teach you what Master Perry and Mistress Bessie never did; to keep your place and to do as you are told. You are indeed fortunate to have someone take an interest in you at all. Whether you are allowed to stay or not depends upon you. Now, go introduce yourself to the housekeeper."

The Vicar opened the gate and, without another glance at Will, crossed his garden and entered the house. Will watched until the door closed, then he followed the fence to the back.

"You, boy, come along." The housekeeper motioned to him.

THE FOUNDLING

He entered the hot kitchen and stood waiting. "We have plenty to keep you busy. The Vicar keeps an open house, and we are always in need of help." She considered Will and shook her head. "Well, one must make do. Cook is at the market. Be sure the kitchen is tidied before she returns."

The housekeeper paused. "Take the broom to the floor now, but a good scrubbing is in order before you go to bed. Cook will tell you the rest of your duties. Oh yes, you may call me Mistress Butterfield, but do not speak unless you are spoken to."

She walked over to a low doorway and opened the door. "Here is where you'll sleep. I've had fresh straw and a blanket put down. You'll receive half a candle each week. There are hooks for your clothes. Cook has already received instructions about your diet."

Will walked into his room. He could reach up and touch the ceiling. When he stretched his arms out, his fingers touched the walls. In the light from the kitchen he saw that he hadn't even a pallet, just loose straw. But it was clean and dry.

"Boy!"

Will stepped out to face Mistress Butterfield.

"Your position as a member of this household is scullery boy. Remember what you are and that the Vicar is good enough to put a roof over your head and we'll have no difficulty. Now get to work. Cook will be returning soon enough."

Will found the broom. While he swept, he thought of the times he'd helped Mistress tidy her kitchen. He swept the dust from each corner and under the cabinets. She said you could always tell a cook by her kitchen: cabinets dusted, each pot scoured clean and put in its place, the floor clean. He pretended he was cleaning for Mistress Bessie. She would be proud of the work he did. Will straightened the chairs around the table. Then he sat and waited for Cook to return.

That night, Will lay on the straw, hugging his blanket. He was cold and the straw poked him. He reached out to open his door to let some warmth from the kitchen in. His hands hurt when they touched the rough wooden door. Cook had made him scour every pot with sand. Only after he was finished had she given him his supper. Finally the warmth of the kitchen reached him, and he fell asleep.

"But it's time for my lessons!"

"You're my scullery boy!" Cook's voice got louder.

"I've finished all the work you gave me!"

"I'll say when you've finished. Now go out and pull the weeds from the herb garden. You do know the difference between weeds and herbs?"

"I'm supposed to go to my lessons. I always went when I lived with Mistress Bessie. You just ask the Vicar."

"Well, the Vicar isn't around now, is he?" Cook caught Will by the arm and marched him out of the kitchen and into the herb garden.

"When you've finished, there's coal to be carried."

"The Vicar will be angry with you."

Cook stepped back into the kitchen. "He'll never miss you."

A porter brought Will's clothes that afternoon, but Will found only one shirt, a pair of breeches, a nightshirt, and some underclothes hanging from the pegs in his cubby.

"Where are my clothes?" he asked Cook.

"Don't shout." She kept kneading. "Mistress Richards gave you what you need, and she'll give the rest to the needy. Most of what you had was too good for a scullery boy."

"Where's my jumper? I'll need my jumper. Mistress Bessie knit it for me. I'll need it when it's cold. And, where's my shawl? That was my mother's shawl."

"You'll have what you need. Mistress Richards is very generous. I don't know about the shawl."

Will pointed towards his cubby. "Those are my worst clothes. They don't even fit me."

"Since you'll be doing the worst work around here, those clothes are just what you need."

"I'll tell Rodgers when he comes to visit."

"I don't know who this Rodgers is, but we're so far from London, no one will have the time to visit you."

THE FOUNDLING

"He's my best friend. He visited me all the time at Mistress Bessie's."

"This isn't Mistress Bessie's, and your playmates aren't welcome here. Especially if they come when you have work to do."

"Rodgers isn't a mate. He's a grown man who likes me."

"Really? I doubt you'll ever see him again. He probably thinks he's well rid of the likes of you."

"He will come! He gave me my top and my horse and knight."

"Those old toys? Falling apart, they were. And the top was all chipped. Your Rodgers couldn't have cared too much for you if that's what he gave you." Cook nodded towards the fire. "We found them and burned them."

"They were mine! You had no right!" Will's breath came in short, hard gasps. "You had no right!"

"No right?" Cook wiped the flour from her hands. "The likes of you has only what he's allowed to have. You've your own cubby, a bit of straw, food, and clothing. You even get a bit of candle. That's what you have a right to. And generous at that." She reached for the broom. "Now you'd best stop whining and be about your tasks, or I'll lay this about your ribs and backside."

Will stood before Cook, trying to understand what she was saying. In the fireplace he thought he could see his horse and knight lying in the ashes. He looked back towards his cubby. He had nothing, nothing at all. Wait until I tell Rodgers, he thought. Rodgers will fix everything. Will shoved his hand into his pocket and closed his fist around the small pouch he always kept with him. No one will ever get this, he thought, no one.

"Why are you standing about?" asked Cook. "There's work to be done." She shook the broom at him.

Will clenched his teeth. He wasn't supposed to be a servant, a scullery boy. He ran for the kitchen door. Cook commanded him to stop, but he ran straight through the garden and out a gate in the garden wall. Long grasses and weeds pulled at his legs. He stumbled over rocks and bits of rotting harness and rusting tools until he finally fell. He never wanted to see Cook again, or Vicar Richards, either. Wait 'til he told Rodgers that his clothes and his mother's shawl had been taken from him. Wait 'til he told Rodgers that they'd burned his toys. "Just you wait," he muttered through his teeth. "You'll be sorry you took my things. The Vicar will be sorry he's not giving me my lessons."

He pushed himself up and pulled his shoe back on. He looked back towards the vicarage. No one had followed him, and he was glad he couldn't see the house. He wasn't going back, at least not right now.

Will surveyed his surroundings. The overgrown lane continued up a small hill and around a bend. On one side was a stone wall with fields beyond. On the other side were farm buildings and some cows and pigs in a pen. Deliberately he turned away from the vicarage and set off down the lane. By the time he'd climbed the second hill, Will decided he was like some of the people in his books who had gone to live in new countries. Just like them, he was exploring the new place where he would have to live.

He heard the rumble of traffic, the clink of harness, the creak of wheels, and the shouts of teamsters long before he reached the top of the last hill. The highway below was so busy, it seemed as if most of the world were coming and going before him. He ran down the hill to the road.

"Where are you going?" he shouted at a teamster.

"London, laddie. Mind the wheels!"

Will jumped back and looked down the road, but he couldn't see the walls of London. He shouted at several other travellers before one heard him.

"How far is it to London?"

" 'Bout five miles."

A long way. Will returned to the top of the hill and watched the traffic. Five miles. What if Rodgers couldn't come that far? I'll never get my clothes or my lessons, he thought. I'll always be a scullery boy and sleep in the cubby on a pile of straw.

His stomach grumbled. He didn't want to go back to the vicarage. He'd be in trouble for being gone all afternoon. But he had no other place to go. So he stood up, and with a last look at the dwindling traffic, he walked slowly back down the lane. He hoped Rodgers didn't think five miles was too far away for a visit.

Chapter 3

Will never did get his lessons. Nor did Rodgers visit. Whenever he could, Will walked down the road towards Mistress Bessie's and sat under an old oak tree to wait for Rodgers. Often Will took out the green ribbon and remembered when he had been a little boy and Rodgers had bought him gingerbread. They'd sat under a tree that day. Rodgers had rolled his ribbon just as Will was doing now. He'd come if he could, Will thought. It's just that he's busy, and the vicarage is a long way from London, five miles by the great road and who knows how long by way of the local roads and lanes.

Summer became autumn, and still Rodgers did not come. Will stopped going to the oak. Instead, he went to the hill overlooking the great London Road. There he sat and imagined where all the people were going. Those soldiers. Look at them, he thought. They've probably fought all over the world. They step out so bravely, their uniforms all clean and buttons polished. Each one a hero. He watched heavy wagons loaded with goods move slowly to and from London and thought it must be wonderful to be a drayman. What a feeling of power, to control the huge horses through the thin bands of leather. Occasionally, coaches of the wealthy, protected by outriders, rolled by.

Someday, if I don't become a soldier, I'll be rich, Will thought. Then I can do whatever I want, go wherever I please. He dismissed the beggars that moved with the traffic. They were always about, always a nuisance. He wondered why they didn't work so they wouldn't have to beg.

He stood up to leave.

"Say there! What's your name?"

Will turned to face four boys just about his own age.

"C'mon, what's your name?" The speaker had fiery red hair and lots of freckles. "I'm Harry. Here's Charles, this is John, and he's Edward. We're all named after kings." Harry's hand swept in front of each boy when he gave his name. " 'Course those aren't our real names. We took them to throw the constables off." Harry winked and grinned broadly. "If you know what I mean."

Will wasn't sure, so he just nodded.

"What's your name?" Edward shifted impatiently.

"Will."

"Want to come with us?" Harry asked.

"Where?"

"We're going to London," said John.

"It's five miles away."

"Not far, and when we get there, we'll have some fun."

The boys smiled and nodded at Harry's proclamation.

"What will you do?"

John spoke. "We'll get us something to eat and see if there isn't a rich man with a few extra coins in his purse."

"You going to work?"

"Never have to if you know how to move quickly enough." Harry laughed. "We do pretty well, we do. Want to come with us?"

"It's five miles away," Will said again.

"That's not far," Edward repeated. "We've already come a hundred at least."

"C'mon," Harry urged. "We'll have a good time."

"Where do you sleep?"

"We sleep rough. It's fun."

"Got cold last night," Charles said under his breath.

Will looked the quartet over. "You could stay here for a while, and we could have fun."

"Doing what?" Charles looked around without much hope. "There isn't even a market near here so we can get something to eat." He swung around to survey the countryside. "Can we eat with you?"

Will shook his head. "The Vicar won't let Cook feed beggars." He looked the boys over more closely. Their clothes were old and torn. Their faces were dirty too. Mistress Bessie wouldn't—

"We don't beg; we take what we need."

"Didn't work too well last night."

"Shut your gob, Charles." Harry turned back to Will. "Sometimes people don't want to help us. Like last night. So we took the bread and ran."

"Couldn't eat it 'til we'd run half the night," said Charles.

"Oh, give over." Harry shook his head. "He's always muttering about something."

"You steal?" Will's voice rose.

"Just what we need and only when no one will help us out."

"You're beggars and thieves?"

"Well . . . " Harry drew the word way out. "Not really. We only take what we need. We can always get more for you if you decide to come."

Will shook his head. "No, I've got to get back."

"Leave him, Harry. We've got to get to London." Edward started to back away.

Harry looked at Will again. "You're sure? It'll be a grand time."

"Here comes a wagon," Edward said. "Let's go. We can jump on the back and the driver will never know we're there." Edward ran to the road. The wagon rumbled past, and the other three ran with him to the wagon.

Harry waved once and shouted something that Will could not hear. A curve in the road took them from sight.

Will kicked at the clump of weeds. I could go to London if I wanted to. I could just wrap my clothes in my blanket, come right down to the road, and jump on a wagon myself. At that moment, five miles didn't seem so far. But it was too late to start today.

Cook met him at the door. "Late again! I'm getting cross!" She stood there with her hands on her hips. "Nothing for you to eat until you've finished carrying the coal."

Will carried the heavy scuttles up and down the stairs. The autumn nights were chilly.

"Boy!" The Vicar stopped him. "Fill the scuttle in the library. I've need of a fire there tonight."

"Yes." Will turned away with a grimace. His arms ached from carrying coal.

"Yes . . . what?"

Will faced the Vicar. "Sorry?"

THE FOUNDLING

" 'Yes, sir' will do nicely, boy."

"Will. My name is Will."

"Oh, yes, the boy from old Bessie's."

"Mistress Bessie."

"What? What was that?" The Vicar frowned at Will. "I'll not stand corrected by a cheeky scullery boy." He waved his walking stick at Will. "Mind your betters, lad, or you'll be out, do you hear? Out! Now be off and don't forget the library." The Vicar entered the dining room and closed the door behind him.

Will fetched the last scuttle of coal and went to the library. He had never been in the room before. It was small and dominated by a large fireplace. After laying the fire and sweeping up the coal dust that always flew about no matter how careful he was, Will looked around. Two chairs flanked the fireplace. Their cushions were a deep purple and looked soft and comfortable. In front of each chair was a footstool, and by the right arm of each was a small table with a candlestick for reading. Along one wall stood a small desk covered with papers and books. Most of them were in Latin. The Vicar's scrawling handwriting covered some of the papers. At the top of one was written "Sermon for the Lord's Day, September 23." Will didn't like the Vicar's sermons much.

He straightened up; he'd already spent too much time here. Then he spied a piece of furniture almost hidden in a corner. It was a beautifully carved bookcase with glass doors. And it was full of books whose leather bindings gleamed in the fading afternoon light. If only I could open the doors, he thought, I could read the titles better. He pressed the door with his finger.

When he took his finger away, the door opened with a snap that made him jump and glance toward the library door. No footsteps. The family was still at supper.

The bookcase door squeaked a bit when he pulled it open. Will ran his fingers along the spines. He breathed in the warm smells of leather and parchment, paper and ink. Most of the titles were in Latin, but he pulled out a small volume anyway to look at it and enjoy its feel. He opened the book and ran his fingers over the heavy vellum, leaving a smudge of coal dust that would not come off no matter how he rubbed it. When he bent to replace the book, he saw another book behind it. In fact, there was a whole row of books behind on every shelf. The Vicar had lots more than a hundred books.

Will reached in and pulled out one of the back books. It was in English and it was about King Richard and the Crusades. He pulled out several more books of stories, legends, tales of foreign lands, and exploration.

Footsteps sounded in the dining room. Dinner would soon be over. Quickly, Will replaced the books, making as little noise as he could. He picked up the last one and read the title again. He looked over his shoulder, then slipped the volume about King Richard into his shirt. He closed the squeaky bookcase door slowly, hoping it wouldn't be heard. At the library door he checked both ways and sped quietly down the hall and into the kitchen.

"Where have you been, you bone-idle scamp?" Cook slammed down a large pot. "Begin cleaning the kitchen. You'll get no supper tonight for your laziness."

Will ran to his cubby, wrapped the book in his extra shirt, and shoved it under his straw bed. He didn't care about supper. He would clean so fast and so well, Cook wouldn't be able to complain. Then he could read.

But it was two hours before he crept into his cubby. He carried a long splinter of wood from the kitchen fire to light a candle. He'd never used any of his candles before, so he grabbed one from the small pile near his bed, lit it, and stuck it to the floor with some melted wax. Will kicked the straw into a pile, spread his blanket over it, and lay down. He reached out and pushed the cubby door shut.

Almost reverently, he unwrapped and opened the book. The leather felt warm and smooth, but the pages were cool under his fingertips. Will rubbed his hands on his blanket to clean them. He turned page after page, enjoying the contrast of black ink on the creamy vellum. When the anticipation was unbearable, he started to read.

Soon he was lost in the world of King Richard I and the Third Crusade. It didn't matter that he already knew the story from the beginning to end from the times when he and Mistress Bessie had read it together. The walls of the tiny cubby disappeared, and he walked through castles and rode through the forests of England and Europe all the way to the Holy Land. With King Richard he charged the Moslems and made a treaty with Saladin the Turk so Christian pilgrims could travel safely in the Holy Land.

He read on and on, shifting from elbow to elbow, rolling on his side, then on his back. Sitting up to read wasn't easy because he had to put the book on the floor between his feet and bend over it to have enough light. Only when the candle guttered did he look away from the page before him and realize where he was and how stiff his muscles were. With a sigh, he closed the volume, wrapped it up again, and hid it behind the door of his cubby. The candle flared up one last time and went out.

The next morning Cook had to pound on his door to waken him. Why wasn't he up and working? Was he sick? No? Well, then, best have breakfast and get to work.

Will rubbed his eyes. He thought they'd never open. His muscles made him wince when he rolled over. He limped into the kitchen, rubbed his sore shoulders, and stretched his stiff back.

Over the following weeks, Cook wondered at the difference in the scullery boy. He often had a faraway expression and was tired in the morning. But he never had to be told to take the heavy scuttles upstairs. She did not notice the occasional bulge beneath his shirt.

By the end of December, Will's supply of candles was nearly gone. Fortunately, the holiday parties and celebrations provided a new supply of partially burned candles, too many for the housekeeper or Cook to count. But holidays that brought him the extra candles also made it more difficult to get into the library because of the Vicar's many guests. Will was happy when everyone finally left and the household settled back into its routine.

During the next three months, he read of Marco Polo's visits to the court of Kublai Khan and a book on the Hundred Years' War between England and France. Will felt rather sorry for Joan of Arc. She was so brave leading the French army that he thought it too bad the English army captured her and burned her as a witch. He found a book by a man named Langland who had walked all over England and written down what he saw. It wasn't as exciting as reading William Shakespeare's plays, however.

Part 2: The Scullery Boy

Then he found a volume of Chaucer's *Canterbury Tales*. The "Knight's Tale" was the best of all, and Will set himself the task of memorizing the passages of the great battles. He memorized up to the last battle of the knight Arcite who had fallen from his horse, hit his head, broken his ribs, and lay dying. Will would have finished, but by the end of March, he was nearly out of candles again. This time it was Cook herself who helped him out. She sent him to clean all the candlesticks in the house and put new candles in them. At any other time Will would have hated cleaning the wax left behind by dripping candles. Now he picked up the large basket and went through all the rooms collecting candlesticks without complaining.

He entered the room of Elspeth, the Vicar's daughter. Will did not like her at all. She was always calling him a maid because he cleaned the pots and pans in the scullery. She bullied him every chance she had and made him do all sorts of irksome tasks for her. Today, however, he decided to be nice, because it was her turn to contribute to his candle collection.

"I say, there. What are you doing?"

Will spun around with a candlestick in his hand. She really is sneaky, he thought. Aloud he said, "Taking this candlestick to be cleaned. It's awfully messy."

"It also has nearly half a candle in it." Her eyes closed ever so little when she smiled. "Are you selling the ends back to the candle maker and keeping the money? I shall tell Father at once."

"No, I haven't been selling the ends back to the candle maker," Will said mimicking her. "You can ask Cook. She sent me to collect and clean these. Now if you don't want this one cleaned . . . " He left the sentence unfinished, shrugged, and moved to replace the candlestick on the mantle.

"Oh, no. Please do clean it," Elspeth fairly purred. "I'm going to follow you, though, until I find out whether or not you're selling those candle bits. This will be more fun than my embroidery and music lessons."

Will watched her.

"You may go." She motioned him away.

THE FOUNDLING

From then on Elspeth appeared at the most unexpected times and places. Will started looking around corners and peeking through doorways before he took another step. Still she surprised him, once with a full coal scuttle. He spun around so fast, lumps of coal went rolling onto the floor, scattering black dust. Elspeth stood over him while he picked up the coal and wiped the floor. She also visited the kitchen more often, much to Cook's annoyance.

Lady Day came and Will went with the other parishioners to hear another of the Vicar's sermons. Lady Day was not only the day the angel told the virgin Mary she would be the mother of Jesus, but March 25 was also New Year's, the first day of 1653. After the service everyone ate in the churchyard and played games. The Green Man visited, decorated with leaves and vines from the woods, to wish good crops for the farmers. When the sun set, a huge bonfire lit the churchyard and the young people sang and celebrated the end of winter. A late shower did not dampen their spirits. It only sent the older folks home to tuck the children into bed.

Shortly after Lady Day, Will finished memorizing his favorite parts of the "Knight's Tale." When the days grew longer and he spent more time tending the herb garden, he recited the battles over and over again. When he escaped down the lane, he used stick knights and horses and set up whole battlefields. He wished he had his old horse and knight back, but he'd swept their ashes out of the kitchen fire long ago.

When summer came, Will frequently went and sat on the hill overlooking the London Road. He took his book with him because he was now memorizing the exploits of King Richard the Lion-Hearted in the Third Crusade. The rumble of the traffic, the shouts and calls of the people became the clamor of great campaigns. And as long as he didn't look up from the story, he lived at the end of the twelfth century and rode at King Richard's side.

Later on he went back to the library and took the volume about King Arthur. So much of King Arthur's trouble was caused by the wicked witch, Morgan le Fay. She reminded Will of Elspeth because they were both sneaky.

Elspeth's spying had kept him from returning to the library as often as he liked. Only by going very early one morning was he able to return the volume about Arthur and remove the history of Charlemagne. Even then, he was certain he heard the rustle of cloth. The squeak from the hinge on the bookcase door sounded like a scream when he pushed the door shut. Will tucked the new book into his shirt and tiptoed down the stairs toward the kitchen.

His hand was out to open the door. Then he froze where he was.

"Elspeth, you leave that boy alone!"

"You can't tell me what to do. This is my house. You merely work here!"

Will stepped back into the corner behind the door. Maybe Elspeth had seen him go into the library. Maybe he hadn't just imagined the noises. He had no time to put his newest book back now. Besides, he wanted to hear everything that was going on in the kitchen. Elspeth was no match for Cook.

"Your scullery boy is stealing everyone's candles."

"Really?" Cook smoothed her voice to the consistency of honey. She frequently found the Vicar's children a nuisance, but Elspeth wanted bunging out the kitchen door for all her high and mighty ways. "I allow him all the candle ends as he digs out of the candlesticks."

"Look what I found in his cubby! Several candle ends and half a good candle as well! I think he's selling the ends to the candle maker."

Will clutched the book in his shirt. What if he had not taken his book back this morning? She would have found it. His heart began to beat so hard that he was sure the whole house could hear. He held his breath and crunched himself farther into the corner.

"That's his half candle he gets each week. If you must know, I give him the odd broken ones as well. Now stop being a silly goose."

"Why does he need these candles? Have you thought of that?"

"You've been into his cubby. How many windows did you count?" Cook snapped back.

"He's up to something. He sneaks around the house, you know."

"And who's creeping about?" Cook's eyebrows flew up. "Put those bits and pieces of candle back where you found them." Cook's knife expertly quartered an onion for the evening's meat pie.

"I'm not going in there. It stinks."

THE FOUNDLING

"You went in there to pry."

Elspeth stood at the door and tossed the candles into the cubby.

"Now you'll go in there and sort those candles out and leave them as you found them. Then you'll leave my kitchen, or I'll put you to work in the scullery." Cook's words were slow and calm. Even if Elspeth didn't realize that Cook had reached the end of her patience, Will knew. From his corner he wondered if Cook would really thrash Elspeth. He hoped so, and he moved closer to the door so he wouldn't miss anything.

"Ugh!" Elspeth came out of the cubby shaking her skirts. "Doesn't he ever change his straw?"

"Once a month or as often as your father allows him new."

Elspeth stood silent for a moment. She knew, as well as Cook, that it was her mother who ran the house. She pinched every penny and would never allow new straw every month. Elspeth had enough trouble wheedling a new bodice for the midsummer celebrations next week.

"Well, doesn't he ever bathe?"

"Once a week except in winter. And if you recall," Cook's tone was not friendly, "it was a long, cold winter." Her knife chopped a carrot in two. "Now, off with you; out of my kitchen."

Elspeth flounced through the door, hitting it so hard that it cracked against the stone wall behind. Will didn't dare move until she reached the top of the stairs. He reached out for the door handle, but thought better of it. He didn't want to have to explain to Cook why he had been upstairs so early in the day. So he tiptoed back up the stairs, slipped out a side door, walked around through the garden, and entered the kitchen through the back door.

"Get about your business, boy."

Will stepped into his cubby to hide his new book. It definitely did not stink in there.

"Get to work, I say." Cook watched Will go into the scullery. When she heard pots and pans clanging and the steady scrubbing of sand against metal, she turned back to the vegetables.

Chapter 4

The long summer days passed slowly for Will. Cook decided that every inch of the kitchen needed cleaning. Will emptied all the cupboards and moved them so the walls and floors could be washed down. Then he dusted the cupboards and polished them with beeswax. He was surprised that Cook didn't make him wipe off the ceiling beams. Even the fireplace and chimney received a cleaning. Will breathed a sigh of relief when a chimney sweep came to do that.

When he wasn't in the kitchen, Will worked long hours in the gardens. There were berries, apples, and pears to be picked. The herb garden needed constant attention to keep the weeds from taking over. The gardener was as hard a taskmaster as Cook, and he soon had Will lopping branches off trees and trimming the bushes and hedges as well.

Will decided he liked the outside work best. It was easier to stay away from the Vicar's family, particularly Elspeth. It was easier to recite the passages from his books too. He had only to look into the tangle of a hedge to imagine himself in a forest. Sometimes he finished his work hardly remembering what he'd been doing.

He tried hard not to think too much of Rodgers anymore. In the year since Mistress Bessie had died and he'd lived at the vicarage, Rodgers had never come visiting once. And when visitors did call, Will was always sent to the scullery or on a long errand. It soon became clear that he was never to be around when guests arrived. So when the wagon wheels crunched in the driveway, or horses' hooves clattered up to the front gate, Will left his work and disappeared for an hour or two.

One late August afternoon when he heard a rider stop, Will picked up his book and set off down the lane. The day was warm under a blue sky dotted with only a few small clouds. In the lane, wildflowers bloomed in the tall grasses and the smell of freshly cut hay blew over the low stone walls.

THE FOUNDLING

He sat on the hill overlooking the highway, reading and memorizing until his eyes began to close. Then he leaned back on his elbows to watch the world passing below him. He saw some boys, but they were not the same ones he'd met last autumn. None of them had Harry's red hair. Will wondered what had happened to Harry and his friends. A few minutes later a man carrying a small boy on his shoulders caught his eye. They were very poor. Their clothes had holes and didn't fit very well. The boy drooped over the man's head, not even bothering to hang on. The man shuffled at the edge of the highway, never slowing down or hurrying along no matter who shouted at him.

Rodgers carried me like that on our way to Mistress Bessie's, Will thought. He could still remember sitting on Rodgers's shoulders and being able to look down on all the people around him. He recalled turning into the lane that led to Mistress Bessie's cottage. Will's mind filled with pictures of the cottage, of Button curled up on the warm hearth, and of Mistress working in her rose garden. He thought of their trips to market for groceries and clothes. He glanced down at his shirt and breeches. His wrists and ankles stuck out because he had grown so much, and he'd had only one new shirt and pair of shoes all winter.

I had proper clothes at Mistress Bessie's, he thought, and all I wanted to eat of bread and preserves and thick stews and meat pies. The memories faded into the churchyard where he had stood with Rodgers at her grave.

When he finally sat up, the traffic moved as it had before under the yellow sun. Nobody looked in his direction. Oxen still bellowed, and dust drifted up from the wheels of the carts and wagons they pulled. Whips cracked. Horses whinnied. Draymen shouted. Will took a deep breath. At least, he thought, I still have this. He patted his pocket and felt the familiar lump made by the pouch and the green ribbon it protected.

"So this is where you come!"

Will jerked up and looked over his shoulder. Elspeth! The book tucked inside his shirt pressed against his ribs. He turned back to the road and slid the book more securely into his waistband.

"Go away."

"I knew I'd find where you ran off to if I followed you long enough." She stood over him. "You should be working."

"Cook doesn't need me until afternoon. Besides, someone called at the vicarage, and I always get sent away."

"The gardener was looking for you."

"He can do his old garden himself."

"I shall tell Father you've been running off. You'll be locked in your cubby—with no candle ends at all."

A carriage of some important man caught Will's eye. Four horsemen protected it. Once it reached the wild countryside, robber gangs might attack. He studied the horses prancing and tossing their heads. They wanted to gallop straight away. Elspeth was still talking, and her tone became angrier. Will's eye was drawn to the livery worn by the outriders. The purple and silver cloth, shining buttons, and jaunty hats with huge feathers were grander than any he had ever seen.

"Ow!"

Elspeth had his ear and was dragging him up. She pinched harder when he slapped her hand.

"Let go!" Will tried to get up to relieve the pressure on his ear. He couldn't get his feet to catch up. When her skirt caught on a piece of rusted metal, she yanked it free without missing a step.

Will reversed tactics. Instead of pulling away from Elspeth, he ran straight at her, his fists waving. He swung twice, but she straightened her arm and held him away. He thought his ear would be torn off. A picture of Mistress Bessie holding tightly to Peter's ear flashed through his mind. He laughed out loud.

Elspeth stopped. "Laugh at me, will you?" She brought her other hand around to slap Will, but the sudden movement allowed him to slip free. He ran back toward the vicarage, half laughing, half crying, holding his ear with one hand and the book in his waistband with the other. He ran through the garden gate, around the vicarage, and stumbled into the hedge at the side of the house.

"You, boy! Get out of there and back to the scullery!"

The Vicar turned to his guest, who had just arrived. "I hardly know what to think of the world today . . . "

THE FOUNDLING

The guest wasn't listening. He was staring at the scullery boy.
The Vicar cleared his throat for a more authoritative tone.

"Be gone, boy. You know you're not to be seen when we have
visitors."

The guest's eyebrows flew up, and he looked quickly from the
Vicar to the boy who was fighting to free himself from the hedge.
"I say, isn't that—"

"My apologies, my friend. Such carryings on are simply not
permitted in my household. Mrs. Richards takes all the help in hand
to teach each one his place, but some are more difficult than others."
The Vicar coughed apologetically. "Elspeth!"

The Vicar's daughter came round the side of the house, bran-
dishing a switch. Her cap was askew and wisps of straight, brown
hair hung to her shoulders. Part of her hem trailed in the grass.

"Where is he? Slap at me, run away from me, laugh at me, will
he? Where is the little toad?" She paused for breath. "I'll give him
a lesson he'll not soon forget." She tripped over a tree root and fell
against the house.

Will collapsed in the hedge and laughed till his sides hurt.

Elspeth righted herself and raised the switch. "I'll sort you out!"
She was nearly shouting.

Will tore himself free of the hedge, ducked Elspeth's switch,
and ran to the back of the house and into the kitchen. He stumbled
into his cubby and collapsed on the straw, still laughing.

Meanwhile, the Vicar was trying to bring some order to what
he could only describe as a social disaster.

"Elspeth . . . my dear! Elspeth, my pet. We have a visitor."

Elspeth stopped in midstride and whirled around. She looked
up. Her face registered her thought: handsome! Elspeth dropped the
switch and ran her fingers around her cap, trying to tuck her hair
in, and kicked the trailing hem behind her. She approached the two
men with what she believed was her most becoming expression, a
slight smile that just showed her teeth and made her dimples appear.
She'd practiced it in front of her glass for hours.

Rodgers looked past her. "I'd like to see the . . . toad . . . if I may."

The Vicar harrumphed. "Yes, indeed . . . Are you quite sure?
Yes, of course you are. Ah, Elspeth, who was that . . . that?"

Part 2: The Scullery Boy

"He's the scullery boy, Father." Elspeth never took her eyes from Rodgers.

"Oh, yes . . . quite." The Vicar led Rodgers up the garden walk. "If you please, sir. Elspeth, please bring us refreshments in the library."

Will didn't care if the Vicar beat him for running from Elspeth or appearing when a guest was present. It was worth it to see that girl all mussed and tattered. He rubbed his sore ear. He still owed her for that.

Cook called him. "The housekeeper wants you to clean the fireplaces this afternoon. See that you don't scatter ash all over. Put any live coals in the kitchen fire."

Will took the canvas, bucket, and shovel and started up the stairs. Ahead of him he could hear the Vicar holding forth on the evils of an unlettered younger generation, and that was why he consented, at great inconvenience to himself, mind you, to take in local youngsters and set them on their way with lessons in reading and writing, both English and Latin. He played no favorites as some did, but taught boys and girls alike. Of course, the girls didn't need as much education . . . The Vicar warmed to his topic.

Will spread the canvas on the dining room hearth. He was supposed to have had those lessons.

"And how is Will coming along? I have been disappointed that he has not been here whenever I have visited." Will turned to stone at the sound of that voice.

Vicar Richards said in his most reassuring voice, "Oh, famously, quite. In a few more years, he'll be ready for the university if that's your intention, or ready to be put to apprentice much sooner."

Will knelt in front of the fireplace, shovel in hand. Rodgers! He's been here before! I've been sent off every time, he thought. Will held his breath.

"And has the allowance been sufficient for all his needs?" Rodgers asked.

"Of course, of course. I immediately turn all monies over to Mrs. Richards, you know. My wife and the housekeeper discuss each child's needs and strive to meet them within the limits of the fees. I must say they do extremely well."

Will wanted to jump up and shout to Rodgers that he was in the dining room. And he might have done it, if he hadn't looked down at his dirty and ill-fitting clothes. Suddenly, he was embarrassed and didn't want Rodgers to see him at all. Not looking like this!

Rodgers spoke again. "You have other children staying with you? Do they get on with Will?"

"None at the moment, but when they're here, they do tend to get on well together. I like to think it's the loving atmosphere of the house. Aha!" Will could hear the smile in the Vicar's voice. "A case in point. My daughter and the light of my life."

"Oh, Father."

Will could imagine her curtseying to Rodgers and wearing that silly expression. He sat waiting for the conversation across the hall to resume.

"No, it's true my dear." In the stillness of the old house, Will heard the Vicar pat his daughter's hand. "A good match you'll be for any young man. Raised with love, yet well educated. A good match." The Vicar paused. "Don't you agree, sir?"

"Quite." Rodgers said. "I'm sure she'll be more than a match for any young man."

"Wouldn't have to be a young man, would it my dear? It is frequently advantageous for a young lady to . . . ah . . . marry a man somewhat beyond her in years, a man settled in his work with more than two coins to rub together. Someone more like yourself, sir."

"Surely, there's a man perfect for her," Rodgers said briskly. "Now about Will—"

"Will you pour, Elspeth, before you return to your duties?"

The clatter of cups and saucers was followed by Elspeth's retreating footsteps.

"Some people have hard hearts, and no mistake, but not that girl. Worrying herself over a stray kitten just yesterday, she was."

"Now about Will." After a moment of silence, Rodgers raised his voice a bit. "The boy!"

"What? Yes, what about him? I believe I've told you all I can."

"I demand to hear him recite his lessons before I leave. I do have a bit of personal interest in him, as does Mr. Perry, and so far we've had no satisfaction that he's doing as well as you say he is."

Not forgotten! Will's heart pounded. Not alone! And Rodgers wants to hear me recite! I could read to him from King Richard but it's in my cubby. I could recite from the "Knight's Tale." That's what I'll do—the part where Arcite dies. Or maybe—

In the library, Rodgers leaned forward and put his cup and saucer on the tray.

"What has he been studying, if you please?" Rodgers said. "He always loved knights, dragons, and all sorts of exploration and adventure."

"Just so." The Vicar wheezed as he rose from his chair. "I'll show you the library available to the boy as soon as he's ready for it. Quite the follower of such reading myself, I am. Mind I keep those volumes in the back. Don't want to appear frivolous or put them before my other, more learned theological studies." He opened the bookcase. "How odd. It appears these volumes have been moved. And just a fortnight ago I found a truly bad smudge on one of the pages of my Tacitus. Most distressed I was and took it right to the printer, for it looked like the result of poor quality ink. Horrible smudge. I'm very particular about who handles my books." He pulled some from the front row. "Notice the quality. Each year I personally set them all in front of the fire to dry the vellum. It absorbs the damp so. What's this? One is missing! Someone has taken a book!"

The Vicar pulled out book after book. Rodgers held the growing stack until it threatened to topple.

"Might I just put these on your desk?"

The Vicar's voice rose. "Look! Look at the condition of these bindings—finger marks, water spotted, pages soiled. Now who—"
He ran to the library door and shouted, "Elspeth, Mrs. Richards, come here at once, and bring the housekeeper. Bring everyone! I will know who's responsible for this. Whoever it is will pay dearly."

Footsteps hurried from several rooms. Elspeth arrived first. "Father, Father," she nearly shrieked, "look what I found in Will's cubby! Your volume of King Richard. And look at the stains on it. Father, he should be whipped! How dare a scullery boy steal, or even presume to read your books!"

Will cringed. Did he dare run? Could he hide?

Mrs. Richards joined her daughter. "Why, Rodgers, good day to you. And how are the Perrys? I understand they've just added a son to their family."

Rodgers bowed slightly. "Thank you for your interest. The Perrys have indeed a new son, a welcome addition, I assure you."

"And the twins?"

"Very well, thank you. They've just turned five."

"Madame!" exclaimed the Vicar. "Kindly bring the amenities to an end. I've called to discover who might have been in my bookcase without permission. Just look at the damage!" He waved the volume of King Richard in front of her face. When she tried to take it, he handed it to Rodgers. "Just look at that!"

"Mother, he'll have an apoplexy!" Elspeth said.

The Vicar's voice nearly rattled the windows. "Where did you say you found this book?"

"The scullery boy. I told you I found that book in his cubby. I knew he was up to something with all those candles."

"Eh? What candles? Look at my books! Get him. Now! Bring him here. I'm of a mind to have him arrested right after I give him the beating he deserves. He'll work off every penny of their value. He'll be in the scullery until he's fifty!"

"Yes, Vicar, let's see this scullery boy named Will." Rodgers snapped the words across the room. "I believe we'll find more problems than a few well-read books." He went to the door and called so the whole house shook. "Will! Will. It's Rodgers. I must speak with you now!"

Will slowly stepped from behind the dining room door and into the hallway.

Rodgers motioned with the book he held. "Will, come into the library . . . Yes, come along," he said when Will hesitated. "Shall we sit down?" He motioned them to chairs. "You too, Will."

"No, he mustn't sit on the cush—" Mrs. Richards began.

"Get him out of my sight. He's worse than a thief." The Vicar sat on the edge of his chair.

"He'll stay while I speak," Rodgers began. "It was with the distinct understanding when you took Will on after Margaret Bessie's death that you would treat him as a family member and continue his lessons."

Rodgers held up his hand at the beginning of a protest from the Vicar's wife. "Master Perry provided you with ample funds for his room, board, and clothing. Indeed I have three pounds, fourteen shillings, sixpence in my pocket to pay last quarter's charges."

"It'll not begin to cover the cost of my books!"

Rodgers ignored the interruption. "Instead what I find is a dirty, poorly fed, abominably clothed boy forced to do the heaviest household labor and to forgo his lessons as well." He turned to Will. "How many lessons have you had this past year?"

"None," Will said and rushed on, "that's why I took the books—"

"Shh." Rodgers addressed the Vicar and his wife. "If you two were in a proper business, you'd be imprisoned for embezzlement and breach of contract. Don't get red in the face. I believe you've misspent the money meant to support Will. Heaven only knows what you've done with the clothing provided for him.

"Because you have not honored your commitment to Will for this past year and more, you will receive no more of Master Perry's money. Nor will he, I should add, recommend you as a teacher in the future. Will, go collect your belongings."

Will looked down at his clothes and shrugged.

"That's it? You have nothing more? . . . One should not leave such a hospitable home with such a thin valise." Rodgers held up a book. "I believe he's earned this and one other of his choice many times over, don't you, Vicar?"

"No, I do not. He's earned nothing and been nothing but trouble. I'll have the constable on you!"

Rodgers stood. "Master Perry could take you in suit before the law for what you've done here. We may no longer have bishops to remove dishonest Vicars, but Parliament can serve the same function."

"My dear, no!" whispered Mrs. Richards from her seat. "I was depending on the last quarter's fees to cover the expenses of a new gown and party for Elspeth for her sixteenth birthday. If we lose our position here at the vicarage, how can we afford—"

"Hush, Barbara!" Vicar Richards looked at Will, then Rodgers. "All right, take the boy and the book and good riddance."

Rodgers smiled and held up two fingers. "Two books."

"He's not touching my books again."

"Very well." Rodgers stepped over to the stack of books on the desk. "Which one, Will? And I will take it for you."

Will stepped over to the desk and bent his head sideways so he could read the titles. "The third from the bottom."

"Of course, you want the thick one at the bottom." Rodgers set the other books aside. "Chaucer, eh? Beautiful binding. Great stories, aren't they? 'Wife of Bath' interest you?"

The Vicar fairly exploded. "Not the Chaucer!"

"The 'Knight's Tale,' " Will answered.

"Not my Chaucer!"

"Correct, it is no longer your Chaucer. Let's be off, Will. It is clear we are in no proper Vicar's house."

Chapter 5

When Rodgers pushed Will into Master Perry's kitchen—dirt, rags, and all—Cook surveyed him head to toe, pronounced him the filthiest boy she had ever seen, and ordered him to bathe and get his hair cut. Will could see Rodgers from the corner of his eye, a wide smile on his face. Two kitchen maids peeked out from the scullery to see who was receiving the scolding usually reserved for them. They giggled and ducked out of sight when Cook looked their way. Will felt his face grow hot with embarrassment.

The old tub still sat in the kitchen corner. Not in the kitchen! Will thought. I'll take a bath, but not here. Rodgers stepped toward the tub.

"Help me move this old thing into the laundry," he said, "so you'll have some privacy." He was still grinning.

"Mind the table!" Cook directed the move. "Don't drag it across the floor. The scraping drives me scatty and leaves marks. Can you get the tub through the door? Don't mar the woodwork!"

Will and Rodgers looked up in exasperation from their labors. Rodgers opened his mouth to speak and immediately changed his mind. He saw Cook standing in the middle of her kitchen with her hands clasped under her chin. She looked like a little girl who had been promised a treat and couldn't wait to get it.

Cook met Rodgers's gaze. "Hurry!" she said.

Will slid beneath the soap bubbles. He scrubbed himself twice, even his hair. Rodgers rinsed him off with a pail of warm water and handed him some clean clothes. Next, Rodgers picked up a comb and scissors. He worked for twenty minutes and then viewed Will from all sides, pronounced his ears straight, and whisked the towel off Will's shoulders, scattering dark brown hair everywhere.

When Will stepped back into the kitchen, Cook was waiting for him at the door. She wrapped him in the tightest hug he could remember. "It's so good to have you back, boy." She ran her hand over his head. As Rodgers left the room she added, "Sit down and eat. And don't worry, we'll get you a proper haircut tomorrow."

The kitchen was just as he remembered. Even the cupboards and shelves looked the same. The tabletop was scrubbed as clean as ever. A pot bubbled over the fire. Will looked at the floor. Clean, of course. He couldn't have gotten it cleaner. When he couldn't eat another bite, he gathered his dishes to clear the table, but Cook swept everything from his hands.

"You're not kitchen help."

"But I know how to wash dishes and scrub floors and scour pots. I did it all the time at the Vicar's."

Cook snorted. "I'm sure that's all very well for the Vicar's house, but I have my scullery maids, lazy twits, both of them." Sounds of scraping and clattering came from the scullery. "I do my best with them, I'm sure I do."

She sat down across from Will and reached out for his hands. "My, you've grown. By my reckoning, you must be about thirteen?"

"Thirteen and a half," Will said and sat up as straight as he could.

Cook went on, her nose and chin nearly touching when she spoke. "And how do the clothes fit? A bit large, seems to me. I didn't have much time to find you proper clothes." She reached up and pulled at the shoulders. "Shoes fit well enough? Did you put those stockings on? They're mine. Mended them myself just last week. Hope they don't wear a sore spot on your toes. The toes always go first for me. Mending stockings all the time, I am. Have to wear two pair at once during the cold. Chilblains, you know."

She sat there, still smiling. "I missed you, boy. Especially after we lost track of you at the Vicar's."

Cook got up from the table. "I have to finish here. Tell me about your living with Margaret Bessie. I knew her quite well at one time."

Will began his narrative while Cook prepared the evening meal. Occasionally she stepped to the fire to stir the pot's simmering contents. The girls in the scullery talked while they worked. Once or twice Will thought he heard the squeals and shouts of children. Footsteps passed the kitchen door several times. Each time he paused, Cook nodded for him to continue.

Will had just finished telling Cook of Mistress Bessie's funeral when the kitchen door opened and a woman entered. Everything about her was thin and severe. Her lips were pressed into a line that turned down at the corners. She held her chin high and her back straight and walked across the kitchen looking neither to the right nor to the left. Her petticoats rustled and her heels clicked hard on the floor. Her light-gray bodice and skirt were perfectly fitted and showed no signs of wrinkle or crease. Her hair was parted in the center and pulled back into a shiny braid coiled at the back of her neck. A small cap perched on brown waves that would not be pulled straight.

Will wrinkled his brow. She was vaguely familiar.

She took what she needed from a cupboard and turned to Cook. "I do hope this is not another waif for me to see to."

"Master Perry has made all the arrangements for Will."

"Will?" The woman looked closely at him. "You!" Her free hand flew to her collar. "What are you doing here?"

"Marie! Remember yourself!" Cook scolded.

Marie struggled to recover. "Yes, of course." She drew herself up and left the kitchen looking, Will thought, like a thundercloud about to brandish some lightning bolts.

"I'm sure I don't know what's gotten up her nose. She's become nastier than she ever was. Getting impossible to live with."

"I slept in her room when I first came here, didn't I?" Will asked.

"Yes, you did. But she has her own apartment now that she's housekeeper. Can't imagine what's made her so contrary. Perhaps because she's not yet married?" Cook winked at Will. "You know, she had her cap set for Mr. Fielding, yes, she did. And wasn't her nose out of joint when he came calling and asked for Gillian?" Cook raised her eyebrows and drew a long breath. "Let me tell you, it was good our Gillian was all caught up with her Mr. Fielding. She never saw all the meanness Marie put in her way, even at the engagement party."

"Gillian's married?"

"About four years now." She saw Will's expression of disbelief. "It's true, every word. There are ever so many changes for you to catch up on. Why, the Perrys have three children now."

"Children?"

"Indeed. We're fair running out of rooms. The twins are five now and lead us all a pretty dance. Always into mischief. And the new baby was just born a fortnight ago. James, one of the twins, reminds me of you. Can't get his shoes on right yet."

"I can too." Will laughed and held out his feet. "Look."

"But you couldn't when you first came. You gave us many a good chuckle."

The kitchen door opened again. "Cook, pardon me, but Mistress Perry would like some sweet biscuits for the twins. They are driving us mad this afternoon. If the weather were a bit better, we'd have them in the garden. As it is, they've completely upset the nursery, and now they say they're hungry." Gillian took down a pottery jar and lifted the lid. "You, boy, hand me that plate."

Will picked up the plate and carried it to Gillian. He remembered her very well, especially hopping around the laundry room. He smiled.

She dropped a handful of biscuits on the plate. "Here, have one or two. Willy, isn't it?"

"Will."

"Yes, of course. You're quite grown." She took a biscuit for herself. "I'm hungry all the time. Happens with every child. This will be number three."

"You have children?"

"Yes, and I'd better get back to the nursery or they will be screaming. Have another."

Will grabbed another biscuit as she swung the plate by him. Then she was gone.

"Those little ones do keep her busy every minute, and she loves it." Cook stirred the pot. "Marriage was the best thing for her. A mite young, I thought, but it set both her feet on the ground."

"I thought she was an apprentice here."

"She was, but a girl's apprenticeship ends when she gets married."

"She lives here?"

"Oh no. She and her husband live over by the London wall. He's a saddle maker, he is, and I hear he does well for himself.

"Gillian is his second wife, so they're well set up. She comes over nearly every day, especially since Mistress Perry was brought to bed with her new son. Helps out more than one would believe, remembering her as I do." Cook replaced the biscuit jar on the shelf. "Yes, marriage made that girl. Barely nineteen and has a fine family, husband who can make his way, and cares enough about Mistress to help whenever she's needed. Who would have thought it?"

Cook put the last vegetables into the pie crust and poured gravy over them. She touched her finger to the gravy and tasted it. "Very nice. Why I thought to make an extra pie, I'll never know. Good thing I did with you around." She reached over and pinched Will's arm. "Didn't they feed you at that Vicar's house?"

Will eyed the pies. "Not like you do. Not one bit."

After dinner, Will followed Rodgers to his room.

"Best to stay away from Marie, Will. She runs the house well, but she becomes more mean-spirited with every passing day. She's housekeeper now, so mind how you go."

Rodgers stopped at the end of the hall and pushed a door open. "Right, here we are," he said. "Just have a seat there while I tend the fire. It's become the coldest August I can recall." Sparks flew up the chimney as Rodgers threw coal on the fire. "I prefer wood, but coal is less expensive, so I'm giving it a go. It certainly doesn't smell as good as wood, and it gets dust all over."

"I carried coal at the Vicar's. It's heavy too . . . Rodgers? Can Vicar Richards make trouble for you?"

"Trouble? What do you mean?"

"Well, you did give me two of his books."

Rodgers chuckled and nodded.

"And you didn't pay him for my last quarter."

"He wasn't spending it on you." Rodgers finally coaxed a flame from the coals. "Besides, he did not abide by his agreement regarding you. He's well advised not to go to court."

"Could Master Perry have him removed from the vicarage?"

"That would take some doing, but yes, he could. Master Perry has many friends in Cromwell's government. Don't worry about the Vicar."

Will looked around Rodgers's apartment. A bed was built into one wall. Heavy draperies could be pulled around it for warmth. By the fireplace were a desk and chair. In the corner shadows he saw a bookcase with more books than Vicar Richards ever had.

"It has been decided that you will sleep here, Will," said Rodgers.

"Here?"

"Yes, your bed is just there." Rodgers pointed across the room. "I'm sorry it is only a cot and not a proper bed. We shall just have to make do."

Will tested the cot. "Soft."

"Soft? What were you sleeping on that you think a cot is soft?" Rodgers asked.

"I had some straw and a blanket. At first the straw poked me right through the blanket, but I got used to it."

"Were you sleeping in the barn?"

"Oh no. I slept in a cubby in the kitchen. It wasn't big enough for a bed, but it had a door, and I could close it and read all night if I wanted to."

"The Vicar's books."

"I tried to be careful with them. I really did. Where are my two books?"

"They're right here. I thought we might be able to tidy them up a bit. You've kept the pages fairly clean. I'll ask Gillian if her husband knows of any way to restore the bindings."

"You have lots of books."

Rodgers glanced at the bookcase. "Yes, I have. I've been fortunate in my travels to find some very fine works. I even have a handwritten copy of Dante's *Divine Comedy*—a real treasure that I found quite by chance last year in Frankfurt."

"Frankfurt?"

"A German city." Rodgers pulled a large book down. "This is an atlas. Whenever you read about a place, you can find it in here. If you need help, just ask."

"Do you mean I can read your books?" Will's jaw dropped.

"Yes, but only with clean hands and only in this room. Agreed?"

Will nodded. He started for the bookcase.

"Just a moment. I have a few clothes here, some of which may fit you." One by one, Rodgers held three shirts up to Will. "Here are two. They're a bit big, but you'll—"

"Grow into them."

They both laughed, and Rodgers said, "At least you'll be warm. Here's a coat and scarf. Shall I have Gillian knit you a cap and mittens? We can tie the mittens together with string so you won't lose them. Do you know, I told Gillian and Mistress Perry about that little trick for the children, and they knew all about it. I must have been the only one in England who didn't know. We'll get you some proper clothes straight away. I don't suppose you know what happened to the clothes you took to the Vicar's?"

"No, and they burned all my toys, even my horse and knight. Even my mum's shawl disappeared. But they didn't get this." He held a small pouch out on his palm.

"What's that?"

"My green ribbon. Remember? You told me how important it was. Then Mistress Bessie made the pouch to keep it clean. I tied the flowers for her grave with it, you know. I don't ever want to lose this." Will put the pouch in his pocket and patted it. "Not like I lost my mum's picture."

"Your what? You had a picture of your mother?"

Will nodded. "I didn't know I had it at first. It was in a pin, a brooch, that opened. But I lost it. I remember her picture. She was smiling. That's all I can remember." Will watched the fire. "What's going to happen now?"

Rodgers closed the wardrobe. "You'll be here a short while until new arrangements can be made, probably for another nurse."

"I don't want another nurse."

"That's really in the hands of the vestry. You needn't worry. Master Perry is Upper Churchwarden again this year, and he'll have to approve all arrangements. Now let's go down for dinner."

Chapter 6

"Wasn't allowed in my day, and that's the truth on it." Old Arthur Dewe rapped his cane for the full attention of the vestry. "Never allowed to complain, so we never did. Just stayed where we were put; minded our betters. Had to, or suffer a good switching." He paused. The wind whistled around the vestry house and through the loose mortar around a window. Goodman Dewe leaned farther into the fireplace.

"Arthur, mind yourself. You're about to catch fire!" Master Perry leaped up. "Arthur, your scarf! Arthur! George, get his scarf out of the grate!"

George Hefield rescued the smoldering scarf and beat the smoking wool with his free hand.

"Mr. Dewe . . . I say." George raised his voice. "Mr. Dewe, your scarf, sir."

Arthur Dewe yanked his scarf back to his lap. "Case in point!" Down came the cane. "This young chap, trying to set my scarf afire; knitted by my late wife, Agnes, it was. Some sort of joke on an old man, no doubt." The cane hit the floor again next to George's toe.

"But, sir . . . "

"Wouldn't have happened in my day. Henry! Someone wake that fool. Henry! Shouldn't have happened today. I sit close to the fire only because Henry has neglected to have the windows reset. Hickford!"

Henry's head snapped up. The action started his slide from his chair. He stopped himself only by grabbing the edges of the chair seat.

"Yes? Well?" He struggled to reseat himself, then straightened his greatcoat and shoved his hands up opposite sleeves. He ignored the muffled chuckles around him. "Well, Arthur?"

"Don't look at me as though you'd just bitten into a lemon, Henry. This," Goodman Dewe waved his singed scarf, "results from your not doing your job."

Henry's eyebrows flew up. "I can't imagine what your scarf has to do with the repair of the churchyard wall." He looked at Master Perry. "And Hudson's price is much too high. I simply will not put out so much of the parish funds to stack a few bricks—"

"Henry!" Master Perry drew a long breath. "Henry, we've moved quite beyond the churchyard wall. Please see what can be done regarding mending the vestry house windows."

"It simply cannot be done until spring. The mortar won't set properly in the cold."

Goodman Dewe's cane rang against the hearthstone. "We will all have chilblains if we must sit and freeze all winter!"

"It's barely September. Surely a short cold spell—"

"Henry, please see to the windows as soon as you may." Perry turned to Goodman Dewe. "Now, sir, are you quite extinguished? Please continue with your original comments."

"What? Oh yes, as I was saying . . . " He looked uncertainly at Master Perry.

"About Will Pancras."

Goodman Dewe cleared his throat. "The lad's behavior is most questionable—must be dealt with." His voice faded. "Wouldn't have been allowed in my day."

"Nicholas, will you look into providing another nurse for Will? We have sent children to Ann Woodward of Shoreditch in the past. Tell her we will pay five pounds, four shillings a year, or two shillings a week. Perhaps she has room."

"Why should he be sent to a nurse? Isn't he old enough to be apprenticed out? He's what, ten or eleven?" asked Nicholas.

"Actually thirteen," Perry said slowly.

"As one of the Overseers for the Poor, I must tell the vestry that we should remove as many from our poor rolls as quickly as we possibly can. Our expenses continue to increase and now include, by order of Parliament, three pounds, ten shillings each year to the poor of the parish of Giles Cripplegate. We still have a number of our own elderly and ill to care for. The latest is Goody Gilbert who fell down her stairs and bruised her head and body. Our rates barely cover costs. This young chap, Will, can read and write, and he is old enough to be put out, saving us that much in nurse fees."

"You're right." Perry sat back and thought a moment. "See what you can arrange, Nicholas. Just keep him out of button-making and cookery and so on. There are so many apprenticed in the women's trades already, the boy will never be able to make his way if we apprentice him there."

"I had Nathan Fortescue in mind. A friend of yours, I believe?"

"He's an ironmonger, Nicholas. I'm not sure the boy's strong enough." Perry leaned over the table again. "If he were older . . ."

"You know he'll not be doing proper ironmongery for several years, James. And it's a good position for the boy, any boy, in fact."

Master Perry looked around the vestry house. Henry had once again fallen asleep, his feet braced against a stool to keep him from sliding to the floor. Goodman Dewe huddled at the fire. Others blew on their fingers or sat hugging themselves trying to keep any bit of heat from escaping their heavy woolen coats.

"Are there any other boys in the parish who should be placed before Will?"

The Overseer stepped closer to the fire. "James, agree to place the boy with Fortescue if he will have him, and let us go home before we freeze to death. We're all agreed, right?" Few of the huddled figures moved, but there was an eager chorus of ayes to the Overseer's question.

"All right. Nicholas, please contact Fortescue and make all necessary arrangements. Gentlemen, let's be done." Perry rose, closing the meeting.

The clerk scribbled his final notes. "And how much of the conversation between Arthur and Henry shall I include?"

"None of it, you young sprat." Goodman Dewe hammered his way across the room. He passed Henry Hickford, who was still snoring softly. His cane flew out and cracked against Henry's stool, sending it across the room. "And don't forget the windows, Henry, my boy," he called over his shoulder. With his footrest gone, the Lower Churchwarden landed on the floor, sitting with his legs buckled under him and his hands up the opposite sleeves.

The candles on the office desks barely held back the gray afternoon. The *Charlotte* had returned from the Indies, and both

Rodgers and Perry were working through the papers that accompanied the end of a voyage.

"How was the meeting?" Rodgers held his pen over the inkwell.

"Overall, much the same as usual." Perry signed an account and looked up. "Old Arthur Dewe nearly burned alive. You should have seen his face when he thought young George Hefield was trying to set his scarf afire. Poor George, he didn't deserve the scolding he got."

"And about Will?"

"We will try to apprentice him to Nathan Fortescue."

"Ironmongery? Is Will up to it?"

"I doubt Nathan would put Will to heavy work for a while." Master Perry shuffled some loose papers into a neat pile. "It really is a fine position. Better than what is given to most foundlings."

"Yes, it is," Rodgers agreed. "Nicholas is making all the arrangements? Of course, Nathan may not take Will. Do you suppose I should speak to him? I mean about the heavy work and all?"

"Why don't we wait until Nathan gives us an answer?"

"Yes, we should have some news in a week or so, I suppose." Rodgers bent over his papers again.

"Quite."

"I shall miss him when he leaves. He is reading through my library when he isn't with Cook. Have you heard him read? He's very good, and I daresay more widely read than most men. He's still keen on Arthur and Lancelot and dragons. Says he conquered the known world several times over with that horse and knight I gave him."

Master Perry looked up. "You gave him toys?"

"No more than you did." Rodgers scribbled a note.

"I may have slipped the odd puzzle or ball in on occasion, but that is all. I thought that with—what's his name?—Peter, so much older, Will would need a little amusement. But, a knight on a horse? A bit over the top, wasn't it?"

"And a fine knight he was too. Had a sword and a lance; he could even be removed from the horse. Couldn't stand alone though. Made of cloth, you know."

"Sounds like some of the old Royalist Army."

Rodgers grinned. "But the horse was the best, all painted and with real horsehair for the mane and tail."

They worked steadily through the afternoon. The fire in the stove snapped and popped. Its warmth did not reach far and both men wore jumpers under their coats, and gloves with the fingers cut off. Muffled calls, thumps, and bumps came from the warehouse beneath them where laborers stored the cargo. The smells of cinnamon, cloves, ginger, mace, and nutmeg rose into the office. A muffled cry of warning followed by a splintering crash brought both men to their feet.

Master Perry muttered in frustration as he dabbed at ink spots that had spattered on his ledgers. Hurried footsteps on the stairs were followed by two sharp raps on the office door.

"Enter!"

The foreman opened the door far enough to poke his head in. "That crash you heard? Well, it weren't but a bale of cotton cloth that got away from us. Rope broke. Fell onto a chest of tea, it did. No harm to either. Jack, now, he's got a few scrapes from not being quick enough on his feet, but nothing to bother yourself about. We're putting it right; be back to work directly." The foreman bobbed his head and disappeared before either Perry or Rodgers could do more than exchange glances.

"You want me to check below?"

"We'll check when we leave. If that had been a crate of oranges or lemons, Jack would have more than a few scrapes." Perry walked to the window.

The crew was back at work in the slow drizzle. The ship lay hauled close to the wharf. From her looks, she would need extensive refitting before her next voyage. The cargo had suffered a minimum of damage from heat and damp, considering that this voyage had been longer than usual. The ship had called at ports in Africa and throughout the Far East.

Not all the trading had been peaceful. The Portuguese and Dutch claimed ownership of some of the ports, but the ship with the biggest guns usually went where it pleased. The *Charlotte*'s log showed two attempts by Dutch pirates to overtake and board. Neither succeeded, and, according to the captain's entry, one Dutch ship suffered considerable damage from the cannonade of the *Charlotte*.

We'll just have to build the fastest, best-defended ships, thought Master Perry. He shivered in the damp air that crept in around the windows. I should have Henry reset these windows too. He grinned.

"Coffee, James?" Rodgers appeared, carrying a tray.

"You startled me. I didn't even hear you leave. Coffee? Capital. Mind if I ask you who made it?"

"I did. See what you think."

"You?" Perry sipped cautiously. "Ahh, good." He leaned over the tray. "Any cakes? Scones? Excellent. You're hired."

Rodgers licked his fingers. "We're going to need a garbler for the cloves. Captain Morgan had to load quickly before the Dutch discovered him. He had no time to check the contents of the casket. There's enough rubbish mixed in to make it weigh a quarter again as much as it ought."

"Are the cloves damaged?"

"No, just mixed with sand, bits of shell, and so on."

Rodgers joined Perry at the window. "Our investors should get a nice return from this voyage."

"Indeed," Perry said. "We've had a marvelous run of luck. I can't recall when we've had less damage."

"A bit extra for the crew?" Rodgers sipped his coffee.

"I should think so."

"Think of it. Will may very well be outfitting our ships one day. Nathan's been doing our work for how long now?" Perry drained his cup.

"Four or five years. Do you suppose we'll get to see Will at work? We might have to visit to see how he's doing."

"We could pop 'round from time to time. Keep an eye on him." Perry looked at Rodgers and laughed. "Who are we fooling? No matter where Will is apprenticed, we'll be like two mother hens clucking after him. Hmm. It's gone quiet below. Let's take a turn through and see that all is as it should be. We'll need to have the cloves accessible."

They straightened their papers and banked the fire, shrugged into their overcoats and descended the stairs. One of the guards approached and pronounced all secure. Perry nodded his good night, and they stepped outside. He turned to Rodgers.

"I'm for a walk. The rain's stopped."

"Mud to our knees, James. Gutters will be full."

"Hmm. I'd still rather walk. Let's hope the scavengers have been out and cleared some of the rubbish."

They set out in silence, stepping carefully on the wet, rounded cobbles and around the collected debris of a busy day in the City.

Rodgers pointed. "Look, just there, at that boy going through rubbish. Reminds me of Will. And look there, another. I seldom noticed them before Will; now I think I must see them all. There are so many."

"We've a couple behind us. Mind your pockets. And to think Will might have lived like this."

"Are you going to tell him about plans for his apprenticeship?" Rodgers asked.

"The vestry has just begun its inquiries. Perhaps when something more definite is known. What do you think? Should he be told right away?"

"I'll leave that to you, James."

"Right."

They crossed Gracechurch Street.

"Perhaps I should speak with him. Less of a shock and all that."

"It might help things go more smoothly." Rodgers stepped around a cart.

When they passed the parish church of St. Pancras, Rodgers nodded. "There's where Crumpton found him. Wonder whatever happened to his mother?"

"Anybody's guess. Probably dead."

"Did you know he actually had a miniature of his mum? If we'd had that, perhaps we could have put them back together."

"What happened to the picture?"

"Says he lost it."

"It really doesn't make much difference. She would have left him in a parish that wasn't hers, most likely."

They climbed the steps and opened the great door to Perry's home. A rush of children and screams of delight welcomed them.

Chapter 7

The next day, Master Perry called Will to his chambers to tell him of his proposed apprenticeship.

"I rather expect you don't remember me," Master Perry began. "But ever since Constable Crumpton brought you here, I've kept a close eye on you, Will. You've done well. Do you remember me at all?"

Will met Master Perry's gaze. "You've given me clothes and had Mistress Bessie and the Vicar take care of me. And you bought me my ribbon, my green ribbon." He pulled the small pouch from his pocket. "Do you want to see it? I've kept it always. I was going to give it to my mum if I ever found her, but I never did." He carefully unrolled the ribbon. "I tied it around the roses on Mistress Bessie's grave. She made this pouch for it. That's why it's still so pretty. I hardly ever take it out, you see."

Master Perry touched the green coils lying on his desk. "And you've kept the ribbon all these years?"

"Yes. It's special. I remember lots of things with it."

"Indeed." After a few moments, Master Perry picked up the conversation. "Rodgers tells me you read very well."

"Yes. Yes, I do." Will wondered if Master Perry knew about the Vicar's books. He bent over his ribbon and coiled it around his finger. "I read a lot when I had the time."

Master Perry laughed. "So I heard. Found the good books too, hidden behind the theology and ancient languages. I wrote to the Vicar just this Monday past, telling him of my disappointment with his actions towards you. He will receive no more references from me. I'm sorry he treated you so poorly, Will. Rodgers told me about your circumstances. That is not what I intended. I wanted the Vicar to continue your lessons, not make a kitchen drudge of you."

"Rodgers let me keep two books. I know a lot of parts by heart."

"I shall enjoy hearing you recite. By the way, you did learn how to cipher?"

Will nodded. "Mistress Bessie taught me."

"It seems we grossly underpaid her. She went far beyond my expectations."

"You paid her?" Will thought of the evenings he spent in Mistress's lap listening to her read and eventually learning himself. It was the best part of living with her. "Is that why she read to me?"

"Mistress was paid, but she did a lot more because she wanted to. She grew to love you, Will."

"Really?"

"She was always telling Rodgers of little things you'd done or said. People don't remember little things unless they love you. I remembered the green ribbon, didn't I?"

Will stared at the candle on Master Perry's desk. The flame danced in the occasional draft. Mistress had loved him. He thought she had, even though Peter was her favorite. The kitchen, the garden, Button, even Peter and Hal appeared in the candle flame. And Mistress was in every picture, smiling, scolding, cooking, pruning her roses, reaching for a book, motioning for him to sit on her lap . . . He smiled at the flame.

Master Perry cleared his throat. "We must talk about your future."

Will refocused his eyes to see the man on the other side of the candle.

"It's been decided that you are to be apprenticed as soon as a proper master can be found. You will live with him and learn his trade. Do you understand?"

"When?" asked Will.

"I think not for a fortnight at least. All boys and many girls are apprenticed to learn a trade. We're not pushing you out, you know."

"I know." Will looked at his lap. "But I like staying here. If I could stay, I would help Cook. I know how to do a lot of things to help."

"Rodgers and I want something better for you, Will. We want to see you learn a trade so you can support yourself and even a family someday. You don't want to work in a kitchen always, do you?"

Part 2: The Scullery Boy

If it were Cook's kitchen, Will couldn't see any reason not to. But it was obvious that was not the answer Master Perry expected. "This will be best for you, Will. I think you already know that."

Best for me? he thought. What if I lose Rodgers again? What if Cook forgets about me? I'll be alone again.

Nevertheless, Will attended the next vestry meeting with Master Perry. When they entered, the fire had not yet taken the chill from the vestry house. Arthur Dewe sat nearly inside the fireplace, holding his hands out to the flame crackling around the kindling. Even Henry Hickford was less interested in finding the lowest chair than in arranging his cloak so no cold air could get down his collar. Master Perry motioned Will to a stool close to the fireplace.

Will studied the men who would decide what was to happen to him until he was twenty-three. Ten years! It was a lifetime. Will shivered.

"I say, can't we meet at the Dolphin? It's right 'round the corner." Goodman Dewe sniffed.

"Might be just the thing." The clerk shook his ink pot. "My ink might freeze here."

"Gentlemen, let's begin." Master Perry seated himself. "My apologies for the cold, but our sexton has taken ill and there was no one to set the fire until a few minutes ago."

"What about the beadle? Seems he could have done it. He does little enough as it is." Goodman Dewe sniffed even louder and leaned further over the fire.

"We'll make this as brief as possible," said Master Perry. "First we must decide whom we will invite to preach our commemoration services on Guy Fawkes Day and Queen Elizabeth's birthday . . ."

The vestrymen argued over which minister to invite. Next, they discussed a pensioner named Goody Ford who was in Newgate. All the while, Will leaned against the warm chimney and hoped the meeting would soon end. It seemed an age before Master Perry tapped him on the shoulder.

"I realize that it is somewhat unusual to bring a parish child before you in this manner. Since Will has been in my house for the last few days, however, I brought him along. Most of you know him only through the reports of Rodgers. We spoke of his apprenticeship last week.

"He was with Margaret Bessie until her death. Vicar Richards in Moorfield assumed responsibility for Will, but only poorly fulfilled his duties. Nevertheless, Will reads well and ciphers. Now we've to decide on his apprenticeship. Nicholas, have you any word from the ironmonger, Nathan Fortescue, east of Tower Hill?"

Nicholas stood again. "Mr. Fortescue consents to take Will Pancras as apprentice for ten years to teach him ironmongery and metal casting. I should say here that he specializes in fittings for ships. Mr. Fortescue requires that the boy read, write, and cipher, and that he have a new suit of clothes at least once a year. He also requires a fee of fifteen pounds, and the usual other—"

"Why, that's highway robbery!" Henry sat bolt upright. "Fifteen pounds to apprentice a parish child, and a foundling at that!"

"You're a miser, Henry. I see you haven't had the windows reset yet." Master Dewe pointed an accusing finger.

"Arthur, I'm taking bids! Do let's get on with this business. Fifteen pounds is over the top!"

"For a ten-year apprenticeship with a man specializing in ship fittings? Really, Henry." Nicholas Vaughan went on. "This is a good position, available within the week, with a master known for the quality of his work." He looked around. "And it will remove Will as a charge upon this parish."

"This position should go to one of our own boys, not to some foundling dragged in off the streets." Henry Hickford wasn't giving up.

Vaughan turned to Perry as if to say "Now what?"

"What will the parish pay, Henry?" Master Perry asked.

"Five pounds, maybe, and that's twice what we usually pay."

"If the vestry agrees, I will make up any difference. Now, please raise your hands if we should place Will Pancras with Mr. Fortescue according to his demands."

"Raise your hand, Henry!"

"No, Arthur, I will not. The place ought to go to one of our own boys."

"None of our own boys is of age." Arthur Dewe elbowed George Hefield. "Raise your hand, boy. Both of them if necessary, because I will be gone to the Dolphin before I freeze to death here."

"An ironmonger? He's not big enough." Cook put her ladle down with a clatter.

"He probably won't be swinging a hammer for years to come. In fact, he may simply learn how to buy and sell to shipbuilders." Rodgers took another scone. "Where are the children today? Usually they are emptying the plate before I get a bite."

"Don't change the subject." Cook scowled at Rodgers. "I don't intend losing track of Will again. I shall follow his every move, and his master's too. If that boy is ever mistreated again—" She twisted her apron into a knot.

"And I shall be right there with you."

Cook met Rodgers's eyes. She smiled and tried to smooth the wrinkles from her apron. "We're a dangerous pair, aren't we?"

Rodgers saluted her with his scone.

"About the children. Gillian took them out. They are taking advantage of the bit of sun we've had today. I fixed them a basket, so they'll be quite happy."

"How does she get them all out for a walk? With one of her own still in arms and the twins to handle?"

"It's beyond me. But she does quite nicely and seems to enjoy the outings as much as the children. I can't imagine what we'd have done without her." Cook poured herself some tea.

"Marie's the hard one. Seldom has a kind word for anyone, let alone caring for the children."

"She does run the household well enough. The odd pleasant word would be nice, though." Cook sipped her tea noisily.

"She's gotten a bit above herself, if you ask me."

"I know why she went off you. It began when she had to brush your clothes after you'd visited the boy."

"What? A quick brush up?"

"Have you ever tried to remove cat hair? Very irritated with you, was our Marie."

"Speaking of—" Rodgers said in a low voice.

THE FOUNDLING

Marie entered, carrying a tray of dirty dishes and a teapot. "Mistress thanks you for the tray. She and Master Perry both compliment your cakes and tea." She set the tray down without looking at either Cook or Rodgers and left the kitchen.

"And good day to you." Cook raised her cup towards the door. "Her behavior has gone off like sweet milk goes sour."

"An apt description."

The kitchen door opened again. "I'm so hungry." Will hugged his stomach and staggered to the table.

Cook set her cup down. "Wondered where you were. Thought you might have gone with Gillian to the park."

Will rolled his eyes and groaned. "Not with all the babies."

"What have you been doing this afternoon?" Rodgers asked.

"Reading." Will spoke around a scone. "Umm, this is so good. The Vicar's cook never made scones. Or, if she did, I never had any. And they could never be this good." He smiled at Cook. "The plate's nearly full."

Rodgers pushed it over. "We were saving them for you. Cook's still trying to fatten you up." Rodgers helped himself to another scone. "So, Will, what are you reading now?"

"You have so many books, I couldn't decide, so I just picked one. It's a book about martyrs. Those monks and judges were awful. Want to hear some of the ways they killed people?"

"Not in my kitchen, if you please," said Cook. "You want to make me sick so I can't fix your supper? Tell me instead about the vestry meeting last night."

Will shrugged. "I'll be apprenticed to Mr. Fortescue. He's an ironmonger." Will turned to Rodgers. "I won't be living here, will I?"

"No, you'll become part of Mr. Fortescue's household. That's why Cook is taking advantage of every opportunity to feed you."

"Doesn't Mr. Fortescue feed his apprentices?"

"I'm sure he does, but not the way Cook feeds you."

"What will happen when I'm apprenticed?"

"It's all quite simple. You will meet your new master and the indentures will be drawn up. That's the agreement about how long you will be an apprentice and what Mr. Fortescue agrees to teach you. The clerk will write the terms twice on one sheet of paper. You, Mr. Fortescue, and the representatives of the parish will swear to abide by the terms and sign both copies. The clerk will tear the sheet in half and give one copy to you and one to Mr. Fortescue. Then you will go live with him."

"Were you ever apprenticed?"

"Yes, to a shoemaker."

"You learned to make shoes?"

"In fact, I learned more about the leather to make shoes, and that's how I met Master Perry. I was buying some leather from him, and he purchased the rest of my apprenticeship."

"So you don't make shoes?"

"Never did. I was a much better factor, or purchaser, for Master Perry's business."

Will thought for a moment. "Are you still an apprentice to Master Perry? You still live in his house."

"I live here because Master Perry has a very large house with an apartment for me, and because we are very good friends."

"But you could live somewhere else if you wanted?"

Rodgers nodded, then drank the last of his tea. "Now I must finish my accounts."

After the door closed behind him, Cook pulled out a bowl and rolling pin. "I think I'll make a spicy crust. How does that sound for a treat for the twins? It won't take long to bake. By the time we've cleared away, it'll be ready."

Within five minutes the kitchen door flew open and the twins ran into the room. One cried, "Spicy crust! We can smell it! When will it be ready?"

"Susan! James! Do settle down." Gillian closed the door behind her. "Mind yourselves or you'll have none at all." She sat the twins at the table, tucked Susan's curls back under her cap, then settled onto a bench by the fireplace.

"Who is that?" The twins spoke together.

"Don't point," Gillian said. "It's not polite."

The fingers disappeared into their laps. "But who is that boy?" James asked again.

THE FOUNDLING

Cook counted out cups and saucers. "That's Will. He'll be here for a few days."

"Will who?"

"Will Pancras." Cook counted the spoons.

"What's he doing here?" asked Susan.

"Visiting with me and helping me with your spicy crust." Cook put water on to boil, then measured tea leaves into a small dish.

"Is he a cook?"

"No, but he has been helping me."

The kitchen door opened again; Rodgers entered.

"I thought you were doing accounts or some such thing," Cook said.

"Isn't it time for another cup of tea?" he asked. "Besides, I had to see my favorite twins." He scooped them up, one on each arm. "What are you two doing in the kitchen? Aren't you having your bite in the nursery?"

"No, Stephen is sleeping and Mummy says we are too noisy," said James.

"I don't doubt that for one minute. Now give us a hug." Rodgers managed to sit while still holding the twins. At his request they told him all they had done outside. When James talked too long, Susan reached up and turned Rodgers's face to her.

Gillian took the opportunity to lean against the fireplace and close her eyes.

The twins giggled.

"Shhh. Let Gillian rest." Rodgers put his finger over first one then the other mouth. "You two lead her a merry chase, you know. Small wonder she needs a nap."

"She snores."

"Yes, I heard. Now sit quietly at the table. Cook has just poured our tea."

Will watched Rodgers with the twins. He doesn't remember I'm here, he thought. Those twins have all his attention. They climb all over him. I would never—

"Will, come, join us." Cook filled a cup for him.

"Come, sit at this end." Rodgers said. "Yes, right across from me so we can talk." He set the twins down on their bench. "Will, did you have a hand in preparing this crust?"

"Cook did it. I just watched." Will sat down. He remembered me, he thought. Even with the twins and—

"Cook never lets us help." Susan shook her head.

"You sat on a pudding once," James reminded her.

Will leaned over to Rodgers. "They really are noisy."

"Indeed, they are. They keep Mistress Perry and Gillian on their toes."

"Did I hear my name mentioned?" Gillian stretched and yawned. "A cup of tea? Wonderful." She sat down with her cup and saucer and sipped slowly. "And how are you, today, Will?"

"I'm fine, thank you." Suddenly he couldn't keep from grinning. "Do you remember that day in the laundry?"

"I remember a good many days in the laundry."

"No." Will laughed. "I mean the time you scalded your foot and danced around howling."

Gillian gave him a stern look. "You remember that performance, do you? You told everyone as I recall."

"Only Cook."

"That's as good as telling everyone." She glanced over at Cook. "I danced around that room on one foot, didn't I?"

Will smiled and nodded.

"My, how our lives have changed since then." She smiled at him over her cup. "Now I must see to the babies. Children—finished? Thank Cook and come along, then. Susan, leave your serviette at the table."

Will rubbed his chin. Gillian was rather nice after all.

Rodgers said, "Would you like to visit the warehouse tomorrow? A ship arrived a couple of days ago from the Orient." He turned to Cook. "You don't mind my taking Will, do you? He said he's been helping out in the kitchen."

"I'll make him work twice as hard all morning. Of course, he can go."

THE FOUNDLING

"We'll bring back some of the tea. Now I really must get back to my accounts if I'm to have tomorrow afternoon free. Be ready at one o'clock." Rodgers pushed away his cup and left.

Will turned to Cook. "Did you hear? I can go to the warehouse and see the tea and spices and the ship and all the things I read about. Maybe I can even go on the ship. What do you think?"

"I'm sure I don't know. Everyone will be busy unloading the ship. Mind you don't get underfoot."

Chapter 8

Marie was not displeased as she went through the Perrys' home, though there were still patches of dust that Charlotte must see to. And why were these pieces of furniture not in their proper places?

She entered the small sitting room where the Perrys frequently relaxed after the children went to bed. Here the maids had followed her instructions to the letter. Cushions nicely brushed. Draperies drawn. Fireplace cleaned and a new fire laid. Fresh flowers and candles.

On through the house Marie walked. Charlotte must be more careful here, pay more attention there. On a whim, Marie detoured past the laundry. Those girls had better be up to their elbows in washing, she thought. She stood outside the open door listening to their chatter over the sloshing of the water.

"There, I didn't think that grass stain would ever come out." Charlotte held up a stocking for inspection. "Elsie, did you get those handkerchiefs clean? Remember, they must be bleached as well."

Elsie! That was the new girl's name. Just ten. Not old enough to be cheeky. Although Gillian, at that age, had been.

"They're finished and soaking in the bleach. I'm doing the serviettes now. They'll need bleaching as well."

"I know. Do what you can with those food stains and hope the bleach will get the rest." Charlotte wrung the sock out. "Don't put your hands in the bleach, Elsie! Stir that kettle with this stick."

Marie moved away, still listening. "We'll ask Cook for some lard for our hands . . . " Just like Gillian used to, she thought. At least I get more work out of them than I did from Gillian. She paused at the door of the playroom. The twins saw to it that this room was always in confusion. A broom and a very large dustbin are all this room needs, thought Marie. That, and a strong hand to teach the children how to behave.

THE FOUNDLING

She pushed the door open. It was as bad as she feared. Toys lay everywhere. Mistress may say what she will, but I can't stand this, she thought. She shook out a cloth sack and soon had it nearly filled with dolls, tops, whistles, wooden and cloth animals, boats, and puppets. Mistress's castoff hats, ribbons, and bits of cheap baubles came next. All went into the sack, now so heavy it dragged on the floor. Half of this rubbish should have been thrown out long ago, Marie thought. She surveyed what was left. There was still enough for half the children of London.

Movement in the garden drew her to the window. If that is some ruffian off the streets having a go with the toys in the garden—her hand stopped at the door latch. Him again! Marie shook herself. She didn't want to be anywhere near Will, even though he didn't know. He never could. Still—

She stepped back from the window and stumbled over the toys. She walked to the door and felt for the latch, never taking her eyes from Will. She saw him jump from the swing and bound up the walk. Just as Will reached the house, her trembling fingers found the latch, and she slipped through the open door.

Marie was nearly running when she reached the front parlor. Only when the carved wooden panels closed behind her was she able to breathe. The silence of the room eased her nerves. The huge fireplace, cherry-red carpets, heavy furniture, and sunlight burnishing the wainscotting invited her to relax. She walked through the room, flicking away a bit of dust here, arranging a candlestick there. Nothing was out of order. The noises in the streets were muffled, soft and comfortable.

She sat in her favorite chair and tilted her head until it rested against the chair back. Much better, she thought. No one knows I'm here. I can forget how much it startled me to see that boy again.

The first time she'd seen him in the kitchen last week had given her a horrible turn. She'd run straightaway to check on the brooch. It had not been disturbed.

She closed her eyes. Why should I still be afraid? It's been years that I've had it. It mocks me each time I look at it, she thought. I'm sure I wouldn't feel this way except the boy is here. As soon as he leaves, I'll be fine. After all, I've had the brooch for so long, it's really mine anyway. I'm no thief. Taking a bauble from a little boy hardly qualifies one as a thief, does it? Besides, it's hidden; no one knows.

The twins are out of the house for the afternoon! Now there's a relief. No screaming or running children upsetting the house. No unexplained crashes and spills to clean. And Gillian with them. The perfect little mum, that's what she's become. Only nineteen and married . . .

Marie stiffened her jaw and gripped the arms of the chair. Why had he married her? Why had he chosen that addlepated girl with the plain features and straight brown hair? She had behaved like a cow from the first day they met. She'd stumbled over him in the front entry and landed in a heap at his feet. Sat there like a rag doll in a dirty apron, and linens scattered all over. Trying to sneak a shortcut, wasn't she, rather than taking the servants' passage?

Rodgers had helped her up and introduced her to his guest. Imagine! Introducing Gillian to anyone. Rodgers and Mr. Fielding even helped pick up the linens! One of them must have made some comment because all three laughed. Laughed! Gillian should have been beaten, and Rodgers too, for encouraging such behavior.

Then it wasn't a fortnight before Mr. Fielding came to call and asked for Gillian. And Master Perry let her walk out with him and she barely fifteen and me fully eighteen. Marie closed her eyes and rolled her head back and forth against the chair. It should have been me. I was older and prettier. I knew how to run a house and care for children. Mr. Perry should have insisted that I step out with Mr. Fielding. Mr. Fielding, of medium height, with blond hair and blue eyes. Such a smile that made the corners of his eyes crinkle. Why did he not notice me?

Marie opened her eyes. This was not why she had come to the parlor. She emptied her mind and let the warm sunlight soothe her. That was better. I shall try to recall only the happy times in this room, she said to herself, and forget Gillian. But one of the happiest times had been the party given by the Perrys for Gillian after the first reading of the banns.

THE FOUNDLING

Friends of the Fieldings had arrived first, Marie recalled. Really, his friends were not of the same social class as the Perrys, but they were nice enough and well dressed. The father was influential in his county, she'd heard. Then Gillian's small family had arrived, all agog over the fine match she had made and incredulous at the comfort and size of the Perry home. When Gillian entered the parlor, everyone had gasped. She wore a lovely blue dress over a white petticoat. Both were made of fine cotton brought all the way from India. The petticoat was decorated with white lace at the hem and white satin bows. The dress had small flowers held by tiny bows scattered on the skirt and waist. Her hair was caught up and back and the straight, brown locks that had never stayed under a mobcap had been coaxed into curls that were truly becoming. She wore little gold earrings that caught the light whenever she moved her head and, at her throat, a golden pin.

Marie tried to calm her breathing and relax again. But she recalled how she had nearly dropped the dishes she was bringing from the cupboard. The room had faded for a moment, and conversations seemed to come from a great distance. When her sight returned and she could breathe again, she put the dishes down and leaned against the table. Had someone asked if she was all right? She really didn't remember.

And I couldn't leave. There was Gillian wearing a dress that should have been mine. And the pin and earrings! Mrs. Perry gave them to her, the woman who has never offered me so much as a farthing for all the work I've done over the years. How dare she reward laziness so beautifully? I wanted to scream and throw every dish at her. Instead, I had to smile and serve punch and cakes—and watch that cow curtsey and accept gifts that might have been mine. And at her side, Mr. Jesse Fielding, who never once looked my way.

And Charlotte chattering on! "Hasn't Gillian quite blossomed since she's fallen in love? Rodgers says Gillian has become quite a fine woman and that Mr. Fielding is fortunate to have found her. Just look at them, so happy."

What did I say? Oh yes, "You can't make a silk purse out of a sow's ear." And still the servant girl kept talking.

"How you talk! You must be happy for them. Aren't you?" Charlotte had arranged more cakes on a silver tray. "And look at the earrings Mistress gave her as a gift. Did she give her the pin as well? It's beautiful."

Mistress had given gifts to a dunderhead who barely knew the business end of a broom. "I'm sure it's none of your concern."

Gillian and Mr. Fielding had approached the table. She will probably spill punch on him, thought Marie. The picture was so funny that she smiled as she handed Gillian a cup.

"Thank you, Marie."

"Yes, thank you," said Mr. Fielding, "especially for your warm smile. I know it carries many good wishes with it, and we appreciate every one."

Marie and Charlotte dropped curtseys.

Gillian sipped her punch. "It's rather warm with all these people here." She set her cup down and moved away to greet another friend.

At least she won't spill it on anyone, thought Marie. Pity.

"Lovely, isn't she?"

Marie looked up into Mr. Fielding's smile. "I'm sorry?"

"Lovely, isn't she?" He motioned toward Gillian. "And making quite an impression on everyone. So gentle, so kind."

Marie opened her mouth. Nothing came, so she just smiled. Lovely, gentle, kind? If that's what he really thought of Gillian, he was a man of poor judgment altogether.

"He has a good future. They'll do well." Rodgers picked up a cup. "Jesse has a good head for business. Why, only last week he was able to purchase a small manor in Sussex."

"Really?" Marie wiped another cup to remove any dust.

"Oh yes. I imagine that soon Gillian will have her own lady's maid. She's come quite a ways, our Gillian." Rodgers turned to Marie. "I'm sure someone will soon discover all your fine qualities, Marie." He smiled and moved to the side of another guest.

Discover? Discover! Marie shouted to herself. As if my qualities are hidden under so much rubbish! I'm prettier by far, have better social graces, a better education, and I can run this or any other house in London.

Her smile had been rather grim when she handed another guest a cup of punch. How dare he?

"Charlotte, get out of my way, or I shall pinch you black-and-blue."

"I wasn't in your way, miss," said the serving girl.

Marie set her lips in a firm line.

Charlotte bobbed her head. "Yes, miss. Surely, miss, 'twas my fault."

"I must leave for a moment. You may serve the last guests, but do have a care not to be untidy." Marie left the parlor. Jealousy washed over her and her eyes filled with tears. Jesse Fielding should be mine. That party should be mine. Gillian's future should be mine.

In her room, Marie had sunk to her knees and sat back on her heels. Her silent sobs bent her double over her clenched hands. Gillian will be a lady, or as much a lady as Gillian can be. Her husband will soon wish he'd chosen me. She grabbed a shoe and threw it against the wall.

"Miss? Miss?" Charlotte rapped on the door. "Are you all right? May I come in?

"No." Marie had to clear her throat before she could be heard. "No, I'm fine."

"Miss, we need you, please, to help us. The guests are leaving."

"I'll be right there. Go along, I say."

Marie did not move until Charlotte's footsteps died away. She got up and splashed cold water on her face. I don't care, she told herself. I don't need them, any of them. Gillian putting on airs. A manor in Sussex won't make her what she isn't. A good-for-nothing tricked out in finery is still good for nothing. And Jesse Fielding chose her. I'm not good enough for him, but Gillian is. He's not so clever as I thought, marrying so far beneath himself.

Marie patted her face dry and studied her reflection. "You're well out of it, my girl. Mr. Fielding obviously has no taste and little desire for the finer things of life. Let him have Gillian. I'll not settle for second best, and I'll do whatever it takes to get what I deserve." She stopped with her hands poised over her hair.

Yes, whatever it takes. And I'll make the Perrys pay for treating me like a common housemaid and preferring Gillian before me. Somehow I'll get even with them all.

Part 2: The Scullery Boy

Marie nodded to herself now in the quiet of the parlor. I've done just as I planned. Within the year I became housekeeper. Now this house runs according to my schedule. Even Cook must have meals ready when I say, and Rodgers stays out of my way. I've saved a bit and been able to invest in some of Master Perry's ventures. I'm not rich, not yet, but I will be. When I go out, one of the maids attends me. I daresay it is hard to tell that I am not a fine lady. I even have a few pieces of jewelry. They aren't of the most expensive quality, but one must begin somewhere. If those pesky Puritans weren't governing, I'd have feathers in my hats as well.

Soon I may be able to wear the brooch. I bought a velvet-lined casket for it. What a sacrilege to have kept it wrapped in flannel under the hearthstone. But one does what one must. And with the brooch lies a small ring and a delicate chain. I truly enjoyed Mistress Perry's distress when she realized the ring was lost. A precious heirloom, a gift from her grandmother. Then a few months later, I dropped the gold chain into my pocket. Too simple, really. She almost believed me when I suggested that it might have been the children who lost it while they played.

Marie brushed a bit of lint from one of her cuffs. "Oh yes, they'll pay for not giving me what I deserve. There is nothing to stop me. No flies in the ointment . . . except for the return of that foundling. They're treating him just like they did Gillian, better than he's worth. He'd better stay out of my way, or I'll make him wish he were still in the streets."

A twinge of the old fear touched her heart. No, she thought, I'm safe. He'll soon be apprenticed. Perhaps I'll have another miniature inserted in the brooch. My own likeness? Why not? Who could say then it didn't belong to me?

Marie stretched her arms over her head. I suppose I must visit Mistress about menus for next week, she thought. Before she left the parlor, Marie paused for a last look. Perfect. "I shall have a room much like this in my own house, someday. Indeed I shall." Her face softened ever so little.

part 3
The Apprentice

Chapter 1

Will sat on his bed. He held his indenture in his hands. By it he swore to obey his new master in all things, never to lie to or to steal from him, to learn the mystery of ironmongery, and never to tell any of his master's secrets. For ten years! And during those years Will was not to return to the parish of St. Pancras, the parish that had given him half his name, and no one from the parish was to visit him or contact him in any way. Did that include Rodgers? Will was sure it did, since Rodgers lived in the parish.

Rodgers had gone with him to the brief ceremony of signing the indentures. If anyone had asked me, thought Will, I'd have told them I want to be just like Rodgers. Will took a deep breath to loosen his chest. Why couldn't I have stayed with Rodgers and Master Perry and learned to be a merchant? he thought. I would have worked hard and done anything they asked me. I can read and write and do arithmetic. What more does a merchant need?

But it had been Rodgers who had told him how proud he was of him and what a good position this was. He had shaken Will's hand, clasped his shoulder, and wished him all good fortune. Good fortune? I don't know Mr. Fortescue. I don't know if I can please him because I don't even know what an ironmonger does. And I'll be twenty-three when I finish learning.

Will furrowed his brow and scrunched his eyes tight. The tears came anyway. He would not see Rodgers for ten years. Or Cook. They'd sent him away, again. He rubbed the tears away with the back of his hand and searched his pockets for a handkerchief. Mistress Bessie always wanted him to use a handkerchief, but he didn't have one. His clothes had been sent ahead and put away for him. They probably took all my clothes, just like at the Vicar's, he thought.

When he opened the wardrobe, however, all his clothes were there, even his new ones. Will found his handkerchiefs. He snuffled hard, discovered he didn't need to blow his nose after all, and stuffed the square of cloth into his pocket.

He still held the indenture in his left hand. There were some wet spots on it. He patted them dry so the ink wouldn't run. There was a huge hollow place in his chest that felt as though it could never be filled up. For a moment he saw, as clearly as if she stood before him, a familiar smile, bright brown eyes, and shoulders wrapped in a blue shawl.

"Mum," Will sobbed, half expecting her to reach out and pull him close. But his memory disappeared as quickly as it had come, and Will stood alone in the center of his room, wanting any small part of her to hold. Everything was gone. The old blue shawl was gone. His mother's brooch—he wasn't even sure any more that he'd ever had it. He tried, but he couldn't bring her image back.

Will reached for the brown pouch Mistress Bessie had made for him. This was all he had. He laid his indenture on the table and carefully unrolled the green ribbon. He ran his finger from one end of the ribbon to the other. He placed the small pouch beside it. "This is all. And my two books." Will looked up to the shelf where they sat. He recalled Rodgers standing up for him in the Vicar's house.

A breeze from the window swept the indenture from the table to the floor. And, thought Will, I have that piece of paper for ten years. He went to the open window.

"If I were free," he murmured, and stopped. What if I were free? Where would I go? I could run away like Harry and his friends. I wonder what they're doing? Of course, if I ran away, I'd have to leave London. Then I would never see Rodgers again.

He studied the courtyard below him. It was bounded by buildings on three sides and a high wall on the fourth. The gate was locked. But it wasn't the locked gate that kept him from running away. Rodgers and Cook and Master Perry had been so proud of him and his new position. He couldn't disappoint them.

The breeze caught his indenture again and propped it against the wall. Will went and picked it up. He tried to smooth the edge where it was wrinkled. His signature stood out in bold, black letters. He admired his penmanship for a moment. No splatters or poorly formed letters. And right next to it was the signature of

Stephen Rodgers. Stephen? Will still felt surprise at learning that Rodgers had a proper Christian name. It didn't sound right, somehow.

"I'm proud of you, Will," he had said. "You've done well." Then he'd walked away without another word.

"Stephen Rodgers," said Will aloud. He went to the table and rolled the green ribbon and put it back in its pouch. After a moment's hesitation, he folded his indenture until it was small enough to slide in beside the ribbon. He smiled and put the pouch in his pocket. "Rodgers is proud of me. He said so."

The next morning after breakfast, Will followed Mr. Fortescue across the courtyard and into a large building. Fires blazed on three hearths, making shadows dance on all the walls. The sound of hammers against metal hurt Will's ears. He could barely hear Mr. Fortescue.

"This is the forge area. Here the metal is heated and then hammered into shape." The loud sizzle of hot metal hitting water interrupted him.

"Hello, Adam. Busy today?"

"That we are, Mr. Fortescue." Adam held up the wet metal. "Slow work, this," he said and picked up a large file.

Mr. Fortescue walked on to a corner where two men pulled thin ribbons of wire through a machine. "This is our wiredrawing area. We don't do much of this, as a rule. But I have an old customer who wants some cable. Couldn't turn him down." The men nodded to Mr. Fortescue and continued their work.

"Over here, Will, is the foundry where we pour melted metal into molds. When it hardens, we remove the casting from the mold, smooth it, and polish it. We've turned out some fine work here over the years. We mostly outfit ships, but we've done locks and clocks as well as buckles and buttons." He called to one of the men. "Are you ready to pour, Tom?"

"Just finished pouring, sir. Ready to remove the mold if you'd care to see."

Will followed his master over to the workbench where Tom opened a mold made of sand. Inside were two sets of hinges.

"Here, young man." Tom picked the hinges up with heavy tongs. The metal was still hot and covered with sand.

"Will you put this in water to finish cooling it?" Will asked.

"No, we don't do that with brass."

"It's not shiny at all."

"There's the real work," said Mr. Fortescue. "Tom, here, will clean off the sand and then spend several hours smoothing the hinges with all sorts of files and then polishing them with grits and rouge. Anything nearly finished for us to see, Tom?"

Tom held up another set of hinges. They gleamed in the light, and Will could see his reflection in them.

"Tom takes great pride in his work. Thank you, Tom."

Mr. Fortescue turned to Will. "Now, my boy, you'd best meet the foreman. He's in charge of all this, and he will be in charge of you. He's in the forge right now."

He called to his master ironmonger and foreman. "Mr. Porch! When you've a minute!"

Work in the forge slowed momentarily as the men looked up to see what was happening.

Mr. Porch set them back to work with a look. "Yes, sir, Mr. Fortescue." He left his anvil and approached.

Will had never seen anyone like this man. He had large hands, heavily muscled arms and shoulders, and a chest like a barrel. When he crossed his arms over his chest, his upper arms seemed to double in size. His heavy leather apron protected him from his neck to his knees. His hair was completely white and cut short. His blue eyes shone out of a face flushed from exertion. When he spoke to Mr. Fortescue, it was as to an equal.

"Mr. Porch, I have here Will Pancras. He is our new apprentice. You'll please put him to work. Will informed me this morning that he has absolutely no idea of the business of metals and forges, but he is willing to work hard to learn."

Will nodded, never taking his eyes from Mr. Porch.

"Oh yes, Will also reads very well, writes passably, and can do arithmetic." Mr. Fortescue turned to Will. "So, young man, step right into the forge. Mr. Porch will be your superior. You are to follow his orders implicitly."

Will nodded again and held out his hand to Mr. Porch. "Good day, sir." At least, he thought, everyone will know I have manners.

Mr. Porch's eyebrows went up a fraction of an inch. Will's hand and wrist disappeared into his grasp. He shook Will's hand solemnly and with some care. "Come along, lad. There's plenty for you to do."

Will looked at Mr. Fortescue, who nodded for him to follow. The workers looked up as he passed. Some smiled encouragement. He followed Mr. Porch to a bench near the pump in the courtyard.

"Sit down, Will. As Mr. Fortescue said, I'm Mr. Benjamin Porch. You'll hear them call me Ben. However, as a youngster, you will call me Mr. Porch."

Will said, "Yes, sir," but his eyes never left Mr. Porch's muscular shoulders.

"You will always keep your hair cut short and your shirttail tucked in. We can't have you catching fire or getting caught in any of the machinery. For the time being, you must wear long-sleeved shirts with the cuffs buttoned. That will help protect you from the heat of the hearths, though you'll not be too close to them for some time." Mr. Porch changed his position and refolded his arms. "Is there something wrong, Will?"

Will shook his head. In his mind he was betting that Mr. Porch could lift anything he wanted with no trouble at all.

"Now as to your actions in the forge. You must never interrupt the men at work. If they wish to talk to you while they are resting, that is up to them. You must always do what they ask unless you are told differently by me. Always obey quickly.

"Until you know your way around, it is best to stay away from the hearths and forges. Always watch where you're going. You could very easily be hit with flying metal or a hammer, or be burned at a hearth."

Mr. Porch flexed one arm and watched Will's eyes widen in admiration.

"Like them, do you? Become a maker of fine metals and perhaps you'll be just like me."

Will looked up. "Me?" His eyes were still wide, and his lips parted in amazement.

Mr. Porch reached over and flexed Will's right arm. He held the muscle between his thumb and forefinger.

"It'll take a few years and lots of work, but it's possible."

When Mr. Porch let go of his arm, Will poked at his muscle. There wasn't much there.

"Now your duties."

Will sat back on the bench and leaned against the wall behind. He crossed his arms so his hands pushed his muscles out and made them more noticeable. "Yes, sir?"

"You'll carry water for the men, and sweep the floors, and run errands as you're told. One last thing. Drinking water is to come from the rain barrels over there. Water for the forges comes from this well." A note of pride entered Mr. Porch's voice. "We are one of the few forges with our own well, put in by Mr. Fortescue himself at great cost."

"The men drink water?" Will could not recall ever seeing an adult man drink water unless he was desperate. His mum had warned him as a little boy of the dangers of drinking water. It carried horrible diseases.

"While they're in the forge, they drink water, so be sure it's the good water from the rain barrels."

Mr. Porch thought for a moment.

"We're busy today. There's work that must be done, and I've no time to do more with you today. So you're to stay out of the forge altogether unless someone calls for water. What I want you to do is tidy the yard. Brooms and shovels are in that shed."

"Mr. Porch?"

Ben Porch leaned forward, his hands on his thighs, his elbows out. "Yes?"

"Will I have a leather apron like yours?"

"You're not working in the forge yet. But, yes, eventually you will have your own apron. Now let's get to work." He pushed himself up and headed across the yard. "And, Will, you'll eat with the men at noon."

Will cleaned the yard every week. He carried water for the men every day. That winter Mr. Porch gave him the task of sweeping out the forge and foundry at the end of each day. Will thought he surely must be making his muscles grow.

During the winter, work in the forge was warm and comfortable. In the hot weeks of summer, it was nearly unbearable. Will worked hard to please Mr. Porch. In the back of his mind he was also working hard to please his mum, Mistress Bessie, Cook, Master Perry, and Rodgers. Especially Rodgers. He knew if he worked hard enough and did very well that Rodgers would find a reason to visit, even though he wasn't supposed to.

At the beginning of his second summer at Mr. Fortescue's, Will received his leather apron. He could now move freely in the forge. It also meant new duties at the hearths. He had to pump bellows to keep fires hot to soften iron or to melt the ores for brass and bronze. While he worked, he saw a sword appear from dull metal that was hammered, heated, folded, and hammered again and again. When it was finished, it had a strong, sharp blade. He saw household implements mended and everything from bits for bridles to rims for wheels come from the forge and foundry. But mostly, the men made metal parts for ships.

During his second winter, Will was given the task of cleaning individual work areas and placing each man's tools exactly as he wanted them. All the time he worked, he waited and watched patiently for Rodgers. Finally, he admitted to himself that Rodgers had too many other responsibilities and interests to visit an apprentice.

At the end of his second year, Will took the small pouch from his pocket and weighed it deliberately in his hand. There was no use carrying it around any more. The people it represented were no longer a part of his life. He would always remember them, but he had new friends at Mr. Fortescue's. And he had met some other apprentices and spent his free time with them. Will opened a small drawer in the wardrobe and placed the pouch holding the green ribbon and his indenture into it. People like you while they're around, he thought, but they forget later on.

He didn't blame Rodgers. After all, Rodgers was simply obeying the agreement in the indentures. I'd best forget too, he thought.

THE FOUNDLING

Even so, it was hard to close the small drawer and decide not to open it again.

Two days later, as he had done repeatedly over the past two years, Rodgers left a book for Will. He had come across it in a stall near St. Paul's Cathedral, a book on maps and map drawing. He bid good day to Mr. Fortescue, pleased at the good report on Will and even more pleased at having found a book he was certain would tickle Will's fancy. Rodgers wasn't permitted to see or speak to Will, but he could provide him with good books, even if Will wasn't to know they had come from him.

Chapter 2

September 1655

Will leaned on his shovel. There wasn't much left to do. He had banked the fire of the largest hearth so it wouldn't go out before Monday morning.

Fires and coals! I've been carrying coal and building fires for someone most of my life, Will thought. And sweeping floors! But not too much longer. I'm over fifteen. Mr. Porch says that I can begin learning about ship fittings. A new apprentice will do the fires and the sweeping.

Will dumped a panful of rubbish into the dustbin. "Well, that's the last of it," he said. His voice sounded hollow in the quiet building.

He had no plans for tonight beyond a hot bath and brushing his suit for Sunday morning services. And that's a good thing, he thought. I'm so tired. Maybe I'll read that new book Mr. Fortescue gave me. Or, maybe I'll . . . Will yawned so hard he had to close his eyes and lean against the door. He shook his head to clear it and finished locking up.

The next afternoon John Battersby, apprentice to Mr. Budgins, the weaver, called from the street.

"Will! Will! Are you coming? The lads are waiting for us."

Will leaned from his bedroom window. He could see John pacing impatiently outside the courtyard gate. "Coming," he called back.

He hadn't intended to be late, but Sunday dinner had not begun at the usual time because there had been two christenings, three readings of marriage banns, and a rather long sermon at church. And then there had been Mrs. Fortescue's birthday celebration. Will pulled on an old pair of stockings and pushed his feet into his shoes.

"Will! Do hurry!"

John could shout loudly enough to shake the walls. He was the tallest of Will's friends. His arms and legs were always too long for his shirtsleeves and breeches because it seemed he never stopped growing. Will thought it fortunate that John was apprenticed to a weaver. At least there was plenty of cloth to make him new clothes. But even Mr. Budgins had given up trying to keep John in clothes that fit.

Will ran down the back stairs to the kitchen. "May I have my lunch?" he asked the Fortescues' cook.

She pointed to a small cloth sack. "I don't know where you put it all," she said and went back to tidying the linen closet.

"Thanks, awfully." Will ran out of the kitchen.

"Don't slam the door," the cook called, but Will had already pulled the kitchen door shut with a bang, run down the hallway, and crashed through the front door.

"Let's go, John."

"I was ready to leave without you."

"Sorry. Had to get the food." He swung the cloth bag in front of his friend, then tied it to his belt.

John patted his coat pocket. "I have something too. Not much, though." They walked on. "We're going to the river. Some East Indiamen came up with the tide yesterday."

The East Indiamen were the largest merchant ships to dock in London. Like Master Perry's ships, they sailed around the world and returned with goods from all over. Their cargoes of cotton, silk, tea, spices, coffee beans, sugar, ivory, and gold were so precious that each ship carried cannon for protection against pirates. More than one vessel had docked in London with a mast and some rigging missing or with its hull patched from a battle at sea.

Robert joined them at East Smithfield. If John was the tallest of Will's friends, Robert was the shortest. But Robert was not small in any other way. Like Will, he was a foundling. He was named after the street where he had been taken up: Throgmorton. Robert Throgmorton. He thought his last name sounded quite important, especially if he rolled each *r* and said "Thrrrogmorrrton." He would have preferred to be a soldier, but he was apprenticed to Mr. Bright, a tailor.

John took up the topic of Robert's soldiering once again. "I was thinking—you can't be a soldier. The army doesn't make uniforms small enough!"

Robert snapped around. "I can make my own uniform, and it would be the finest in the army. So fine that all the officers in the service of England would come to me for one just like it."

"How will you have the time to be a soldier if you're so busy making uniforms?" Will asked.

"Don't worry. I will."

"If your uniforms will be done up so flash, none of the soldiers will want to get them dirty fighting," said John. "What kind of army will that be?"

"A good one for parades," said Will.

Robert looked from John to Will. "Oh, that's right. Just because you've no plans or ambition, make fun of mine."

The conversation lapsed. The boys reached the river.

"There's Sam." Will pointed out a seated figure. "Sam! We're here!"

Sam waved for them to join him. "Look. That must be a new ship from the yards."

"Just launched, I'll bet." John whistled his appreciation.

"What a ship!" said Robert. "Wouldn't I just love to go aboard even for a few minutes."

"Makes all the other ships look so . . . bad. Wonder who the owner is." Will's eyes followed the graceful curve of the hull. "Look at all those gun ports. I bet pirates will think twice before trying to take that one."

"There are the East Indiamen." Sam waved his arm. "Look how low in the water they are. They must be full of all sorts of fancy goods."

Along with the merchantmen anchored in the Thames were smaller ships that travelled along the coast of England and traded to Europe. Some were slow barges that brought coal from Newcastle to London. They were favorite targets of Dutch privateers because they were slow and easy to sink. In return, English privateers attacked Dutch ships and sank all they could, so Will thought they probably came out about even.

"What do you think, Will?" John asked. "Where have they been?"

"Sorry?"

"The merchantmen. Where have they been?"

There was really no way to tell, but it began a guessing game that kept them busy each time they saw a vessel return.

"India and China."

"I wish I'd been aboard," Sam said, "and away from the smell of tanning leather."

Sam was the youngest of the friends. He was apprenticed to the tanner, Luke Falconer.

"Not me. I wouldn't be a sailor for anything," said John. "Remember that sailor we met once? He hadn't but one eye, most of his teeth were gone, and he had scars all over his face and arms. He smelled just awful." He held his nose.

"But think of the places he's seen," Sam said.

"I think mostly he saw the inside of taverns when he went ashore," said John.

"If I were a sailor, I would really try to see things wherever I went," said Sam. "I would write about them, like Marco Polo. He saw things so wonderful that no one believed his stories when he came home." Sam wasn't going to give up easily.

"I read that book," said Will. "I liked it."

"I still don't want to be a sailor." John shook his head. "I can't swim. Besides, can you see me trying to climb up one of those rope ladders?"

"Ratline," said Robert.

"What?"

"Those rope ladders are called ratlines."

"All right, ratline, and the ship tossed about in a huge storm? Can you see me doing that, really?" asked John.

"You get a sick stomach sitting on a fence. You're right, John. Better stay home." Robert tossed a stone into the river.

Sam leaned back on his elbows, then lay flat on his back. "I wonder what would happen if I ran away and went to sea?"

"Mr. Falconer would have to get another apprentice to beat and starve," said Will. "I don't know how you stay with him."

"I don't have much choice, do I?" asked Sam. "But let's not think about that right now. Look there. Where's that ship been and what's the cargo?"

And their game began again.

Some time later, they were interrupted by the rumble of John's stomach. "It must be time to eat." He rubbed his middle.

"For me too." Robert stood up and brushed himself off. "I really hate to go. It's been just about a perfect day, hasn't it? No rain at all. Nice and warm." He looked at the sky. "Hardly even a cloud."

"It's back to Master Budgins for me." John held his hand up. "Give us a tug, Robert."

Robert pulled and John scrambled to his feet.

"Do you really like being a weaver, John?" asked Sam. "I mean, is it hard work?"

They walked away from the river.

"It's better than being a tanner, I suppose. It's sure better than being an apprentice to the likes of your master."

"Will, now, has the best apprenticeship of all," said Robert. "He'll soon be working in the shipyard."

"If we're wishing," said Will, "I'd wish to be a goldsmith and be rich."

"Goldsmith! And sit all day bent over a workbench? Not you." John slapped his friend on the back. "You want to travel."

"Here's where I leave." Sam stepped toward a narrow street.

John took a small bundle from his pocket. "Here, Sam. It's a good thing you're smaller than I am. I can't wear this shirt anymore."

Will untied the sack from his belt. "And I have this for you. Hide it so it won't be stolen again, or eat it now."

"Me too," said Robert. "I have these stockings. They're too big for me."

"They don't look too big," Sam said.

Robert grabbed Sam's hand and put the stockings in it. "Besides, I'm a tailor and I can mend my old stockings—if I have to."

"You, mend stockings? That's funny, it is." Will laughed. "You'd stab yourself with the needle."

Robert lunged toward Will. "C'mon, John. Let's blow him up with one of his own bellows!"

THE FOUNDLING

Sam backed down the alley. "I really must go. You know he's angry if I'm the least bit late. 'Bye, and thanks." He ran off, untying Will's sack as he went.

"What'd you give him, Will?" John asked.

"Just some bread, an egg, a bit of meat, and a pickle."

"Where did you get all that?" asked Robert.

"We had a big dinner today. Mrs. Fortescue's birthday."

"I'm going to become an ironmonger," said John. "Master Budgins hasn't had a celebration since he took me on."

"You can sweep and tend the fires for me anytime. And carry water and clean the courtyard too."

John thought a moment. "I guess not. Tending looms isn't half bad if you can stand the noise. 'Bye!" He waved and ran across the street.

Robert fell into step beside Will. They walked along, enjoying the late afternoon sunshine. "How long do you suppose Sam can keep going on what little we're able to bring him?"

"I don't know. Mr. Falconer is a hard man, a mean, greedy man. I hope Sam can keep those stockings you gave him. He'll need them when the weather turns. And that won't be long."

"I wish he wouldn't beat Sam. He doesn't deserve that." Robert stopped.

"We'll keep doing what we can," said Will.

" 'Bye. See you next week."

" 'Bye, Robert."

Chapter 3

The next week Mr. Fortescue received an order for steel. A wagon brought the wrought iron bars Monday morning, and Mr. Porch supervised their arrangement on a bed of carbon in one of the furnaces. Will's job was to keep the furnace hot enough to bake the bars until they absorbed some of the carbon. By the end of the first day, he was covered with black soot.

While the smiths took the finished bars from the oven and put new ones in, he ate a meal and took a short nap. Then he went back to heat the furnace once again. At the end of four days and nights, enough bars had been baked to fill the order.

Will staggered out to a huge barrel of water, took off his leather apron, shirt, and shoes, and poured water over his head. The water ran down his face, but it didn't rinse away the soot. He rubbed his arms, but that didn't get him clean either. He leaned against the barrel, too tired to finish. He could hear the smiths hammering the bars flat, folding the metal over on itself, and hammering it again to distribute the carbon evenly throughout the iron.

I really should be in there helping, he thought. The sooner I get cleaned up, the sooner I can get back. He found a cake of soap and a washing flannel and climbed into the cool water in the barrel. It felt so good after the heat of the furnace that he leaned his head against the edge of the barrel and relaxed.

"Lads! Look what I've found! Here's our boy sleeping in a tub of dirty water!"

Will woke up just as Mr. Porch's hand came down on his shoulder.

"Shall we help him, lads? Seems he missed a few spots." Mr. Porch made a great show of pulling Will's ears out and looking behind them. He stuck out his lower lip and wagged his head. "A sorry case, this one. A sad case. A sad and sorry case if ever I saw one. Poor Will needs our help to clean behind his ears."

THE FOUNDLING

He plunged his hand into the tub and came up with one of Will's feet. Will lost his hold and slipped underwater. "Look at these feet." Mr. Porch ignored the splashes and splutters coming from the barrel as Will fought his way to the surface. "Why, there's soot between each little, pink toe. What do you say, lads? Do we have enough brotherly kindness left after a hard day's work to help a fellow creature?" He tapped the bottom of Will's foot just so it tickled. Will tried to get his foot away, but Mr. Porch held it higher as an example of how he and the other smiths could help a friend.

"You're right, Ben. Hand me that flannel and soap."

"No! . . . Oh, no!" Will gasped before he splashed back underwater.

The smith laughed, pulled Will up, and began on his ears. Then he passed the flannel to the next man, who scrubbed an arm until it was pink. He passed the flannel to another and so on until most of Will had been scrubbed clean and Mr. Porch was working very hard on his feet and toes.

Finally they tipped Will out of the barrel.

"My, he's clean." One of the men whistled.

Will wrapped a soggy towel around himself and stood as straight as he could. "I thank you for your help in my bath, gentlemen. Now, if you'll let me pass, I must dress for dinner."

The men laughed and one called, "Good one, Will. You sound just like a gentleman."

"Do gentlemen stand wrapped in wet towels in the middle of a courtyard?" another asked.

"Your clothes, my lord." Tom draped Will's dirty clothes over his shoulder and put his shoes in his hand. Will's wet feet slapped the stones when he walked across the yard. Everyone laughed.

"We're done for the day, lad. See you early tomorrow." Mr. Porch slapped a friend on the back. "Does a body good to help a friend in need, now, doesn't it?"

Will heard the men laughing over the splash of water. They were refilling the barrel so they could wash up before going home. Will dropped his clothes in the laundry and climbed the stairs to his room.

He nearly fell asleep again over supper. But he was hungry enough to wake up and eat three helpings of stew.

"To bed, Will." Mr. Fortescue shook him awake.

"Yes, sir." Will went slowly up the stairs, pulling himself along on the railing with his hands. He was asleep almost before he fell onto his bed and felt the cool pillow beneath his head.

He tumbled out of bed in time for breakfast. He didn't have to dress because he'd slept in his clothes. And he didn't have to straighten the bed covers because he'd hardly moved all night.

In the forge the men were busy hammering the carbon into the bars.

"Say, Will, these bars are done proper," Mr. Porch said when he walked in. "We still need you at the bellows today so we can finish hammering the carbon in."

Will nodded and stuffed bits of cloth into his ears against the noise of the hammers. While he worked the bellows, he thought about ways to help Sam. It was too bad Sam wasn't an apprentice of Mr. Fortescue's. The work was hard, but there was always enough food and warm clothes. But there was no way Sam could change apprenticeships. What if Sam ran away? Some apprentices did that. He and Robert and John could hide Sam somewhere and take him food. Will shook his head. How long could that last? Someone would see him, some constable or nosey old busybody would turn him in. Sam could go to prison. It really couldn't work anyway, with winter coming on.

What if Sam could get back to his mum? She could go to the vestry and demand a new master for him. That's been done. Wonder where his mum lives? Will thought. Then we'd be in trouble for helping him leave his master. There really is no good solution. He pumped the bellows again.

Will took an extra meat pie from the table and added it to the loaf of bread he'd already begged from the cook. Now if Robert remembered the cheese, and John the fruit, Sam would do well this week.

The four met in East Smithfield and walked around the Tower up to Lion Quay, just below London Bridge. From there, they could watch the small ferries shoot the bridge. The great pillars that supported the bridge were so close together that unskilled ferrymen often dumped both goods and passengers into the muddy waters of the Thames. Some passengers made the ferryman pull to shore on the upriver side of the bridge. They walked to the downriver side while the ferryman took the boat through the pillars. Then they got back in to continue their journey.

The boys understood why ladies might want to get out and walk, but why would men? Shooting the bridge with the river's current and the tide pushing the boat along, racing through the great piers of London Bridge, had to be too exciting to be missed.

Sam whirled around. "Where's Will?"

"He'll be along. He's found another shop that sells maps," said John. "He's trying to see in the windows."

"Has he ever been to the bookstalls over by St. Paul's?" asked Robert. "I'll bet he could find everything he ever wanted over there."

"Most of the mapmakers are down by the docks. Will knows all of them. He even has an old map on the wall above his bed. Some old copy. But he's added to it so it's nearly complete. He's even made corrections on it. You know, things that weren't drawn quite right. Well, he's got them right on his map. I've seen it."

"Sure, John. As if you'd know," said Robert.

"You'd know too, if you'd seen it. It's a right piece of work, it is." John's fingers drew a delicate line in the air. "All inked in, so perfectly. You just know he's got it right."

"So that's why we're always losing him," said Robert.

"From all that reading, you know. Made him daft." John tapped his head.

Sam smiled. "I'd like to see that map. When I used to read, I wanted to know where all the places were. Some I learned, but now I dare not read at all. Mr. Falconer says it makes people think they're better than others; high-minded, he calls it. He took my last book away. Says I don't need to read."

"Probably because he can't read himself," said Robert. "Why, I'll bet he's jealous of you."

"Me?" Sam looked at Robert. "He has all the nice clothes and house. Makes no sense for him to be jealous of me. I think—"

Will ran up. "I'm back."

"Did you see anything?" asked John.

"Not really. He has some nice old maps, but not much up-to-date."

"Nothing to add to your map?"

Will shook his head. "No great discoveries this week."

"We think Mr. Falconer is jealous of Sam," said Robert.

"Jealous?"

"Because Sam can read and Mr. Falconer can't."

"Maybe he can read," said Sam. "I've just never seen him do it." He sighed, "I just wish I didn't have to stay with him for twelve years."

"I've been thinking, Sam."

"Oh no, Will's been thinking." Robert rolled his eyes.

"Do shut up, Robert. What about, Will?" asked John.

"Of ways to help Sam out. First of all, here's a bite or two. There's a meat pie in there."

"And I have some cheese here." Robert dropped a smaller package in Sam's lap. "Sorry, it's the real hard kind."

John emptied his pockets. "I brought apples and pears from Mr. Budgins's trees. He doesn't mind. Here, we can all have some; I brought enough for all of us."

Robert slapped Sam on the back. "Eat now, if you're hungry."

"You don't mind? Where's the meat pie? I should eat that before it goes off." Sam took a large bite of the pie and kept on talking between chews. "Thanks awfully for the stockings, Robert. I wore them on Tuesday when we had that cold turn. I washed my feet before I put them on. They're that nice."

"Cold turn? When?" Will asked.

"The weather really freshened midweek, Will. Where were you?"

"We had an order for steel, so I tended the furnace for four days and nights. It might have snowed on Tuesday and I wouldn't have known."

"Hey, here comes a ferry. Want to bet whether or not it'll make it?"

"Robert, you don't have anything to bet with."

"We could just take sides."

"Here he comes!"

Sam shook Robert's arm. "Look at that! You'd have lost your bet."

"Lost! How do you how I'd bet?" Robert asked.

"You always bet they'll tip over—"

"Capsize," said Robert. "And I do not always bet they'll capsize."

"Capsize, that's it, tip over." Sam licked his fingers. "Yes, you do, and you know it. Thanks, Will. That was a delicious pie."

"Our cook's pies are the best."

"Were you able to keep the shirt?" asked John.

"Well, I had to get it dirty and give it a nasty tear."

"What? Why?"

"It was too nice for me, or so Mr. Falconer would say. He'd take it and sell it. I've seen him do it to another apprentice, and he's older and bigger than I am. Don't worry, the dirt will come out and the tear isn't where it will show if I tuck it well in."

"If Mr. Budgins treated me that way, I'd run away."

"I'd go home straightaway, I would," said Sam, "if I ever ran away."

"No, you'd be found and sent right back. That's not the answer," said Will. "What if we could find you a good hiding place? We could bring you food and clothes."

"Could we bring enough?" asked Robert. "We wouldn't be able to bring anything during the week. You'd probably have to do some begging," he said to Sam.

"And if you're caught, you'd be thrown into Newgate." John grimaced at the thought.

"No, he wouldn't," said Robert.

"Yes, he would. I've seen it happen. If you don't have a license to beg, you can be arrested as a sturdy rogue. And that's enough to get you into prison." John settled back.

"Could your mum complain to the vestry and have them find you a new master?" asked Will. "Sometimes it's done."

"But not for poor folks like me. The vestry has found me a place. They won't pay Mr. Falconer to release me from my indentures and then pay for a new master."

"You could complain to his guild," said Robert.

"If he belonged to one."

They lapsed into silence.

"Here comes another ferry!" John stood at the edge of the quay. "Look there! The current's too fast for him! He's slipping sideways! He'll never make it! Watch! . . . There he goes!"

None of them breathed until the small ferry reappeared on the other side of the bridge, half full of water.

"Wants a bit of practice, I'd say," said Will.

"Maybe that's what he's doing," said Robert. "I don't see that he has any boxes or passengers aboard."

"Say, what would we do if a ferry sank? Anybody besides Robert swim?"

"No."

"I'm not jumping in after anybody."

"Me neither. Except maybe to pick up the packages and boxes that float to the banks," John said.

"What a brave chap!" Robert taunted John. "You're so big, you probably wouldn't float anyway."

"Who'd want to swim in that dirty old river? Not me, I'm sure." John sniffed as though he were offended. "You should know by now, Robert, that water is not good for you."

"That's true," said Will. "I can remember seeing people sick in the streets when I was a little boy. Someone told me they were sick because they drank the water from the public well. Mr. Fortescue allows his men to drink only pure rainwater."

"Well, I learned to swim in the country where there is some good water. I went swimming a lot when I was little. It didn't hurt me," said Robert.

"That's what you think!" John looked at each one in turn. "We've finally discovered why Robert is a bit off the latch! Swimming! What a pity."

THE FOUNDLING

Robert stood and brushed himself off. "It's going to rain. Look at that cloud. I have to get back." He tucked his shirttail in. "What can we really do for Sam?"

Will turned to Sam. "We can keep bringing some food and the odd bit of clothing each week."

Sam nodded. "That's as good as my mum could ever do, poor as she is. You've been grand to help me out all this time."

Will put his arm around Sam's shoulders. "We'll each bring what we can each week. Right? We'll get you through another winter somehow."

Chapter 4

In late November Mr. Fortescue took Will out of the forge to the dockyards to begin his training there. "You must learn all the parts of each kind of ship," he said. "If you're going to do the best work, the kind of work that guarantees orders," he added, "you must know more than just your special area. Learn where each piece of hardware is used and how it is used. Listen to sailors if any come into the yard. They use the hardware in all conditions and sometimes give us good suggestions for improvements."

He led Will aboard one of the ships in dry dock for repair. "By the end of this week, I want you to learn everything you can about this ship. Let's get you started with a quick turn through the decks so you'll know where you are. I'll speak with you on Saturday, and you can show me what you've learned." He walked across the deck to a hatch opening and climbed down the ladder.

"What about my work at the forge?" asked Will when he joined Mr. Fortescue on the gun deck.

"The lads will have to get along, at least until I can get another apprentice to replace you . . . You should talk to the men in the forge too. You may see some of them here from time to time. They're good men, and Mr. Porch, the best." Mr. Fortescue stepped around some barrels of pitch. "Knows every piece of hardware on a ship. Probably invented some of them. When you've finished here, you'll have a basic knowledge of what goes into a ship. Then I want you to get into the yard and learn shipbuilding from the keel up. They're expecting you."

"Really?" Will followed his master deeper into the ship.

"Really. I pay the yard a fee for your education here, but it is up to you how much you learn. So take advantage of all you can. Talk to anyone who has time. Now let's go through the cabins and back up on deck."

Will came up the last steps and onto the deck. He turned slowly. This ship had lost a mast in a pirate attack and needed general refurbishing, as well, after a yearlong voyage.

How could he ever learn all Mr. Fortescue wanted him to in just one week?

Mr. Fortescue led him by the carpenters. Some of them nodded in recognition. Will heard snatches of conversations as they walked past.

"Davits pulled right out, I say, and the wood not rotten. Must have been quite a storm . . . "

"Split the length, it was. All the timber will have to be replaced . . . "

"Say, there's Mr. Fortescue. See what he thinks about the fittings for the main hold when he's free . . . "

"Harry! Where's the timber I ordered for . . . "

Will straightened his shoulders, proud to be walking beside a man who knew so much and whose opinion was so important to the workers.

"Judging by the smile on your face, I imagine you'll enjoy yourself," Mr. Fortescue said. "Just don't enjoy yourself too much. I'd not like losing you to the trade of ship's carpenter."

Will looked up. "Oh, yes, sir. I mean, no, sir."

"I think I know what you mean. I felt the same way when I started. This is truly an exciting place. Almost wish I were back here sometimes myself.

"Now here's a copybook and a pencil. Make notes of everything you see or hear, boy. Draw pictures of the hardware and the pieces of wood to which they're attached. And make them good. You will need to refer to them someday and you'll want to be accurate."

Will took the small book of blank pages and the pencil. He had seen the books of the men in both the forge and the foundry. They were soiled from use and were sometimes the source of forceful discussions because of differences from one diagram to another. No man let his book out of his sight.

"Put your name in it, lad."

"Yes, sir." Will wrote his name inside the cover.

"You might as well begin here and now. I'd begin by drawing a general plan of each deck of the ship. Then you can go through and discover what is needed in the way of hardware one deck at a time." Mr. Fortescue shook Will's hand. "I'd start below today. Keep out of the weather that way."

"Yes, sir."

That week Will surveyed every deck and cabin for fittings. He sat or lay for hours, measuring, drawing, and labelling. He frequently had to ask one of the refitters the name of a piece and its use. A carpenter named Bill Bowles said, "You must be one of Fortescue's. He's the only one I know who trains his apprentices this way. Good idea, I always thought. Know what you're about before you start." He looked through Will's book page by page. Then he led Will to the main deck and explained the tangle of ropes that were the ship's rigging.

"Course, some's missing 'cause she was dismasted, and the rest is pretty much a jumble, but look here." And he drew a simplified diagram that Will copied into his book. "Stop by any time."

Will often ate his lunch in the empty hold where he could hear the creaking of timbers and the wind whining through the rigging. It was in ships like this that Master Perry's goods came, with the caskets and boxes and bales lashed to rings set in the deck so they wouldn't shift. This was like the ships John, Robert, Sam, and he watched and dreamed about. And he was on one! In his imagination, the fitters' shouts above became the shouts of sailors, and Will was sailing the Indian Ocean. A crash followed by shouts shattered his dream. He got up and went to the cabins to draw the hardware used there.

On Friday, Will rolled his map up and took it to show to the men in the shipyard.

"Look at this. Didn't know I'd been that far away from home!" For over an hour, fitters and sailors showed where they'd been and told stories of their voyages. Some were good navigators and knew ports of call exactly. Others "couldn't find their heads with their hands" according to their friends.

Will made notes of new ports, islands, and coastlines.

"Now see here," Bill Bowles pointed out, "you've drawn Java in, and a right fine job you've made of it, but it's shaped longer and thinner. And just to the north of Borneo—a big island, that. To the east lies the Celebes. That island has a funny shape. Part of it looks like a cat's tail."

He sketched a small map in the back of Will's copybook. "A Dutch ship chased us around this island. Dangerous waters, full of reefs. Rip the bottom of a ship right out."

"Over here, Will." Mr. Fortescue waved to him from a table by the fire. "Have a seat. Glad you got my message to meet here rather than on the ship. What'll you have to drink?"

"Anything hot, sir," Will said and sat down. "Here's my book."

"In a few minutes. Tell me first what you think of this past week and what you did."

"There's so much. I know all the fittings on the *Fair Wind*."

"Tell me about them."

The examination continued through the afternoon. Mr. Fortescue finally picked up Will's book, and the questions became specific about the fittings for the gun decks, the hold, and the crew's quarters. Will was sure they'd covered every square inch of the ship. When Mr. Fortescue asked about rigging and the hardware used there, Will silently thanked Bill Bowles for his diagram and his suggestions that Will visit a ropewalk to learn about the different kinds of rope used on a ship.

Mr. Fortescue finally leaned back and called for stew and bread and butter for both of them. "You've done well. A few weaknesses, but nothing major. Your book is nicely done. I see you've already been refining your drawings. Glad you've taken advantage of the knowledge around you."

"The only reason I knew about the rigging was because of Bill Bowles. He knows a lot and told me to go to the ropewalk."

"Bowles was a good seaman in his day. Has a story about every port and ocean, I'm told. Rough reputation, though."

"I took my map to the yard yesterday. He gave me lots of information and even drew some maps for me. I hope he's accurate. A lot of what he says isn't even on the latest maps in the shops."

"As far as information goes, trust him. Bowles has a good eye."

"Do you know him?"

"Rather of him. Rumors only. Still, be careful. I'd like to see this map of yours when you have drawn in all your information. Always wanted to travel. Yes, indeed."

"Just as soon as I've finished, I'll show it to you. Someday, I want to take it to Mr. White over near London Bridge and see what he thinks of it."

"Who's Mr. White?"

"He sells maps and lets me look at them and sometimes watch him when he's drawing. He has a huge map of the whole world all colored in. It's beautiful. I'd like to do that to my map someday."

Mr. Fortescue pushed his empty bowl back and patted his stomach. "Better. Much better. Now, Will, you'll be in the yards for the next few months. Learn all you can about building a ship. And get on board as many different kinds of ships as you can. We'll get together every fortnight to check your progress. And be sure to keep in touch with Mr. Porch every day. From time to time he may need you in the forge."

"What we need, Will, are trees growing in the actual shape," the carpenter told him. "The yard has men travelling all over England looking for trees growing just the right way. The trees are marked for the Royal Navy, and anyone caught chopping one down is guilty of treason."

"For chopping a tree down?"

The carpenter nodded. "Good thing for those who are wood choppers that there aren't too many such trees left in England." He returned to his work.

"So where does all this timber come from?" Will asked.

"From the east, my boy—Sweden." He straightened and waved his arms to include the world east of London. "Sweden. Sends tar and timber. See those spars there? All of a piece they are, one tree for each. Tall and straight those trees must be. We don't have many left like that, either." He set a peg and hammered it in. "Each ship carries extras in case one snaps. Doesn't happen often, but when it does, the crew wants something to hang its canvas on. Storms, you see, or pirates sometimes."

"I've read about the New World. There are great forests there."

"Too far away and too expensive to compete with Sweden." He hammered another peg in. "There, that's done." The carpenter stood up again. "You're Fortescue's apprentice, aren't you? Bowles told me about you."

Will nodded.

"Come with me and I'll show you how the wood is seasoned. You've not seen that yet?"

"No, sir."

"Follow me. Let's see how much we can do before the rain begins again." He stopped midstride. "I like the title *sir,* and it's proper you should use it, for I'm the master carpenter here. Pete Goodcole's the name. But Pete will do. Mind you say it with proper respect. Now, come along, my boy."

They went to a part of the yard that was new to Will. Pete pointed out stacks of fresh-cut wood. From there he took Will through the stages of curing many kinds of wood. Will trotted along, writing as fast as he could, trying to remember what the various woods looked like as they cured, and how to know when each was ready to be used.

Pete looked up. A raindrop hit his eye. "Wouldn't you just know it? Here, I've only half done. Close that book, my boy, and let's get in out of the weather."

Will closed his book and folded an oilcloth around it for protection. Only half done. He let out a long breath. He'd need to paste more pages in his book soon.

Pete ushered Will into a public house called the Mermaid and led him to a table by the fire. "I'm beyond hungry," he said, looking around. "Richard? Richard, you old windbag. Where are you? Two bowls of whatever's in the kettle."

When Will protested, Pete held up his hand. "My pleasure, my boy, but when Richard comes, would you kindly call me 'sir'? That'll get right up his nose, it will." He slapped the table and chuckled. "Ho, Richard, we could perish here."

"Of course, I knew it was you." Richard stepped into the room. "Who else would make all that noise? I've a good mind to turn you back into the rain, you old—"

Pete held up his hand. "Mind what you say, we've a lad among us." He closed his eyes, pushed out his lower lip, and shook his head.

"If that boy has been around you for more than half an hour, he's heard worse." Richard bent over the kettle hanging above the fire. With great care he stirred its contents, inhaled the savory aroma, and looked sideways at his customers. "Two bowls, you say. Don't know as I've enough."

The smell of food caught Will off guard. He'd had no idea he was so hungry. Surely no public house would run out of food! They were supposed to have food on hand all the time. The law said so.

Richard stirred the pot again, lifted the wooden spoon to his lips, and tasted. A low "ahh" of satisfaction followed.

Pete turned his full attention to Will. "We've had quite a day, haven't we?" When Will hesitated, Pete raised his eyebrows.

Will had to swallow twice before he could answer. Whatever was in that kettle had his full attention, and he was nearly choking in anticipation.

"Huh? Oh, yes, *sir,*" he finally managed.

"So much to be taught; so much to be learned. It's a miracle a man's head can hold up all that knowledge." Pete nudged Will until he stopped staring at the kettle. "So much, isn't there, my boy?"

Will cleared his throat. "So very much, sir, yes, sir." If this was the price of some food, Will hoped he'd soon have said enough "sirs" to pay. "And from such a knowledgeable teacher as you, sir."

"What's this 'sir' business, then?" Richard asked. "I can tell you this much. He's just an old—"

"Language, Richard." Pete held up his hand again.

"—tar," Richard finished his sentence. "He comes in here and shouts the house down; treats me like his servant, he does; and persuades some stripling into calling him 'sir.' As if he were Somebody." Richard looked at Will. "Guess I'll just feed the poor, misled lad and let you starve, sir."

Richard put a large wooden bowl full of stew in front of Will. "Bread's right here. Warm from the hearth." He cut two thick slices.

"Thank you, sir." Will picked up his spoon.

Richard roared his laughter. "There you are, Petey. You've an uncommon mannerly student there. Certainly it's the only reason he'd ever call you 'sir.' Here's a bowl for you, but I think I'll charge you double, you—"

"Language!"

"—scoundrel!"

"He's not half as bad as he sounds." Pete picked up his spoon. "But he does have a certain command of the English language that Mr. Fortescue probably never intended to be a part of your education."

"One of Fortescue's boys, eh? They all have books." Richard held his hand out. "Let me see yours, boy. I can always tell the good ones by their books."

Will looked at Pete.

"It's all right. Richard's been a sailor and worked in the ship-yards before he found his life's calling."

Richard looked through the pages, nodding at some, pointing out refinements on others. He handed it back. "Fortescue is the only man who trains his apprentices this way. Known along the water-front, he is. When he's finished with an apprentice, that man can practically build a ship himself."

He nudged Pete. "Remember old Harley? Built a ship of green wood. When the wood dried, it shrunk and there were odd bits and pieces of metal rolling about the ship." He paused resting his chin on his fist. "As I recall, that ship foundered off the Cape Verdes."

"Didn't the shipwrights know the wood was still green?" Will asked.

"Oh yes," Pete said, "but the investors were in such a hurry, wanted the ship finished day before yesterday, you know, that they never listened to those who told them. And they wanted to save a few bob up front, so they bought the cheapest timbers. Green. Properly cured timber costs."

"When word got 'round the docks, there wasn't a sailor who would board the ship, let alone sail her. Had to make the crew up of pressed prisoners, they did. All lost at the Cape Verdes." Richard shook his head.

"How'd they get prisoners for crew?" Will wiped the bottom of his bowl clean with his last piece of bread.

"Lots of men in for small debts. The investors pay off the debts, with the understanding that the men will work off what they owe. Problem is, they're not sailors. Most get seasick watching the tide come up the Thames," said Pete. He finished his bowl and sat back. He hooked his thumbs into his belt and belched.

"See who you've been calling 'sir'? Shocking. And he calls me on my use of the King's English."

"King's dead." Pete yawned.

"His son isn't," said Richard, "and it's him I mean. Mark my words, he'll come back to England someday."

"Don't tell Cromwell. He'll have you drowned in your own kettle for treason."

"Probably."

They sat staring into the fire. From time to time, Richard left them to serve other customers. The rain drummed on the roof and ran through it in several places. The men slid down the benches to drier spots or moved their stools. The room filled with the low rumble of voices and the clatter of wooden spoons on wooden bowls. The smell of wet wool joined that of the stew. Small gusts of wind came through bad joinings in the walls.

Must have been built with green wood, thought Will.

"Penny for your thoughts," said Pete.

"I was just thinking that the wood used to build this must have been green for all the cold air it lets in."

"No. Mostly that's where Richard has had to mend the walls. Sometimes the, uh, gentlemen get a bit rowdy." He pointed. "Why, I've seen most of that wall knocked out. Usually it's only a board or two, though."

They lapsed back into silence. Richard sat down again.

"I see, lad, that you've an interest in maps. Some nice ones in your book."

Will nodded. "I have a large map at home that I'm filling in with discoveries."

"Accurate?"

"I hope so. I've no proper training, so I use the maps in the shops as guides. But I've learned more from some of the men here in the yards than from anyone else."

"Ever want to see all those places?" Pete asked.

"Sure," Will said.

Richard nodded his head. "Maybe you will."

"Not while I'm an apprentice."

"You could stow away and be gone before old Fortescue knows it."

Will thought a minute. "No, I owe too much to Mr. Fortescue. In fact I'd best get back. I'll be missed." He stood up. "Thanks awfully for the stew, Pete . . . sir."

Richard harrumphed.

"Glad to tide you over, my boy. And better company you are than his nibs, here. See you tomorrow?"

"That depends on what's being done in the yards. But I must see you again to finish."

"There's others you could see, but you're right. I'm the best." Pete clapped Will on the shoulder. "Off with you. Mind how you go."

Will turned at the door to wave goodbye, then stepped into the drizzle.

Pete looked at Richard. "What do you think, you old pirate? Was Bowles right?" His voice barely a whisper. "A likely lad. Smart too. Maybe a bit small. Likely, though. Don't lose track of him."

"He'll be back. Fortescue will see to that."

"How much for him?" Richard poked at the fire with the toe of his boot.

"We should get more, the boy being so well taught and all. Still, he'll only be another tar before the mast. And he is a bit small, as you say. Probably the usual six pounds."

"When will the ship be ready?"

"April, sometime."

Richard stirred the kettle and sat down. "Can you keep track of the lad until then?"

Pete nodded. "Well, that's one then. How many does Mason want?"

"Four or five, no more. Too hard to handle."

"The captain going soft? He knows how to handle the boys we get for him."

"Keep your eyes open, Pete. The authorities have looked in our direction more than once when boys have gone missing. And we've enemies in the yards."

"Yes, but wasn't Bowles right about this one?"

Chapter 5

"Mr. Porch! I say, Mr. Porch! A moment, if you please." Mr. Fortescue hurried across the yard, holding his greatcoat closed with one hand and waving a paper with the other. He stopped breathless inside the door.

"The wind fairly steals the breath from your mouth." Ben Porch slammed the door shut behind his employer.

"Indeed. Indeed it does. And cold as the North Sea itself." Mr. Fortescue shivered, then stepped closer to one of the hearths. "I trust we won't be in the way here?"

"Not a bit. This hearth isn't being used just now. In fact me and the lads banked the fire and set a kettle on. Fancy a cup of tea?"

Mr. Fortescue smiled. "All the comforts."

The foreman dropped tea leaves into a wire sieve and dragged the kettle out of the coals. He poured the hot water over the tea leaves and into Mr. Fortescue's cup, then filled his own. "Milk? Sugar?" He pushed a small tray along the hearth to Mr. Fortescue. "Mind the spoon. I saw one of the cats cleaning it off earlier."

Mr. Fortescue breathed on the spoon and polished it on his sleeve before stirring sugar into his tea.

"I wouldn't have rushed right in, but we have an order for some brass work." He nodded at the paper he'd laid on the tray. "Take a look. See what you think." Mr. Fortescue sipped his tea from the spoon. "Perfect."

"Of course we can do the work. And we've time enough." Mr. Porch looked up. "Is there a problem?"

"Not really, Ben." Mr. Fortescue took a gulp of tea. "Not really. I happen to know who's going to captain this vessel, and I hate to do anything to make him happy."

Ben smiled and hit the paper with the back of his free hand. "I can tell you who this is for. There's only one man can demand fittings like these for his cabin and have the East India Company agree. It's Walter Mason."

THE FOUNDLING

"It is."

"Because he knows he'll get value for money from us."

"I put it to you, Ben. Should we accept that old scoundrel's business?" Mr. Fortescue held his cup out for more tea.

"Who's money will we be taking?"

"Oh, the East India Company's, of course."

Ben poured water through the tea leaves. "As I see it, the Company will have the fittings from someone, and it might as well be us. If Captain Mason were paying, I wouldn't take a farthing of his if I were a beggar in Houndsditch." He picked a tea leaf from his tea. "And that's my thoughts."

The two men sat on the hearth, the fire at their backs. The pumping bellows, clanging hammers, and occasional calls filled the air around them. Mr. Fortescue wrapped his hands around his cup.

"Can't warm your hands on a wooden cup."

"But the drink stays hot longer."

They lapsed into silence amid the activity in the forge. "How's Will coming along? Enjoying the shipyards, is he?"

Mr. Fortescue grinned and nodded. "He's quick. Interested in everything. The lads at the yard say he has more questions than three boys. Once he's told, though, he seldom forgets."

"I suppose it's a nuisance for them having an apprentice around. Still what a boy can learn about ships in the yard is ten times more than he can learn from a book or even here in the foundry."

"It's worth the fee, I agree. That is, so long as he doesn't run off to sea." Mr. Fortescue shook his head. "Remember young Hughes?"

Mr. Porch nodded. "Did he really run away? He always said he was kidnapped."

"I heard. Put aboard Mason's ship, wasn't that what he said?"

"Nothing was ever proved." The foreman stopped in the middle of a stretch.

"What?"

"Little enough. I just recalled that one of the lads at the yard said that Will has been spending time with Pete Goodcole, the carpenter. Word is that he and Mason are mates. Pete's been thought to pick up a boy now and then for Mason's ships."

"I've heard. It's possible that Hughes's story about being kidnapped was true. Better warn Will. Perry would hang me from the nearest gibbet if I lost that boy." Mr. Fortescue rubbed his back. "That heat feels good. Hate to leave."

"So we're doing Mason's fittings?" asked the foreman.

"Yes, if we have the men free to do it."

They both stood and walked to the door.

"I tell you, Ben, the *Lady Eleanor* will have the best-furnished captain's cabin on the seas." Mr. Fortescue started to open the door, then hesitated. "Why don't you have Will learn a bit about molds during this bad weather? He's not done anything there yet."

"Right, you are, sir. We'll set him to work."

The wind seemed to pull Mr. Fortescue out when he opened the door.

At breakfast the next morning, Will was told to report to Mr. Porch. He wasn't at all disappointed about the message. Yesterday he'd been buffeted by the wind all day and, in the afternoon, the wind drove a fine mist through all the layers of his clothing until his skin was clammy.

He ran to the forge and struggled to open the door far enough to squeeze in. The wind slammed it shut behind him.

"Step into the foundry," one of the smiths told him. "Mr. Porch'll be in there."

Will found the foreman at his bench, studying a page of diagrams.

"Mr. Porch, sir." Will pulled his leather apron on.

"Come here, Will, and take a look at this."

Will studied the drawings for hinges and drawer and cupboard handles.

"It's for the captain's cabin on the *Lady Eleanor*. Some captains take their luxury with them, and that's a fact." Mr. Porch pulled a box of wooden patterns to him. "You can see we've done work like this before. Here are the patterns for the molds. We'll work together, you and I, for the next few days."

"Really?" Will's face lit up.

"Let's get you started on a proper mold." Mr. Porch pulled a container of sand and clay to him. "Now grab a handful of that sand

and squeeze it. See how it holds its shape? That is special fine sand mixed with a bit of clay and a bit of water."

Will crumbled the lump of sand and clay back into the box.

"Now here we have a solid brick of the sand and clay. I'll arrange these patterns on it and use these rods to form the passageways for the molten brass." When all was arranged to his satisfaction, Mr. Porch handed Will a cloth bag.

"Shake that over the patterns," he said. "It's parting powder."

Will shook the bag and a fine powder fell on the patterns. "What's it made of?"

"Not too much! Shake it evenly!" Mr. Porch took the bag and handed Will a soft brush. "Even that out a bit." He pointed to the patterns. "It's talc and ground charcoal. Others use what pleases them. It keeps the patterns from sticking to the mold we're making." He inspected Will's work and pointed. "A bit more there."

Will brushed again and stepped back.

Mr. Porch picked up a rectangle made of metal. "This is a flask. It holds the sand in place on our patterns. Now hand me that riddle. We'll sieve the first layer of sand onto the patterns."

Soon the flask was full of packed sand. Then Mr. Porch gave Will a small wooden paddle weighted with lead pieces to pack it down. "Strike the sand with the flat side."

"How's that?" Will hit the sand with a smart whack.

"Evenly all over."

"How's that?"

"Now use this mallet." Mr. Porch cocked his head. "Strike a bit harder. Doesn't sound quite as it should."

"What do you mean?"

"I can tell by the sound of the mallet on the sand if you have a good mold. Now you're going to lift the mold you've just made off the pattern. Just put your fingers here and lift this end. Tap the mold gently with the mallet to free the patterns."

"What if I break the mold?" Will lifted the flask full of packed sand and tapped it gently with the mallet.

"We'll have a workbench covered with sand . . . That's right . . . lift . . . tap it gently."

Will tapped the mold again and a pattern piece fell out.

"You see the pattern can stick even with the parting powder." Mr. Porch leaned down to get a closer look. "You still have a pattern stuck. Now, you can either tap the mold or—"

Will lifted the mallet and let fall again. There was no warning, no little cracks spreading through the new mold. It simply collapsed on the patterns, on the workbench, and in Mr. Porch's face. Will froze, the empty flask in one hand, the mallet in the other.

Mr. Porch brushed the sand from his beard and straightened up. "Umm." He surveyed his workbench. "Not the first time it's been covered with sand. Every apprentice I ever taught left me under a pile of sand at one time or another. Though I must say, I thought you had it."

"I must have hit the mold too hard." Will lowered the flask and mallet to the workbench. He never took his eyes from Mr. Porch. "I'm very sorry, sir. I'll just clean this off." He grabbed a bucket and pushed sand into it. "It'll never happen again, sir."

Mr. Porch spat some sand from his lower lip and looked up. "Oh yes it will." He spat again. "It's just that my face won't be under the flask next time. You clean up here—don't lose the patterns, mind—while I comb the sand from my beard."

He walked away, running his fingers through his beard and shaking his head. Will looked around the foundry. The men were watching. And they were all smiling. Tom waved before he returned to his mold. Will felt his face get hot. He wanted to fall through a hole in the floor. Instead he busied himself with brushing the sand off the workbench and cleaning off all the patterns. When Mr. Porch returned, Will stood ready.

"Now let's see what you remember." Mr. Porch stood to one side.

"Me?"

"That's right. Start from the beginning. I'll watch."

Will brushed off the hard brick and laid the patterns on it. His fingers shook so badly it was hard to arrange the patterns properly.

"Few men get it right at the first go. Even if they do, it still takes years of work to get it right every time. That's why we have long apprenticeships."

"You aren't angry? Even about your beard?"

"I'll be more careful where I put my face."

THE FOUNDLING

With a fingertip Will nudged the patterns until he was satisfied with their positions. When it was time to lift the new mold, he hesitated.

"The packing sounded good," Mr. Porch said. "Lift carefully and tap gently." He stressed the last word. "If all the pattern pieces don't fall loose, turn the mold over, and I'll show you how to pick them out."

Will picked up the mallet and tapped the new mold lightly. I'm not hitting this again, he thought. He put the mallet down and taking hold of the other end of the flask, he turned the new mold over. The impressions in the sand looked nearly perfect. All the patterns had fallen free.

"Lay it down, and I'll spray it lightly with water. You use those small bellows to blow away any loose sand."

Mr. Porch studied Will's handiwork. "Couldn't have done much better myself."

Will let out his breath. He hadn't realized that he'd stopped breathing.

"Good work. Yes indeed. And you know I don't say so unless it's true. That's half our mold."

"Half? We have to make another one?"

"That's right. See what you can do. I'll watch." Mr. Porch took his position at the end of the bench.

Will nearly forgot the parting powder, and one of the patterns stuck to the mold, but a light tap with the mallet sent it bouncing out. By noon the two halves of the mold were clamped together, ready to be used.

Will ran his hand over his forehead. He was exhausted.

"Let's eat, Will. Cook sent this over for you." Mr. Porch held up a package wrapped in oilcloth.

"Yes, sir!"

The men had set a large kettle in one of the hearths and had drawn benches around to sit on.

"Enough cups for all of us?" Mr. Porch asked.

"Righto," said Tom.

The men grumbled about the weather. They all listened for a moment as the wind gusted and rattled the building. When the fire on the hearth started to spit and sizzle, they knew the wind was driving rain ahead of it. Each of them would have a cold, wet walk home. Their conversation progressed to their wives, their children, the price of coal and wood needed for warmth and cooking. Then they talked about the work of the day. Amazing, one said, how the work kept coming from the shipyard with the weather so nasty and all.

"Say, Will. You've seen this new ship, the *Lady Eleanor?*"

Will straightened up. "She's tied in the basin for final fittings."

"When was she launched?"

"Last Thursday. Two of the masts are up now." Will wished he knew a lot more about the *Lady Eleanor*. "She'll be tied in the basin until the fitters are finished."

One of the smiths asked no one in particular, "Isn't that the ship that's supposed to be the pride of the East India fleet?"

"So I hear," answered another. "I'm surprised they're still building, business being what it is. I mean this war with the Dutch and all. Who would put a new ship to sea just to be sunk?"

"She's supposed to be fast and has two gun decks," said Will.

"Two? That's a man-of-war, not a merchant ship."

"I'll wager the *Lady Eleanor* has a successful maiden voyage," said Tom.

"Ha! Two bob says she gets sent straight to the bottom," said another.

"Say, Will, aren't you making some molds for the *Lady Eleanor?*"

Will nodded. "For the captain's cabin."

"Who's that?"

"Mason."

Tom harrumphed. "I'm surprised he's not sacked. He must cost the Company a penny or two with all his demands and high-and-mighty ways."

"He also brings his ships home." Mr. Porch emptied his cup. "And it's good business for us."

As if the foreman's empty teacup were a signal, the men stood, moved the benches back to their places, and returned to work. Mr. Porch led Will to the hearth near his bench.

"Build us a fire using coal and charcoal. We'll need it for at least an hour." Mr. Porch gathered bits of castoff brass and a small brass ingot and put them in a crucible. "Ready?" he asked Will. "Right, I'm going to put this into the fire. You must keep the fire white-hot for the next hour."

Will grabbed the handle of the bellows and began a slow, even pumping.

"What's that white flame, Mr. Porch? It's right over the crucible." Will changed hands on the bellows.

"That's zinc burning off. We'll have to replace it before we pour the mold."

Will pumped the bellows and watched the brass in the crucible and the white flame dancing above it. Not a good day to be in the shipyard, he thought. Think of it, these fittings will go on the *Lady Eleanor*. I've watched men working on her. Wonder if I could board and see the captain's cabin?

"Let's add that zinc. I'll skim this slag . . . and . . . add the zinc." Mr. Porch watched the crucible closely for a minute, then caught it securely on the end of a long rod and pulled it out of the fire. He stepped to Will's mold and poured the molten brass in.

"Always fill right to the gate entrance," he said, "because the metal shrinks as it cools and it will draw from the channels to keep the mold filled."

As he had predicted, the level of metal in the gate fell a bit and its color changed as the brass hardened.

"How long will it take?" asked Will.

"To set? A few minutes. But it will still be hot. Always wear your gloves when pouring and removing molds."

Will hovered over his mold. He could see no further changes. What if it didn't turn out right? He checked along the sides of the mold to see if there were any leaks. There weren't any. Maybe the mold would be good. He shifted his weight from one foot to the other. He didn't know what to do with his hands while he waited, so he stuck them in his pockets.

"Looks like you're doing the sailor's hornpipe." Mr. Porch bent over the mold. "Stop jumping around. We can undo the clamps." He opened the mold and picked out the hardened metal with the tongs and carried it to his bench to brush the sand away. "Nice work, Will."

"I'm sorry about the mold."

"What's that? The mold? Why are you sorry about that?"

"We'll not be able to use it again. Look at all the sand that stuck to the brass."

Mr. Porch brushed sand from the other side of the casting. "They're only good for one use. Sand always sticks to the casting." He handed Will some heavy snips. "Here, cut the pieces apart . . . Now the real work begins. Use this file and take off all the rough edges and scale. Tomorrow we'll use lighter files, then pumice, and finally rouge to polish these pieces. They'll shine. Oh yes, they'll shine, and you'll swear your fingers are being worn off. We'll drill the holes when you're finished."

While storms from the North Sea beat the City, Will polished the fittings for the *Lady Eleanor.* When the weather finally broke, he had made four successful molds and nearly half of the fittings for Captain Mason's cabin.

Chapter 6

End of March 1656

The weekly meetings of the four friends might have stopped that winter except for Sam. The colder and wetter the weather grew, the more he needed the help of Will, John, and Robert. John provided another shirt and a castoff woolen scarf. Robert and Will added lumps of coal to their sacks of food once they discovered that Mr. Falconer didn't provide his apprentice with heat. Even with all this help, Sam was frequently hungry and cold. And now he had a bad cough.

Will turned his collar up against the mist that somehow found an opening and drizzled down his neck. He hadn't left his room more than ten minutes ago and already he felt wet, right to his skin. He turned to the usual meeting place on the south side of East Smithfield.

"Will! Will!" The call came long and loud down the street. John ran to catch up and fell into step with his friend. "Beastly day to be about. Seen Robert and Sam yet?"

"There's Sam." Will waved.

Sam ran to meet them. "Where's Robert?" He huddled farther into his coat.

"We haven't seen him," said Will. "Maybe he can't come. Let's find a place out of the weather to wait."

They stepped into a large, deep doorway.

"It's just too much to expect to see the sun, I suppose. Do you realize we've seen no sun for a fortnight?" Sam turned to Will. "Tell me, where in the world does the sun shine all the time, if there is such a place."

John laughed. "It isn't England."

Will thought. "I think you'd be wanting the Indies. According to the men in the yard, at least those who've sailed, it's warm there all the time."

"Let's go," said Sam. "I was ready last October." He shivered. "Will we ever be warm again?"

"Doubt it, or dry." John wiped his face with the end of his scarf. "We need to find a drier place out of the wind if we're going to stay out today."

Will leaned out of the doorway and looked up and down the street. "I don't see Robert yet."

"We've waited long enough. He'd be here by now if he could get away. Let's find a warmer spot." John began hopping from one foot to the other.

"He's right, you know." Sam's teeth chattered. "Robert could talk his way through a brick wall. If he's not here by now, it's because he can't get away."

"Right. Then where shall we go?" asked John.

"I know. The shipyards. There are some old buildings there. We could get out of the rain and even build a fire." Will stepped out of the doorway. "Let's go."

"Just a minute." John hadn't budged. "How do we get in? The gate's locked."

"There are lots of places to get in. It's not hard. No one will see us." Will waved for his friends to follow him.

"I didn't bring anything to start a fire," said John.

"I did." Will patted the sack he carried over his shoulder. "And the reason I did," he lowered his voice to a conspiratorial whisper, "is because I have sausages to roast."

"Get off. Where'd you get those? Raid the larder?"

"No. Look." Will opened the sack.

"Well, what's that other lump?" John pointed.

"Bread. Can't have sausages without bread."

"And the small packet?"

Will smiled. "Do you want to eat or not?"

"I'm hungry," said Sam from his corner. "Let's go."

"Got a knife to slice that bread?" asked John.

Will nodded.

"Aren't you just the perfect host?" John sniffed.

"Apparently not." Will surveyed the contents of the sack. "I've forgotten the serviettes. Sorry."

Sam laughed. "I'll wipe my chin with my shirttail, thank you." He coughed into his sleeve.

"I was going to keep this for a surprise," said John, "but since you have that sack, Will, I hope you won't mind carrying it." He brought out a well-wrapped package.

"What is it?"

"Soft cheese."

"Soft cheese? Like the rich folks have? Is it yellow?"

John dropped the package into Will's sack. "Let's find a dry spot, then you'll see. Lead on, Will. The yard it is. Let's go before the rain starts falling even harder."

Will tied the sack shut. All three tightened scarves and turned up coat collars. They were silent as they stepped into the rain and hurried through the streets. Even though Will followed narrow alleys that kept the wind from reaching them, they all felt the damp.

Without looking up, John and Sam followed Will through a loose board in a wooden wall.

"Here we are."

Ahead of them were the frames of two large ships and a smaller ferry. The ships' skeletons shone against the dull gray-blue sky. They creaked and groaned in the wind.

"Look like those sea monsters you hear about, don't they? They even sound alive." John stepped forward for a better look.

"Stay back." Will pulled him back to the fence. "There might be guards about."

"They won't be out today, if they're smart," said John.

"Maybe not, but follow me. We'll soon be out of the wind and wet." Will stepped sideways behind some piles of timber covered with canvas. He followed a winding path between buildings and across a small work area. Finally he opened the door of a small shed.

"Here we are. There's plenty of wood just there." He pointed to a corner.

"Close the door, Will."

"Not until we light the fire. This shed has no windows, and we couldn't see to do anything."

John and Sam immediately gathered a pile of dry wood chips and broke an old box into pieces.

THE FOUNDLING

"Start the fire, Will, and hurry." John's teeth were chattering as loudly as Sam's. He stood holding his hands over the wood chips, waiting impatiently for the first heat to rise.

Will struck a spark with his flint. "There," he said when the chips caught. "Keep it going, John. Sam, hand me that crate there. Yes, that one. It will be our table." He emptied his sack on it.

Sam split a wooden slat into long thin sticks so they could roast their sausages. "However did you get so many?"

"Mr. Fortescue gave us Lady Day off and a celebration besides. He does things right. Loaded the table, had a quick bite with the men, and left the rest to us. Whatever was there was ours, and we cleared the table. The men took extra to their families, so no one blinked at me rolling a bundle up." He picked up the smallest packet and tossed it into the air a couple of times. "Dried apple slices."

John and Sam had already skewered sausages and were holding them over the fire.

"Want me to start one for you, Will?" Sam turned his sausage to inspect its progress.

"I'll just cut this bread, then I'll do one." He worked for a moment. "You know what's really good? When you wrap the bread around your sausage, put an apple slice in it too. I must have eaten five or six like that last week."

"These are really good." Sam swallowed. "Real meat. We get sausage of cereal flavored with grease. Once Allen and I split the casing of one of those sausages Mr. Falconer gives us and tried to find a bit of meat. Couldn't. We were still hungry enough so we scraped the bits and pieces together again and ate it anyway."

"How many apprentices does Mr. Falconer have now?" John licked his fingers.

"He's only supposed to have two. I mean that's what the guild would allow him if he were a member. So he says he has only Allen and me. But he takes one or two others in on the sly. They're real poor boys or foundlings who have no one who will complain about how they're treated. Mostly the vestries are so happy to find someone who'll take them out of the parish, they never ask questions." Sam skewered another sausage. "You know how it is, Will."

"Not really. I've met lots of apprentices who were foundlings, and I'm beginning to realize just how lucky I've been. Aside from the Vicar Richards, I've been treated well."

"Look at those juices sizzle." John stared at his sausage, now golden brown. "Say, Sam, before you get another sausage, would you slice off a strip of that cheese and lay it on a slice of bread?"

"Apple too?"

John nodded. "I think I'm going to have a feast."

Will and Sam waited while John tested his recipe. He rolled his eyes in satisfaction.

"Good, huh?" Sam asked. "I'm going to try that."

Within twenty minutes each of them had eaten three sausages garnished with apples and cheese. Will wrapped the rest of the food and set the sack by Sam. They all leaned against the crates, their hands folded over their stomachs, and enjoyed the growing warmth in the shack.

"Could use a drink after all that." Will licked his lips.

"Simple," said John, "stick your head out the door, lean back, and open your mouth." He cocked his head and listened to the steady drumming of the rain on the roof. "Careful you don't drown."

Sam rolled over. "Good shed, Will, tight and dry. I could go to sleep. First time I've been warm in ever so long."

"What's in this shed anyway?" John peered into the corners. "Can't see anything without a candle."

Will got up and pushed some broken crates aside with his foot. There were more crates thrown in the corner. He lifted them one by one. "All empty. Maybe they just throw old broken crates in here. It's perfect for us. There's enough wood here to last through spring." He piled the crates back in the corner.

Sam sat up. "I can't see anything over here, either," he said. "Just more crates, a coil of rope. That's all."

John sat up. "It's stopped raining. Let's walk around and see the ships up close. I've never seen one being built." He looked at Will. "Can you get us close?"

"There are supposed to be guards in the yard, but most likely they're half-asleep in some corner."

Sam coughed. "Are you sure?"

John pulled at Sam's sleeve. "C'mon. It'll be fun and we may never get another chance."

"All right. Let me get my coat and scarf on."

"I hate to get my shoes and stockings wet again. They take forever to dry." Will shoved his feet back in his shoes. "The leather's stiff as a board."

"Rub grease into them," said Sam. "Animal fat, oil, something like that."

"Won't his shoes smell like grease?" asked John.

"Only on real hot days. Besides, who do you know who would notice?"

"There he goes calling into question the good name of my friends. That includes you, Will." John wrapped his scarf around his neck.

Sam crunched the last embers of the fire out with his shoe. "If you move in such high circles, nobility and such, there's refined oils to use. You wouldn't believe it, but some folks buy oil special from the apothecary with lavender or musk mixed in to rub on their shoes." He stood back and picked up the sack. "That's the lot. I'm ready to go."

Will opened the door and looked out. Sam bumped into him. "Don't push."

The rain had stopped, but a steady wind blew low clouds across the sky.

They walked among piles of stores under canvas. No one challenged them, and soon they stood looking up at the ship's frames.

"What kind of ships are these?" John whispered.

Will glanced over his shoulder to assure himself they were alone, then he led them past the first ship. "This one will probably carry coals from Newcastle. It's really more like a big barge with sails."

"Look at this one!" Sam ran ahead. "This is no barge."

"It's a merchant ship, isn't it, Will?" John started walking backwards so he could take it all in. "Where'll she go, do you suppose?"

Will shrugged. "I don't even know who's having her built."

"I'd give anything to board her when she's finished."

"Well, there is one just launched in the basin. Mr. Fortescue's men, uh, we are doing the metalwork."

"Can we go on it?" John asked.

"There's a guard aboard. Sorry. Besides, you get seasick."

"Not while it's tied to the pier. I'm sure I wouldn't."

They walked past another ship. "The hull's nearly boarded up on that one. She'll be launched soon."

"It," said Sam. "Ships are things, not people."

"She," said Will. "The men here all say 'she.' "

"Well, that's silly, if you ask me."

"No one did, and ships are called *she*s," John said.

"Why?"

"Why, Will?"

"I don't know."

"Why not? You work here." Sam coughed again.

"I'll ask tomorrow."

"Then I'll have to wait 'til next week to find out. I'll bet ships are called *it*s."

John looked at Will. "Shall we thump him now or save him for our late afternoon entertainment?"

"Let's get him now."

All three ran through the yards, Sam well in the lead. They stopped only when they reached the basin and saw the *Lady Eleanor* tied to the pier. Sam whistled. John stared.

"How close can we get?" John asked.

Will scanned the yard and the pier but saw no one. "The rain must be keeping the guards inside. But mark my words, we could all land in the Tower for this."

"The Tower?" John spread his arms wide. "For what? We aren't doing anything but looking. If we're caught, they'll throw us out, if they can catch us." He skipped backwards a couple of paces. "Let's go!"

"I'm going to see how close I can get." Sam ran toward the pier.

Will jogged slowly after the two, half sorry he'd brought them to the yard. But he wanted to board the *Lady Eleanor* too. He'd hoped to go aboard during the week and use Mr. Fortescue's instructions as his excuse. If I can look around on Monday, he thought, I guess I can look around on Sunday. His decision made, Will ran to catch up.

Sam stood on the pier and leaned as far over as he dared to see the deck. "Can't see much from here."

Suddenly John crouched low, pulling Will and Sam down with him. "I saw a guard!"

"Where? Did he see you?" Will wished again he'd never come.

"No. He was onboard, lying down. Well, sort of propped up against the ship. He must be looking the other way." John stood halfway up. "He's still there and paying us no mind."

"How do we get out of here?"

"The same way we got in, Sam." Will straightened up a bit. "Where is he, John?" His eyes followed John's finger. The guard was there. He had a blunderbuss across his lap and two pistols tucked in his belt. He raised his head and looked directly at the boys who immediately fell flat on the pier.

Nothing happened.

John looked at Will. "Well," he whispered, "what now?"

"I don't know. You're the one who wanted to get this close."

"Right. Blame me. Who brought us here in the first place? Against the law and all that?"

"We needed a place to get out of the weather. You've never found a place as good as that shed."

"You'll get us killed, you will. We'll be hanged! We'll never even see the Tower. Right to the gallows, that's us."

"Oh, do be still!" Sam cocked his head. "I'm trying to listen."

"Clever boy, isn't he? Wants to hear the guard coming to arrest him."

"No, he's right. Listen, John. What do you hear?" Will stretched up to look for the guard. "He's lying in the exact same place. Hasn't twitched a finger."

"He looked right at us," Sam reminded him.

"I don't think he really saw us. C'mon; get up. See that bucket by his side? I'll bet that's why he's so comfortable. Richard's pub is right over there."

"You mean the guard—"

"—will be asleep for quite awhile."

"So we can go aboard. Just so we don't do anything to disturb him." John headed for the gangplank.

Will followed, still watching the guard. Sam came last, ducking low behind Will.

John stopped. "You go first, Will. After all, it's your ship."

"It isn't my ship." Will looked closely at his friends. "You scared?"

"I don't see your foot on that board."

"Gangplank."

"Whatever. You going to go?"

"Go, Will, go." Sam gave Will a slight push.

"We're right behind you." John assured him.

Will took a deep breath and went up the gangplank. He dropped lightly to the deck and turned to warn his friends to be quiet. John was still on the pier, and Sam was pushing him. "Go, John."

"No, you go."

"You're the one who wanted to get on that ship."

Will walked back to his friends. "Change your minds?"

"Wipe that grin off your face. I'm coming." John looked at the plank again. "Not very wide, is it?" He gulped and looked down to the water below. "What if I fall?"

"You won't fall. Just don't look down and walk in a straight line." Sam stood back with his hands on his hips. "Robert would go if he were here."

"He isn't afraid of high places, and he can swim." John swallowed hard.

Will held out his hand. "Hold on. I'll help you."

"I'll hold on to your coat."

"Let go if you slip." Will backed up the gangplank.

John inched up the plank, teetered, and seemed about to fall, but Will pulled and Sam pushed. Finally they all reached the deck.

Sam looked at his taller friend. "Really brave, that's what you are. You going to be able to get back across to the pier?"

John groaned and straightened up. "I'll do it when I have to."

THE FOUNDLING

"Are you two quite finished? I've checked the guard. He's been to the pub all right, probably two or three times. He'll give us no trouble. Let's go."

The first tour took only half an hour as they ran from deck to deck, cabin to cabin. Then they started over and gave the ship a minute inspection.

"I made some of the brass for the captain's cabin. Let's go there and see if it's been put in." Will headed toward the stern of the ship. He led John and Sam down a short ladder and through a door opposite into the captain's cabin.

"Doesn't look like they've done much of anything in here," said Sam.

"None of the fittings I made are up yet. Wonder when it'll get done. I heard the men say that the *Lady Eleanor* was to sail soon." Will could not hide his disappointment.

"Don't worry, Will. You'll probably get to see the pieces you made once everything's finished." Sam walked to one of the portholes and looked out. "Just imagine being the captain and sailing all over the world."

"I think I'd like going to sea." John leaned against the door.

"You'd have to be able to go up the masts to furl and unfurl the sails," Will reminded him.

"Not if I were a passenger."

"This ship doesn't carry passengers unless they're supercargo for the shipping company."

"If I were a passenger, I'd make sure the ship was going someplace warm." Sam coughed and shivered. "I've been cold my whole life."

"The Indies, Barbados, Jamaica, Africa, India, South America." Will listed the places.

"All warm?"

"I think so."

"We'd better be getting back," John said. "The wind's freshening, and it's probably going to start raining again."

They followed Will on deck.

"I'm going to check the guard. Just to make sure he's still there," said Will.

Part 3: The Apprentice

"What if he's gone?" asked Sam.

"That means someone else has taken his place and we'd better get out of here . . . No, he's still there. Let's go."

"If it rains, he'll get soaked. Maybe we should move him."

"Right, Sam. If he catches us, he'll shoot us. He has three guns, you know."

"Sam's right," said Will. "He could take sick. Let's be quick about it."

Will leaned over the guard. He reached out and lifted the arquebus slowly, carefully from the guard's lap. When he had it, he motioned for John and Sam to grab the guard's hands and feet. They dragged him as gently as they could to a more sheltered spot and covered him with a piece of canvas. Will placed his arquebus by his side.

"That's all we can do," whispered Sam.

They tiptoed toward the gangplank.

"Thankee, boys, for helping Old Jim."

Will and Sam stopped dead. John took off running.

"You two get after your mate and never let me see any of you again."

Will and Sam followed John down the gangplank and across the yard until several sheds were between them and Old Jim.

"Stop! I can't go any further." Sam was bent double, coughing and gasping for breath. When he had enough breath, he fell to his hands and knees laughing. "Did you see John go down that plank?" He gasped again. "His feet never touched the board at all."

"That's the way to do it, John." Will was laughing so hard he could barely stand up.

"It's fine for you two—" John began. Then he joined them and laughed until his sides hurt. "Say, do you suppose Old Jim saw our faces?"

Will stopped laughing. "I hope not, because I still have some time here."

"You won't get in trouble, will you?" asked Sam.

"I'll just stay away from the basin for a while."

"And the gangplank."

And all three started laughing again.

243

Chapter 7

April 1656

"So your time's about up here, is it?" Pete pulled his lower lip. "That's too bad. Help me stack these planks here."

The planks rattled into place, and Pete threw a piece of canvas over the pile.

"Make that fast on your side."

Will knelt to tie the canvas down.

"Now let's take a turn through the timbers again. Some more things to show you."

The sun threatened to break through the clouds. Sea gulls wheeled through the air and landed to fight over crumbs where the crews had eaten. Work on the three hulls was progressing rapidly. The coal ship would soon be launched. The hull of the merchantman was nearing completion as was that of the ferry. The *Lady Eleanor* still rode in the basin. But now, two weeks later, her spars were in place and her rigging was nearly complete. Ropes hung everywhere, and Will wondered how they would ever be sorted out. Pete stopped to watch.

"When will she be ready, Pete?"

"Cannon haven't arrived yet. Let's go aboard. You should see the final fitting anyway. I allow as how Mr. Fortescue would want you to see that."

"Do you suppose the captain's cabin is finished?"

"I heard you've an interest there. We'll look in."

Once aboard the *Lady Eleanor,* they dodged and ducked workmen and their burdens, and stepped over coils of rope and piles of metal rings and tackle. On the gun decks sat cannon mounts for the small guns and iron rings to which the larger guns would be chained.

"Why aren't the larger cannon mounted?" Will asked.

"Recoil," said Pete. "Larger cannon are set on wheels so they can recoil after they're fired. Chains through those rings keep them from going too far." He shook his head. "Not the place to be during a fight. Smoke rolling in so you can't see your hand in front of your face and you can hardly breathe."

"Were you in any battles?"

"A few. Once a ball came through the side of the ship, flew by me, killed two gunners, and went right out the other side. That wasn't quite as bad as the one that hit our powder. The explosion tore the ship apart."

"Did she sink?"

Pete nodded. "And 'tween decks is the most dangerous place to be 'cause there's no way out. The ship rolled over—at least the part I was in rolled over. I escaped through one of the gun ports. Most of my mates weren't so lucky."

"Who attacked you?"

"Believe it or not, it was an old Portuguese trader, half-rotten in the timbers. Never seen a more derelict ship in my life. Had quite a captain as I recall. He'd taken that ship all the way around the world, and he was blasting anything that got between him and Lisbon. Been gone over three years."

"Did he bring you back?"

"Clapped us survivors in irons, he did. When we reached Lisbon, we were put in the galleys. Took me a year before I escaped."

Will whistled.

"That's why," Pete continued, "I decided to put my earlier training as a carpenter to good use." He took a last look. "Let's get out of here. I'm feeling a might cramped."

They went to the main hold. The fitters were finished there. Iron rings hung from beams and were set in the floors. From there Pete led the way to the crew's quarters. Bunks lined the walls of the tiny room in the bow of the ship. A table was bolted to the floor in the center.

"What are these hooks in the ceiling for?"

"Mostly the sailors like the bunks. But some have brought back a new contraption for sleeping. Just hang it from the hooks and climb in. In a rough sea, you don't get tossed around in your bed; the hammock just swings back and forth."

"Hammock?"

"From the South Seas, it is. Hello! This looks like one. Must belong to Old Jim. He's the only man I know who uses one in port."

Pete untangled the hammock and hung it up. "Have a go."

"Where's Old Jim now?" Will looked over his shoulder.

"He's here only at night and Sundays when the crews are gone."

"Oh. Sure? I wouldn't want to upset him by trying his hammock." Will looked toward the door again.

"He won't mind. He's a mate." Pete patted the webbing hanging from the ceiling. "Have a go, then."

"I don't know. Will it hold me?" Will tugged on one of the cords.

"Watch." Pete pulled the hammock sides apart and fell into the webbing. He stretched out and put his hands behind his head. "Like a baby in a cradle." He rolled out. "You try."

Will stepped up to the hammock and pulled the sides apart. He gave a little boost as Pete had done, balanced for a moment, then flipped over and landed on the floor.

"Try again." Pete ran his hand over his face.

"Are you laughing?"

"I'm not; I swear I'm not." Pete held up his hand, but he stepped into some shadows.

Will held the hammock wide and gave a little jump. He hooked one leg over, then rolled over headfirst. One hand and a foot tangled in the webbing. The rest of him landed on the floor.

"Pete? Help me. Pete!"

But all Will heard was wheeze after wheeze and Pete slapping his knee.

Will pulled his hand free and untangled his foot. He lay on the floor.

"There now, my boy. I'll hold it for you," Pete said when he could speak again. He grabbed the hammock and spread it wide. "Now just set yourself down and roll back easy-like. I'm holding it, trust me."

"Trust you? You think it's funny to see me hanging upside down."

"You'll laugh too, in the end."

"Hold it steady!" Will sat on the hammock and slowly lifted his feet. Soon he was stretched out and swinging gently from side to side.

"This is nice. You go on without me." Will stretched his full length.

The noise of the fitters began to die. Pete listened for a moment. "Must be noontime. Hungry? Or do you want to stay here and starve?" He headed for the cabin door.

"I'm coming." Will rolled over and so did the hammock. He grabbed the webbing and hung on upside down, staring at the floor. "Pete!"

Pete shuffled back. He stood in silence for a moment. "Guess I should have told you about that," he said and bent double wheezing again.

Will dropped to the floor. He looked from the hammock to Pete. "No one could ever get a night's sleep in one of those. And if, by chance, he did, he'd kill himself getting up the next morning."

Pete unhooked the hammock and put it back in its cupboard. "You have to admit that it was nice when you lay still. Imagine relaxing on a balmy night with the ship moving through calm waters, and you swinging gently like you were in your mother's arms."

"Maybe. But I don't remember my mum flipping me over and dropping me when I woke up."

"What do you say that we make a stop in the captain's cabin before we go eat?"

Pete went down the ladder and threw the door open for Will. "What do you think?"

Will could hardly believe the changes in two weeks. The cabin was nearly complete. The captain's bed was built into the wall. A carved and decorated table was bolted to the floor and chairs to match were strapped in place. But it was the cupboards that pleased him most because on each door were two of his hinges and a small doorknob. They gleamed against the fine wood. Will pulled one of the doors open and found the shelves filled with table linens.

"Best not open any more, Will. I didn't realize Mason had begun bringing his belongings onboard."

Will stepped back and turned to see the whole room. The brass was the perfect finishing touch, he thought.

"You have a right to be proud," Pete said. "As fine work as any I've ever seen."

Will couldn't stop a smile. "You think so?"

"I just said so."

"Thanks, Pete. I did want to see how the cabin would look . . . My very first pieces, you know."

Pete clapped him on the shoulder. "And worthy of a fine lunch. Let's go, my boy."

They went to Richard's and, while they ate, Pete described Will's losing battle with the hammock. The men laughed, though many agreed with Will that a bunk was certainly safer.

"Black-and-blue all over, I was," volunteered one large man. "Every time I turned over, I found myself with my nose on the floor." He shook his head. "Dangerous, they are."

"Aye, right dangerous. Near broke my arm," said another.

General debate on the merits and dangers of hammocks lasted for a short while. Richard refilled cups and bowls and rejoined Pete and Will.

"How's the *Lady Eleanor?*" he asked. He pulled his own bowl over and began eating.

"Beautiful," said Will.

"Will did the brass in Mason's cabin."

"I made the molds and everything. The polishing was the hardest."

"I'd like to see that, surely I would," said Richard. "When will she be ready to sail?"

"In about ten days, depending on the cannon and her canvas."

"Canvas not furled yet?" Richard seemed surprised. "There's a lot of work getting the canvas on. How much will she carry?"

Will listened to the discussion of jib sheets and mizzen mains and how the *Lady Eleanor* ought to be rigged.

"Mason likes to fly every square inch of sail he can," said Richard.

"This ship will take all he can give. She's one of the best ever to come from this yard." Pete scraped his bowl with his spoon. "Have you heard whether the crew's complete?"

Richard shifted his weight. He glanced at Will, then answered. "Not quite. I told Mason we might be able to direct some his way. Those not signed to a ship but might like to be." He reached over the table and took Will's bowl. "Let me get you more, lad. How about you? Fancy a berth on the *Lady Eleanor?*" He stirred the stew. "That is, if you were free to go to sea."

"Sure. So long as I got a proper bed. But my apprenticeship won't be finished for six more years."

"A long time." Richard filled his bowl. "If you were free, would you go? You know, just saying you were free."

Will shrugged and took a drink. "I have to be back in the forge this summer." He looked out the door left open by a customer. "I'd miss the yard, that's for sure, and all the friends I've made here."

"You've still a short while here?" Pete asked.

Will nodded.

"How long?"

"A week, maybe two. I don't know. I'll have to ask Mr. Fortescue."

"Have any mates who would like to see the yard before you go?" Pete took a drink.

"Of course. They all think I have the best apprenticeship ever."

"How many mates?" Richard asked and glanced at Pete.

"There's four of us. But we can only get together on Sunday afternoon."

"Surely they could get away some other time to see the yard. I hear that apprentices run off all the time."

The thought of Sam escaping his master for even an afternoon was unlikely. Poor Sam who wanted only to be warm. "Say," Will leaned over the table. "Where's the *Lady Eleanor* bound for?"

"The Spice Islands, according to Mason," said Pete. "I spoke with him just yesterday. Why?"

"Just asking."

"You want to see the Spice Islands?"

"Not me," said Will. "Not now, anyway."

"A mate?" Pete lowered his voice. "We might be able to help a friend get one of his mates signed on. Mason and I, well we know each other, you see."

Another customer entered. "Will!" Mr. Fortescue's voice boomed in the small room. "Heard I'd find you here. Come along, lad. I need your strong back this afternoon."

Pete touched his cap. "Begging your pardon, sir. Will he be back? We have more to do."

"Tomorrow. I'm in a bit of a hurry just now. Gentlemen." He left with Will following.

Pete waited until the door closed, then he leaned far over the table. "What's with all the questions, you idiot?"

"Me? What about you?" Richard jabbed a finger at Pete. " 'Want to sail on the *Lady Eleanor?* Want to bring your mates to the yard?' He's a smart lad, bound to catch on."

"He'll never know until it's too late. I'm his friend, remember?"

"I was wondering about that. Seems you're getting too friendly with him. Maybe you couldn't go through with it."

"He's the best I've taught, and that's the truth. But he can use what I've taught him anywhere in the world, wherever ships are built. He doesn't need to be here. Besides, I need the money. And Mason will pay plenty if we can get all four of them."

"It sounds like we may have to take them on Sunday and hold them till the *Lady Eleanor* sails. Risky."

"Maybe." Pete hunched further over the table. "We've got the cellar. No one knows about it. Our first problem is to get Will to bring his friends to the yard."

"Old Jim says there were three boys here not so long ago."

"Three? Do you suppose one was Will?"

"You know Old Jim. Can't see straight half the time and sleeps the other half. What's it matter?"

"Nothing." Pete sat back. "This Sunday?"

"Only Mason sails next week. I don't want them in the cellar for more than two or three days."

"Once they're on the ship, they're his problem. He's managed before."

"Listen, Pete." Both men leaned over the table again. "I want them gone as soon as possible." Richard held up his hand when Pete interrupted. "Until Mason has them down the Thames, we aren't safe. Just one word or pointed finger and we'll be on the gallows.

THE FOUNDLING

So this Sunday it is, if Mason is sure he's leaving. Otherwise we put it off."

Pete studied the tabletop. "It's true the cannon haven't arrived and the canvas isn't up." He looked up. "We'll wait until we're sure. But I don't want to lose these lads. It'll be easy money." He picked his teeth with a splinter of wood. "You have the ropes?"

"Everything's ready here."

"I have to get back to the yard." Pete stood up. "I'll talk to the boy tomorrow."

"Sunday, then, unless you say differently." Richard rose and began clearing empty wooden bowls from the tables. His business was over for the day.

The next Sunday, Will, Sam, and John stood on the south side of East Smithfield. Their coats hung open because of the warm weather.

"I don't want to go without Robert." Sam coughed several times. "He wasn't with us last time, and it wouldn't be fair."

"Pete said he'd show us around if we came today. No worries about guards and he can show us lots more," Will said.

"Can't he do the same next week? Robert can come then . . . Listen, let's eat anyway, and we can make up our minds afterwards." John shook a cloth sack in front of his friends.

"You're right," said Will. "We can eat. Where shall we go?"

"Not too awfully far. I'm really tired today." Sam coughed again.

"The Bridge? That's not too far." John turned toward the Thames and his friends fell into step beside him.

The streets were wet from an earlier shower. The cobblestones glistened in the sunshine. In small gardens, blades of green struggled into the sunlight. Early wallflowers bloomed in window boxes. The City looked cleaner in the April sun.

After eating, Sam stretched out on the warm ground, now dried from the sun, and fell asleep.

"Guess we won't be going to the yard." John looked down at his friend. "How much longer do you suppose we can keep him going?"

"I don't know. Summer's coming. It should be easier for him, except that he's sick all the time now."

"Do you suppose it's the consumption?" asked John. "I knew a family where everyone had it. They were really thin too, just like Sam, and they coughed a lot."

"Maybe he has just a bad cough from winter that'll get better this summer." Will studied his sleeping friend. "Whenever my face was all flushed like Sam's and I had chills, Mistress Bessie used to give me the world's awfullest medicine." He shivered at the memory.

"My mum had some stuff like that. Her 'special tea' she called it. Smelled like tar. We got better really fast."

"You know, we could get something like that from an apothecary. I wonder what we'd ask for? We could give it to Sam next week."

"Even if we had money for a cure, it wouldn't be enough, not with the beatings he gets." John was silent for a long time. He pretended to watch a small boat below London Bridge. When it finally disappeared, he breathed heavily. "Sam was limping today."

"I saw." Will threw a stone out into the river. "Mr. Fortescue never lays a stick on me. I'd want to die if he did. The men in the forge have laid into me a time or two, but I deserved it. I was stiff and sore for a week, once. Not like Sam, though."

"Mr. Budgins came after me last week for nearly destroying the loom. I swear I'd never seen such a complicated pattern before and we had to add two heddle shafts. It was awful with all those parts crashing to the floor around me. I think Mr. Falconer enjoys making Sam miserable."

"Maybe," said Will. "One thing's sure, there's no way to stop him."

"Did you hear about the master who killed his apprentice? The court told him just to be more careful in the future."

"Didn't he say his apprentice had stolen from him?"

"I don't know about that," said John.

Sam rolled over. "Ouch! I am so stiff!"

"Go back to sleep."

"No, I've slept enough. Sure felt good." Sam sat up and rubbed his left shoulder.

Will flopped back on the grass. He studied the clouds moving across the sky. How could clouds move so quickly in the sky when he felt no breeze at all?

"Sam?"

"What?"

"You ever think of leaving Mr. Falconer?" Will asked.

"You mean run away?" Sam answered slowly. "Yes. Why?"

Will continued to study the clouds. Finally he rolled over on his side and propped his head in his hand. "Just asking. Why haven't you?"

"Lots of reasons."

"Name them," said John.

"My indentures. I am an apprentice, you know."

"But would you leave if you could get away?"

"There's lots worse than Falconer. He's given me a home since I was six or seven."

John leaned over until his face was just inches from Sam's. "Given you a home? Are you addlepated? What home? Who feeds you and gives you clothes? Not that old miser. You're sick all the time because of the way he starves you."

"Summer's coming. I'll be better."

Will spoke softly. "I think I have an idea. You can run away and not be caught."

"You don't know Master Falconer. There's a story of him chasing an apprentice all the way to Norfolk. Brought him back in shackles, he did. He'd find me wherever I went."

"Not if you were on the *Lady Eleanor*." Before Sam could protest, Will continued. "I have a friend who knows the captain and could get you signed on."

"Your friend would be breaking the law helping an apprentice leave his master," said John. "We'd be breaking the law."

"I don't think Pete draws too fine a line." Will sat up. "Shall I ask him? He wants all of us to visit the yard anyway. Four will go, three come back."

"The *Lady Eleanor*?" asked Sam.

"I was aboard her again with Pete just last week. She's about ready to sail. The cannon hadn't arrived yet, but as soon as they're aboard and the sails are up, she'll be off to the Indies. There won't be time for Falconer to find you."

"And even if he does," said John, "will he follow you to the Spice Islands?"

"I don't know anything about sailing."

"Pete says some crews are pressed out of prison. What could they know? They learn at sea."

"Hold on." Sam started laughing. "My sides hurt! Think of this. You want me to run away from my master who is rather nasty and go to sea with a boatload of prisoners?"

"Doesn't sound like much of an improvement, when you think about it, Will," John said.

"Prisoners aren't pressed for merchant vessels, just for the navy when not enough men sign up. What I was trying to show you," said Will, "is that obviously anyone can become a sailor."

"Sure," John said. "You can read and write too. You might become an important person on a ship."

"I don't think your friend Pete will help me after we've left him waiting at the shipyard today."

"I'll explain what happened when I see him tomorrow. I'll apologize too, if that'll help get you a place on the *Lady Eleanor*."

Sam stared out over the swiftly flowing waters of the Thames. "Do you really think your friend will help me?"

"He said he would."

Sam was silent for a few more minutes. Then he said, "It won't hurt to ask him, will it? I mean if he would still be willing?"

"I'll ask him tomorrow."

Chapter 8

"They didn't come."

"No, they didn't."

"There goes our chance for an easy twenty pounds."

Pete's shoulders sagged. "Probably."

They walked across the yard toward the basin.

"The easiest twenty pounds we ever would have made."

"Do you mind just shutting up?"

"Well, you're certainly no fit company. I'm going to see Old Jim. At least he's civil." Richard turned toward the moored *Lady Eleanor*.

Together they boarded the ship and found Old Jim fully armed, fast asleep.

"He's not civil; he's cupshot," said Pete. "He won't see the light of day for several hours."

Richard nudged Jim with his toe. "Wake up, old coot."

Old Jim groaned and tried to roll away from the nudging. His arm hit his bucket and spilled the rest of its contents.

"Look at that. He's closer to bucketshot, if you want my opinion. Too bad. I was hoping he could tell us the sailing date." Pete squinted and looked up at the sky as if it held a clue.

"Huh." Richard walked away. "Who would tell that old man anything?"

"He hears a lot, you know." Pete followed Richard down the gangplank. "We could have at least got Will, but you didn't want to keep him in the cellar for a few extra days."

"That's right! That boy has a master who looks after him. If Will disappeared, the first place Fortescue would come would be here. If we ever take that boy, he goes right aboard ship. Let Mason take some of the risk, I say."

Their feet stirred up little clouds of dust as they crossed the sunlit yard toward the Mermaid.

THE FOUNDLING

"The worst thing," said Pete, "is that we could have had twenty-four pounds for the four. Twenty after we gave Bowles his money for putting us on to Will in the first place."

"Maybe the next ship."

"Will's going back to Fortescue's soon. Twenty pounds!"

They stopped at the door of Richard's pub. "Ten of that would be mine," he said, and pushed open the door. "Want to wet your whistle?"

"Got anything to eat?" Pete stepped in. The room was dark after the bright sunshine.

"I asked if you were thirsty, not could I feed you." Richard pulled the door shut.

"You do have something in the kettle?"

"I always have something in the kettle. For paying customers."

"You certainly have a lot of them today," said Pete, glancing around the empty room. He stumbled over a stool. "Don't you ever straighten this place up?"

"Why should I?" Richard lit a candle, let some wax drip on the table, then stuck the candle in it.

"Open the door a bit. We really could do without the candle if you'd leave the door ajar."

"Unwise." Richard carried cups and two wooden bowls to the kettle. "If Old Jim sees that door ajar, he'll try to come off that ship to get his bucket filled. In his present condition he'll never make it down the gangplank, and I'll have the death of a dear friend on my conscience." He looked up as if to say "I knew you'd understand perfectly" and continued filling the bowls.

"Are those bowls clean?"

"What? Here you are sitting in my public house, eating a free meal, and enjoying a cup, and you ask if the bowls are clean?"

"Well are they?"

Richard put Pete's bowl down so stew slopped onto the table. "Not any more," he said. "Eat."

They ate in silence and drained their cups. Richard leaned back and patted his stomach. Pete hooked a toe on the leg of a stool and pulled it over so he could put his feet up.

"See what I mean?" asked Richard, pointing to the stool. "No sense setting them straight. Just leave them where they are and those what wants to prop their feet will find them."

For a few minutes all that could be heard in the small room was the crying of the gulls.

"Well?" Richard stared at the candle flame.

"Well, what?" Pete's eyelids were closing.

"What are we going to do? Mason's expecting those boys."

"He's not going to get them. At least, not those four."

Richard looked around the shadowy room. "I really could use the money. I want to fix this place up. You know, a window maybe." He nodded. "Over there."

"I wouldn't waste the money," said Pete. "Just don't replace the wall after the next fight."

"Do we really have to have those four boys? Think about it, " said Richard. "What are they, fourteen and fifteen years old? They could be a handful. Why don't we snatch four others? Younger. Easier to handle. Easier to keep until Mason wants them."

"Got any in mind?"

"No, we'd have to go hunting like always."

"That was the beauty of these four." Pete pulled his footrest closer. "They would come straight to us. No work. No fuss."

"We can get four boys just about anywhere. There are so many wandering the streets. To take a few and put them to work would be a public service."

"Well, that's true enough. The City of London was taking donations to send a shipload of the little beggars to the New World. Virginia, it was. Gets them off our streets and puts them where there's work to do."

"Recollect as how my ship called at Virginia once."

Pete laughed. "As a legitimate trader, or was it that pirate ship you sailed on?"

"That was no pirate ship. We were privateers going after enemies of the King."

"And when you couldn't find any enemy ships, only then did you raid the settlements."

"We needed fresh water and food."

"Was that all?"

"In Jamestown it was. I never saw a sorrier place in my life. Half-starved, half-massacred by the Red Indians." Richard shook his head. "A wretched place to send anybody, if you ask me."

"Somebody thinks it's a good idea. But where do you propose we pick up four lads for Mason?"

"St. Bride's? There's thousands there."

"And carry them clear across the City?" Pete shook his head. "No, not for me."

"You're getting lazy."

"No, I'm not. We've taken boys from that parish before. There's folks who know our faces already."

"Once we get out of there, it'll be smooth sailing."

"Not really. Remember Crumpton, that constable near Soper Lane? He knows us. If he sees us with so much as a child's shoe, we'll be hard put to save our lives."

"He's not so dangerous."

"He can bellow like an ox and raise the hue and cry before we could get away."

"What for? Seems like we're helping him get rid of the strays so to speak. Less trouble for him."

"I think he's a bit balmy when it comes to the little gutter-crawlers."

"Well, we sure can't pick them up around here." Richard got up. "Want more to drink? All this chin wagging has made me dry as a bone."

Pete handed his cup for a refill. "Not around here," he agreed. "We're too well known."

"Twenty pounds!" Richard put the filled cups down and sat again. "Wonder why the boys didn't come?"

"I don't know. Boys, you know. They hardly ever have a serious thought for long. Fine day like this, they're out having a good time."

"Speaking of this fine weather, I'm going out and sit in the sun." Richard stood up and hitched up his trousers.

"I thought you didn't want Old Jim to see you," Pete reminded him.

"It's a shame to let this sun pass by. Tomorrow may be cold and rainy, probably will be. You stay here if you want to. I'll sit in back."

Pete pinched the candle out and followed Richard. They settled down with their backs against the wall.

Richard stretched his legs out in front of him and laced his fingers across his stomach. "Just close your eyes and feel the warmth sink right to your bones."

"Nice," Pete agreed. "If it weren't for that bit of breeze, it would be almost too warm."

"I've been in lots warmer places."

"So have I, and I didn't like them much."

"Now, Java, for instance—"

"Shhh!"

They dozed in the warm sun.

"Heigh-ho! I say, it's me—Jim. Hoped to find you. You awake?"

Richard raised one eyelid. "No."

"Does he have his bucket with him?" Pete asked.

"It's a miracle, no."

"Well, he's not after a handout."

Jim put his arquebus down and slid down beside his friends.

"Aren't you supposed to be on the *Lady Eleanor?*" Pete still hadn't opened his eyes.

"Captain's aboard with the owners. They don't want the likes of me around."

Richard groaned. "Twenty pounds."

"He all right?" Old Jim asked.

"More or less," said Pete.

"Sounds awful."

"He lost some money."

"On the boys you were going to get for Mason?"

"How'd you know about that?" Pete's eyes flew open.

"You do your best by Mason each time he's in port. Didn't think this time would be any different."

"Well, it is," said Richard. "We don't have anyone for him. And he's sailing soon."

"I may be able to help you there. Ah, for a proper consideration." Jim smacked his lips and leaned toward Richard.

"Forget it."

"You might want to think again."

"Why should I?"

"Richard, give him a cup, or he'll never shut his gob."

"Tell us first." Richard opened one eye again.

Old Jim rubbed his chin. "Well, I guess I'll have to trust you for that cup."

"Guess so."

"Would you spit it out?" Pete sat up, now wide awake. "Before I —"

Old Jim held up both hands in front of his face. "Now, don't do that. I thought you'd want to know the *Lady Eleanor* sails Tuesday week."

"Nine days sure?"

"Sure as I'm sitting here."

"Another Sunday!" Richard pushed himself off the ground. "Always said you were a good old coot to have around. Guess I'll just bring us three cups. Yes indeed, I'll have me a window yet."

Chapter 9

"Will, my boy! Missed you yesterday. Wasn't sure I'd see you again." Pete stood up from his work.

"I'm—we're all—sorry. One of my friends couldn't come, so we decided to wait until he could. You aren't angry with us?"

"Angry? I should say not. In fact, Richard and I want you and your friends to come next Sunday. We'll show them the whole yard, we will."

Will let out his breath. "That's good, because I want to know if you will still help one of my friends sign on the *Lady Eleanor*."

"Wants to be a sailor, does he?"

Will nodded. "He's an apprentice."

"Running away?"

Will nodded again. "We'd be breaking the law, you know."

Pete clapped a hand over Will's mouth. "Shhh! Not here. There are those who take young men such as yourself against their will and sell them to ships' captains." He took his hand away. "We wouldn't want anyone thinking such things of us, would we, now?"

"We're not selling Sam," said Will. "He wants to run away and we want to help him. We're just not quite sure how to go about it."

"Has he had a bad time of it?"

"His master beats him awfully."

"Bad. That's bad." Pete picked up his tools. "Wants to go, does he now? That makes it a lot easier."

"Makes what easier?" asked Will.

"Getting him onboard ship—the place he wants on a ship, that is." Pete turned toward the Mermaid. "Have time for a bite?"

"Always."

"Good. But before we go, I have to hand in these figures for the new keel that's being laid. Merchant by the name of Perry. Likes everything to be—but what's that to you?"

"Perry? James Perry?"

Pete nodded. "I'll be back in just a few minutes. Wait for me."

Will could hardly wait.

"Tell me about James Perry," he said when Pete returned.

Pete took Will by the arm and steered him to the Mermaid. "Nothing to tell. Wants to build a ship. I had to inventory the timbers we have and tell the shipyard owners what they'll need to buy. In we go. Mind the step."

Pete pulled the door open and pushed Will in. "Richard! What did I say just yesterday? That our good friend Will certainly would not forget us." Pete pushed Will into a chair. "Have a seat."

"What about James Perry? When was he here? Was there another, rather tall man with him?" Will started to get up.

"Sit down, Will." Pete pushed down on Will's shoulder.

"If it isn't our Will!" Richard rushed over and tried to clear the table of cups, plates, and crumbs with one sweep of his arm.

Will nodded. His mind raced. Master Perry here in the yard and I missed him. Didn't even know. Was Rodgers with him? It's been three years. Remembering the warehouse, Will breathed deeply. He could almost smell the spices. Later they had boarded the ship and met the captain. I'll never forget his broken nose, thought Will. Halfway down it took a marked jog to the left.

"Will! Will, I say, where are you?" Pete dug an elbow into Will's ribs. "We're trying to have a polite conversation and you're leagues away."

"Sorry." Will pulled his thoughts back to the small room of the Mermaid.

"Clean bowls and spoons." Richard nodded. "Saw to it myself, I did."

"How much longer will you be at the yards?" asked Pete.

"Actually, today is my last day." Will pushed his thoughts of Master Perry and Rodgers aside. "I go back to the forge tomorrow. Really, I'm here today to say goodbye to my friends and pick up some things for Mr. Fortescue at the office."

"The forge. Hot, noisy work. Not sure I'd want to work there." Richard shook his head. "Still, we're happy you thought to come by and see us, Pete and me."

"I couldn't leave without seeing you. Anyway, the forge is a good living. Mr. Fortescue started out as an apprentice and look where he is now. Owner of his own business."

"I'm with Richard. In fact both of us prefer hearing wind whistle through the rigging," said Pete.

"Why aren't you signed on to a crew?" Will studied the older men. "I mean, if that's what you really want."

"My time in the galleys convinced me to stay at home. I never want to be chained to an oar again, thank you. Besides, I'd been apprenticed to a shipwright before I went to sea. Taught me about all I know when it comes to timber." Pete sighed. "It's a living here in the yard, but I'd rather be aboard ship."

"What about you, Richard?" asked Will.

"My last ship sank off the Skeleton Coast. Bad currents, lots of fog. Barely made it to shore—don't swim, you know—and when we made it to shore, it was desert. Would you believe it? Desert right down to the water. There was plenty of food—fish, birds, and such. One night we even heard lions roaring. But we had no fresh water, you see. And cold, so cold at night and the fog settling on our skin. If we hadn't been picked up within a few days, we would have died right there of either thirst or cold or both."

"Where's the Skeleton Coast?" Will leaned forward.

"On the west coast of Africa about"—Richard stopped to think—"twenty degrees south latitude. Called that because of all the ships wrecked there. You can see their hulls in the sand and lying offshore. And I suppose because of the men who died there. Desert right to the water's edge," he said again. "Just sand and rocks. We climbed one of the hills of sand to see what was inland. Hardest climb I ever made. Take one step and slide back two it seemed."

"What did you see?" Will was storing every bit of information for his map. It had been quite a while since he had been able to add something new.

"More hills of sand as far as the eye could see."

"I don't believe the part about the lions," said Pete. "If you didn't have water, then they didn't either."

"We saw one, yes, we did." Richard shook a finger in Pete's face. "A lion did come right to the water's edge and fed on the carcass of a beached whale." Richard's finger went straight up as though he were taking an oath. "Truth! You ask my mate when he's next in port."

"How were you rescued?"

"Well, boy, it was a good thing we climbed that hill of sand, because we could see way out to sea. Those on a passing ship saw us, with a glass no doubt, waving and jumping. They put out a boat and we raced down to the water. Just that lucky, we were. But I never much fancied sailing around Africa again."

Will whistled. "Some tale."

"And all true."

Angry calls from the rest of the patrons broke the spell. Richard jumped up to tend empty bowls and cups.

"Fancy an adventure like that?" asked Pete.

"Sure, if I could be certain of rescue."

"Earlier, when we were in the yard, you, ah, mentioned a friend . . . " Pete let the sentence trail off.

"You mean Sam?" Will broke off a piece of bread. "Sam needs to get away. We, his friends, have been helping him for a long time now. His master—" Will stopped. "Anyway, Sam needs to get away, and we told him we'd help him. But, as I said earlier, we really don't know how."

Richard sat down, ready to tell another story. He thought better of it when Pete caught his eye and gave a small shake of his head.

"Now, Will," Pete began slowly, "I don't want to put ideas in your mind, especially since helping an apprentice leave his master is a serious offense, but I have some information that might interest you. Just might be of interest, mind you. I couldn't say what you'd do with it; wouldn't want to be involved if there is something illegal afoot."

"What is it, Pete?" Will was whispering. "Please tell me; I'd never mention any names of who helped us."

"What do you think, Richard? I'm not sure about this."

Richard stared at the tabletop. He tried to run his fingers through his hair, but tangles forced him to give up.

Will looked first at Pete, then at Richard. He was on the edge of his stool, leaning on the table. He opened his mouth to beg one of them to say something, but Richard cut him off.

"It's true," Richard said. "We know the captain of the *Lady Eleanor.* From time to time he helps lads escape to the sea. Takes them, he does, at great risk. For a small fee."

"Fee?" Will felt his heart drop. He spread his hands. "We haven't a penny among us." He took a deep breath and pushed himself away from the table. "I should have known. We thought he could just sign on as a sailor. We'll have to think of something else. Thanks for the food, Pete."

Pete looked at his friend in astonishment. As soon as the door closed behind Will, he reached over and grabbed Richard by the front of his shirt and dragged him halfway across the table.

"Fee? What fee? There's no fee, never has been. Our twenty pounds has just walked out the door." Pete was as close to shouting in a whisper as he could get. "I should throw you through your own wall! I had the boy on the hook. He'd have brought his mates to the yard next Sunday!"

"Don't be so high-and-mighty with me," Richard whispered back. "Will's a smart lad. He knows such favors don't come free."

"You idiot!" Pete dragged Richard closer until their noses nearly touched. "We're supposed to be his friends!"

"I thought we might get a couple of quid from the chaps, seeing how they're so eager to help their friend." Richard pulled away and sat down hard. He jerked his shirt back into place.

Pete leaned over the table so he could keep whispering. "I'm going out there and try to catch Will and see if I can't set this up again." He stopped and looked around the pub, wondering if anyone had overheard. No one had even looked up.

Pete left the Mermaid and stood outside looking for Will. He ran after a distant figure who walked with his head down and his hands in his pockets.

"Will! Will! Hold on!" Pete ran to Will and pulled up, gasping for air.

"I have to get back." Will kept walking.

THE FOUNDLING

Pete grabbed Will's elbow to stop him. He needed to catch his breath. "Like I said, Will, I know the captain. Let me speak to him. He's helped me many times before."

"We don't have any money."

"I'm sure he'll help when he hears your friend's story. If you were to bring him by the yard Sunday next, we could probably do something for him."

"Not if we have to pay a fee."

"This captain owes me. I've done him a favor or two in the past." Pete held Will's elbow even tighter. "This is your friend's chance. Let me speak to the captain. Now let's go sit down, and I'll tell you what I have in mind."

Pete guided Will to a low pile of timber and sat down, dragging Will down beside him.

"You and your mates can go out as usual. I can get the guard to let you in, even if I have to bribe him." Pete looked closely at Will. "See how eager I am to help you? Just like I said I would."

"I know lots of ways into the yard. You won't need to bribe the guard."

"You come right to the gate to the shipyard. Richard and I will take you all to the ship so you can see your mate safely aboard." Pete rubbed his hands together. "It'll be all over as quickly as that."

"Sunday?"

"Sunday at the yard."

"You're sure? No fee?"

"I told you the captain owes me."

Will stared at the toes of his boots. It seemed simple enough. He looked out over the yard toward the *Lady Eleanor.* She was nearly ready to be towed into the Thames for her trip downriver. "Sunday it is, then."

"All four of you?"

"I should think the fewer of us that come, the better."

"I was only thinking of you. Perhaps I should have said bring no more than four on Sunday. We can't afford to draw attention to ourselves, can we? Can't afford a procession."

Will chewed his lower lip.

"Having doubts, are you?"

Will nodded. "What if we're caught?"

"We, Richard and I, would never let that happen." Pete's tone was fervent. "Believe me, you mean just that much to us. You have to trust someone, my boy. And after knowing you these past months, I'd like to think we have a friendship of sorts. I mean, Richard and I, two old broken-down tars, don't look like much, but we value your good opinion of us." Pete studied the backs of his hands.

"I'm sorry." Will pushed himself up and stood in front of Pete. "Here's my hand on our friendship."

"Thank you." Pete stood and shook Will's hand. "Now be gone. We'll look for you on Sunday, as many as can come—up to four."

"We'll be here. Thanks. I have to go now."

"Even if your friend decides not to sign on the *Lady Eleanor,* we'll have us a lark."

"Thanks."

Pete watched Will go. "And thank you, my boy." He tilted his head back, to the blue of the sky, to the warmth of the April sun. "I do believe I've all four coming. Pete, you're a clever one, you are. Richard, we'll soon have our twenty pounds and no one the wiser!"

Late that afternoon, Will sat staring at the new notations on his map. The Skeleton Coast. That must be a sight, he thought. He'd also written the word "desert" right on the coast. Sam might get to see this.

And Sam would need a kit. He couldn't walk out of Mr. Falconer's with his belongings. On second thought, Will doubted that Sam had anything to pack. What kind of things did a sailor need?

Will's wardrobe yielded two shirts, a jumper, a pair of breeches, two pair of stockings, and an old pair of shoes. He checked the soles. Not too bad. Besides, Sam wouldn't be doing a lot of walking on a ship. He added a piece of soap, a washing flannel, and a small towel. Perhaps Sam would want to write a letter. Will added two quills and a penknife to sharpen them. He folded three pieces of paper and put them beside the pens.

THE FOUNDLING

What else might Sam need? Will went through the wardrobe again. A cap? A belt? A small leather wallet? Will searched each shelf and opened each drawer.

The pouch still lay in its small drawer and, for a moment, Will stared at it in surprise. He had forgotten it was there. Almost forgotten, anyway. Memories sprang forward in his mind. Mistress Bessie's cottage. Flowers in the garden and roses draping over the doorway. For a long moment, Will wanted to touch, to prune, to tie up the roses. He saw the fence, whitewashed, but with two rails missing. Button with her cloud of orange fur. Mistress reading, knitting, stitching the small pouch. The crackling fire with chestnuts roasting on the edge of the coals. Peter running in, dropping his books and coat on the floor. Visits from Rodgers . . .

It seemed right that he had opened the drawer today, the day he'd heard his first news about Master Perry and Rodgers since being apprenticed. He pulled the drawstring and opened the pouch. Visits from Rodgers. He pulled out his indenture and carefully unfolded it and laid it on his table. Stephen Rodgers. Playing at conkers. Walks to the market, sometimes talking, sometimes enjoying quiet company. The man who rescued him from the vicarage and stood with him when he signed his indentures. Stephen Rodgers. The tall man with dark brown hair and smiling eyes. A quiet voice that laughed quickly, understood, explained, admonished, and made a little boy want to be just like him.

Will held the rolled ribbon in his palm. The store full of flowers and Master Perry who bought it for . . . Mum. She could have put the brooch on it and worn it around her neck. Her laugh seemed to whisper through his room. No face. Will squeezed his fist tight around the ribbon. He could remember no face. He opened his hand. The satin still gleamed.

This is it, he thought. All I have. He put the ribbon on the table beside the pouch and his indenture and sat back in his chair. The sun dropped behind the trees, roofs, and church spires. They, like the last birds going to their roosts, appeared in silhouette against the golden evening sky. The sky turned deeper gold, then orange, and finally deep blue and purple. The first stars appeared, and lights of the City twinkled away to the horizon.

A slight, chill breeze made him shiver. He looked around his room as though he could not recall where he was. He put the ribbon back into the pouch. Then he refolded his indenture and put it beside the ribbon. When he stood up to close the window, he deliberately put the pouch deep in his pocket and patted it into place.

He felt a mild surprise at how happy he was at that moment. This may be all I have, but it's more than Sam has, he thought. I shouldn't have put my best memories in a drawer and tried to forget them. If I never see my fam—friends again, they're still mine. He smiled into the dark, and thinking of them, he went to bed.

When Will dressed the next morning, he patted the small pouch in his pocket. He felt as though he'd met some old friends and spent a pleasant evening getting to know them all over again.

He straightened the blanket on his bed and stuffed his nightshirt under his pillow. Then he put the clothes for Sam in a small sack and put it in the bottom of the wardrobe.

For the rest of the week Will did little more than beat pieces of scrap metal flat. Controlling the heavy hammer was much more difficult than it looked. All the while, Mr. Porch stood by, telling him when to reheat the metal, how to hold it with the tongs, and when to cool it in the tub of water.

Each night Will fell into bed right after supper, too tired even to read or to worry much about Sam. By Wednesday Will's hands were blistered, and his arms and shoulders ached. In the mornings he was so stiff he could hardly put his shirt on or pull on his breeches. Now he knew why the men in the forge had such rough hands and bulging muscles.

On Saturday afternoon, Will held up a piece of iron. He turned it over several times so he could admire what a good job of work he'd done flattening it. Mr. Porch came up and clapped him on the shoulder. Will's sore muscles gave way, and he dropped the tongs and his metal piece.

"Admiring your work?"

Will bent over to pick up the tongs and metal. "Mr. Porch, I say, sir, give me a hand up."

"Stiff?" the foreman asked. "I don't wonder. A hot soak will put you right." He stood with his hands in his pockets.

THE FOUNDLING

"I can't straighten up." Will reached up to his workbench with one hand and tried to pull himself up.

"Don't forget your tools and your work on your way up." Mr. Porch grinned. "Welcome to the forge, Will. I'm off to supper."

Will reached out for the metal and the tongs and pulled them closer. He was still hanging on to the edge of his workbench. Finally he pushed and pulled himself straight. The men stopped clearing their benches and applauded and whistled.

But even then, he remembered the contentment that had followed him all week. The men wouldn't have paid any attention to me if they didn't like me, he thought. He winced and limped to the bath barrel. He soaked until his skin tingled and turned bright pink from the hot water. He thought of how silly he must have looked trying to stand up. They tease me like I'm a younger brother, he thought. Yes, that's it. We're like a big family. Just like Mum, Mistress Bessie, Cook, Master Perry, Rodgers, Master Fortescue, Sam, John, and Robert are all my family. It surprised him how large his family had grown since he was a little boy.

Chapter 10

Sunday was overcast, though, at odd moments, the wind pushed the clouds aside and the sun shined through. Will and John hugged their coats around them and hurried down the street.

"See, I told you," Will said. "Look at him, John, barely able to walk. I've brought some clothes for him, and Pete says he can get Sam signed on a ship today."

"Does Sam know this?"

"No. I haven't seen him since I talked with Pete on Monday."

"What if Sam doesn't want to go?"

"You've heard him talk. He wants to leave."

John stopped to face his friend. "We'll be in trouble if anyone finds out we helped Sam run away. I don't want to cause any difficulty with Master Budgins. I may not be ever so keen on the weaver's trade, but he has been good to me."

"Nor do I want to get in trouble with Mr. Fortescue." Will stepped closer. "But you know as well as I how badly Sam has been treated. We've fed and clothed him for over two years."

"Yes, but—"

"Besides," Will went on, "who's to know? We'll be as surprised as everyone else that Sam's gone."

John stared at the pavement.

"Are you with me in this?" asked Will. "Will you help?"

"Let's catch up with Robert and Sam and talk to them. If Sam decides to go, I'll help. Does it have to be today?"

"Pete says so. Besides, how much longer can Sam stay where he is? Look at him!"

John looked and saw Sam leaning against a wall, his right hand holding his left side.

"You're right." But John didn't sound convinced.

Robert waved for them to catch up. When Will and John reached them, they all turned towards the shipyard.

"Finally," said Robert, "I'll get to see the yard. It hasn't been fair that you've gone without me. Say, don't go so fast. Sam isn't up to it."

"Sorry." Will slowed his pace.

"What were you two talking about back there? We were nearly freezing waiting for you." Robert hunched farther into his coat.

"I was telling John that my friend Pete will be able to get Sam on a ship, if he wants to go."

"He can?" Sam stopped so quickly that Robert nearly bumped into him.

"Yes, he can."

Sam thought a moment. "When?"

"If you're caught, you could be sent to prison." John looked sideways at Will.

"Even Newgate can't be as bad as staying with Mr. Falconer. I can't take much more of his temper. You should see my ribs, all black-and-blue. When?"

"You've really decided, then?" asked Will.

"I guess I have. How long will I have to wait?"

"You won't have to wait at all. Pete says you can leave today. Really, you have to leave today because the *Lady Eleanor* will be going downriver to pick up her cargo in just a couple of days."

"Today?"

"Pete will hide you until the ship leaves." Will swung the sack from his shoulder and out in front of Sam. "I even brought a kit for you."

"Today? You're sure?" Sam limped on, staring at the pavement.

"Pete said the captain still needs some crew and will sign you on. No fee."

"Even though Sam's ribs are broken?" asked John.

"Your ribs aren't actually broken, are they, Sam? I mean, you couldn't walk around if they were, could you?" asked Robert.

"I'm just stiff and sore. I'll be right as rain in a few days." Sam didn't look up.

When they reached the gate to the yard, Will looked through the peephole. "Hmm, I don't see Pete."

"I don't want to stand waiting in this wind." Robert turned his back to a strong gust.

"We'll go in through the fence." Will led them to the opening they had used before. "Shall we eat first, then find Pete?"

"Let's just get into that shed." John's teeth chattered when he spoke.

Will led them to the shed and opened the door. "It looks just like we left it." They all hurried to get out of the wind.

John pulled two candle stubs from his pocket. "This time we'll be able to see what we're doing," he said. He lit the candles and stuck them on a crate with some melted wax.

Robert squinted into the corners. "Nice. You came here before?" He emptied his pockets and placed their contents next to John's package.

"I found it while I was exploring one day." Will dragged sausages and a loaf of bread from his sack. He tossed the bread to John. "You brought your knife?"

John nodded and set to work.

Robert broke a crate into kindling and lit the fire.

Sam searched for the sticks they had used before to roast sausages. When he had all three, he paused. "So it has to be today?" he asked again.

"Pete says so." Will unwrapped the sausages. "There was no way to get word to you, you know. You don't have to go, Sam. It's up to you."

John sawed on the loaf of bread. "If we're caught . . . "

"Will you go?" Robert dropped a broken crate by the fire. "If I were you, I'd go in a minute. No, in a second." He snapped his fingers.

Will heard John mutter, "We'll be caught."

"Fire's ready. Here, Sam, cook while you're thinking." Robert handed him a sausage.

"It's hard to actually decide. Seems like there should be more planning or something," Sam said. "And I'll be leaving all of you." He turned his sausage slowly over the fire. "You've packed for me?"

Will nodded. "We'll miss you, Sam, as much as you'll miss us."

"Maybe even more," said Robert, "because you'll be so busy learning to be a sailor."

"I don't know anything about being a sailor. That's for sure." Sam rolled cheese around his sausage and put it in a slice of bread.

"Pete says the *Lady Eleanor* is bound for the East Indies. It's warm all year there," said Will.

"Go, Sam, go." Robert spoke around a mouthful of sausage, bread, and cheese. He swallowed. "Here's your chance. No one but us will ever know." He turned to John. "Don't you say a word."

Sam turned to John. "What do you think?"

John spoke slowly. "I don't know. We will miss you a lot. Maybe it will be better for you. But what if being a sailor is worse than being a tanner? And you said you knew nothing about—"

"Pete says you learn to be a sailor right on the ship," Will said.

"Pete says a lot," said John. "But why isn't he a sailor anymore?"

"His ship was sunk, and he was captured by the Portuguese. He was in the galleys until he escaped, but that doesn't happen very often." At least Will hoped it didn't.

"Right, then," Robert said, "prison for us and capture by pirates for Sam. I'd rather be captured by pirates. At least then I'd have a fighting chance."

John laughed. "They'd make you walk the plank straightaway, they would."

"What do you mean?"

"No pirate captain would want a troublemaker like you aboard."

"I would go down fighting!"

"The *Lady Eleanor* has two gun decks and her captain is known for bringing his ships back." Will joined the laughter at the thought of Robert on a pirate ship. "Really, Sam, everyone says the *Lady Eleanor* is the best ship our yard has ever built."

"Let me meet your friend Pete and see the *Lady Eleanor,* and then I'll finally make up my mind." Sam reached over for a dill pickle. "Very good, these." He waved the pickle once, then took a bite.

They finished eating, then lay or sat propped against the crates, enjoying the fire.

"I don't want to go out in that wind again," said John.

Robert cocked his head. "It doesn't sound so bad right now."

Will wiped his hands on his breeches and stood up. "Finished? We should go find Pete. He's probably wondering where we are since we missed him at the gate. He's eager to meet Sam."

"Let's get going, then. This is my first time here, and I want to see everything." Robert stomped on the small fire to put it out.

"They're not coming, I tell you. Not coming!" Richard slumped in his chair. "The second week in a row too. I stood at that gate, blown by the wind for an hour, and they never showed up."

"You weren't gone more than half an hour." Pete slapped the table between them. "You missed them, that's what. Just because you couldn't take a little breeze. There goes our twenty pounds. You should've waited longer."

"You go stand in that wind."

"It's not that cold."

"The wind's fierce. And why was I out there waiting at the gate? You're the one who said he'd meet them."

"I had thinking to do."

"You never thought this much before. Just snatched them, got our money, and left. No thought to it."

"This is different. We may have to keep Will and his friends in your cellar for a day or two. At least until Mason can take them aboard."

"Just how are we going to do that with no one finding out?" asked Richard.

"That's what I was thinking about."

"We've been over this half a dozen times. Ropes and gags. What more do we need?" Richard spread his hands, palms up, over the table and rocked his stool back on two legs, then brought it crashing forward. "If they give us any trouble, there's a board down there too. A crack over the head solves most any difficulty." Richard sat with his arms folded across his chest.

"And how do you propose to get them all down into the cellar easy-like? I'm just assuming you don't want a brawl up here." He looked around the small public house. "Some of the furniture might get broken." •

"Oh. Well, have you come up with anything since you're the great thinker?"

"Maybe."

"You'd better go find them. They're expecting you. You can think while you're looking for them."

"All right, all right. Keep your shirt on." Pete pushed himself to his feet. "When things begin going wrong, don't blame me."

"Me and that board can handle whatever comes up."

"There's Pete!" Will waved his arm and urged his friends into a trot. Even Sam shuffled along.

"Pete, here are my friends, John, Robert, and Sam. Sam's had a beating, and he's got sore ribs, but he's ready to go. We even have his kit ready."

Pete shook the hands held out to him. "It's a risky business we do, and no mistake, so let's move to the Mermaid."

"Could we see the ship?" Robert asked. "We know Will did some of the fittings for the captain's cabin. Could we see them? Or maybe just walk on the deck? This is my first time here. I want to see everything."

Pete looked Robert over. A bit small, but he'll grow. Quick tongue and puts himself forward. A few days on board will cure him of that. Aloud he said, "We might get on the deck, but supplies are aboard and the captain has moved his belongings to his cabin. No one goes there without invitation."

The group rounded a building.

"Look!" Will pointed to a ship. "There's the *Lady Eleanor!*"

"Where is everyone?" asked John. "I thought there would be sailors all over getting ready to leave."

"Not supposed to work on the Lord's Day," Sam said.

"That's how we got on the ship before; no one was here. Except the guard, but he was sleeping off a trip to the pub." John swaggered a bit. "We went through the whole ship. That was before Will's fittings were done. We saw everything else, though."

Sam chuckled and bent nearly double, holding his side. "Remember John going up the plank? Almost on his hands and knees, he was." Sam gasped, leaning against Will.

Will held his friend up. "He didn't have any trouble getting off, did he? Flew right down that plank without touching it." Will demonstrated with his free hand how fast John had run. "He thought the guard was after him."

Even John smiled. "There's more than a board there, now, isn't there? I mean, they've had to put lots of supplies on board, and cannon. Surely there's a wider board now."

Pete motioned them to follow him onto the dock. "There, how's that?" He waved to a wide gangway.

The worry in John's eyes turned to relief. "That's fine. Can we go aboard now?"

Pete nodded. "Go aboard. Have a good look." They all clattered up the gangway.

Sam turned slowly, studying the deck and rigging of the ship. "Well?" asked Will.

"This could be home for quite a long time." Sam looked up into the maze of ropes again and sighed. "Where do all those ropes go? Will, I haven't a clue about sailing."

"You'll learn, and rather quickly, I should imagine." Will followed Sam's gaze. "You'll have to tell us all about it after your first voyage."

"Lads, we must leave the ship. Up to the Mermaid with you. Richard and I have prepared a meal." Pete turned and walked quickly back down the gangway.

"We just ate—" John began to call after him. Robert's elbow in his stomach cut him off.

"Well, I'm hungry," Robert said.

"You're always hungry."

"My master told me never to turn down food." Robert stepped onto the gangway. He ducked a swing from John, and the two ran to the dock with Will and Sam following.

"Where's Pete? Where'd he disappear to?" Robert's stomach grumbled. "It's rude to invite someone to supper then disappear."

THE FOUNDLING

"What do you think, Sam? Are you going to go? You can still change your mind, you know." John faced his friend. "Once your name is signed on the ship's books, you've no choice."

Sam looked past John and studied the ship. "I really do want to go."

"There's Pete," said Will, looking across the yard.

"Let's go eat. Where's the Mermaid?" Robert patted his growling stomach.

"It's that way." Will pointed, and they walked across the yard towards Pete.

"So you're going for sure?"

Sam nodded. "Don't worry, John. Even if I'm caught, I'll never give your names."

"I'm not worried. I'll miss you."

"No one to feed each week, right?"

"You can put it away—almost as much as Robert."

"No one can eat as much as Robert."

They caught up with Pete. "We must get out of sight. Quickly, into the pub. If we're seen, tongues will wag." Pete took a quick look over both shoulders.

"I don't see anyone," said John, but he stepped into the dark pub as soon as he could.

"I thought I saw two men coming up from the other direction." Pete closed the door behind him. "We stayed far too long on the ship. Always the odd chap who shows up and ruins the plan." He opened the door a crack and peered out. "I really can't see anything from here."

Richard brought out two loaves of brown bread, some yellow cheese, and bowls and spoons. "Washed them in your honor," he said, and he set the table with a flourish.

The aroma from the kettle brought everyone to the table.

Pete dunked his bread in his bowl. "Here's the plan. Sam will have to stay here until I can meet with Captain Mason. We've a cellar under us, and Sam will be safe. He can also rest and let his ribs mend a bit. Just before the *Lady Eleanor* is towed to anchor in the Thames, we'll take Sam, here, aboard."

"Usually we charge a small fee for this," said Richard, "seeing as how we're putting ourselves at odds with the law."

"But, I thought you said—" Will began.

"Right," Pete interrupted. "Right. Usually we do ask a small payment for our pains, but Will's a mate of mine. How could I put a few coins in our friendship?"

"Usually? You do this often?" Robert looked hard at Pete then at Richard. "Are you spirits? I've heard of them. They steal children and sell them to captains."

"Spirits? I know the word, but we're not stealing Sam, here. 'Twas Will who first mentioned Sam to us," Richard said.

"So you're doing this out of the goodness of your heart?" Robert wasn't going to be put off.

"I'm sure Captain Mason will drop a coin or two in our palms for providing a bright, likely lad to him. But what does it matter as long as Sam gets aboard the *Lady Eleanor* and away from his master?"

Will stood up. "We'd best say goodbye to Sam and be getting back."

"Don't you want to see the cellar?" Richard jumped up. "That is, don't you want to see that Sam will have all the comforts while he waits here?"

Pete went to the corner and pulled some boards up from the floor. "Surely, you want to see."

John shook his head. "I don't."

"Me neither." Robert held up a hand. "Small dark spaces give me the creeps. You go, Will."

Will took a candle from Pete and went down a makeshift ladder. "Watch out for the third round, Sam. It slants to the left a lot."

Pete grabbed some of the dirty bowls from the table and carried them to a large tub across the room. Richard followed him.

"Well?" Richard whispered.

"Well? What do you mean, 'Well'?" Pete whispered back. "We've two of them in the cellar."

"And two that won't go near it."

"Let me think." Pete dropped the bowls into the tub.

THE FOUNDLING

Back at the table Robert watched the men and leaned toward John. "What do you suppose they're whispering about?"

"I don't know. Why are we whispering too?"

"I don't trust either one of them. This whole arrangement feels dodgey to me."

"Nothing's gone wrong, yet, but . . . " John rubbed his neck. "I can't put my finger on anything. After all, Sam wants to go."

Meanwhile Will and Sam explored the cellar. There were a few crates, two barrels, a small table with a candle holder and, in the corner, some rags and coiled ropes.

"The floor's dry, anyway," said Will. "And you won't be here for long."

"Guess I could put the boxes together and sleep on them," said Sam.

"We'll move them before we leave, and we'll get you a blanket as well. I'll ask Pete for a brazier to give you some heat. I guess that's it."

They stood silently for a few moments. The candlelight flickered and threw dancing shadows on the clay walls.

"That's it," said Sam. "I might as well stay here right now. Best if I'm not seen anymore." He held out his hand to Will. "You've been a good friend, the best anyone could have. I probably owe my life to you, John, and Robert."

"I don't want to leave until I know you're safely aboard the ship."

"I'll be fine. You'd best get back up there. There'll be enough questions for you to answer without missing curfew." Sam sat down on a box. "I'll be fine, really. Goodbye, Will."

Pete's heavy steps crossed to the cellar entrance. He scrambled down the ladder. Richard followed.

"Pete, Sam needs a blanket and a brazier, if you have one."

"Isn't there a blanket over here?" Pete stepped behind Will, picked up a board, and knocked Will over the head. Before Sam could yell, Richard grabbed him from behind. One arm circled his chest, pinning his arms to his sides. Richard's free hand came down over his mouth.

"Stop struggling, or I'll finish breaking the rest of your ribs," Richard said in Sam's ear.

Sam kicked out with both feet, but he couldn't shake Richard's hold around his chest. And the hand over his mouth made it harder and harder to breathe.

Richard loosened his grip only when Sam hung limp in his arms. Pete tied and gagged Will. "The simple plans are always the best. You tie up yours, and I'll tell the others Sam wants to bid them goodbye."

Richard bent to his work, and Pete climbed the ladder until his head appeared above the floor. "John. Robert. Come on down. Sam wants to say goodbye to you."

"You go, John. I'll stand at the top of the ladder and wave," said Robert.

As John climbed down the ladder, Richard said, "Have a care there on that third rung. Here, let me help you."

Two strong arms grabbed John from behind.

"Robert, run!" cried John. "You were—" A sharp blow from a board cut him off.

Robert hesitated only an instant. He jumped over one stool and stumbled over another. His hand closed over the latch at the same moment that Pete threw his weight against him and pinned him against the door.

Pete wrapped a rope around Robert's chest and arms and then around his knees. He picked him up, kicked the stools out of his way, carried Robert to the cellar opening, and dropped him, head-first, through to Richard. Soon Robert was lying on the floor with Will, Sam, and John.

Richard dusted off his hands and winked at Robert. "You'll be happy to know you'll not have to say farewell to your dear friend. Each of you is worth too much money to break the set. Six pounds each, from which we must give Bowles his due." He blew out the candle, climbed the ladder, and pulled it up after him.

"Here, drop this down before you put the boards back." Pete threw the bag Will had packed for Sam across the room. "Can't leave anything lying about."

"Right you are." Richard dropped the sack into the cellar and replaced the boards.

Pete poured himself a drink and sat by the fire. "Not too bad. Not too bad at all, eh?"

Richard joined him. "Had me going for a minute there. But your plan to get the other two—" He took a drink. "That Robert was a handful."

"We'll need to keep them tied and gagged until Mason wants them. Maybe you should close the Mermaid for a couple of days. I'll say you're sick. Fever. It'll keep the folks away."

Richard agreed. "When do you see Mason?"

"Tomorrow evening, late."

"Maybe we could ask for more for the lads."

Pete shook his head. "No. Mason comes to us because we don't ask much. There's others he can go to if he chooses. Best keep our demands a bit lower. Besides, Bill Bowles would want more."

Richard picked up his mug. "To our good fortune."

"And ten pounds each." Pete knocked his cup against that of his friend. "Here's to easy money."

Chapter 11

Something pushed against Will again and again. He groaned and tried to roll away. The pushing continued. He tried to speak, to protest, but his mouth wouldn't open. When he turned his head, it felt like a walnut split open with a hammer.

This is an awful dream, he thought. If I could just wake up! He was sure he had opened his eyes, but he couldn't see a thing.

Still the pushing continued. Am I awake? he wondered. He tried to lift his right hand. It was caught behind him and the more he pulled, the less it moved. What was going on? He let his head fall back. It hit a hard clay wall, not a soft pillow. He groaned.

The pushing stopped for a few seconds, and Will decided to keep dreaming until his head felt better. Something hit him hard on his ankle. I'm awake now, he thought. He pulled at his hands. Tied! They're tied! And my feet too! I'm gagged! How? Something pushed against Will again, and he shoved back hard. Out of the dark came a muffled sound almost like a growl.

Will's head felt like someone was hitting him again and again. Holding still helped a little and allowed him to think. He'd been with John, Sam, and Robert. They'd gone to the yard, met Pete, gone aboard the *Lady Eleanor*. Met . . . Pete and Richard. Pete and Richard! They did this!

He sat straight up and immediately fell back with a moan. He stopped thinking and waited for his head to stop throbbing.

But then, he thought, where's Sam? Is he gone? Is Pete afraid the rest of us will say something that will get him arrested? Where, where are John and Robert? What or who has been pushing me? Maybe I wasn't dreaming. Will turned his head from side to side, rubbing his chin against his chest and the back of his head against the wall. The gag didn't budge.

Something nudged him again. He slid sideways to find out what it was. Using his hands and digging in his heels, he was soon leaning against someone. Will squinted hard and leaned forward.

He couldn't see a thing. He leaned farther, and his cheek brushed the rough wool of a coat. At least, he thought, it's a human and not one of those huge river rats.

The person next to Will was moving. What's he doing? thought Will. Clammy fingers touched his hands and fumbled for the ropes around his wrists. Will jumped. That's it! He turned as quickly as he could so his back was to his neighbor. The fingers pulled at the ropes, trying to find a free end, a loose place, anything. After a long effort, tired fingers tapped Will's hands. Will took it as a signal that he was to try to untie his neighbor's hands. But he had no better luck.

Exhausted, the two leaned against each other, back to back. Will's cramped muscles slowly relaxed. He dozed off briefly; movement awoke him. Will's partner was lying down with his head near Will's hands. Will's hands fumbled over a head of curly hair. Robert!

Will set to work on Robert's gag. He couldn't budge that knot either, and he couldn't leave Robert lying with his face in the dirt for long. He reached back down and his finger caught the edge of the gag on Robert's cheek.

He tried pulling the knot over Robert's head. The gag was too tight. Next he tried pushing the gag down off Robert's face. The rag moved a bit, only a bit. Will grabbed at the bottom of the cloth and pulled. Robert wiggled and pushed in an effort to help free his mouth. It took more tries than either counted, but the gag at last moved and slipped free. Robert gasped a full breath.

Say something, anything, Will wanted to shout. He struggled wildly against his bonds and sank back exhausted.

"Shh. It's me—Robert." Robert rolled to a sitting position. "I'm going to try to get your gag off. Hold still. No, don't lie down. My fingers are too sore to pull it off. I'm going to get it with my teeth as soon as I can move my jaw properly."

Robert's curly hair brushed against Will's cheek. Robert caught the bottom edge of the cloth and began tugging. Will tried to pull his chin in. The gag slipped farther. Robert gave one last tug and fell against Will's chest as the gag finally came off.

Will breathed in again and again, filling his lungs. "Robert," he whispered, "are you all right? Where are John and Sam? What's going on? Where are we?"

"Shh!" Robert rolled back to a sitting position. "Richard's still upstairs. Or maybe Pete. We're in the cellar. At least, I think we're all here. We were when I was dropped through the floor. All three of you were trussed up like geese at Christmas and out cold. I was tied up and dropped in the corner. We must all be here, but I haven't heard any noise from Sam or John."

"I should have known! Mr. Porch warned me. It looks as if we're all going to sea on the *Lady Eleanor.*" Will clenched his teeth. If he ever got his hands on Pete—

"What should we do? I don't think we can get these ropes off."

Will shook himself again. "You were right, Robert. They're spirits. I'll see Pete and Richard in the Clink for this, and Captain Mason too."

"We have to get out of here first. I can't see a thing, can you?"

"No."

They sat quietly.

"I'm going to try to move around and find Sam and John."

"Right," said Robert. "You go to the right; I'll go to the left."

Will rolled to the right and moved along the wall propelled by his hands and heels. After a few feet, he had to stop to rest. When his heart stopped pounding and his breathing returned to normal, he heard the soft scuffing sounds of Robert moving along another wall.

Will continued scooting and rolling. He turned a corner and bumped against a stack of crates. He would have to go around them. He opened and closed his fists several times to return feeling to his hands. All the moving and shifting and struggling hadn't loosened the ropes a bit. The cool clay floor felt good on his palms. He heard Robert mutter under his breath. He'd run into something too.

Will moved his hands under his hips to boost himself away from the crates. On the next boost his hands gave way, and he collapsed on them and nearly rolled onto his back. Why hadn't he thought of it before? Will rolled back and pulled his hands under his hips. It was harder than he'd thought because of his coat. But when he rocked back up to a sitting position, he had his hands behind his knees.

Just get your feet through now, he told himself. Perhaps you can untie your feet or even untie your hands with your teeth.

If his feet hadn't been tied together, Will could have easily pulled them through the circle of his arms one at a time. Instead he pulled and strained and rolled on his back again.

"What are you doing?" The hoarse whisper sounded a long ways away. "It sounds as if you're rolling about like a madman."

"I am." Will's breath came in short pants. "Got it!"

"Got what?"

Will caught his breath. "Got my hands in front of me. See if you can do it. Roll back and pull your hands under you."

Scuffing, wiggling sounds filled the small cellar again.

"I've got them behind my knees."

"Roll way back, until your head rests on the floor and pull your legs way up," Will whispered into the dark.

Robert scuffled around again. Finally Will heard "Got mine too. Now what?"

"Can you untie your feet?"

"I can't even feel my feet," Robert said.

"If we can walk, we'll be able to find Sam and John faster." Will felt around his ankles for any loose bit of rope. "My fingers are all swollen, and I can hardly feel anything."

"Me too. But I found a loose end." Robert worked for a moment in silence. "What a knot! I'm not sure I could untie this even if I could see it."

Will's numb fingers slid over the ropes around his ankles. He found the knot down low just above his heels. The only way to get to it was to get his hands behind his feet again. Will rocked back and slipped his hands over his feet. It could have been minutes or even an hour that he worked on the ropes on his ankles.

"Any luck?" Robert's whisper came through the dark.

"Yes! I just loosened something. Wish I could see."

"Wish I could feel! My fingers aren't working right."

A low moan sent icy chills down Will's spine. That has to be Sam or John. Surely they should be awake by now. I bet they'll have horrible headaches too, he thought.

"That John?"

"I think so." Robert listened for another moan. "I must be close to them. Where are you, Will?"

"Behind some boxes. I'll have to get around them. Say! The knot's loosening."

"I'm going to get to Sam and John to get their gags loose."

"Right. Something's giving way here." Will felt one coil of the ropes loosen. The skin underneath itched, but his numb fingers weren't very good for scratching. Another coil loosened, then another. What he thought would be wonderful relief became pounding pain as the ropes fell away and allowed free circulation again. He nearly cried out.

Will rubbed his ankles as fast and hard as he could. The pain lessened to a dull ache and thousands of prickles. He pulled off his shoes and rubbed and scratched until the prickles went away and he could feel his feet again. The cool floor felt good through his stockings.

"What are you doing over there? I've found John, and I think Sam's lying next to him. C'mon, John, wake up."

John's groan rewarded Robert's efforts.

"Shhh. We're in the cellar of Will's friend, all trussed up. We think he's going to sell us all to Captain Mason."

"What?" John flopped around. "What's going on? Oh, my head."

"Precisely," said Robert. "Shut your mouth and lie still."

"Is he all right?" asked Will.

"I think so. I hope he doesn't make too much noise. What were you groaning about just now?"

"Wait 'til you get your ropes off. You'll find out. And Pete's no friend of mine. If we get out of this, I'll see both him and Richard in prison."

"Found Sam. There, his gag's off. I have to rest."

For a long time no one moved. Will thought he might have slept awhile because when he opened his eyes, he saw a thin line of gray at the top of the cellar wall. He could make out the outline of the pile of crates against which he was leaning. He tried to stretch, but his stiff muscles did not want to work. Will wiggled his feet. Most of the ache was gone, and he could feel his toes. He leaned forward to search for his shoes. They had been right by his feet. His hands hit them, but his fingers couldn't grasp them. There was no feeling left.

The line of light brightened slowly. Will could see the ceiling beams and the hole in the corner that led to the pub above. How could he have been so stupid? He'd heard the rumors.

Because, thought Will in surprise, I rather liked him. He taught me a lot. We were friends. Will nearly snorted out loud. Friends! And Richard! Big, slow Richard. A good cook and harmless, I thought. I should have known. And now I've got myself and my friends in this mess. Will looked down at his lap and was surprised to see what his hands looked like. They were swollen and dark.

I've got to get these ropes off, he thought, and started searching for the knot. He found it underneath his hands. At least he could see it and grab the ropes with his teeth. He had to get these ropes off and help the others. Sam! Poor Sam! He must be in a sad way. Already beaten by Mr. Falconer and now treated like this!

Will tugged at the knot and felt it slacken. He bit another part and pulled. The rough ropes scraped his lips and chin. Sam, Robert, and John were all here because of him. Somehow he had to get them out.

The knot was getting wet. Pete had told him that wet ropes shrink as they dry. It didn't matter how sore his lips were now, if he gave up, the knots would dry and shrink even tighter. Will tugged and pulled until his teeth hurt and he could taste blood.

Robert called softly to him.

A boot scraped on the floor above them.

"Will!" Robert whispered again.

"I'm working on my wrists." It was hard to make the words come out through his swollen lips.

"Sam doesn't look too good. Neither does John, for that matter."

"I can't stop now," Will whispered back. "The knot's loosening. I'll come 'round as soon as I can."

The cellar became a little lighter. Will could tell from the rustling noises that Robert was working on his ropes too.

Another section of the knot loosened. I may not have any teeth left, thought Will. Or lips. He pulled the loose end through the knot and stopped to study the ropes. If he could just reach that bit there. He twisted his hands over as far as he could and reached around with his teeth. The muscles in his neck strained and popped as he pulled. But when that rope began to slide through, the whole knot loosened. Will pulled again and strained to pull his wrists apart. The coils fell loose, and within a few seconds his swollen hands lay in his lap. For a moment he just looked at his freed hands; then he almost wished he'd left the ropes on. The blood began to flow, and he thought he could not stand the pain. He rolled over on his face with his hands under his chest and bit the sleeve of his jacket to keep from crying out loud. The throbbing in his hands was much worse than it had been in his feet. For a moment he thought of Sam. How would he be able to stand it? The throbbing subsided a bit, and Will lay with his cheek against the cool floor.

"I have my feet untied, Will. Oh! Ow!" Robert groaned and sucked in air through his clenched teeth. Will could hear him rocking back and forth trying to be quiet.

"I have my hands free," Will said.

"Come give us a hand then," Robert gasped.

Will rolled over and sat up. "I can't feel anything yet. Give me a minute." His hands felt like two large, wet lumps of clay. A tingle of feeling delighted him even when it was followed by a thousand prickles. He shook his hands only once. The movement made the prickles feel like thousands of needles; he rubbed his hands together. When his hands were more red than purple, Will walked on his knees around the boxes to Robert.

"You look awful!" Robert was massaging his feet. "Had to take my shoes off."

"Me too." Will sat back on his heels. Robert didn't look so good, either. Neither did Sam and John, but they were awake.

"Can you untie us?" John asked. "I'm really stiff and sore."

"So am I," Sam whispered.

"I'll bet you are." Will looked at the ropes that tied his friends. "Let me try." He tried to grasp the ropes that bound Sam. "My fingers won't work. At least, not right now. Is there anything . . . ?"

THE FOUNDLING

He and Robert peered around the room. There was nothing on the small table to help them. Robert and Will saw the bag on the floor at the same time.

"Is that my bag? The one I gave to Sam?"

"Richard threw it down before he covered the hole."

Will crawled to the bag. "It's here, I know it. Where is it?" He muttered to himself. He pawed clumsily through the contents and finally held up the penknife. "It's part of the kit I packed for Sam. Now, let's see those ropes, Robert."

Robert held out his swollen, purple hands and Will sawed part of the knot in two.

"Your hands will hurt worse than your feet," Will said. "At least mine did . . . Here goes."

The ropes fell from Robert's wrists. He fell back against the crates, gasping for breath. He rocked back and forth, making no sounds, just staring at his throbbing hands. Will reached out and rubbed first one hand, then the other. When Robert settled back and could rub his hands together, Will moved to Sam's side. "I'm sorry about all this."

"Not to worry," whispered Sam. "I'll be quite all right once these ropes are off, I think."

Will cut through part of the knot. Nothing happened. "Don't pull. I have to cut this part, I guess." Another length of rope parted and the coils loosened. Will pulled the pieces of rope away and helped Sam sit up.

Sam caught his breath and clenched his teeth together, trying not to cry out. Will grabbed one of his hands and began rubbing it gently to help restore circulation. "This is all my fault, Sam," he said. "I'm sorry I got you into this. I was stupid; I should have known. I ought to—"

"That's not so." Sam spoke through clenched teeth. "I decided to run away from Mr. Falconer. And I'm not sorry about that one little bit. I am sorry that all my friends are in trouble because of me."

"We had to help." Robert chafed Sam's left hand. "Could we have let you run away alone? No. We're mates, and mates help each other no matter what the problem. Pity we've helped ourselves right into this cellar, though." Robert looked up and smiled. "Still, it's a grand adventure, isn't it?"

"Right. No matter what happens, we'll help each other," John said.

"Right. We will." Will patted Sam's hand. "All right?"

Sam nodded, and Will turned to John. "You're next."

"Do Sam's feet first."

"The blade is losing its edge. I'll do your hands, then Sam's feet." Will sawed through the ropes. The color was almost normal in his own hands, though his wrists were sore where the ropes had bruised and rubbed on them. Soon John gasped with the pain of returning circulation.

Will tested the blade on the ropes around Sam's ankles. "The knife's too dull to cut anymore. We'll have to untie your feet by hand."

It took much longer, but eventually all of them sat cross-legged on the floor massaging hands and feet.

"How long have we been here?" asked John.

"Last night and this morning, or whatever time it is now," Robert said.

"Are you sure? Seems like weeks." Sam clenched and un-clenched his fists.

"I'm sure. I was the last one. Pete caught me at the door, picked me right up, and dropped me through the floor into Richard's arms. He trussed me up before I could squeak. So I lay over there the better half of the night hoping you weren't dead. Then Will came around. We got our gags off and began to look for you."

"Pitch black it was too," Will said.

"I woke up once; couldn't see anything. My head hurt so badly, I went right back to sleep." John rubbed first one foot then the other.

"I never woke up at all until this morning," said Sam. "And I'm glad I didn't."

"How are you?"

"No worse off than you are, except my head is splitting." Sam pressed his palm against his forehead. "Don't worry about me."

John took off his jacket. "Here, put this around you. You're shivering. This'll warm you up."

"Wait a minute! Don't give me your coat. You'll freeze your-self." Sam tried to shrug John's coat from his shoulders, but his muscles were stiff and sore from being tied up all night and from Mr. Falconer's well-placed blows. "Will, John's cold. Look at him. Make him take his coat back."

"No. It's his to give. I should have thought of giving you my own. Now put your hands in your pockets, and I'll button the coat around you."

"Will, didn't you say you put some clothes in the kit you made for Sam?" Robert dragged the sack in front of him and dumped it out. "We could use this shirt like a scarf. And stockings. Are you wearing any, Sam?"

"None of your business." Sam tried to pull his feet under him. John pulled Sam's legs straight and took off one of his shoes. "Ouch!"

"Shhh! I'd say ouch too. Look at those blisters. That's what comes from wearing no socks. And your feet are cold as ice." John rubbed Sam's foot. "Here, Will, you do his other foot. Robert, toss those stockings over here."

Robert, John, and Will sat back to admire their handiwork. Sam was so bundled up he could do little but grin back.

"Thanks. I really do feel warm."

"You rest," said Will. "We'll try to find a way out of here." He surveyed the cellar. "Look at the light coming through up there. I'll bet we could dig our way out."

"This clay's awfully heavy." Robert knocked lightly on the wall.

"Will's right," John said. "We could dig a hole large enough for us to crawl through right below that beam." He pointed to the penknife and added, "Will even has a shovel."

"Let's start now." Robert tried to stand but flopped against the wall. "As soon as I can feel my feet better, that is."

"Um . . . If it's all the same to you," said Sam, "I don't really want to escape if this is my only chance to go to sea."

"What?" All three spoke at the same time.

"You see, don't you, that if I escape from here, I'll have to go back to Mr. Falconer. And since it is Monday already and I'm not there, he'll beat me within an inch of my life every day for the next week if I go back."

"But you're to be sold to a ship's captain." Will spoke almost too loudly.

"Does it really matter how I get onboard the *Lady Eleanor?*" Sam asked.

"He's right." John shifted to rub his other foot. "If Sam escapes with us, he'll have nowhere to go except to run to the country. If the runners catch him, he'll be sent back and likely land in prison. Happened to a friend of mine. He died of jail fever."

For a moment Will remembered Harry and his friends, each named for a king, on the great road to London. He often wondered what had become of them. Their life had seemed so daring and so much fun. Now he realized how dangerous it had been: stealing to eat, sleeping under hedges, trying to stay one step ahead of the law. There really was no help for it. Sam's best escape was to be sold by Pete and Richard to Captain Mason.

"I guess we could leave you here," Robert said.

"Why couldn't you go to the captain of the *Lady Eleanor* and sign on like any other crew member?" asked John. "I mean, you're this close."

"Sounds good to me." Sam settled back. "Just so I don't have to go back to Mr. Falconer."

"That's settled." Will stood up and started piling the crates against the wall. "If you, John, and Robert will steady these crates, I'll start digging. We have a long way to go."

"Wait! I have my knife and it's sharper!" John reached deep into his pocket. "I forgot about it."

"I wish we'd remembered you had that," said Robert.

"We could never have gotten to it. Besides, now we have a sharp shovel. We won't have to use this." Will threw the small penknife into the sack. "Hold on to these crates. Hand me the knife, John."

Chapter 12

Rodgers stepped to the door of Perry's office. "Nathan! Do come in! May I take your hat and coat?" He draped Mr. Fortescue's coat over his left arm and motioned him to a chair. "Please be seated. James and I were just going to have a coffee. Will you join us?"

"Indeed, I shall. Where is James? Downstairs in the warehouse?"

"Actually, no. He's with our foreman looking over some crates on the docks . . . Aha, here's our coffee. And I see three cups."

"Yes, sir. I saw your guest arrive and assumed he'd join you." The old man set down the tray.

"Quite right. Thank you."

"I'll send my girl around in an hour for the tray." The man accepted his payment and backed through the door.

"He makes the best coffee." Rodgers hung Mr. Fortescue's coat up. "James and I have tried to do it ourselves. Sometimes we even get it right. But that man's never made a bitter cup in his life. Roasts the beans himself, he does." He joined Mr. Fortescue at the window.

"Busy today?"

"We've been busy for the last ten days, Nathan. Two ships going out, the *Fair Wind* and the *Raven*."

"You know, the *Lady Eleanor* sails tomorrow."

"Finally got her ready, did they? She's a fine ship. As good as any I've seen. Didn't Will do some brass work for her?"

"Yes, he did."

They watched the laborers carrying bales of woolen goods aboard the *Fair Wind*.

"Stopping off in Europe on the way? With the woolens, I mean?"

"We've a new venture with the New England colonies," said Rodgers. "Here comes James." He moved to pour the coffee. "There are upwards of twenty thousand people there. Their winters are abominably cold, we hear, so we thought we'd have a go and ship clothing and a few household items. Then it's off to the sugar islands of the Caribbean."

"You're not shipping on the *Lady Eleanor?*"

James Perry closed the door behind him. "Still a nip in the air." He held his hands over the stove. "We'll not ship anything with Mason. He's a good ship's captain, but he's dishonest, crooked as a dog's hind leg, and I'll say so to his face."

"I hear," said Nathan, "that he's gone to buying from spirits."

"Why? He shouldn't have trouble getting a crew."

"It's not a matter of trouble—more like money. Kidnap victims don't show up on the ship's books. Don't have to be paid, you see."

"Greed has driven him so far? But, come, let's have our coffee."

Each settled into a chair around the stove. Rodgers placed the cakes on a small table. Mr. Fortescue went on. "Speaking of spirits, did you hear about the woman who sold her husband? Just a fortnight ago, it was."

"No. How did she do it?"

"Well, James, she knocked him on the head and had her friends carry him in a old barrow to the river and dump him in a boat. Rowed him out to the ship herself and struck a bargain with the captain. Dead of night, but they hauled the poor soul on board like a sack of meal. Unfortunately for her, those who helped her found there was a reward for turning in a spirit. So they turned her in and collected. She's in prison now."

"What happened to her husband?" Rodgers asked.

"He went to sea with the tide."

Rodgers chuckled. "Let all married men beware!"

"There are those who snatch children right off the streets and sell them." Perry poured himself a second cup of coffee.

"Aren't some of them purposely collected and sent to the New World?" Rodgers flicked a crumb from his shirt.

Fortescue nodded. "Taking those who would probably end up in Newgate. From what I hear, there's a need for laborers over there. They're indentured—like an apprentice."

"How do they fare, Nathan?"

"I hear they are awarded land and a cow at the end of their service. More than most of our apprentices will ever get." He held his cup out for a refill, then stirred the milky brew thoroughly. "In fact, I'm here about our favorite apprentice."

"Really?" Rodgers stopped chewing.

"Quite. This isn't entirely a social call. I was hoping he'd come here or perhaps to your home, James."

"Nathan, do be plain. I haven't seen Will since Rodgers and I were at the yard, and then only at a distance."

"He's missing. Didn't come home yesterday. You know, he's out with his mates each Sunday. But he didn't come home for supper, and he's still not returned. I don't mind telling you, I'm concerned." Mr. Fortescue stirred his coffee again. "I know one of his friends, a John Battersby, apprentice to Budgins, the weaver."

"And?" Rodgers leaned forward resting his arms on his knees.

"I stopped by Budgins's shop this morning, and John has gone missing as well."

"Has this ever happened before?" asked Perry.

"Never. That's why I'm worried."

"Any difficulties, ah, trouble, that we should know about?" Perry set his cup aside. "You know, a disagreement in the foundry that might make a night away seem necessary to a boy?"

Mr. Fortescue shook his head. "No. That's not Will's way. He'd speak to me directly. Not to say we haven't had our misunderstandings, but they were settled at the time. I daresay any master in London would be pleased to have Will." Mr. Fortescue stared at his coffee. "I really thought—hoped—he'd be here."

"He could be out on a lark. He's at an age when boys do foolish things without thinking." For all his attempts at optimism, Perry didn't sound very sure.

"Nathan." Rodgers clasped his hands between his knees. "Have you any idea where the lads go?"

"What is there for a boy and his mates to do? It's not as though there were bearbaitings or games any more." Mr. Fortescue thought. "He's mentioned London Bridge and—oh yes—one of the guards saw three chaps at the yard walking about. He thought one of them might have been Will. That was some time ago."

James went to his desk. "Should we send runners out?"

"Let's not do that. If they find him, they're just as likely to clap him in jail for breaking his indentures as bring him to us."

"But where do we start to find him?"

James turned to look out the window. "Nathan, perhaps you should return to the foundry. Will might have returned, or word might have come."

"What will you be doing?"

"I'm not sure. Rodgers?"

"Thinking."

The cries of the gulls came clearly through the air, providing a melody punctuated by the uneven rhythm of thumps and thuds from the warehouse below. Mr. Fortescue broke the silence.

"Must be getting back. As you say, perhaps Will has returned." He pulled his shirtsleeves back around his wrists and followed Perry's gaze out the window. "I confess, James, sometimes I think I'd like to sail to the Indies, East or West, but only as supercargo, mind you. None of this running up and down ropes for me."

"I'll keep you in mind if ever I need another factor." A smile crinkled around James's eyes.

"What brings that smile?"

"I just pictured you hanging from the ropes of the *Raven* some blustery day off the Lizard."

Rodgers smiled briefly, then turned the conversation back to Will.

"James?" Rodgers spoke slowly. "Will wouldn't sign on a ship, would he?"

The men at the window stared at Rodgers in surprise.

"You mean—just—just take off?" Nathan Fortescue raised an eyebrow. "No. No, he wouldn't. Besides, several ships have already left. Why wait until now?"

Rodgers went on patiently. "Which ship would have the greatest interest for Will? He must have been proud of the work he did for the *Lady Eleanor.* He may have even met some of the crew. Perhaps they persuaded him?"

"If Will were going to do that, would he have taken a friend along?"

Rodgers frowned. "Yes, there's that."

"Mason sails tomorrow with the early tide. There's still time—"

"Mason!" Rodgers cut Mr. Fortescue off. "He's the captain? That's why both boys are missing!" He jumped to his feet. "It's possible. Listen to this. Will probably went to the yard on Sundays. Perhaps several times."

"That's a guess."

"I know, James. Hear me out. He visits yesterday with his friend, John. They go to the basin to see the *Lady Eleanor.* Perhaps Will asked permission to go aboard? Don't you see?"

"Mason. A captain rumored to complete his crews with kidnapped boys so he won't have to pay them!" Master Perry nearly shouted.

Mr. Fortescue slapped his forehead with his hand. "Pete Goodcole! Why didn't I think of that immediately? I had Ben warn Will against that man. Pete is the master carpenter, and Will had to spend a lot of time with him. There are rumors that he is a spirit. Even if Will didn't go near the *Lady Eleanor,* there's still a chance that Goodcole has him and John. Both could end up on Mason's ship by the turn of the tide tomorrow." In three strides he crossed to his coat.

Perry and Rodgers shrugged into theirs as quickly. Perry ran down the stairs. "Have to tell the foreman—" he called over his shoulder.

Rodgers snuffed the candles and checked the stove. He stopped for a last sip of his coffee. Cold. His upper lip curled. He took one more sip before setting the cup down with a clatter. "Come, Nathan. We'll meet James at the gate below."

The trio stormed through the busy, narrow streets, sidestepping puddles, rubbish, carts, and other hurrying pedestrians.

"Wait!" Perry stopped. "We have no plan. If we go careening in as we are now, Goodcole, Mason, or whoever has Will and his friend will soon discover what we're about and hide the boys more carefully."

"What? Plan? What do you mean, 'plan'?" Nathan stared at his friend.

"We have to hurry, James." Rodgers moved to continue. "We need time to search the yard; it's a big place."

"And the *Lady Eleanor,*" added Fortescue.

. "Right! And which of us should do what? Let's find a quiet place to think. We don't want to make matters worse for Will and his friend than they may already be." Perry looked around. " 'The Three Tuns.' That should serve us nicely." He herded his friends through the door of the public house.

"James!" Rodgers protested as they sat down.

Perry held up his hand. "I know; I know. If I had wings, I'd be flying, and so would Nathan."

"If Mason gets his hands on Will—"

Mr. Fortescue slammed his fist on the table. "He won't! I've friends in the yard. If necessary, they'll make sure he never sets sail."

Perry leaned over the table. "First of all, one of us has to get onboard the *Lady Eleanor*."

"I'll go," said Rodgers.

"No. It can't be you. There's no reason for you, or me, either, to go aboard."

"I can." Nathan Fortescue grasped his cup. "It won't be any problem for me. We did all the fittings for that ship. I can always do a last check. And I can get right into the hold, the whole ship." He flung a hand out.

"You probably shouldn't go alone."

"We're not that far from the foundry. I'll stop by and pick up a couple of men. Six eyes are better than two, eh?"

James turned to Rodgers. "You will go to the area of the yard frequented by Goodcole. It's a large area, lots of sheds, piles of timber."

Rodgers nodded. "If anyone asks, I'll say I'm checking the timber for our new ship. I may even find Pete Goodcole, master carpenter."

"Don't punch him till you find Will," said Fortescue. He turned to Perry. "Perhaps we should send a couple of men with him to protect Goodcole."

"I will go into the yard offices and around the ships," said Perry. "I'm frequently there anyway, so my presence will arouse no curiosity."

"And if—when we find Will?" Mr. Fortescue asked.

"If you can, get him out immediately. He's an apprentice who's broken his indentures. That's reason enough. We can't give anyone enough time to move him while we go find help." James looked at his friends. "Ready? Let's go."

Nathan Fortescue hurried off towards his foundry. Rodgers and Perry set a steady pace towards the yard.

"If Will's been harmed in any way . . . " Rodgers stopped. "What if we're wrong, and Will is somewhere else in trouble or hurt and we're wasting our time here? What if—"

Perry's voice was quiet. "I believe this is the best place to start. You must too, since it was your idea."

"Yes."

"As soon as we've done here, if nothing comes to light, we'll send out runners."

"Yes." Rodgers let out a long sigh. "Sorry, James. He's become my family, the one I look out for even before myself. Do you—"

"—understand?" Perry's expression was grim. "Oh yes, I do."

They entered the yard without waiting for Mr. Fortescue.

"Back at the main office in an hour?" Perry asked.

"Better give me an hour and a half. There are lots of sheds out there."

Rodgers disappeared behind some low storage sheds. Perry went to the yard offices.

"Ah, good day, Laurence," he said to the yardmaster. "I had a little time on my hands. Thought I'd see how the new hull is progressing."

"The carpenters are still selecting the timbers. Would you like to see?" Laurence Winter was always ready to guide a good customer through the shipyard. "I hear you have two ships preparing to sail."

"Yes, but there's nothing that my foreman and the ships' captains can't handle."

"Let's walk, James. You know Mason's ready to sail tomorrow. His ship's still at dock, but she'll be towed into the Thames early tomorrow. Catch the afternoon tide. He's picking up cargo farther downriver." They strolled into the yard. The rasp of saws and the sharp cracks of hammers mixed with the calls of the men. "Didn't Mason sail for you at one time?"

"Only once. A good captain, but greedy."

"And one of your men broke his nose? Improved his looks by all accounts."

Perry half-grinned. "Yes, and it did. Now I hear he's taken to filling his crew with boys who never intended to go to sea. A bad business, that."

They stopped to watch the raising of part of the skeleton of a hull. "There is word that Mason lacked five crew members last Friday. Now he lacks but one," said Laurence.

"When did you hear this?"

"Only this morning."

They walked on, each with his hands clasped behind his back, like two elderly university dons debating an obscure point of philosophy.

"I'll tell you, Laurence, this isn't just a visit. A friend and I are missing two boys, each about fifteen or sixteen. One of them is Will Pancras."

"I know him. Hasn't been around for a week at least. His time here must be about up."

"We're afraid he may have been taken aboard the *Lady Eleanor*," said Perry. "Or that a chap named Goodcole may have him. Do you know of the rumors that he's a spirit?"

"Plenty of stories about him. None proved. And that mate of his, Richard. Now there's a character. Runs a pub at the edge of the yard. A rough place. I wouldn't doubt a few unfortunates have passed through their hands. Hope Will's not caught up by them."

"I have Rodgers looking over that part of the yard, but he may not know about the pub."

"He shouldn't go in there alone. Better warn him."

"Not to worry. Rodgers can handle himself."

"Still, you should warn him."

As if in agreement they turned their steps toward the piles of timber.

"Is that him?"

Perry waved and called out to a distant figure.

Rodgers hurried to meet them. "Any news?"

"None."

"Me neither."

"There is a pub near the basin, and—" Laurence began.

"—Pete Goodcole haunts the place," finished Perry.

"Where?"

"Along the fence," said Laurence. "It's a rough place." He pulled his lower lip. "Master Perry, if you and Rodgers go to the pub—well, face it—men such as yourselves wouldn't darken the door of such a place. If you show up . . . "

"It might look unusual, but we'll think of a good reason to be there."

Laurence looked at Perry. "Really, sir? If Goodcole has your boys, he probably already knows of your connection to Will." Frustration, anger, and despair passed over the faces of Rodgers and Perry. "I could check the pub for you."

"Wouldn't your presence there be just as suspicious as ours?" Perry asked.

Laurence shook his head. "I stop by on the odd day to remind Richard just who allows him to run the Mermaid. The owners of the yard wouldn't like any trouble. And Goodcole should be stopped. I can't stand alone against him, but with your help, here's a chance to knock him off his high sawhorse."

Master Perry shook hands with Laurence. "We can't thank you enough for your help. We'll be back at the offices."

"I don't want to just sit and wait, James."

"Laurence is right; we daren't go near this pub. We might endanger Will further with our presence."

Rodgers stood as though he carried a great weight on his shoulders. Finally he stretched out his hand to Laurence. "Look ever so carefully, won't you?" he asked.

Laurence touched his hat. "Upon my word, I'll do all I can."

Rodgers watched him go. Then, without a word, he followed Master Perry.

Chapter 13

The main office at the shipyard was seldom so crowded. Master Perry and Rodgers arrived first and sat in two corner chairs. Master Perry drummed his fingers on the chair arm and stared out the window at the busy yard. Rodgers never took his eyes from the fire in the grate. In spite of the warm weather earlier, the office now was cool and damp. Neither man spoke until Mr. Fortescue and two of his men returned from the *Lady Eleanor.*

Rodgers jumped up. "What did you find? Any sign of Will or his friend?"

Mr. Fortescue shook his head. "Nothing. Mr. Porch, here, insisted on poking everywhere from the bilge to the captain's cabin. Even saw Mason."

"He's up to something, he is." Ben Porch's voice carried the tone of knowledge.

"Why do you say that?" asked Master Perry.

"Because he insisted on going with us. He was too accommodating by half."

"But no boys," said Tom, who had left a mold unpoured on his workbench. He had insisted on helping find Will. He ran his hands over his hair as though to smooth it. "I agree with Mr. Porch. Mason's hiding something."

"We've shot our bolt with him. We have no excuse to go onboard again." Mr. Fortescue looked from Master Perry to Rodgers. "I'm sorry. There was nothing to find. Nothing."

Laurence entered. "Gentlemen, please find seats, because while I found nothing, the back of mind says perhaps—just perhaps—"

"Laurence, do say what you mean." Rodgers sat on the edge of his chair, his hands clasped so tightly his knuckles were white.

Laurence poked the fire and added some scraps of wood. When it burned to his satisfaction, he replaced the poker on its hook and turned to the waiting men.

"As you know, I went to check out the Mermaid. It's owned by a friend of Goodcole's, a Richard Simons. Not a man many would want to call friend. Your Will worked closely with Goodcole. He took Will any number of times to the Mermaid. You found him there once yourself." Laurence nodded to Mr. Fortescue, who nodded back and made an impatient gesture.

Laurence held up his hand and continued. "I went to the Mermaid and couldn't get near it before Pete ran out, waving me off. Said that Richard had a fever and I shouldn't come closer. When I asked if a doctor were needed, he assured me he would call for one if the fever was not abated within a day or two."

"You sound as if you don't believe him," said Mr. Porch.

"Not altogether, but given the kind of men who go there, Goodcole's friend could have a fever from any quarter of the world. I think we should keep the Mermaid under guard at all times, really, I do."

As the yardmaster spoke, another figure shuffled through the door. He wiped his nose on his sleeve and cleared his throat. "I saw that river rat in my ward, slithering around corners, looking for boys. He's a spirit, Richard is, and so's that barnacle friend of his, Goodcole. Known it for years." Constable Crumpton drew himself to his full height. "I came as soon as I heard. I knew you could use all the help you could get."

The men stared at the Constable.

"Thank you for your offer of help, Constable, but—" Laurence took Crumpton's arm to usher him out of the office.

"Offer? Offer? This is no offer to be accepted or not. I'm here and here I mean to stay. I belong here twice over. I found the boy on the porch all those years ago. Yes, I did, and 'twas a fierce night, at that." He removed Laurence's hand from his sleeve. "And I've been chasing those spirits from my ward for years. Yes, I have." Crumpton looked around the office, challenging each man there.

"He's right. We'll need every pair of eyes." Master Perry stood. "Gentlemen, this is Jack Crumpton, long-time constable of our ward."

"Thank you, sir. I was worried you might not think me fit because of my age and all." Crumpton rubbed his grizzled chin.

"Indeed, Constable. If there are arrests to be made, you will be just the one we need." Master Perry motioned the Constable to a chair. "Now, where were we?"

Rodgers laced and unlaced his fingers. "We know two boys are missing. Will has worked closely with Goodcole who, rumor has it, works with the owner of the Mermaid to spirit boys aboard ship."

"The yard's been searched. My men went over the *Lady Eleanor*. They're not on board. I'll swear to that." Mr. Fortescue looked around. "And they won't be taken on without my knowing. I left one of my men in the basin to keep an eye on the ship."

"We'd best decide what to do soon. The afternoon's half gone. The whole yard's been searched. What's to be done?" Master Perry paced in front of the fire.

Constable Crumpton held his cap in both hands, alternately crushing and stretching it.

Laurence Winter scowled and glanced out the window in the direction of the basin. "I should have gone in that pub, anyway. But with fever about . . . "

"It's a bit early for plague." Rodgers stood. "I'll go in whether both are dying. It's the only place left, isn't it?"

Ben Porch spoke. "If you'll permit me?" He paused, but continued at Master Perry's nod. "We have enough men here to surround the pub while some of us search it. I'd enjoy the privilege, sir."

"Sounds good to me. Let's go." Rodgers started for the door. "We should go immediately before any word can reach them about our meeting here."

Mr. Fortescue stood. "Rodgers is right. We should move right now."

"What about the fever?" said Crumpton.

"I don't believe there is any fever. Goodcole is saying that to keep everyone away from the pub. The boys may be there right now. We should search every inch of the place before evening allows them to move Will and his friend. I say let's go now." Mr. Fortescue looked around the group.

"Right."

"Let's go!"

"I can't wait to—"

"A moment." Master Perry's voice demanded attention. "If Will is at the pub, he probably is in little danger until he and his friend are moved. There is no reason to rush out willy-nilly and search the pub."

"James!" Nathan Fortescue stepped forward. "I say, James—"

"No, listen to me. Will is as important to me as he is to any of you. But think! Here's an opportunity to take the captain as well as two spirits."

"You'll not catch Mason."

"We will, Laurence, if we catch him with the boys on his ship. And we can do that with some careful planning."

"James, this is Will. Do you really want to wait?" asked Rodgers.

"No, I don't. But, if no money has changed hands, the boys are most likely in good health. And we have a real chance to send Mason to Newgate."

"Mason will go aboard shortly before the ship is towed to the Thames," Laurence said. "Then he won't come ashore for anything. I know him. The boys will probably be brought aboard last."

"Then we'll have to be aboard as well," said Master Perry. "Nathan, we'll need more of your men. Can you get word to them? Will they come?"

"For a bit of a dustup in a good cause? They'll come. Besides, there's not a man but holds Will in some regard. Right, Mr. Porch?"

"I'll see to it myself. When shall we come and where?"

All heads turned towards Master Perry.

"Tell the men to come as quickly as possible and meet here. They should be dressed like sailors." Mr. Porch turned to leave. "Ben, tell them they may be out all night."

"Mr. Porch! Tell those who come tonight, they'll be paid," Mr. Fortescue called.

Mr. Porch touched his cap with his right hand. "That guarantees a fine turnout, I should say," he said and closed the door behind him.

"James, what do you have in mind?" Rodgers's expression showed a bit of hope.

"I think we should take the place of some of the sailors on the *Lady Eleanor*."

"What?"

"Precisely."

"Not you two," Laurence said. "Pardon me for speaking so boldly, but the sailors will hear your manner of speaking."

"We'll not miss this, speech or no. We'll just have to remain silent."

"Begging your pardon again, but those are rough men and—"

" 'Twas Rodgers here who broke Mason's nose. Not to worry, Laurence." Master Perry looked Rodgers over. "Think you can handle it, old thing?"

"I can. But you'd better not tell Amelia or you'll have to fight your way out of your own house."

Master Perry chuckled. "Too true. Now let's be on our way. Best not to leave all at once."

The men left by ones and twos and finally the office was empty.

Pete looked worried. "There were at least six or seven. Nathan Fortescue was there, Perry and his partner. Even old Crumpton showed up. They know something, else why would they all show up in the yardmaster's office?" He leaned over his cup. "I tell you, they know something," he repeated.

"Did anyone else see you? You're supposed to be taking care of me."

"No one saw me. No one who matters, anyway."

"What did they say?" asked Richard.

Pete shrugged his shoulders. "Couldn't get close enough to hear."

"What'll we do?"

"Follow our plan; wait 'til dark, take the boys down to the ship in barrows if we have to."

"Think they'll be back?"

Pete nodded. He chewed on a fingernail while he thought. "But no one knows about your cellar, and half the yard probably thinks you have the plague. Laurence'll spread the word, the old busy-body."

They sat in silence, watching the candle burn.

"Word is Fortescue and some of his men were aboard the *Lady Eleanor* today. Told a mate of mine it was a final check of the fittings. I'll bet they searched that ship from stem to stern."

"Looking for the boys." Richard shifted his position. "Good thing we didn't take them to the ship as soon as we caught them."

A muffled thump came from the cellar.

"We'd better check on them."

"They're trussed up like Christmas geese. One of our better pieces of work. They couldn't move." Pete started on another fingernail.

"That's true. I used every knot I ever knew. It's the waiting that drives me mad."

"It's always like this."

"Worse this time. Someone wants those boys back. We don't usually snatch boys that'll be missed."

"If we stay with our plan, we'll be fine." Pete inspected the second fingernail. "The ship will be towed to the Thames at first light. That leaves us all night to move the boys. No matter if there is a plan afoot to rescue them, we can choose the best time. Dark. Safe. No one about. Collect our money and be gone, all while they're still planning."

"I suppose I'll have to lay low a day or two to recover from my fever. I'll lose that much custom."

"You'll have ten quid! What's the loss of two days' custom?"

"Money is money," Richard said.

"You're getting greedy."

Another thump came from the cellar.

"Think we should check on the boys?"

"You check on them," said Pete. "I'm going to walk around a bit. See what I can see."

"That's right, you go walking about enjoying yourself while I can't leave this room."

"If you aren't going to stick your head in the cellar, lie down and take a nap. After all, you're a very sick man."

Richard watched the door close. "That's right. I do the hard part. It's always me what does the hard part."

Chapter 14

"How are you doing?" John steadied the pile of crates.

"No faster than before." Will cut another chunk of heavy clay free and let it fall to the floor. "This knife is getting dull. Who's next?"

"I am." Robert took Will's place.

Will sat down next to John and propped himself against the crates.

"I really thought we'd have a hole dug out of here in a few minutes. It's been a couple of hours at least." Will tried to clean his fingernails with a long splinter of wood.

"Are we digging at the back of the pub?"

"No, at the side."

"Is it safe? Shouldn't we dig at the back?"

"Is any place safe? Just look at the mess we're in. We're in trouble no matter where we dig or even if we dig."

"Right." John rubbed his forehead.

"Sorry. I'm angry with myself for getting us into this mess."

"You were only trying to help me, Will. If anyone is to blame—" Sam gestured towards himself.

"Well, it really doesn't matter does it?" Robert whispered over his shoulder. "We're in this together. We all decided to come along." He dropped a handful of clay on the floor.

Sam sat up and leaned against the crates.

"How are you feeling?" asked John. "You don't look so good."

"Too bad there's no mirror down here. I'd show you someone else who doesn't look so good," Sam said.

"Still, you should rest all you can."

"I can't sleep anymore. I should be helping."

John's stomach growled. "I'm hungry and thirsty. I can't wait to get out of here so we can eat."

"Mé too, but let's not even think about it until we're actually out." Will licked his dry lips. "How are you coming, Robert?"

"I think the hole is big enough, even for John. I just stuck my head out and there's no one around. Let's get out of here!"

"When you get out, run for the fence," said Will. "We'll hide in the shed until after dark, and then Sam can go to the ship."

Robert had his head and shoulders out of the cellar when he stopped.

"Go on!" said John. "We have to move fast!"

"What's wro—?" Will began. Then he heard a familiar voice.

"A nice piece of work here, boys. I hope you haven't weakened the foundation of Richard's public house." Pete stood astride the hole, his hands on his hips. He threw back his head and laughed. "Richard! Richard, I say, see to the comfort of our guests!"

The boards rattled at the cellar opening. Richard dropped down. "Now, my lads, we can fight, and you will be hurt, or you can do as you're told. I don't much care. I'll be paid either way."

"You down yet?" Pete called.

"I am. Cover that hole and come on down before someone wonders what you're doing staring at the side of a building."

A minute later Pete dropped into the cellar. He picked up the board he and Richard had used on the boys the night before. "Tie them up," he said.

"You don't need to tie me up. I'm the one who wants to go to sea," said Sam.

"Do you now?"

"Yes, sir."

"Well, then, why don't you help me with your friends here?" Richard's voice was soft. He held new ropes out.

"Oh no. You'll have to do your own dirty work." Sam backed away.

"Then I guess you're first." Richard caught Sam's arm and soon Sam lay on the floor again, unable to move.

Will stepped forward. "You can't do this!"

"Not another step!" Pete brandished the board.

Richard grabbed Will and, before any knew what had happened, he too lay on the floor. Robert and John soon lay beside him.

Pete pulled at the ropes around John's wrists. "Nice and tight. Good. Now, don't worry boys. As soon as it's dark, you'll be stowed away safe and sound on the *Lady Eleanor.* That should suit Will fine, him with his maps and grand ideas about the world."

"You'll return to London as men. Yes, you will." Richard tied the last gag in place. "Someday you'll thank us for this."

"Come on, Richard. Let's get back upstairs before Bowles arrives. I don't want him thinking we've run out without paying him."

Richard stood beneath the opening and jumped to catch the edge of the floor. He pulled himself up and Pete did the same. Before putting the boards back in place, Pete stuck his head through the opening. "Patience, boys, patience." He disappeared and dropped the boards in place.

Will wished he were dead. They'd been so close to freedom. All that work, and he was so tired. None of them had eaten or had a drink since the evening before. It would be so easy to give up and go to sleep. He looked at his friends and found they were watching him. So he gave one curt nod and, as if that were a signal, each one rolled around trying to free himself. They had to escape before dark, and it was already late afternoon.

Will and Robert soon had their hands in front of them, and started working on the ropes that bound their hands. The westering sun provided less and less light, and the ropes were barely giving way to their efforts.

Sam and John worked together and, like Will and Robert, had to bend closer and closer to the ropes to see what they were doing. Almost suddenly, they could see no more.

We're beaten, Will thought. We'll never get out of this before dark. It is dark. He hung his head.

It won't matter at all. Even if we free ourselves, surely one of them is guarding outside. It's late. No one is here to come to our rescue. Worse yet, I'll never see Mr. Fortescue or Mr. Porch again. They might even think I ran away! So might Master Perry and Rodgers. The thought that Rodgers might believe he'd purposely broken his indentures and run away was the last blow. Will's whole body slumped, and his hands fell into his lap. He moved his arm to flatten an uncomfortable wrinkle under his coat. No matter what he did, it would not flatten. That's no lump. That's my pouch!

Would Mistress Bessie have ever quit? Not if there were a broom left in London. And Rodgers, Master Perry, even Sam. Will straightened up and began working on his ropes again. Even if we go to sea, we'll make it. I'm going to fight all the way. He pulled a rope end free.

The boards were thrown back and the ladder lowered. Pete came down with a hooded lantern.

"You're not going to believe this, Richard, but they're at it again."

Will sat straight up and stared at Pete. The other three did the same.

"Still some fight left, eh? Good. You'll need it to stay alive. Richard, come help me with these ropes. We'll let these roost-cocks walk to the ship if they have so much energy."

Pete and Richard untied the ropes around the boys' ankles.

"That's right. On your feet." Richard nudged John with his toe.

Will caught John's eye in time to warn him against anything here in the cellar. He was glad to see John was as angry as he was, but they needed more room to run.

John slowly got to his feet and walked toward the ladder.

"Here comes the big one," shouted Richard to someone up in the pub. Footsteps crossed the floor to the ladder.

"I've got him and no problem."

Robert, Sam, and Will followed John into the dark public house. In the dim lantern light, Will saw Bill Bowles.

"You see this pistol?" he asked. "I'd hate to use it because I'd probably hit one of you and there would go some of our profit. But, just so you'll know, if anything happens, this one goes first." Bowles pointed the pistol at Sam's head. "Whether he lives or dies is up to you."

Richard put a loop of rope around each of their necks and pulled them towards the door. He opened it and peered out. Then he stepped out and tugged on the ropes.

"Mind your manners, children," he said as they stepped over the threshold.

He gave the ropes holding Sam and Will to Pete. And beside Sam walked Bowles.

The fresh air revived Will. He looked around as much as he could without turning his head, but he could see no one in the basin. The walk between the Mermaid and the *Lady Eleanor* had never seemed so short.

They walked up the gangway and onto the deck. Will felt a tug at his neck.

"Hold up, there," said Pete. "I'll go see the captain."

Richard stopped Robert and John five or six paces away. Bowles kept his pistol pointed at Sam.

Will looked around the deck. There were two sailors standing guard. One looked curiously at the boys, then turned away.

I'll wager he's seen more than a few just like us, thought Will.

Occasionally a sailor crossed the deck and disappeared below. Other sailors sat or lay in the shadows.

Will looked up. All the sails were furled and the rigging complete.

Pete reappeared on deck and called to one of the lounging sailors. "You. Help bring these lads below. Captain wants to see them."

The burly sailor stepped forward. His beard was short and scruffy. He wore a patch over one eye and a striped cloth tied around his head. He looked Will over with his remaining, glittering eye. His smile reminded Will of a drawing of a wolf he'd once seen.

I'll bet he wins all his fights, thought Will. The sailor took the ropes and pushed the boys towards the captain's cabin.

Captain Mason sat at the table in the center of his cabin. Some china and crystal had been set to one side to make room for a ledger and a small locked box. Will wished he'd never done any work for the *Lady Eleanor,* especially for Captain Mason. Still, it was hard not to notice how the brass fittings gleamed in the lamplight.

The captain ordered their gags removed. Then he stood and walked around the table to look Will and his friends over.

"All sound?"

"Aye, sir."

"Been to sea before?"

"No."

"They look strong enough. Especially this one. What's your name?"

"John."

"That's 'John, *sir.*' "

"John, sir."

"That's better." He stepped in front of Sam. "And your name?"

"Sam, sir."

"Running away from your master, I'm told."

"Yes, sir."

"Running away from your captain is mutiny and a hanging offense. Don't even think about leaving, because I will see you hanged and your body thrown to the sharks."

Sam glanced at Will as if to say this wasn't what he had in mind. Aloud he said again, "Yes, sir."

"And you." Captain Mason stepped in front of Will. "The mastermind of this attempted flight of an apprentice?"

Will stood silent.

"Fortescue's apprentice. And ties to James Perry, I'm told. See what breaking the law brings to a man? Your life on my ship will be worse punishment than any prison. And since you seem to be the leader of your mates, remember what I said about mutiny."

Will looked Captain Mason in the eye. He had four or five quick retorts ready, each of which would probably get him a beating. But they died on his lips when he saw the captain's broken nose.

"What's this? A smile and no appropriate response?" The captain brought his hand around and hit Will on the ear. The blow resurrected every bit of Will's headache from the night before.

One of the sailors in the shadows stirred, then settled back.

"See that this one is kept on bread and water for a while until he regains his manners." The captain moved on to Robert.

Will hoped Robert would behave. But Robert drew himself up to his full height and looked as though he'd spit in the captain's eye. Mason smiled at him and rested his chin on his thumb.

"Mr. Coker, five lashes here, as a preventative. Then throw him in with this one." He motioned to Will. "Shackle them all until we're at sea."

Pete stepped forward. "These are the best we've ever brought."

"That they are."

"We do need our money so we can be away. It isn't wise for us to spend too much time aboard."

Mason went to his desk and opened a small box. He dropped a sack of coins into Pete's hand. "See that you spend it wisely. A bath might be a good start." He raised a scented lace handkerchief to his nose. "Now get out of here. Mr. Coker, we're ready to be towed into the Thames at first light."

Chapter 15

The one-eyed sailor tugged on the ropes he held and led the boys back on deck. He sneered at Robert.

"So, you're to receive lashes? I hope Mr. Coker gives me the honor. It's a pleasure to help a young chap like yourself learn his place."

Will thought Robert might explode from trying not to say anything.

"You really don't need to punish him," said Will. "He did nothing wrong."

"He was disrespectful to the captain," said the sailor, "and that's reason enough."

They passed Pete and Richard talking to one of the crew members. Pete turned and gave them a mocking salute.

"The captain's rather foul-minded, if you ask me."

Sam, Will, and Robert turned to stare at John, who always made it a point to stay out of trouble.

"John—" Sam began.

"I've had enough. We've been knocked on the head, tied up twice, not given food or water, and now Robert and Will are to be punished for nothing." He stopped and faced the sailor. "If you're going to punish them, add me."

"And me," said Sam.

"I can't tell you how important discipline aboard ship is, lads." The sailor's voice was soft and menacing. "Now hold out those hands so I can check your ropes."

He pulled out a small knife. Its blade was blackened so it wouldn't gleam in the light. As he talked he cut the ropes, but held each one's hands together as a signal to make it look as though they were still securely bound.

"Yes, discipline," he said, "is a necessity on a ship. The crew without it will soon be lost and its ship at the bottom of the sea. It's a smart sailor who learns this quickly. It'll save him many an uncomfortable night in chains, mark my words."

He lowered his voice. "There boys. On my signal, you run for the gangway and straight to the yard offices—"

Will gasped. "Mr. Porch?"

"Shut your mouth and walk on before I deliver a blow to your other ear."

Will stood rooted to the spot. He looked closely at the man in front of him. But before Will could open his mouth, Mr. Porch raised his voice so everyone on deck could hear.

"Are you challenging my orders, boy?" He spat the last word out, then said under his breath, "Turn around and walk! Now! And don't smile!"

"Need any help?" another sailor asked.

Mr. Porch pushed the boys down the deck. "Naw. They just need to learn who their betters are, and I'll be pleased to teach them. You there!" He poked Robert. "Walk faster!"

The other sailor fell into step. "These boys Mason takes on don't know stem from stern. They're a trial, they are." He stepped closer to the boys. "But these look better than most of—Say! Their ropes are cut. What—"

"Run, boys! Don't stop!" Mr. Porch pushed them hard the last few steps to the gangway.

Will grabbed Robert, John almost picked Sam up, and they ran down the gangway to the dock. Their feet pounded across the planks and onto solid earth. Behind were shouts of surprise and a splash. A pistol shot cracked over the basin and echoed into the night. Any thoughts Will had about going back to help Mr. Porch flew from his mind. Instead, he yanked the rope from around his neck. The ropes on his wrists hung in loose coils. He brushed them off. He was free!

The boys ran across the yard. Will thought he could run forever. How grand to be free! He looked over at John, whose long legs carried him into the lead. Robert, as short as he was, kept right up. And Sam—Will stopped so quickly, he nearly fell over. He whirled around. Where was Sam?

Part 3: The Apprentice

"Stop!" he shouted at Robert and John. His throat was so dry he had to swallow and shout again before they heard him.

"We're not . . . to stop." John bent double, his hands on his knees.

"What's wrong?" Robert's voice cracked.

"It's Sam! Where is he?"

They stood looking back toward the *Lady Eleanor.*

"I heard a splash when we came off the dock," said Will. "You don't suppose—"

"He was with me then," said John. He straightened up slowly.

Robert held his side and panted. "We have to go back."

"Let's go. Spread out a little." Will waved his hand. "We don't want to miss him."

They started back towards the basin, looking into every shadow. Will stopped and held up a hand for silence. "I heard a cough. Sam? Sam! Where are you?"

"Over here." A weak voice called out and coughed again.

Will, Robert, and John found Sam on his hands and knees, trying to get up. John and Will helped him to stand and supported him while he regained his breath.

"That was some run, wasn't it?" asked Sam. "You go ahead, and I'll be along. I'm fine now that I'm back on my feet."

Robert pulled the last pieces of rope from his wrists and threw them as far as he could. Then he took the rope from his neck and threw that too.

"I'm free!" Robert croaked. He helped Sam get rid of his ropes.

"C'mon, Sam. We'll help you." Will put his arm around Sam. "Lean on John and me. Robert, you watch to see if anyone follows. The offices are right over there." Will pointed to the candle-lit windows.

They had to stop twice so Sam could rest, but finally they reached the office. Hands reached out to help.

"Tom! What are you doing here? And Mr. Porch is on the ship!"

"We came to rescue you. But let's take care of your mate first." Tom lifted Sam and carried him to a chair.

"He's been sick for a long time," said John.

"My friends, Tom. This is John; that's Robert. You have Sam."

THE FOUNDLING

Tom unbuttoned Sam's coat. "Are the rest of you safe and sound?"

"We're fine. It's just that Sam has been sick for so long and the run from the dock was too much for him." Will watched Tom working over Sam. "He'll get well, won't he?"

"I don't know about that. He needs a drink. Get me a glass of cider from that bucket over there."

"Cider?" John swung around. "We haven't had anything to eat or drink since yesterday afternoon."

"There's food on that table by the wall. The kettle's on the fire if you fancy a cup of tea." Tom took the glass of cider Will held out to him, and put it to Sam's lips. "Here you are, young man. Just a sip or two at first."

Will made sure Sam drank some of the cider before he took a drink himself and joined Robert and John at the table. When their plates were filled, they went and sat near Sam.

Tom continued to give Sam small sips from the glass. Sam struggled to sit up straight. "Thanks, awfully," he said slowly. "I'm rather hungry."

They all offered their plates to Sam. He laughed and took a slice of cold meat pie.

Robert said, "Tell us about our rescue. I had just been sentenced to five lashes for a lack of manners, and I'm ever so grateful."

"I'll tell you what I can." Tom leaned against the wall. "When Will didn't come home Sunday afternoon, Mr. Fortescue was concerned, but not terribly worried. As he said, Will was old enough to stay out. But when he didn't come home the next morning, Mr. Fortescue went straight away to Master Budgins to see if John had returned."

"Mr. Fortescue knows Master Budgins?" John looked up in surprise. "Was Master Budgins worried?"

"Yes, he was, quite," said Tom. "I believe he thought you might have run away because of a recent thrashing he gave you."

John swallowed. "I wouldn't run away from Master Budgins. He's good to me, really. The loom just fell apart around me."

"Then Mr. Fortescue went to Master Perry. And Rodgers helped them puzzle out where you might be."

"Rodgers! How could he know?"

"He knows you've been working in the yard. Mr. Fortescue mentioned the work you'd done for the *Lady Eleanor*. Captain Mason is known for kidnapping. Then you'd spent so much time with Pete Goodcole—"

An old man rose and crossed the room. "—and Richard Simons, that rat he calls a friend. They're spirits, they are. I've been chasing them out of my ward for years."

"Will, here's someone you should meet. Perhaps you remember him?"

Will looked closely at the man. He wore a greatcoat two sizes too big. A scarf hung around his neck. His trousers were held in place with a piece of rope and his shoes seemed about to fall apart. He grasped a knit woolen cap in one hand and held the other out to shake Will's hand.

"Sir?" Will shook the man's hand, which was covered by a glove with no fingers.

"Constable Jack Crumpton, at your service."

Will looked at Tom, puzzled.

"The Constable found you, Will, on the church porch and took you to Master Perry's house."

"Yes, I did, I surely did. And 'twas I who heard your first words giving your name." He looked Will over again. "A mighty fine young man you've become, mighty fine. But I could tell when I found you that you would be a credit to—"

"Constable?" Tom nodded that he wanted to finish his narrative.

The Constable cleared his throat. "Begging your pardon for the interruption." He poured himself a glass of cider.

Tom picked up his story again. "Anyway, they gathered men from the forge and came to the yard where the Constable joined us. But the plan to rescue you was Master Perry's."

"Master Perry? He's here? Where? Where's Rodgers?"

"Why, they're on the ship dressed as sailors. After you were safely off, they were going to capture Pete Goodcole and his friend Richard and arrest Captain Mason."

"Will, I hope they get that Bill Bowles," said Sam. "He was in on our kidnapping too."

"They're fighting right now. I sure would like to see that captain punched out," Robert said.

"He already has a broken nose," said Will. "Did you see it? He was captain of one of Master Perry's ships before I was apprenticed."

Constable Crumpton went to the window. "Here they come! A crowd carrying torches is coming this way. They probably have prisoners. That's why I'm here, you know, to make the arrests all proper-like." The constable pulled his coat straight and buttoned its one remaining button. "Excuse me, but I'm needed out there," he said and left the office.

Will, Robert, and John would have followed him, and even Sam tried to get out of his chair, but Tom called them back.

"You're to stay here until I know exactly what's going on out there. Master Perry put me in charge of your safety, and I'll not take any chances."

In a rush all five went to the windows.

"They got him! Look, Pete's all tied up!"

"Richard's over there. He doesn't look happy."

"Serves him right."

"There's Mr. Porch!"

A moment later Mr. Porch grinned and waved. He grabbed his eye patch and waggled it at them.

"That's my foreman," said Will. He couldn't hide the pride he felt. "And look—there's Captain Mason!"

"All tied up," said Robert. "He doesn't look so grand now, does he?"

"Looks like he dropped his lace handkerchief." John's voice dripped with false concern. "Pity."

"Who's guarding the Captain? It must be a sailor who doesn't like him very much. Looks like he's just waiting to tear Mason limb from limb."

"Maybe he's one of our rescuers," said Will. "Tom, who is he, do you know?"

"Sorry."

Captain Mason turned to speak, but the guard's hand came down heavily on his shoulder and spun him around so he couldn't speak to anyone. Will almost wished he had gone to sea just to be able to meet this sailor.

"Look at him," Will said. And everyone did. He wore yellow and black striped breeches. They were tucked into red leather boots that gave him an added swagger when he walked. He wore a black vest with silver buttons and trim over a white shirt. His gold earrings gleamed in the dim light of the torches. He held one pistol, a mate to the one tucked in his wide leather belt. He was clean shaven except for a magnificent mustache which he stroked every so often.

The sailor looked up at the window. Evidently satisfied with what he saw, he raised his pistol in a salute, then returned his full attention to his prisoner.

They saw Constable Crumpton approach another of the sailors.

"That's Mr. Fortescue," said Tom. "He had us search the *Lady Eleanor* for you earlier today. Believe me, he didn't overlook one square inch of that ship. Of course, there was nothing to find, was there?"

Mr. Fortescue's costume was almost as grand as that of the sailor guarding Captain Mason. He was dressed all in black, except for his light blue shirt. A sword swung at his side and a dagger hung from his belt.

"I think he'd make a good-looking pirate, don't you?" Tom asked.

Will smiled. "He's a little roly-poly, don't you think?"

Tom poked Will in the ribs. "He's your master. Show more respect."

"Look! They're getting ready to move off. Who's that talking to the Constable?" asked John.

"That must be—yes, it's Master Perry," said Tom.

"Where's Rodgers?"

"Rodgers? I assume he's out there somewhere. If I were Mason, I'd not want Rodgers anywhere near me. He swore to see Mason hanged, drawn, and quartered if you were harmed, Will."

Rodgers had remembered him! Will's heart felt as though it filled his whole chest. To make sure he'd heard right, he said, "It's been so long. I haven't seen him in three years." He turned to Tom.

"He remembers you. Men who forget don't usually pace the floor with worry. I'm sure he'll be around soon."

The prisoners were taken away by Constable Crumpton, Mr. Fortescue, the sailor in the red boots, and the rest of the rescue party. "I don't see that Bill Bowles out there," Sam said.

They searched for the shadowy figure of Bill Bowles.

"He's the one who put Pete onto us," said Will. "But he must have slipped away."

"Who slipped away?" demanded a voice from the door.

"Master Perry! So good to see you again, sir!" Tom crossed the room and shook Master Perry's hand. "How did everything go, sir?"

"Couldn't have gone better." He looked at the boys. "I thought we came after two."

Will stepped forward. "Captain Mason bought all four of us, sir."

"Will! Is that you? Come over here, young man."

Will stood in front of Master Perry, whose costume made him more handsome than Will remembered. He wore a red shirt and dark blue breeches. Around his waist was a yellow figured belt from which hung a sword. His boots and the leather sash across his chest were of soft brown leather. He wore a red and yellow kerchief over his head and one gold earring that was actually attached to the kerchief.

"Will! Don't you remember me?" Master Perry took one step forward and caught Will's arm. He swept off his kerchief and earring.

Will's smile became laughter. "Yes, sir, I do." Will shook the hand held out to him. "Thank you for rescuing us. You make a fine sailor, sir."

"Well that's not quite what Mrs. Perry said when she caught me sneaking out of the house earlier today." He looked down at his costume. "Not bad, though, is it? Did you see Rodgers's costume? I have absolutely no idea where he came up with those yellow and black breeches."

"That was Rodgers? The one stroking his mustache?"

"He was stroking it because the glue was letting go. Rodgers went along with Mr. Fortescue to assure that our chickens could not fly the coop. He can't wait to see you." Master Perry looked up. "Tom, did I hear someone had slipped away?"

Sam stepped forward. "Bill Bowles, sir. He put Pete and Richard onto us. He held a pistol to my head when we walked to the ship. And he was paid a pound for each of us."

Master Perry shook his head. "I don't know him."

"I do," said Tom. "We'll put the word out among the workers in the yard. If he shows his face here, he'll be caught."

"I'll see that runners are sent after him as well," said Master Perry. "Now, who are these young men?"

"This is Sam—" began Will.

"I'm the cause of all this trouble."

"Shhh. And I'm John Battersby, Master Budgins's apprentice."

"I'm Robert Throgmorton, Walter Bright's apprentice."

"Whose apprentice are you?" Master Perry nodded at Sam.

"I'd rather not say, sir, because I'm not going back."

Master Perry's eyebrows went up. "You don't have a choice, you know."

"He's a cruel master, sir." John stepped forward. "We were helping Sam run away. That's why we were here." Sam began to cough. He stumbled to a chair with John's help. "And he's very ill too, sir."

Master Perry rubbed his brow. "You're all in on this?"

They nodded.

"You realize you've broken the law?"

They all nodded again.

"You must return to your masters and take whatever punishment they give."

"Not Sam," said Robert. "And we'll keep helping him until he can run away."

"You too, Will?"

Will nodded. "And we can't get in much more trouble than we already have."

"Tom, is there any water left in that kettle? A cup of tea is what I need right now. I'm actually going to listen to what these young men have to say." Master Perry dragged a chair to the fireside.

Chapter 16

1656

"Beautiful evening for April, James. A shame we'll have to spend it in the vestry house." Rodgers looked around the garden. "Nice to have a few moments to relax, isn't it?"

"Look at that sky. Not a cloud."

Marie carried coffee to a small table. She didn't trust the housemaids to serve the Perrys after the last accident had left a plate of spicy cakes scattered from Mistress Perry's lap to the far corners of the dining room.

The twins had laughed and even crawled under the table to help retrieve the cakes. Three-year-old Stephen had found one the next day and stuffed it in his pocket to eat later. It was found, unfortunately, after his clothes were in the great cauldron, boiling clean. Mistress Perry had laughed and wouldn't let Marie give Elsie the switching she deserved. Marie poured the coffee and left the table.

I won't be here much longer, she thought. I have nearly enough saved to find my own place. She never allowed herself to say "stolen" when she thought of the bits and pieces of jewelry she had tucked away over the years.

Why, Mistress Perry seldom misses them, Marie thought. She has so much! No, each coin, each bauble, is owed to me for all the work I do that goes unnoticed. It won't be long and I'll be able to spend that money freely and wear that jewelry. I'll move to another part of London and support myself by offering to train girls in the fine art of housekeeping. My services will be sought after by all the finest families in London.

Through a window, she watched the men relaxing, chewing on sweet biscuits, and enjoying their coffee. Soon you won't have me to serve you, she thought. You can chase your spicy cakes all over the house for all I care.

Rodgers swirled his coffee in his cup. "She gets colder every day, James."

"I confess the children do not like her, and Amelia is constantly less pleased with her work. Ah well, let's move on to more pleasant topics."

"I went to see Master Falconer as you requested. Sam didn't tell us the half of it. Falconer's other apprentices, which he was not supposed to have, were in worse shape than Sam was."

"It's amazing how those boys kept Sam alive for over two years, isn't it?"

"Two members of the Tanners' Guild went with me. They were scandalized. Falconer's boys were removed immediately. One went with Sam into St. Thomas Hospital for a cure. The other was given a small gift of money and sent home. Falconer will have to defend his actions before the Company Court. Added to that, he has a tanning business without a license from the Company, and he'll have to pay quite a fine."

"He'll be able to continue his business?" asked Master Perry.

"There's really no way to keep him from it. But he'll have to do all the work himself."

"The Company will make sure he abides by their decision?"

"So they assure me."

"What about Sam?" asked Master Perry.

"He'll never be able to do heavy labor even if his cure is complete. But he should be out of the hospital by midsummer. I told the hospital warden that we would undertake to pay for his cure. I say, James, he reads, writes, and ciphers. Can't we find a place for him?"

"We have no need of another clerk, but I'll ask around. Surely there's a good place available somewhere. I also sent Mrs. Dove, his mother, a small gift. The messenger said she was most appreciative of all we've done for her boy."

"The vestry will want to know if we intend to undertake his support permanently," said Rodgers. "They're going to want a guarantee that he'll not be a charge on the parish."

"I guess we have taken this on ourselves. Want to divide the expense? Won't be much, just finding him a new master and buying the odd suit of clothes." Tiny wrens landed in the garden near the table, waiting for crumbs.

"Is everything settled with the other boys?" asked Rodgers.

"Their masters have taken them back. Both good men, willing to pick up where they left off. And both John and Robert have promised to stay out of trouble."

"You know good intentions and young men, James."

"Indeed . . . Well, it's nearly time to collect Will and be off to the vestry." Master Perry paused. "But another minute won't matter, will it?"

"No one is more deserving of a bit of respite than we are, surely."

Master Perry called to one of the serving girls. "Would you tell Marie we'd like another coffee, please? There's a girl."

They both shifted in their chairs and shook the crumbs from their serviettes.

When Will entered the vestry house, it was as though he were repeating his earlier visit. Nothing had changed, except there was no fire in the grate. Everyone could have been frozen in time since I was here last, he thought. Master Perry directed him to the same stool by the fireplace.

Even the vestry business hadn't changed much. There was debate on how much to spend on a new roof for the church, who was to be hired to lop the trees in the churchyard, and whether new fees should be levied for burial in the church aisle. Pensions for the elderly and poor were reviewed and allowed.

The light slowly faded outside. One of the younger men lit the candles, and the meeting continued.

"The Constable found an infant placed at Mr. Saunders's stall," Nicholas Vaughan was saying. "Probably not a year old."

"Bring him to my house, Nicholas—if he's in good health, that is."

"We don't know how long it will take to find him a nurse, James."

"We'll be happy to have another baby in the house even for a short time."

THE FOUNDLING

"Of course, the parish will pay for his care and clothing. We'll begin looking for a nurse immediately."

This is probably the way they talked about me, Will thought. He studied the faces of the vestrymen more closely. I'll bet they wish parents would stop leaving their children to the charge of the church. It must be a terrible nuisance. He watched and listened even more carefully. Surely someone would comment on the trouble, the expense, the inconvenience of providing for this new foundling. But no one did.

After all had been settled, one of the men said quietly, "Poor little chap. To be left alone among strangers . . . "

They care, Will thought. They really do care. Just like we cared for Sam. To his surprise, it was Sam's name that came up next.

"I know of a young man, Sam Dove's his name, who is taking a cure in St. Thomas Hospital," Master Perry began. "He reads, writes, and ciphers well and should be ready to leave the hospital by midsummer."

"Is he the one our Will tried to get onboard Mason's ship?" someone asked.

"The same. He won't be able to do heavy work, but he's a sharp lad and will make a fine clerk. I've undertaken to find a position for him."

"The parish cannot be responsible for him, James."

"I quite understand. Rodgers and I are undertaking his expenses entirely. To prevent his being in need in the future, we hope to find adequate employment, or even an apprenticeship for him. If you hear of any position that might suit, please keep us in mind."

"How old is he?" asked young George Hefield.

"Fourteen, I should think."

"Bring him 'round to see me when he leaves the hospital. Fourteen's a bit young, but I've been looking for a lad to begin training in my shop. He could learn bookbinding and how to keep the accounts."

Sam would love that! thought Will. All those books for him to read. And he would learn how to bind them as well. Will looked Master Hefield over. Yes, he had a kind face, an easy smile, a quiet manner. Sam will get on well with him. Warm clothing, enough food, kind words, and lots of books. Sam will think he's in paradise!

"And now about Will, if you please, James. What is going on here and how does it affect this vestry?" asked the Upper Church-warden. "I see you've brought him along."

"Yes, gentlemen. I brought him along so you could see the results of your investment over these last ten or twelve years. Will? Please stand up and be introduced."

Will stood. He felt as though every eye in the City of London was looking at him, evaluating him. His face got warm, and he hoped he wasn't looking too embarrassed.

"Heard he broke his indentures," Henry Hickford said. "That's a serious action. What about his master? Will he still have him as an apprentice?"

"The boy was kidnapped, Henry!" Master Perry paused to calm himself, then continued. "Mr. Fortescue has agreed to keep Will and continue to teach him ironmongery. In fact, he said Will was one of the most promising apprentices he's ever had."

"In my day," Henry continued, "if a lad broke his indentures, he was publicly punished and could even be thrown into prison or sent to Virginia to make his way there. Isn't that right, Arthur?"

Arthur Dewe sat next to the fireplace even though there was no fire. He stared at the empty grate and appeared not to hear Henry.

"Arthur, isn't that right?" Henry insisted.

Old Mr. Dewe ignored Henry. He smiled and nodded at a private memory. His hands rested on the polished crook of his cane.

For once, it seemed Henry had the advantage over old Arthur, and he wasn't going to let it pass.

"Such carryings on as these wouldn't have been allowed in your day, would they, Arthur?" Henry raised his voice to be sure he was heard. "Ship all the troublemakers right over the ocean. Right? Or throw them in prison."

Arthur smiled and nodded. "No," he said quietly, "they wouldn't have been allowed, but they did happen. Yes, they did." He looked at Will, who was still standing. "Good luck to you, boy. I see a bit of myself as a lad in you."

"What?" Henry nearly exploded. "Are you encouraging him to—"

THE FOUNDLING

"Oh, do shut up, Henry." Goodman Dewe turned to Master Perry and Rodgers. "Perhaps you gentlemen would tell us of your part in this adventure."

"Have we quite finished with our business?" asked Mr. Vaughan. "Yes? Then, let's adjourn to the Dolphin and hear this tale in more congenial surroundings. I think we should invite Will along so he can testify to the truthfulness of what we're about to hear."

"Will!" Mr. Porch's call rang through the forge. "Mr. Fortescue would like to see you when you're finished here."

"Yes, sir." Will laid his hammer aside and took off his apron. He'd been back at the forge for a month. He went to find his master.

"Will, I need a special errand run." Mr. Fortescue took him over to a corner of the courtyard and lowered his voice to a whisper. "You know that Mrs. Fortescue's birthday comes in September. And every year I try to surprise her with a special little gift. Few men have been blessed with such a wife as I have. But nearly every year she discovers what my surprise for her will be, long before her birthday. This year I'm bound that she'll not know until her celebration dinner. I'm swearing you to secrecy. Can you withstand her wiles? She'll be after you with all kinds of questions, because I see her right now behind that window watching us. Can you do it, Will?"

Will smiled. "I'm sure I can, sir."

"I'm depending on you. If she drags the secret from you, I'll have you making horseshoes for the rest of your life."

"You can trust me, sir. I'll not say a word to anyone."

"Right." Mr. Fortescue put a folded piece of paper in Will's hand. "Take this to the jeweler on Aldermanbury Street, up by the London wall, at the sign of the Gold Cock. He's expecting you. Wait until he's looked this over and assured you that it can be done. I'm sure there will be no difficulty, but ask him definitely if he can have this ready by Mrs. Fortescue's birthday."

"What is it, sir?"

"A fine gold chain with a pearl pendant. Your Master Perry had the pearl purchased especially for me in the Orient. He's kept it for me all these months."

"So Mrs. Fortescue couldn't find it."

"Precisely! Now off with you. And not a word to anyone, mind."

The walk to Aldermanbury was a long one. Will enjoyed the bustle of the City. He checked out the displays of the map shops, dodged wagons, and jumped over rubbish missed by the scavengers. Eventually he passed the Tower and turned into Eastcheap Street. He went up Bow Lane to Cheapside and from there turned up Milk Street to Aldermanbury. It was a quiet section of London and well guarded. The goldsmiths did not take any chances with their valuable wares. The sign of the Gold Cock glittered in the afternoon sun.

Will opened the door to the shop. Before he could step in, a woman brushed by and hurried away. Will watched her retreating figure, certain he had seen her before. But when a young maid ran to carry her basket, he shook his head and thought probably not. He certainly wasn't acquainted with women who visited goldsmiths and were accompanied by personal maids.

Will entered the cool, quiet shop and went to the counter.

"I'm delivering a note from Mr. Fortescue to the owner of the Gold Cock," he said.

"Yes, indeed, young man," said the goldsmith. "I've been waiting to hear from him. His wife's birthday? Does she know yet? No? That's amazing in itself." He held out his hand. "Let's see what he has in mind this year."

Will handed the folded paper to the goldsmith. "Mr. Fortescue would like your definite opinion as to whether you can have this ready in time for his wife's birthday."

"Of course. Just let me see . . . " The goldsmith unfolded the paper. "Have a look around if you wish. Mind, don't touch anything." He went to his bench. "This pearl—where is it?"

Will's head was bent over some of the most beautiful work he had ever seen. "Master James Perry has the pearl. He will release it to you as soon as he receives a message from Mr. Fortescue to do so."

The goldsmith went back to his calculations. "Does he want to know what this will cost?"

"He didn't say so, sir. But, if you can give him an estimate, I'm sure he'd appreciate knowing."

The goldsmith filed the paper away in a small cubicle above his bench. He wrote a figure on a small paper and added a date underneath. "There's the estimate and the date he may expect the chain to be ready."

Will took the paper and put it in his pocket. "Excuse me, sir. This brooch is beautiful."

"Yes, it is, isn't it? The woman who left just as you entered brought it in. There's a miniature inside that she wants removed." He picked up the brooch and opened the delicate piece of jewelry. "You don't often see this type of work. High quality, probably made in France. It's a shame to change it in any way."

He laid the brooch in the palm of his hand. "Look at that portrait. It's a shame to remove it."

Will stared at the portrait. It seemed that the world had stopped around him.

"Are you all right, boy?" The goldsmith withdrew his hand and closed the brooch.

"No! No, please, open it again!"

The goldsmith slowly did so, being careful not to hold it too close to this young man whose manner had so changed.

Once again Will looked into the smiling face. "That's my mum! That's the brooch she gave me! I thought I'd lost it! That's my mum!"

"I'm sorry, but I find it hard to believe that an apprentice could ever have owned such a piece."

"My mum gave it to me when I was a little boy to remember her by. Please, may I hold it?"

The goldsmith quickly closed his hand over the brooch. "I think you'd best be on your way," he said.

"Please, sir—"

"Be off, or I'll call the guards!"

Will backed slowly from the shop. Once the door was closed after him, he looked back into the shop. The goldsmith waved him off.

When Will was gone, the goldsmith opened the brooch and compared the picture with the face of Mr. Fortescue's messenger. The eyes were the same, and something of the smile. But Master Perry might take an inquiry amiss.

He pursed his lips. A housekeeper with such a thing, though. Almost as unlikely. "Well," he said to himself aloud, "I do have my reputation to care for." He snapped the brooch shut.

"Christopher! Christopher, come at once. Master Perry's housekeeper has just delivered an unusual piece into my hands. Before I work on it, I should like to have some questions answered." He scribbled a short note, folded it, and handed it to his apprentice. "Take this to Master James Perry, if you please."

Master Perry and his wife were laughing at a wild account from the twins of what had just transpired in the kitchen.

"And Marie was all red in the face, like this," young James said. He puffed out his cheeks and held his breath. "And then the cats—"

The door swung open and Rodgers appeared. The Perrys turned to him, still laughing. But his expression checked them. Perry looked a question at his friend.

"You'd better hear this," Rodgers said. He glanced at the children.

Mrs. Perry said, "Run and tell Cook I said to give you a honeycake each," and the twins bolted for the door.

Rodgers stood aside and the goldsmith's apprentice appeared. "Show Master Perry what you just showed me," Rodgers said.

The young man handed over the note. Perry scanned it. His head jerked up. "Young man," he said, "fetch the Constable here." He turned to Rodgers. "Bring Marie."

Epilogue

The Master

In April of 1716 the children of Master Will Pancras met in their father's house. Slowly they went through his possessions, dividing them as he had instructed in his last letter. Finally, nothing remained but a small, red lacquer box that he had purchased on one of his many trips to the Orient. They felt the contents must be of considerable value because they had found the box in a safe meant to protect a man's greatest treasures.

When the box was opened, however, it contained only a small, brown cloth pouch. Inside the pouch were a faded green satin ribbon, tightly rolled; their father's apprenticeship indenture; and a golden brooch. And when they opened the fine old brooch, a beautiful lady—with eyes like their father's—smiled out at them.